Other Books & Stories
by Lynn Bohart

NOVELS

Mass Murder

Murder In The Past Tense

Grave Doubts

Inn Keeping With Murder

A Candidate For Murder

All Roads Lead To Murder

SHORT STORY BOOKS

Your Worst Nightmare

Something Wicked

ALL ROADS LEAD TO MURDER

An 'Old Maids of Mercer Island' Mystery

By
Lynn Bohart

Dedicated to the fans of Julia and the Old Maids.
You give me the motivation to keep these stories coming.

Cover Art: Mia Yoshihara-Bradshaw

Published by Little Dog Press

ACKNOWLEDGEMENTS

Disclaimer: I apologize in advance if you are familiar with I-90 and the towns and locations it passes as it winds its way across country. This book is a work of fiction and while many of the businesses, locations, and organizations referenced in the book are real, they are used in a way to fit the storyline. I admit that I took a fair amount of liberty, while still attempting to capture some of the grandeur of this great land we live in. I hope you can still find it in your heart to enjoy the story.

Acknowledgements

Once again, I have an army of friends, co-workers and experts to thank for helping me to bring this book to you. First and foremost I need to thank my writing group who methodically reads my books two chapters at a time over a period of ten months. Some of their feedback is hard to hear, but they help to clarify the storyline and characters, they challenge me on specific details, eliminate things that just don't work and highlight internal 'gems' I didn't even know I had. Case in point: they liked Jake so much in this story that I've decided to bring him back in another book as a potential competitor for David's affection towards Julia. Whoa! My thanks go to Tim McDaniel, Michael Manzer, Gary Larson, Irma Fritz, Jenae Cartwright and Brian Beckley.

I also rely on a group of "beta" readers to give me honest feedback. They volunteer to read the book from cover-to-cover and not only catch mistakes, but identify inconsistencies in the storyline, things that might confuse the reader or things that just don't make sense (yes, sometimes I do that.) This time around my thanks go to

Karen Gilb & Bill Dolan (fine writers in their own right), Traci Dysart and my daughter, Jaynee Bohart.

I was so happy this year to meet Rex Caldwell, Police Chief, retired, who spoke at my Rotary club. Never shy about finding the right people to give me advice on technical aspects, I asked Rex for help. He readily agreed to read the entire book in order to make sure I wasn't taking too much literary license on law enforcement issues. After all, it was a challenge to take the girls on the road, crossing multiple state lines and interacting with a variety of law enforcement agencies. I appreciate his help in helping to preserve the humor and yet avoid horrendous mistakes. I also appreciate Rosie Lizaola who reviewed my rudimentary Spanish in the book and Richard McSwain, a martial arts instructor who graciously reviewed the section where the girls get self-defense training and gave me some of the technical terms.

As always, I would be lost without my friend and colleague, Liz Stewart. In her real life, Liz runs the Renton History Museum, staging first-class historical and cultural exhibits in the greater Renton area. She also just happens to also be a great editor.

Once again, thanks to my friend, Mia Bradshaw, for another terrific cover. I decided long ago to keep the St. Claire Inn as the main focal point on every cover and only change things in the foreground to highlight the new storyline. Mia is very patient with me. She is a wonderful craftsperson and shows/sells her work in Seattle. Please check out her website at www.miayoshihara.com.

PROLOGUE

It was midnight. The clock tower in the middle of campus had just finished its slow, mournful chime of the hour. The massive academic buildings sat eerily quiet, while the college lay cloaked in shadows. Although it was late, the Florida temperature still hovered near 85 degrees, with suffocating humidity.

Eric had stayed in the dorm that night to study rather than joining some friends at an off-campus party. He was just about to go to bed when there was a soft rap on his door.

He opened it to find a fraternity brother–a kid named Peter. They'd met at an initial get-together during rush week. The two boys shared an interest in science; Peter wanted to design prosthetics, while Eric hoped to become a doctor.

"Let's go," Peter said with a curt nod.

"What? Where?"

"Never mind. Just follow me."

Peter had lost his affable countenance. As a pledge to the Kappa Sigma Fraternity, Eric had been told to expect some good-humored tests of loyalty. He assumed that's what this was. Though a history assignment loomed large in his mind, he turned back into the room.

"Let me get my shoes."

"No," the other boy said. "Come as you are."

Peter didn't wait for a response, but started back down the hallway. With a shrug, Eric closed his door and followed dressed only in an old t-shirt, boxer shorts and socks.

They left the air-conditioned comfort of Albert Hall at Temperance College just outside of Tampa. Eric skipped casually down the steps from the antiquated building and joined three other pledges huddled in a group surrounded by five young men wearing Kappa Sigma Polo shirts.

He had pledged the fraternity the week before, and he recognized the brothers from rush week. Two were juniors and on the football team. Three were seniors, including Peter. One of the seniors, the one they called J.R., was president of the fraternity. J.R. wasn't well-liked, and behind his back some of the boys called him the Bully Master. There were a multitude of stories about him. As a winning member of the debate team, J.R. was pretty full of himself. Eric had been told how J.R. enjoyed berating anyone less verbally agile than him. In fact, he had publicly humiliated a freshman from another fraternity just because he stuttered.

No, J.R. wasn't well-liked, and Eric didn't have any illusions about them becoming friends.

"Get in line," one of the football players ordered.

The four pledges did as they were told. Eric stepped into the back of the line. The humidity was merciless and already creating moisture under his armpits, which made his shirt stick to his skin.

"Now, move out," the same young man said. "And no talking."

The four pledges began to march in a line toward the east side of campus. None of them were wearing shoes. One of the boys, a short, overweight kid named Jeremy was actually in his pajamas.

The campus was quiet, except for a chorus of crickets singing from the pond tucked under the eaves of the library. As they walked in lock step into the commons, Eric swatted at a bevy of mosquitoes that dive-bombed his sweat-laden neck.

Security lights accented doorways and walkways like small glow bugs, but there was no one about. Their procession was witnessed only by the moon and the gargoyles staring down from the giant clock tower above.

They passed the brick-covered library and the cafeteria, eventually taking a side path that angled off towards Trinity Lake. Eric's older brother, Mark, had warned him about hazing. He and his best friend, Jack, had been members of the Kappa Sigma fraternity at Temperance College until they'd graduated three years earlier.

"The hazing's not so bad," Mark had said. "Just suck it up, do what they say and get through it. The other guys will respect you if you do."

Ordinarily, Eric wasn't the type to join a fraternity, but he idolized Mark. As a child, Eric had suffered from asthma and was prone to colds and various ailments. Mark had always looked-out for him, coming to his aid on a number of occasions when older boys bullied him at school. Once, when a kid pushed Eric into a locker and stole his homework, Mark had tracked the kid down, punched him in the face and gotten Eric's homework back.

Now, Eric hoped to follow in Mark's footsteps by joining the fraternity. He might even make Mark proud if he could ascend to a leadership position.

As the line of boys turned towards the lake, Eric's casual attitude turned to anxiety, however. He silently prayed that whatever his fraternity brothers had in mind, it wouldn't involve getting into the water. He couldn't swim.

Eric swallowed a ball of spit.

The group continued until they neared a small picnic area that overlooked the lake. They passed a park bench and then veered off the path into a copse of trees. The full moon filtered through the branches, giving them enough light to pass safely, but the boys began to grunt and groan as their bare feet encountered sharp stones and briars.

"Shut up!" J.R. snapped. "Quit being a bunch of babies."

"Where are we going?" Eric asked. A nervous quiver had snuck its way into his voice.

"What's a matter?" a boy named Ralph snapped. "Afraid of the water?"

Eric dared not admit to his Achilles heel unless he had to; that would give the older boys something to hold over him. His heart rate sped up though, as the lake came into view, the moon glistening off its surface.

The boys left the tree line and approached the water, passing a rack of canoes and paddles students used on lazy weekend afternoons. J.R. stopped when he reached the entrance to the dock.

"You're going to take a little swim," he said with an evil twist to his mouth.

"No!" Eric blurted out. "I...I can't."

"What's a matter?" one of the football players asked. "Is it your period or somethin'?"

"Yeah, do you have cramps?" another one taunted him.

The brothers laughed, and Eric was nudged forward. He could feel sharp stones and pebbles poking through his socks, cutting into his feet, but he was impervious to any pain. His entire focus was on the water lapping gently against the shore.

Eric's sweat had turned cold.

"I just had pneumonia recently. I…uh…"

"No excuses," J.R. snapped.

"But I could get sick again." Eric's mind was spinning. He had to convince them to give him a pass. "Seriously. I…I almost went to the hospital."

The boy named J.R. spun around and stepped to within inches of Eric's face. "I don't care how sick you were. You're a pledge. You belong to me."

Eric stared into the blackest eyes he'd ever seen. There was no compassion there, and this monster seemed to see into Eric's soul. He had to steel himself. He had to find a way to do this. He couldn't let Mark down. So once again, he swallowed and kept quiet.

"You're lying," J.R. suddenly said. "You didn't have pneumonia."

"Sure I did," Eric lied.

"No you didn't. You can't swim."

That prompted another burst of laughter from the other boys as Eric began to tremble with fear.

"I don't swim too good, either," Jeremy said with a brief raise of his hand.

"Too bad," J.R. said, never even looking at him. "Like I said, you're all going for a little swim tonight."

He turned on his heel and walked onto the dock. His fellow fraternity brothers surrounded Eric and forced him forward. Even Peter.

Eric began to hyperventilate, attempting to dig his heels into the beach. "Okay. Okay. I can't swim," he admitted in a panic. "Please. I nearly died once."

J.R. didn't stop. He kept going without a word. The other three pledges followed, glancing over their shoulders at Eric. The dock swayed as he was pushed after them, forcing the taste of bile into his mouth.

"Listen, I'm not kidding," he said, taking deep gulps of air. "I really can't swim. In fact…in fact, I…I…put it on my application. I had an accident when I was young…"

J.R. stopped at the end of the dock and turned back. "I know all about it. Too bad for you."

He knew? And yet, he'd still force Eric into the water?

"Okay," J.R. said. "Strip."

"What?" Jeremy erupted.

"You heard me. Take off your clothes."

The football players stood behind Eric, preventing his escape. Jeremy nervously pushed his glasses up his nose, as the other two boys began to pull their shirts over their heads.

Eric couldn't move. He was frozen with fear.

"What's a matter, probie?" one of the seniors said. "'Fraid we'll see your wee wee?"

That prompted more laughter, but Eric remained still. The bile had pooled in the back of his throat. His eyes were staring blankly at the water, as the sweat trickled down his neck.

"Get your clothes off," J.R. said. "Or my men here will hold you down, and cut them off." He held up a pair of scissors, which glinted in the moonlight.

Someone shoved Eric's shoulder.

He took a deep breath. If he didn't do as they said, he'd have to quit the fraternity. He couldn't do that. What would Mark say? He had to find a way to do this. *Suck it up,* as Mark had said. *Suck it up.*

He glanced back to the shore. *It couldn't be that deep*, he thought. He could probably touch the bottom. With trembling fingers, he began to take off his shorts. By the time he'd removed everything, tears had formed in the corners of his eyes. He didn't feel the mosquitoes anymore. He didn't feel the sweat. His body had shut down.

He was going in the water.

Thoughts blurred within his mind. The picture of Hallerton Lake in upstate New York appeared, and he was eight years old again.

"C'mon," his dad said. "Let's walk out onto the dock."

"I'm afraid, Dad," Eric whined.

"We'll just take a look. I'll hold your hand."

Eric took a deep breath and reached out and grabbed his father's hand. They stepped onto the dock, and Eric's stomach rolled as the dock rocked underneath their weight.

"No, Dad, I don't want to," he said, pulling back.

His father held him in a firm grip. "Eric, don't be a pansy. We're just walking onto a dock. Do you want the other kids to make fun of you?"

Eric looked over his shoulder at the other families gathered on the beach. Several of his brother's friends were throwing a football, but his brother, Mark, was standing at attention, watching them. His friend, Jack, was behind him.

Mark and Jack were inseparable, often leaving Eric behind to nurse a pang of jealousy. But Mark had never let him down. Many times he'd stood up to their dad when he'd tried to make Eric do things he couldn't. Maybe Mark would do it again.

Eric turned back and allowed his father to lead him further onto the long dock. He was breathing heavily now. They reached the end of the wooden planks just as a motorboat swung by. The waves slapped the dock making it tip and sway. Eric tried desperately to pull away from his father again.

"No," his father snapped, yanking his arm. "You have to get over this fear of the water. And it's time you learned to swim. It's not that big a deal."

"No," Eric said, beginning to cry.

"Oh, for heaven's sake. Stop that!" His father suddenly picked him up and threw him into the lake. "You'll learn to swim just like I did!"

Eric splashed into the lake. Instead of swimming though, every muscle in his body tensed, and he sank like a stone. When his feet hit the bottom, the mud sucked them under. He kicked to free them, but his flip flops were stuck.

In a panic, he opened his mouth and inhaled. Instead of air, he gulped down a big swig of algae-laden lake water. His belly expanded, and his throat burned. He choked, taking in more water. He flailed his arms and kicked frantically, his eyes opened wide. The dirty water swirled around him until his vision began to go dark.

Then, someone was there with him, pulling his arm, dragging him back to the surface.

He'd passed out that day, and his brother had not only pulled him out of the lake, but given him CPR. As afraid as he was of the water before his father had thrown him in, the incident had left Eric terrified of it.

Now, someone was shoving him toward another large body of water, and this time, he was going to die.

One of the pledges, a boy named Arthur, turned around and gave Eric a brief smile. "Just move your legs and arms like an egg beater, and you should be okay."

"Time to get in," J.R. said.

"I can't do this. I won't pledge the fraternity. I don't care," Eric said. His body had begun to shiver as a chilled current passed through him, leaving his legs wobbly.

He turned to flee, but the fraternity brothers grabbed him and wrestled him to the dock. Before he could stop them, they each had an arm and leg and hoisted him up. He struggled, but they were too strong.

J.R. just stood back, smiling. "Throw him in," he said with a casual nod toward the water.

"No!" Eric screamed and struggled more.

The boys tossed him into the lake just as his dad had once done. He didn't sink this time. He splashed around, coughing and yelling for help.

The fraternity brothers lined up on the edge of the dock and jeered at him.

Eric reached down with one toe, hoping to touch the bottom. There was nothing there, and his head dipped beneath the surface.

Once again, he took in a mouthful of water.

He choked and sputtered, splashing more. Full-blown panic took hold. His arms and legs flailed faster and faster.

On the dock, he heard Peter yell. "J.R.! He really can't swim. Shouldn't we go in and get him?"

"No," was the last, heartless word Eric heard.

Before his head went under water a second time, he stared with abject fear at the boy who had so callously sealed his fate. J.R. stood on the deck and just glared back at him with a sick kind of triumph etched into his dark features.

Eric sucked in a second gulp of lake water and began to sink.

Blackness swirled around him. There was no rescue this time. His brother was in New York in dental school. Even Jack was gone—in the Army. And his father was dead from a hit and run accident two years earlier.

Eric was alone and sinking fast, feeling a deep sense of remorse for having failed his brother.

His brain began to fog over as resignation overtook him. The muscles in his body relaxed, while his determination to win, to succeed, or to live flat-lined.

He sank, floating like a feather at the will of the water's movement. It was oddly comforting. No fighting. No competition. Just acceptance for what would be his fate.

And then a bright light pierced the depths of the dark green water, making Eric look up. His father's voice drifted down to him from somewhere above.

"Reach out, Eric," the voice commanded. "Grab my hand. This time, I promise I won't let go."

CHAPTER ONE

By the end of June, things at the St. Claire Inn had returned to normal. And by normal I mean that no one had tried to kill me or any of my friends within the last few weeks.

Yes, I said that.

Murder had become a rather normal part of my everyday life.

Case in point.

My friend Doe and I had recently been abducted by two insane people, one of whom had a history of torturing and killing young women and had threatened to do the same to me. The other was going to turn Doe into mummy dearest from Alfred Hitchcock's *Psycho*–literally.

But I digress.

Although summer in the Northwest is unpredictable, July held the promise of a string of 80 degree days. This brought a flurry of activity to Lake Washington, which serves as the backdrop to the St. Claire Inn situated on Mercer Island, just outside of Seattle.

I own the inn and run it as a bed and breakfast with my business partner, April.

By June, April and I had finished the plans for a new reception hall to replace our old barn, which had been torched a few weeks earlier by one of said crazy people. Construction was scheduled to begin right after the Fourth of July.

The fire had consumed the barn and April's prized bakery, relegating her to the big, homey kitchen in the main building to do all of her cooking and baking. She was at the big farmhouse sink when I rolled in from a trip to the store.

"Okay, I got everything you need for tomorrow morning's frittata," I said, dropping the grocery bag onto the counter.

My two miniature Dachshunds, Mickey and Minnie, pranced around my feet, demanding attention. I leaned down to give them each a pet. The kitchen door swung open behind me and José, our maintenance man, followed me in with two more bags clutched in his muscular arms.

"Where do you want these Ms. Applegate?"

"Thanks, José. You can put them on the table." I pointed to our drop-leaf table in front of the multi-paned window that overlooked the lake.

He did as I asked and then turned to me. "I plan to power wash the back driveway today, unless there's something else you want me to do."

I glanced at April, whose back was to me. She was wearing baggy jeans and a long, brightly colored tunic that reminded me of her African heritage. "April?"

"Nothing for me," she said with her hands deep in the dishwater.

"Sounds good, then," I said to José.

He started for the back door, but stopped short when the door swung open in front of him. He stared at it for a moment and then turned his deep brown eyes to me. "Chloe?"

"Probably," I replied.

José just shook his head with amusement and left without closing the door.

The door closed quietly behind him.

"On second thought…" I said, staring at the door. "That was probably Elizabeth. Chloe would have slammed the door."

When I said things had returned to normal, I meant that things had returned to *our* normal. That included the fact that the St. Claire Inn was haunted.

In 1962, the inn had been the home of John St. Claire and his wife, Elizabeth. A fire that year destroyed much of the home. Elizabeth, their six-year old daughter, Chloe, their ten-year old son, Fielding, and their dog, Max had all perished. And yet, their spirits had remained.

Multiple owners since then had reported a myriad of odd occurrences and sightings around the property and moved out quickly as a result. We had become used to them, even complacent.

April chuckled at my comment. "Shakespeare clearly never lived at the St. Claire Inn."

"Why do you say that?"

She turned from the sink, her dark eyes glinting. "I remember a line from *Henry the Fifth* that lamented about so many horrid ghosts. No one would say our ghosts are horrid. I think they're rather nice."

"I agree. I just wish they could help out more around here. I need the carpets shampooed in my apartment."

A chair at the kitchen table fell over backwards, slamming against the black and white tiled floor.

"Elizabeth," we acknowledged in unison.

"Guess you'll have to shampoo the carpets yourself," April said with a smile.

"Story of my life."

I replaced the chair, but the dogs still demanded attention. I opened a drawer and grabbed two doggie dental bones. Mickey, my black and tan male, began spinning in circles. Minnie bounced up and down, her little red body vibrating as she tried to grab the bone from my hand.

"Minnie, sit!"

She stopped jumping, but didn't sit. Mickey, on the other hand, got too dizzy to spin any longer and came to a sudden halt, listing to one side.

"Okay, here you go," I said with a chuckle.

I handed them each a snack. They retreated to their bed tucked into the old hearth on the far wall.

I watched them for a moment, glancing up to where white-washed block letters spelled out 'GOOD EATS' over the arched, brick opening to the old fireplace.

"I love this big kitchen," I said. "In fact, I think I love my life right now."

"Things are going pretty well with David, I take it," April said. She had returned to her dishes.

I smiled to myself. "Yes, they are. Plus, I have you and the dogs. What could be better?"

"And Blair, Doe, and Rudy," she added.

She had just named the members of my book club and the people I spent the most time with outside of work.

"Of course. I love spending time with them. Speaking of…" I said, opening a cupboard to put the food away. "I talked to Doe today. She and Rudy have postponed their trip to Mexico and will be driving one of those big luxury motorhomes across country instead. They've talked Blair into going with them."

April chuckled as she turned off the water and dried her hands. She turned to me with a broad smile.

"I'm not sure I'd trade sipping margaritas in Mexico for climbing behind the wheel of a big bus."

"No kidding," I said, putting a jar of preserves away. "But Rudy's neighbors, the Aberdeens, sold their house and moved to Wisconsin. They need someone to bring their motorhome to them."

"And Doe and Rudy decided they wanted to be the ones to do it?" April asked in surprise, as she hung her favorite fry pan on the pot rack over the kitchen island.

"Don't forget Blair."

"I doubt anyone could forget Blair," she said with a laugh. "Why is Blair going? That doesn't sound like a Blair sort of trip."

The five of us were all in our mid-to-late sixties and as different as the days of the week. My passion was finding and restoring antiques to sell at the inn. April had a degree in culinary arts and was happiest with her hands dusted with flour. As a retired journalist, Rudy spent much of her free time with her hands around a good book. Doe ran her late husband's multi-million dollar waste management company, and yet had an aversion to dirt.

Then there was Blair.

Blair was the youngest of us at sixty-three and often dressed like a high-class hooker. And I mean that in the nicest of ways. Fortunately, she had the figure to pull it off and used it to her advantage whenever she was in the presence of a man—any man. In fact, she reacted to men the way I reacted to chocolate. While others might allow chocolate to melt on their tongue, I had a tendency to swallow it whole.

"Blair plans to meet Mr. Billings in Chicago after they drop off the motorhome," I said. "There's a big foreign car show there. Anyway, the girls will be gone a week." I paused to close the cupboard. "They want me to go…but, I'm with you. I'd rather sit on our deck when I have a free minute, preferably with David, and try to forget the horrors of the last few months."

Detective David Franks of the Mercer Island PD was my new boyfriend. Truth be told, there hadn't been much 'alone' time since we'd started dating in January. In fact, we'd met during the investigation into the murder of my friend, Martha, and had only been able to sneak in one quick weekend at the coast in between a second and third murder investigation.

Remember how I said my life wasn't normal?

To be honest, I was disappointed I wouldn't be going on the road trip with my friends.

"I think you should go," April said. She hung the towel on a hook and turned her espresso eyes toward me. "You need a break. Your life has been pretty overwhelming for the last few months. David will be here when you get back. Why don't you do something just for you for a change? Something that doesn't include chasing killers all over the place."

"Oh, for heaven's sake, I can't go," I replied with a disingenuous wave of my hand. "The inn is booked solid through the summer, and we're about to begin construction on the reception hall."

I silently hoped my argument wouldn't convince her. After all, I couldn't bear the thought of my entire book club going without me. If nothing else, a romp across country in a big motorhome would be good for a few laughs.

"Oh, Julia," April said with a scolding tone. "I have Crystal and José, and we could bring Lynette on full-time for a week. I think we could survive without you. When it comes to the reception hall, all they'll have time to do is break ground. I'll email you pictures. So, go."

I gave her an expectant raise to my eyebrows. "What about the dogs?"

"I'd be happy to take care of them. You should go."

"You think?"

"I think," she replied.

CHAPTER TWO

The girls were thrilled when I announced I would join them on the trip. There was, however, the little matter of learning how to drive the big motorhome—a not so comforting prospect for me since I had a reputation for being accident prone.

Rudy had checked state license regulations, and the states along our route didn't require a special permit. Good news. Nathan Aberdeen, however, didn't care. He wanted us to practice before we took his precious RV on the road.

I couldn't blame him, since I'd been in several accidents recently. But I was a little nervous about this part of the deal. In my defense, the accidents had all been caused by nasty people chasing or shooting at me. My nervousness stemmed from the fact I was only 5' 2" tall and feared I couldn't adequately reach the pedals. The image of me driving the big rig off a cliff was a very real possibility.

I pushed down my anxieties though and joined the group a few days later when we piled into Doe's big Mercedes and headed out to meet Nathan at Safeco Field in downtown Seattle. We chatted about the trip and living the life of nomads until we pulled up to where the RV was parked.

The chatter ended.

Blair peered out the window, her pretty face pinched with disgust. "Jeez, that's what we're traveling in? It's the Incredible Hulk."

I followed her gaze. The RV was large enough to carry an entire NFL team, plus gear. It was also downright ugly. The exterior was painted a dreadful Army green with a black swirling stripe that ran from front to back like a hardened scar.

"At least we'll be inside looking out most of the time," Rudy said, staring at it.

The screen door opened, and Nathan Aberdeen stepped out the moment we emerged from the Mercedes. He was medium height, slender, with a long nose, glasses and receding brown hair. Rudy introduced us.

"Good to meet all of you," he said with a nod. "This is my baby." He turned and placed the flat of his hand on the side of the big rig and glanced up at it as if he was admiring a beautiful woman. "Isn't she gorgeous?"

Silence.

Count to three.

"Yes," Rudy said, filling the dead space. "It sure is. We can hardly wait."

Nathan's angular face beamed with pride. "Mary and I hope to retire in this baby. We just want to be footloose and fancy-free when I finally hang it up."

Nathan worked for a big motor parts company and had been transferred to Wisconsin.

"So…you ready to wheel this thing around the parking lot a few times?" he asked, looking directly at me.

I pressed my lips together, hesitating. "Um…sure."

He climbed the steps and swung open the door, and we followed him into an alternate universe.

While the outside looked like a prisoner transport vehicle, the inside was another matter. It could have competed with a high-end Manhattan apartment.

"Wow," I muttered.

There was a complete bedroom with two single beds accented with patchwork quilts and a small brass lamp secured to a center bedside table. I opened the bathroom door to find a sink, a toilet and a glassed-in shower. The kitchen was graced with marble countertops, polished cherry wood cabinets, a microwave, a glass stovetop, and an oven.

The dining table seated four and Nathan showed us how it broke down into a double bed. In between the kitchen table and driver's seat was a rich leather sofa, which also converted into a double bed. Across from the dining table were two leather swivel chairs, offset by a small game table with an inlaid checker-board. I glanced up to where a built-in flat screen TV hung above it.

"Look at this carpet," Doe murmured. "It's nicer than what I have in my living room."

She was staring at a deep, plush carpet with a rich geometric design in bold colors.

"This is amazing," I said, running my hand across the burnished wood of the dining table.

"They don't call it a luxury motorhome for nothing," Nathan said. "It even has an air conditioner mounted on the roof. You'll have everything but a fireplace."

"So much for rustic camping," Blair said, fingering a floral patterned pillow on the sofa.

"Oh, you'll still be able to roast marshmallows over a campfire. You can just cook, eat, and sleep in comfort."

Nathan gave us a brief explanation about the motorhome's dashboard, the GPS, and how to use the big rearview mirrors. We followed him outside to learn how to hook up water and electricity and dump the waste water. Lastly, we were each required to take a turn driving around the parking lot before demonstrating how to park and back up.

I swallowed.

The moment of truth had arrived.

Nathan had set up two curved lines of orange cones to serve as a practice track. For a half hour, Doe, Rudy, and Blair navigated them without mishap and then showed how easily they could back up and park the giant monstrosity.

Then it was my turn.

In the course of a few minutes, I knocked over two cones, flattened a second cone and dragged it behind me, almost wiped out a small truck parked alone in the back of the lot and then backed the big rig into a parking slot six inches over the line on the far side and slammed it into the fence behind me.

Needless to say, Nathan was polite, but firm; I would not be allowed to take the wheel of his motorhome.

Oh, well, I thought. *Disaster averted.*

CHAPTER THREE

We were set to leave on Sunday morning. Since I was on call at the inn the night before our departure, David and I scheduled dinner in my apartment to say goodbye. He called to let me know he would be late, so I settled on a simple meal of homemade tacos and rice.

He arrived just after seven o'clock dressed in dark slacks and a tan, long-sleeved crew neck shirt. His badge hung from a lanyard around his neck.

The dogs followed him inside from the back door, whining and pestering him for attention. He handed me a bottle of wine and then leaned down to greet them. In my home, the dogs usually came first, so I accepted this affront with a smile. Once the dogs' needs had been met, he put his arms around me and gave me a warm kiss.

"I'm sorry about being late," he said when we separated. "I got caught up in a case, and I'll have to go back to the department after dinner."

He went to the sink to wash his hands.

"What's going on?"

"Senator Owens' daughter disappeared from Luther Burbank Park this morning."

Owens was a Republican U.S. senator from Spokane and a rising star in congress.

"You're kidding. What happened?"

"All we know is that she was scheduled to join some friends. She never showed. Her car was found later with her beach bag and keys on the ground outside the driver's side door. We canvassed the park and found someone that witnessed a girl matching her description with a man wearing a ball cap. He was putting her into a dark van. The witness said she appeared sick or drunk, because he had to help her into the vehicle."

"Wow," I said, perching on one of the counter stools. "I just read an article about Senator Owens a few days ago. He's angling to be the next majority leader in the Senate, but no one likes him. I understand he loves to sue people for the slightest insult until he gets them to back down and apologize. Seems like a bully to me. I wouldn't wish violence on anyone, though. Do you have any leads?"

David popped the cork on the wine bottle. "Our witness was able to give us a good description of the van. It had vanity plates. We were able to track it down, but it was stolen last night."

"Of course it was," I said with a sigh. "Wouldn't kidnapping be a case for the FBI?"

"Not necessarily, but this is a U.S. senator, so they've already been notified. She has a boyfriend, so we're hoping to talk to him."

"What about her father?" I asked with a hint of expectation.

"He's not a suspect, although Owens is not only high profile politically, he's very wealthy. Two potential reasons someone may want to kidnap his daughter."

"I thought I read that he'd remarried."

David nodded. "He did. His daughter lives with her mother and stepfather in Seattle. He lives in Spokane–that is when he's not in D.C." He sighed and put his arm around me. "Let's not talk shop. How can I help with dinner?"

"Pour the wine," I said. "And then you can put this on the table." I pointed to a divided platter with cheese, lettuce, and tomatoes. "I'll get the meat."

We spent the next twenty minutes chatting while we enjoyed dinner. When the topic turned to the trip, David reached over and grabbed my hand.

"I'm going to miss you, you know, even though you'll only be gone a week." He gave me a shy smile as if he'd gone too far in expressing his affection.

My heart fluttered as a big grin spread across my face. I turned my hand over and laced my fingers through his.

"Let's face it; with me gone your life will slow down for a while. At least you won't have to rescue me from some crazy killer."

He chuckled and tilted his head to one side, his brown eyes dancing. "To be honest, I'll miss that, too."

"Be careful what you wish for," I said, smiling. "I feel almost guilty leaving you, though."

"No, it's a good thing you're going," he said, letting go of my hand and sitting back in his chair. "You need some fun in your life, away from the hectic running of the inn, and…" he stopped and shrugged. "Everything else."

"Having a bit of normalcy would be good," I agreed. "No murders. No adventures. No ghosts. Just my friends and a few evenings spent around a campfire under the stars." My spoon slid off the table onto the carpet. I glanced down. "I'll miss you, too, Chloe."

David knew about the ghosts, but never said much about them. I think his cop brain had trouble accepting the whole concept. As proof, he ignored the spoon.

"You're not taking the dogs?"

Mickey had his feet on David's leg, begging. David reached down to pat his head.

"No. April will take care of them. I'll miss them too, though. I don't think I've ever been away from them for more than a day or so."

"I'm kind of envious," he said, reaching for his wine. "Sitting around a campfire under the stars sounds pretty good."

"Hey, why don't you meet us in Chicago? You and I could spend a long weekend together. After all, you never finished telling me about your early days at the police department in Detroit." I smiled and reached over and rubbed my foot against his leg, imagining running my fingers through his thick gray hair. "And maybe we could have a repeat performance of that little game we played at the beach."

He nearly choked on a sip of wine. "Well, I, uh," he sputtered.

"You're blushing," I teased him.

"No, no I'm not," he blustered. "You just took me by surprise."

"Never been propositioned by a woman, I suppose."

He grinned, revealing his dimples. "Oh, I've been propositioned by plenty of women, just not one so brazen."

"Sure," I said with a brief laugh. "With all the women of the night you must come across?"

He shrugged. "I come across a lot less of those since coming to Mercer Island. But…I'll take you up on that offer," he said with a warm smile. "Depending on what happens with this investigation, that is. I'll check flights into O'Hare for next Saturday. Have you ever been to Wrigley Field?"

"Wrigley what?"

He frowned. "C'mon. You have to know what Wrigley Field is."

I snickered. "Of course, I do. They make gum, don't they?"

We shared a good laugh, and then he reached out and took my hand again. "What time do you leave tomorrow?"

"Nine o'clock."

"Are you all packed?"

"Yep. I'm ready to go."

"Well then, I'd hate to mess up that pretty auburn hair of yours, but any chance I could give you a proper goodbye before I head back downtown?"

CHAPTER FOUR

I was up by 6:00 a.m. the next morning to help April with the guests' breakfasts and then finish last minute packing. It was just after 9:00 a.m. when the dogs alerted me to the arrival of the RV.

Our circular driveway slopes down from the street to the front of the inn, and my rose garden fills the large patch of ground in between the two curves of the drive. By the first of July, the roses were in full bloom, but Rudy had parked the Hulk so it blocked most of the garden and the big house across the street.

As I dragged my rolling suitcase through the front door and onto our wraparound porch, April met me with a box of freshly baked cinnamon rolls and a bag of brownies.

"Thanks," I said, taking them from her. "You know me too well. Listen, I have my cell phone, so don't hesitate to call if there's a problem."

"Are you kidding? I don't plan to bother you at all. Go have fun." She reached out and drew me in for a hug. I smelled the familiar scent of coconut oil she used daily to keep her dark skin velvet soft and felt a nostalgic sense of warmth overtake me.

I pulled back. "You have the Butlers and the Griffins checking in tomorrow," I said. "Between them, they have four kids. It's going to be crazy around here."

"Never mind that. Just take care of yourself," she said. "Don't let them leave you behind at a gas station or something."

"We should put a bell around her neck," Blair said, coming up the steps.

Even though we were about to set out for several days of camping, Blair had chosen to wear a skin-tight, sparkly red tank top, black leather crop pants, and red and white polka dotted high heels.

"I don't need a bell. I'm not a cow," I responded.

"Yes, but it would be good to know where you are at all times," she said. "You do have a tendency to get yourself into trouble. Where's your sleeping bag? I'll take it to the Hulk."

"The Hulk?" April asked.

Blair's pretty face tensed as if she'd bitten into a lemon. "That's what we're calling that big green hunk of metal behind me."

"Who cares what the motorhome looks like?" Rudy said, joining us.

"I have a reputation to keep," Blair said, throwing her chin in the air. "Who wants to be seen in some giant rusty tin can with a motor?"

Rudy snorted. "I doubt they make motorhomes with the kind of turning radius you're used to."

Blair's first husband (first of four) had been a race car driver and had taught her the finer points of driving at high speed. Her current husband, Mr. Billings, owned a string of foreign import car dealerships, giving her the pick of cars to drive. It was usually a Porsche.

"Speaking of drivers," April said. "Who's going to drive that thing?"

"We'll share the driving," Rudy said.

"Not me," I blurted out. "I was deemed inadequate."

"Not inadequate," Blair said. "Just dangerous."

I didn't disagree since they were all well aware of my reputation for causing mishaps.

Case in point.

When Doe and I recently went to interview a woman at an assisted living center, I bumped into an old woman sitting behind me in a wheelchair on the outdoor patio. Someone had forgotten to lock the wheels to her chair. Not my fault. Her wheelchair lurched forward and slammed into a nurse's aide, forcing the poor woman to somersault over a wall and down a steep slope towards the lake.

"I'm happy to just be a passenger," I said, shutting off the memory.

"We decided Julia can be in charge of the map," Blair added with a smug smile.

"Funny. My sleeping bag is by the front desk," I said, pointing behind me.

Blair stepped past me into the foyer, her heels clicking on the hardwood floor.

"What route are you taking?" April asked Rudy.

"I-90 most of the way," she said. "We'll spend our first night just outside of Spokane. Then we travel across the top part of Idaho into

Montana. I hope to make Missoula the second night, maybe even Billings. If we have time, we'll swing down through Yellowstone and then back onto I-90 into South Dakota."

"Can we stop at Mt. Rushmore?" I asked. "I've never been there." I felt like a little girl going on a field trip.

"I don't see why not," Rudy said.

"How about Joe's Bar and Grill in Billings?" Blair asked, coming up behind me with the sleeping bag in her hands. Her crystal blue eyes sparkled at the suggestion.

"You want to stop at Joe's Bar and Grill in Billings?" Rudy asked with a smartass curl to her lip.

"Don't tell me," April said. "That's where you met Mr. Billings."

"It was where we had our first date," Blair confirmed with a brilliant smile.

"Date?" Rudy said, spitting out a breath. "What's the name of the motel next door?"

"The Billings Mote…oh, very funny," Blair replied with an arch to her neck.

Blair was infamous for her ex-husbands. Mr. Billings had come into the picture after Blair had dumped husband number three. She was in Billings to visit her aunt when they met. Though separated, Mr. Billings wasn't yet unencumbered from his then-current wife. That hadn't stopped them from beginning a relationship however, probably in that motel next door to Joe's Bar and Grill.

Thereafter, although his name was actually Jack Wentworth, Blair referred to husband number four as Mr. Billings. Well, that's not exactly true. He hadn't earned the nickname because of the town where they'd met. It had more to do with a nickname she'd given a singular part of Jack's body she loved the best. And I don't mean his brain.

"Where will you spend the Fourth of July?" April asked, bringing our attention back to the trip.

"Hopefully, Rapid City, South Dakota," Rudy replied. "There's a big campground there that puts on a fireworks display. Then we spend our last night in Onalaska, Wisconsin. We'll drop off the motorhome in Madison the next day and spend the night with the Aberdeens before renting a car to drive to Chicago."

"Stopping first in Waukegan to drop off my mother," I added.

The fact that my mother's ashes had been on a shelf in the garage since she'd died from emphysema a year and a half earlier had been a constant source of amusement for my friends. There was also the fact that she'd begun calling me on my cell phone during the first murder investigation, usually to warn me of some impending danger.

Yes, I said that, too.

My dead mother calls me on my cell phone. The calls are short and very much to the point. She knows, or can feel somehow, that I'm in danger. On occasion, she's intervened with elaborate distractions, giving me the opportunity to get away.

The problem was that I'd now gotten used to hearing from her in times of trouble, and I had mixed feelings about returning her ashes to her home town. A part of me was afraid that locking her away in a small metal box would sever my ethereal ties to her—that I might never hear from her again. And yet, I'd promised to take her home. And a promise is a promise.

"You realize there's a big Republican meeting in Chicago right around the time you'll be there," April said.

I sighed. "I know. They're calling it the Freedom Conference. All the Republican governors will be there, as well as most of the Republican leaders of Congress."

"Is Graham going?" Blair asked.

My ex-husband was the current governor of the state of Washington—an anomaly if there ever was one since Washington is such a 'blue' state. Though divorce often ripped families apart, our separation had been undramatic. Graham and I remained on good terms, though on different sides of the political aisle.

"Yes. He'll be there. I spoke to him last weekend."

"I think Senator Owens is making the keynote address," April said.

"That turd?" Rudy said with a grimace.

Like me, Rudy was a staunch liberal and didn't think much of Senator Jim Owens. Besides being a bully, he was a hard-right conservative, making Rudy's small brown eyes glint with anger.

"Didn't you read the paper this morning?" April said. "His daughter was abducted."

"David mentioned it last night," I said. "Really sad."

"Julia!" Doe called from the motorhome. "Did you remember to bring a lantern?"

"José should be here in a minute with our camping stuff," I called back.

At the mention of his name, José's lean figure appeared around the corner of the garage carrying a big cardboard box.

"Right on cue," Rudy said. She left the porch and moved over to the side of the motorhome to open a large storage compartment. "Here. You can put it in here."

I clumped down the steps with my jean jacket thrown over my arm as José slid the box into the compartment.

Rudy peeked inside. "You brought marshmallow sticks."

"They're about a million years old," I said, coming up behind her. "But they'll work. I have a bag of charcoal in there, a couple of flashlights, the lantern, and of course, Mother."

Blair erupted with a chuckle. "She won't be too happy about riding back here with the charcoal."

"She won't care," I said. "She's going home."

I felt myself choke up a bit. Rudy saved me.

"I brought lawn chairs," she said, changing the subject. "They're strapped onto the back of the RV."

"I brought my bug zapper," Doe called out from the RV.

"Guess what Blair brought?" Rudy asked with a mischievous smile. She turned to Blair, who still held my sleeping bag in her arms.

"My oversized, battery-operated makeup mirror," she said, flashing her perfectly white teeth. "We can all use it. I'll throw this on the bed inside."

She disappeared into the RV.

Rudy turned back to me with a raised eyebrow.

She and Blair had a friendly and yet adversarial relationship–probably because they were so different. Rudy had been a jock in college and spent her entire professional career as a pit-bull journalist. She was small and wiry and didn't even *wear* makeup. She also didn't take guff from anyone.

On the other hand, although Blair had a photographic memory and was smart as a whip, she down-played that part, focusing instead on her looks. Add her carefree attitude toward life, and it was a perfect setup for the two of them to butt heads.

"This trip should be interesting," Rudy said, grabbing the handle to my suitcase. "The four of us have never traveled in close quarters before. Between Doe's obsession with cleanliness, my lack of patience, Blair's focus on the opposite sex, and your..." She stopped mid-sentence.

"Clumsiness," I said with resignation.

Her weathered face broke into a grin, making her small brown eyes dance. "Well, let's just say, if we all come back friends the trip will be a success."

"I have no doubt we'll come back friends."

"Julia, I forgot to bring Lysol. Do you have any?" Doe called through the RV window.

"And so it begins," Rudy said with a cynical expression.

I laughed and shook my head, turning to José. "José, I have a bottle of Lysol spray under the sink in my kitchen. Can you grab it for me? Also that box by the front door?"

"Sure," he said and left.

As I pulled my arms through my jacket, Rudy took my suitcase into the motorhome. José returned a minute later with the spray cleaner and box, which he stowed in the storage compartment.

"What's in the box?" Blair asked, coming back down the motorhome steps.

"Three bottles of wine and all the condiments and spices we'll ever need."

She grinned. "Awesome."

We were in the process of saying our goodbyes to April and José when my neighbor Caroline and her daughter Amelia appeared around the back of the motorhome. They lived in the house across the street. Amelia was only five and a Downs Syndrome child. She had a bright and happy personality and was dressed in blue denim shorts and a matching blouse embroidered with strawberries.

"Hi, Julia," she said, running forward to grab my hand.

"I'm glad we caught you," Caroline said, coming up behind her. "You look like you're all ready to go."

Caroline had formerly worked at Microsoft as a programmer and now worked from home. She was tall and slender, with short, curly brown hair.

"Yes, we were just about to leave."

"How far do you think you'll get today?"

"We plan to stop in Leavenworth and then head over to Spokane," I replied.

Leavenworth was a touristy Bavarian-style town in the Cascades, about two hours east of Seattle.

"I thought you might like to take these." She handed me a pair of binoculars. "They're Jack's. He does a lot of bird watching. Since you'll be traveling through some beautiful country, I thought they might come in handy."

"Thank you," I said. "We'll take good care of them."

"Tell her, Mommy," Amelia whined, squinting up at her mother and pulling on my hand.

"Tell me what?" I asked, handing off the binoculars to Blair.

Caroline glanced at our expectant faces. "Uh, well...it seems that..." She paused, making Amelia bounce up and down in frustration.

A small whirlwind of dust began to circle us. I suspected it was Chloe again. She often showed herself in this way. Chloe liked to play tricks on people she didn't like, or show her displeasure in unsuspecting ways. None of us had ever seen her, although her mother's gossamer image had often appeared inside the inn. Elizabeth had even once accompanied me in the car, warning me in advance that I was about to hit a deer.

Although none of us had seen Chloe, Amelia seemed to see her all the time. She even had conversations with her–or so she said.

"Tell her, Mommy!" Amelia insisted, watching the small whirlwind. "It's important."

Caroline reached into her pocket. "Amelia wants you to take this," she said, handing me the small object.

I took a small folding knife from her hand. It had a tiny compass embedded in the handle. As I turned it over, I asked, "Why this?"

Caroline shrugged, as if embarrassed by the gift. "I'm not really sure."

The whirlwind grew larger, swirling dust and leaves. Everyone looked around with surprise now, and stepped back.

Amelia was the only one who ignored Chloe's presence. She simply said, "Chloe wants you to take it. She told me."

And with that, the whirlwind evaporated. The leaves floated to the ground.

There was a pause, as I'm sure each of us wondered what might happen next.

Nothing did.

I turned to Amelia. "Did Chloe say why she wanted me to take this?"

She shook her head, making her curls flop around. "No. She just said that you had to take it and keep it with you. You have to promise."

There was a sense of urgency in her voice, giving me a slight chill. Rudy and Doe had joined us, and I looked at my companions and the resignation on their faces. *Did this portend of some impending danger?*

"Okay," I said, slipping the small knife into the pocket of my jacket. "I'll keep it with me at all times."

Amelia's face brightened. "Okay. I wish I could come with you."

"Sweetie, we'll be going to the beach soon," Caroline said, grabbing her hand.

Amelia kicked her foot into the gravel. "I know. But Chloe's going. I want to go, too."

"Oh, dear," Caroline said, giving me an apologetic look. "Uh...sorry. Look, we better get going. Drive carefully and be sure to do some sightseeing."

I thanked her and watched as she and Amelia disappeared around the end of the big motorhome.

When they were out of earshot, Blair spoke up. "What the heck did that mean?"

My fingers fiddled with the knife in my pocket. "I don't know. I think Chloe's just being cautious. Having a compass isn't a bad idea when you're traveling across country."

"Do you think Chloe's coming with us?" Rudy asked.

I chuckled. "Not without Elizabeth."

"Great," Blair said with a huff. "Well, they're not getting *my* bed." She turned and stomped into the motorhome.

CHAPTER FIVE

Doe drove the first leg of the trip, taking us up into the Cascades on I-90, through Snoqualmie Pass and eventually into Leavenworth. We stayed in the picturesque town long enough to stroll down the Bavarian main street and browse through a few shops. We stopped for lunch, and then by two o'clock, we hit the road again and followed the Wenatchee River down the valley, past the small town of Cashmere and over the bridge that spans the mighty Columbia River.

Since most of the rain clouds blow in off the coast of Washington State and dump their load before crossing the Cascades, the other side of the mountains is high-desert dotted with apple orchards, wineries, small towns and signs for Grand Coulee Dam.

As the afternoon wore on, I felt the stress from the last few weeks begin to drain away. Thoughts of murderers, crazy people and serial killers faded into the background. *This trip was a good idea*, I thought.

It was almost four o'clock that afternoon when David called. I was checking my Facebook page and put my iPad down to answer the phone.

"How's everything going?" he asked.

"Great," I replied. I was sitting in one of the leather swivel chairs and turned to look out the window at the flat, dry landscape. "This is pretty sweet. We can grab a drink or something to eat any time we want. No need to stop even to go to the bathroom. And all in first-class style. How's your case going?"

"Not so good. There's been no trace of the girl. Her mother is distraught. Her stepfather seems almost relieved she's gone. And her birth father is a prick."

I erupted with a short laugh. "David! That doesn't sound like you."

"Sorry. But he is. He's in D. C. and even though we'd like to talk to him, he won't make the trip back to this Washington. Too busy, he said. He just wants us to do our job and find his daughter. Like I said…"

"I got it," I said. "Any suspects? Don't you always look at the family first? What about the stepfather?" I realized I sounded like something out of one of the many mysteries I read.

"He could be good for it. His company is in trouble, so he might need cash. We're checking him out now, but the girl's boyfriend is also missing. A kid named Dylan Masterson. According to her mother, Amy broke up with him Friday night."

"Does he have a troubled past?"

"Some involvement with drugs," he said. "He's a bit of a bad boy. That doesn't mean he's good for it, though. We have a task force set up between us, Seattle PD and the FBI. So it's all hands on deck. But, hey, no more talk about crime stuff. I miss you, Babe."

"Babe? I like that," I said, blushing.

The cupboard above my head popped open and a bag of potato chips fell onto the table in front of me.

"Oh!" I said in surprise.

"What is it?"

I began to chuckle. "I think Chloe came on the trip and wants us to hang up."

"Well, I have to go, anyway. I just wanted to check in."

"Listen, good luck with the case," I said. "And get some rest, too. I plan to keep you plenty busy in Chicago."

"Whoa, I like the sound of that. I'll give you a call tomorrow."

We hung up and I went back to relaxing.

The afternoon waned to early evening as we passed through Spokane on I-90, the interstate that would serve as our yellow brick road to Wisconsin. Spokane sits about twenty miles from the Idaho border. Most of us had been there multiple times, so even though it was the site of the 1974 World's Fair, there was no reason to stop.

We kept going, heading for Coeur d'Alene, a posh community just beyond the border in Idaho. Rudy had made reservations at an RV park on the lake there.

It was just after 5:30 p.m. when we checked in at the Wolf Creek Campground. It sat in a gulley with a small stream running along the backside and trees surrounding everything. A single-lane paved road ran through the campground, with RV slots on both sides. The lake glistened to our left as we drove in.

We were assigned slot number 28 on the far side, away from the lake. A bank of trimmed bushes separated each RV slot, giving privacy to the campers, and most sites were shaded by trees. Each campsite offered a picnic table, fire pit and a well-used barbeque.

Since Rudy was driving now, Doe climbed out to act as guide. Rudy expertly backed the enormous vehicle into the slot, stopping with a jerk when Doe gave her a wave. While cool in the RV, the temperature outside hovered around 85 degrees. The difference hit me as we got out of the RV to prepare it for the night. We hooked up the electricity and water and brought out the lawn chairs and lantern.

Once we were settled, Rudy walked up to the store, which sat at the front entrance. She wanted firewood. We had each put $500 onto a debit card that would be used to pay for gas, food, campsites and anything else we needed. If there was money left over when we got back, we'd split it.

I had volunteered to make dinner our first night out and got a pot of Italian spaghetti sauce simmering. I used one of the fancier bottled brands and then added cut-up veggies and my own combination of spices and a little red wine. To top it off, Doe had brought homemade meatballs.

Blair came up behind me as I worked at the small counter. "You need help?"

"No. I've got this."

"Okay. I'm going to change."

She disappeared into the bedroom as I began to make garlic bread. I was wrapping aluminum foil around a loaf of French bread I'd already lathered with butter and garlic salt when Doe came into the RV. She pulled out a blue and white checked table cloth and a small basket of silk flowers from one of the cupboards.

"I thought we were eating outside."

"We are. But no reason we can't be civilized." She smiled, grabbed a sponge and the bottle of Lysol and climbed back out to dress the picnic table.

A moment later, Blair came out of the bedroom wearing denim crop pants and a V-necked t-shirt that showed enough cleavage to make a strong man whimper. She sniffed the spaghetti sauce.

"Smells wonderful. God, what is Doe doing?" she said, leaning over the sink to peer out the window.

"What does it look like? I've always thought her home could substitute for a clean room at a research facility."

She chuckled. "You know she has two cleaning ladies that come each week. Then she spends most of her free time cleaning up *after* the cleaning ladies."

I spied Doe's crisp white slacks and sleeveless print blouse and smiled. "I know. She's clean and perfect right down to her toenails. Even when she's camping, she looks perfect."

Besides being a clean-freak, Doe was a workaholic. I suspected she had brought work with her; we just hadn't seen it yet.

"I wonder if she brought an iron," Blair murmured.

As Doe shook out the tablecloth outside, Rudy appeared from around the end of the motorhome with an armful of firewood. She dumped the wood next to the fire pit and shook off her dirty hands.

I watched her, thinking once again how different we all were. Doe never had a hair out-of-place, while Rudy was usually dressed for the sport of the day and often smelled of suntan oil. Blair dressed from head-to-toe for men, while I liked my loafers, denim shirts and jeans.

I left the sauce to simmer and followed Blair outside. I noticed she had on her three-inch heels. Once again, I smiled.

"I guess we are who we are," I said from behind her. I was looking at her shoes.

She glanced at me and then down to her heels. "Hey, why shouldn't I look good for the resident wildlife?"

"And by resident wildlife I assume you mean the local squirrels and other rodents?" Rudy quipped.

"You're just jealous," Blair responded. "With your bad knees you can't wear high heels anymore."

"Just one bad knee," she said. "The one I had replaced is as good as new." She shook out her left leg to demonstrate.

"Let's face it. You were never much into heels, anyway," I said. "You've always been more of an Adidas kind of gal."

"Adidas schmidas," Blair said with a shrug. "My feet don't feel the same in anything but heels."

"It never even dawned on me to bring heels or anything fancy," I said.

"Did you happen to bring a lighter?" Rudy asked me.

"Yeah. It's in that box."

"Okay, I want a fire later." She went to the side compartment.

"I'll bet Rudy will be the first one to snap on this trip," Blair said, watching her.

"Snap? In what way?"

"Get mad." Blair turned to me. "What's the longest period of time any of us has been together?"

I hunched my shoulders. "I don't know. Maybe five or six hours."

"Bingo. We're going to be together for six plus days. I might have to restate my prediction."

"What do you mean?"

"I think Rudy will be the first one to try and kill one of us." Blair smiled sweetly and said, "I'll get the plates and silverware."

As she returned to the motorhome to get the dinnerware, I watched Rudy carefully stack the wood in the fire pit, wondering if Blair was right. Would we all be at each other's throats by the end of the trip? I couldn't imagine that. We'd been friends for years and despite the difference in our personalities, we got along great.

Twenty minutes later, we were positioned around the checked tablecloth, serving spaghetti and garlic bread onto blue Melamine plates. Doe had made a small salad, and I'd opened a bottle of wine.

"Here's to an *un*eventful trip," I said, my glass raised high.

"Here, here," Doe said, joining in the toast.

Rudy held her glass up and then paused. "And by uneventful you mean…"

"No one trying to kill us," I said.

She grinned. "Okay, I'll toast to that."

We dug into dinner with the sounds of a crowded campground as our backdrop. I glanced around, relishing in the comfort of my friends and just being outside.

"This is delightful," I said, swallowing a mouthful of spaghetti. "Everything smells so fresh. I wonder what those trees are over there." I pointed to a thicket of trees just beyond the rim of the park where a breeze had kicked up the rattle of leaves.

Doe looked up. "Quaking Aspen, I think," she said. Doe loved to garden, despite her anathema towards dirt. "I brought my plant encyclopedia with me. I'll look them up later. So far, I've seen a Bitter Cherry tree next to the store, and that's a Garry Oak," she said, pointing across the road.

I smiled to myself. It appeared we might also get a running commentary on the surrounding plant life as we moved from state to state.

The sound of raised voices made us look up with a start.

Across the road was an old, dirty white Jayco RV parked under the branches of that Garry Oak. The RV was shorter than ours with faded red and blue stripes, accented by rust and dirty water streaks at the upper corners. A stocky man with thick dark hair and a short beard slammed open the door and stepped out. He was wearing a stained undershirt and turned back and yelled inside, "Just keep...quiet."

The middle part of his sentence was lost, but a female voice responded with something that sounded like *asshole*, making him snarl and storm off toward the store.

"What were you saying about the resident wildlife?" Rudy asked Blair.

She smiled. "Not my type."

Rudy scoffed. "I didn't know you had a type."

"Quality versus quantity," Blair said.

We all chuckled, and then Doe said, "Have you heard anything else about Senator Owens' daughter, Julia?"

"No, except her boyfriend is now missing."

"Was he abducted, too?"

I shrugged. "I don't know. They just want to talk to him, but can't find him. He and Amy broke up the night before she disappeared."

"What's his name?" Doe asked.

"Dylan Masterson," I replied.

Rudy's eyes lit up. "I wonder if he's related to Joe Masterson. Elliott plays handball with him."

Elliott was Rudy's ex-husband and a man we all suspected might be worming his way back into her good graces after leaving her for a mid-life crisis.

"Do they think the kid had anything to do with it?" she asked.

As someone who spent most of her time outdoors, Rudy's skin looked like soft, tanned leather. When she smiled, deep lines accented the corners of her mouth. Right now, she furrowed her brow.

"I don't know. They just want to talk to him."

She seemed lost in thought for a moment. "I might call Elliott later and see what he knows."

The burly guy with the beard from across the way returned a few minutes later with a paper bag in his hand. He climbed noisily into the motorhome and once again, slammed the door. We were treated to more raised voices, but it didn't last long.

"I won't be sorry to say good-bye to them when we leave in the morning," Doe murmured. "I want only quiet, contemplative days on this trip."

"Then you'd better take a nap when Blair drives," Rudy said. "I have a feeling she's going to get frustrated the Hulk isn't a sports car."

Blair merely smiled to herself as she swirled spaghetti onto her fork. "The Hulk is like any other man. You just have to know what to stroke and when to stroke it."

"Blair!" Doe said, spitting out a mouthful of wine.

"Maybe we should rename the RV," Rudy said, laughing. "Instead of the Hulk we could name it Tom Cruise."

"I'd prefer Sean Connery," I said with a chuckle.

"How about Kevin Costner?" Doe added.

"No. No," Blair demurred. "It has to be the Hulk. After all, the Hulk would have the biggest…"

"Blair!" we all yelled in unison.

She smiled and wrapped her lips around the forkful of spaghetti.

After dinner, we chatted about potential side trips. Rudy brought out her Atlas and pointed to the Big Horn National Recreation Area as a possibility. We decided to stop there if we had time, but ruled out Yellowstone since once again most of us had been there.

Dessert was the bag of brownies April sent, something Blair had to ignore because of her diabetes. The rest of us were savoring the chocolate decadence when Rudy said, "Now there's a sight you don't see often."

I glanced up. A young girl on a pink bike with training wheels came rolling by. Her mother was jogging slowly next to her, her triple D+ bosom bouncing up and down like giant water balloons.

"Gee, do I smell a whiff of sarcasm in that remark?" Doe said, waving her hand in front of her nose as if someone had farted.

"Well, that's gotta hurt," Rudy said, watching the woman disappear up the road.

"You're just jealous," Blair sniped.

She was referring to Rudy's less than robust chest.

Rudy turned to Blair with a steely-eyed glare. "At least I don't trigger a seismic event when I exercise."

"No, it would hardly register on the Richter scale," Blair sniped back.

Rudy waved a dismissive hand in the air. *"Don't waste words on people who deserve your silence,"* she said, before pretending to zip her lips closed with two fingers.

"Who said that?" I asked her.

"Mandy Hale," she replied. "I'm sure Blair has never heard of her. She wrote *The Single Woman*. A book Blair would never read."

"Humpf," Blair snorted. "Since she's a favorite of yours, I thought she must have written *Little Women*."

Doe and I burst out in laughter. Rudy was only an inch taller than me, without an ounce of fat on her.

"You have to admit, that was a good one," I said to Rudy.

"Maybe," she said with a reluctant smile. "Hey, look over there." She pointed across the road to where a small dog wandered around the Jayco RV campsite. "That guy didn't look like the type to own a dog."

"Maybe it's not his," Doe said.

The dog sniffed underneath the picnic table, picking up scraps left over from other campers.

"Looks like it might be a stray," I said.

The door to the RV opened and the stocky man came out with a beer can clasped in his meaty hand. He spied the dog under the table and scowled.

"Get outta' here," he said with a jerk of his chin.

The dog looked up and came out to sit at the bottom step of the RV.

"Scram!" he yelled.

When the dog didn't respond, he threw the full beer can at it, clipping the dog in the shoulder. The poor thing yelped and ran away. The man spun on his heel and returned inside the motorhome.

"Nice guy," Blair said. "He yells at his wife and kicks a dog. Definitely not my type."

"He didn't kick the dog," Rudy countered.

Blair gave her an exasperated look. "I know that. I was just making a point."

"Point made," Rudy said.

"I wonder where the dog went," I said, straining to see around the motorhome.

"There it is," Doe said, pointing to the road.

The dog was trotting in our direction. A moment later, we had a guest.

It looked like a cross between a poodle and some kind of terrier with dirty white fur, a soft curl to its tail, and a fluffy face. I got up and skirted the table in its direction, hunkering down so as not to spook the little thing. Instead of running away, the dog dropped its head and came forward, wagging its tail.

"Hello little boy…uh, girl," I said, glancing around to her hind legs.

The little dog sat down and raised a paw.

"Oh, my goodness," Doe said. "Someone has trained this dog."

"I bet she's hungry," I said. The dog whimpered and scooted forward, begging. "Doe, can you put a couple of meatballs into a bowl?" She did as I asked and handed the bowl to me. "Here you go."

I put the bowl down. As the little dog bowed her head to eat, I noticed a turquoise collar embedded in her fur.

"She has a collar on."

I knelt down and patted her head while she ate. She flinched at my touch, but kept eating.

"She's hungry," Rudy said. "She must be a stray. It's clear she hasn't had a bath in a hundred years."

I kept petting her until she finished and then scooped her up into my arms. I returned to the bench and reached under her chin to find a tag.

"Her name is Tinker Bell, but there's no phone number." I flipped the tag over. The back was blank. "Jeez, what idiot puts the name of the dog on the tag, but no contact information?"

"Why don't we walk around after dinner and ask people?" Rudy said. "Maybe we can find her owner."

"Sounds good," I said. "Did anyone bring a leash?"

"No," Blair said. "Handcuffs, but not a leash."

We all stopped and stared at her, mouths open.

This time, she burst out laughing.

CHAPTER SIX

Rudy found a length of clothesline to use as a leash. We left Blair and Doe to do the dishes and walked down to the store with Tinker Bell, passing campers out barbequing, building fires, playing games, or doing dishes.

"God, I love the smell of campfires," I said, pulling in a deep breath. "It just enhances the taste of everything and makes me so nostalgic."

"Yeah, somehow just being here relaxes me," she said. "Life is slower. No hassles. Nothing to do. Just relax."

It took only a few minutes to get to the store, which was the size of a mini-mart. Firewood was stacked against the wall outside, along with a place to fill propane tanks. I picked up the dog before we went in.

Inside, there were shelves stocked with everything from food to small pots and pans. It even had an entire section for gloves, flip-flops, t-shirts and socks.

A young woman with spikey black hair sat on a tall stool behind the counter, helping a couple of teenage boys.

"I need some decaf coffee."

"I'll wait here," Rudy said.

I found the aisle with coffee and tea and grabbed a small jar of decaf. When I came back, Rudy was still standing near the door, smiling.

"What's up?" I asked.

The two boys passed us on their way out, laughing and gesturing at the girl behind the counter.

"God, what an idiot," the taller one said as the screen door closed behind them.

I glanced at the girl. She was focused on her phone now, her fingers flying.

"What happened?"

"They asked her if she had any Sudoku. She said they only had Top Ramen."

"Oh, dear," I said with a grimace.

We stepped up to the counter. I put the jar of coffee down, which triggered a response. Without a word, the girl rang it up, put the jar in a small paper bag and handed it back to me. I gave her cash, which she threw into the register and then went back to her phone.

"Um...excuse me," I said. She looked up with a bored expression, her dark eyes blank. "Have you ever seen this dog before?" I asked, holding up the little pup. Tinker Bell wagged her tail.

"Sure. It's been wandering around here for the past week or so." She turned back to the phone in her hand.

"No one has inquired about her?" Rudy asked. "Or come looking for her?"

The young woman didn't even look up this time. "No. But people come in to complain about her. She keeps stealing hot dogs off the barbeques."

I gave Rudy an exasperated look. "So you have no idea who she might belong to?"

"I already told you, no," she said without taking her eyes off the small screen in her hands.

"Okay, thanks," I said, turning away.

Rudy reached out and placed her hand on the girl's wrist. The girl looked up with alarm.

"I hope you haven't been staring at that thing all afternoon," Rudy said with the perfect look of parental concern gracing her face.

"Why?" the girl asked.

Rudy glanced at me. "I guess she hasn't read that study."

"What study?" the girl asked. "What are you talking about?"

"There was a Pew research poll that confirmed that staring at a cell phone for too long can damage the corneas in your eyes. Something about the plutonium in the microprocessor. Several kids have nearly gone blind."

The girl's eyes widened. She put the phone on the counter. "I only picked it up a few minutes ago."

Rudy leaned in and peered into her eyes. "I don't know. I see some redness. If I were you, I wouldn't look at it again for the rest of the night. Short periods of time seem to be okay."

Rudy turned away from the counter hiding a smile, and we left the store.

"The Pew research poll?" I said with incredulity. "You're a wicked old woman, you know that? They don't put plutonium in cell phones."

"You know that. And I know that," Rudy said with a smirk.

"Like I said, a wicked old woman." I glanced down at the dog in my arms. "So what do we do now?"

"Let's ask around," Rudy said.

We walked the entire circuit of the campground, knocking on RV doors and stepping into each campsite, with the exception of the RV across from us since it was obvious they didn't want the dog even it if was theirs. No one recognized her other than to say they'd seen her running around. We returned to the Hulk discouraged.

"No luck?" Doe asked when we returned.

She was sitting in one of the lawn chairs reading from her Kindle.

"No," I replied.

I untied the rope from the dog's collar, expecting her to run away. Instead, she took a running jump and landed in Doe's lap. Doe's hands jerked to the side as if she'd been electrocuted.

"What? Uh...Julia, come and get her," she said in a strangled voice.

I had never known Doe to have a pet. After all, they shed and made messes. Right then the pitch of her voice was her alarm bell going off. The little dog was leaving dirty paw prints all over her crisp white pants.

"Come here, Tinker Bell," I commanded, slapping my leg.

The dog ignored me, continuing to wag her tail and climb up Doe's chest, reaching out to lick her face.

"I think she likes you," Rudy said with a grin. "By the way, where's Blair?"

"Inside," Doe replied, her voice straining as she leaned away from the dog. "She wanted to take a shower and check her blood sugar."

Blair had type 2 diabetes, which she controlled through diet and exercise. And yet, she still had to check her blood sugar levels every couple of days.

"What should we do with the dog?" Rudy asked, grinning at Doe.

"I hate to just leave her on her own," I replied, watching the pup terrorize Doe.

"Perhaps one of you could help me," Doe said, shooting us an irritated look and flicking dirt off her arm.

I walked over and lifted the dog out of her lap and placed her on the ground. Doe quickly stood and attempted to wipe off her pants, while Tinker Bell sat at her feet, whimpering.

"She likes you," I said. "Maybe you're soul mates."

"Very funny," she said. Doe pointed a finger at the dog. "No jumping in my lap." The dog barked and wagged her tail. "Silly dog," Doe said with the flicker of a smile.

I glanced over at Rudy and we shared an amused look.

"Why don't I give her a bath?" I suggested. "We can keep her tonight and decide what to do about her tomorrow."

"Sounds good to me," Rudy said.

While Rudy watched the dog, I walked back up to the store and bought some flea shampoo, dog food and a pink leash. When I returned, I pulled a plastic tub from under the sink in the motorhome and grabbed a towel. Then I took the dog to a faucet at the edge of our campsite.

I spent the next ten minutes giving the little dog a bath. She seemed to enjoy the attention, pushing against me as I massaged her back. When I finished, I used the towel to rub her dry while she wiggled beneath me. When I let her go, she ran in circles, rolling around on the patch of grass that lined our campsite. Her antics made the three of us laugh.

I returned to the motorhome and found some scissors and then put her on the picnic bench to cut mats from the backs of her legs and trim the fur around her face. A few minutes later, her sweet eyes emerged from tufts of white fur.

"She looks adorable," Blair said, stepping down from the motorhome. Blair had wrapped her hair in a towel and thrown on pajamas and a robe. She carried a bottled Daiquiri in one hand and a plate in the other. "Anyone want cheese and crackers?"

Rudy was at the fire pit, stuffing rolled paper in between logs to start the fire as the sun began to dip below the horizon.

"I'd take one of those Daiquiris," Rudy said.

"Me, too," I said.

Blair put her drink and the plate down and went back inside, while Doe went to get the bug zapper from the compartment at the side of the RV.

As Rudy got the fire crackling, we pulled up chairs around the fire pit. Tinker Bell sat at Doe's feet begging for attention. Doe tried to ignore her, but finally relented and invited her back into her lap.

When I chuckled, Doe shot back, "What? My pants are dirty already."

"I think you ought to keep her," Rudy said. "You need something in your life besides work."

"I don't need a dog," Doe said, gently patting Tinker Bell's back. "Anyway, I can't take care of her. I'm gone too much."

"Oh, for heaven's sake, lots of people who work have dogs," I admonished her.

"Easy for you to say," she countered. "You get to have your dogs *at* work."

Blair emerged again with three bottled drinks. "I vote you keep her. She looks good on you."

"Funny," Doe said, blowing some dog hair from her upper lip.

"Hey, by the way, I was listening to the news. They still haven't found Senator Owens' daughter," Blair said, coming to the table.

Blair passed out the drinks and then plopped into the only empty chair. "I guess she was about to leave for college."

"And they're sure she didn't just run off?" Doe asked.

"Someone saw her shoved into a van," I said.

"Well, I'd want to run off if Owens was my dad," Doe said.

Rudy chuckled. "Me, too. But she wasn't living with him anyway, was she?"

"No," Blair said, pulling the towel off her hair. "Her father, the senator, lives in Spokane when he's not in D.C."

"How old is she?" I asked.

Blair began to comb out her damp hair. "Seventeen."

"What else did the report say?" Rudy asked, poking the fire and sending up a spray of embers.

"That her car was found in the parking lot and her belongings were on the pavement outside of the car, along with a half empty carton of Marlboro cigarettes."

"Well, that should help," I said. "They can get fingerprints off the carton, but David also said a witness who saw her lifted into the van thought she was drunk or sick."

"I wonder if this will derail Owens' bid for majority leader," Rudy said.

"Maybe that's why his daughter was taken," Doe speculated.

"That would be pretty extreme," Blair said. "Abduct his daughter just to make him give up his ambitions."

"David said Owens has a lot of money," I added.

A girl's voice cried out from somewhere in the park, just as a young couple and their two children passed by on roller skates. A group of teenagers also chased each other around in front of the campsite next to us.

"Oh, to be young again," Doe said, watching the kids torment each other.

Across the way, the door to the Jayco motorhome opened and a slender man with a ponytail emerged carrying a little blue cooler. He slammed the door and stumbled as he came down the steps and fell onto the picnic bench. He pulled a can of beer out of the cooler and then dropped the cooler onto the ground. He popped the top of the beer can and took a long swig. Then he lit a cigarette. A moment later, a petite woman with red hair came out and sat next to him, sharing his smoke.

"Interesting group to be traveling together," I murmured, watching them. "I mean are they friends...neighbors...related?"

"Why do you care?" Rudy asked.

"I don't. Just curious."

"You're too cynical, Julia," Doe said.

"Well, they don't look like a normal family taking a vacation," I said in my defense.

"What does a normal family look like?" Blair asked, swiping a cracker off the plate.

I shrugged. "Good point."

We continued to chat until the sun dipped below the trees and sounds around the campground softened. As a cool breeze rose up, I announced I was going inside to get a sweater. While I was inside, I grabbed the bag of marshmallows.

"Anyone up for roasted marshmallows?" I asked, coming back out.

"Not me," Blair said.

"I know. Sorry, Blair."

"That's okay. I lost my sweet tooth a long time ago."

As Rudy dropped another log on the fire, she said, "I'm in."

I broke out the marshmallow sticks and shoved one of the sugary treats onto the end of one. I dragged my chair over to the fire and sat down, leaning my elbows on my knees to position the stick over a hot coal.

"I'm going to get a jacket," Rudy said. She stood up and disappeared inside.

"And I'm going to take Tinker Bell for a potty run," Doe said, getting up.

She snapped on the new leash and took the dog to a grassy area behind the Hulk. Meanwhile, I rotated the marshmallow over the crackling fire, allowing the outer layer to brown.

"Have you talked to David today?" Blair asked me.

Even in pajamas, Blair looked regal sitting in the lawn chair with her blond hair falling loosely around her shoulders, her long legs crossed and dangling pink, fluffy slippers.

"Yes. Earlier this afternoon," I said, twirling the marshmallow so it didn't burn.

"I suppose he misses you."

I smiled shyly, remembering David's new nickname for me–Babe. "Yes. He does. But I know that besides the abduction, they also have a couple of burglaries they're working on. So even though I'm gone, I don't think he'll have much time to think about me."

Blair allowed her right hand to drape over the side of the chair as she held her Daiquiri. "You know, I'm hoping this trip will help you to relax a bit. Are you still having nightmares?"

"Occasionally," I replied with a sigh. "I keep seeing that basement in my mind whenever I close my eyes at night."

It was the basement where Doe and I had been held captive and where the serial killer had tortured his victims. He'd threatened to do the same thing to me.

"Well, here's to campfires and Daiquiris," Blair said with a lift of her bottled drink.

"Hear, hear," I said, taking a swig from mine. "Ooh," I said, spilling some on my blouse. I put the drink on the picnic table bench. "Darn it. I was hoping I wouldn't have to do laundry before we got to Chicago." I tried wiping the liquid off with my free hand.

"Better get that," Blair said, nodding toward my blackening marshmallow.

"Oh dear!"

I snapped my arm back. The flaming, gooey marshmallow flew off the stick and sailed over my head just as I heard the RV screen door open behind me.

There was a soft *splat*.

Blair gasped and her hand flew to her mouth

"God, don't tell me."

I made a 360 degree turn.

Rudy stood on the bottom step, as Doe appeared from behind the motorhome. The remnants of the blackened, sticky marshmallow had begun to slide off Rudy's chest and onto the ground. I watched it plop into the dirt with a sinking feeling, just as Tinker Bell swooped in to make it disappear.

Rudy glanced down at the dog and then at me, the weathered lines in her face set in a picture of angered restraint.

I got out of my chair. "Rudy, I'm so sor..."

"Not a word," she said, holding up a hand. She spun on her heel and returned inside the motorhome.

As the door closed, Doe chuckled and said, "I think you might be on dishwashing duty for the remainder of the trip. Come here, you naughty dog. That's not good for you," she said to Tinker Bell.

I slumped back into my chair as Doe came forward and sat down, putting Tinker Bell in her lap again.

"Why is it always me?" I said, tossing the marshmallow stick onto the picnic table.

"She'll get over it," Blair said.

"So that's it for marshmallows?" Doe inquired.

"You can have one," I said. "I don't need the calories, anyway."

Rudy emerged a few minutes later wearing a clean long-sleeved denim blouse.

"I don't suppose you still want a marshmallow, do you?" I asked, as she approached the campfire. "I'll roast it for you."

"No," she said, holding up her wallet. "I'm going to walk up to the store to get a Hershey bar and some graham crackers."

I jumped up. "Oh, I never thought about making s'mores. I'll go." I hurried into the motorhome and grabbed my wallet.

When I came back out, Rudy said, "Julia, don't worry about it. I can get them."

"Don't even think about it. I'll be back in a jif. I can use the exercise."

Since the office and store were set off to the far side of the park entrance, the quickest route would be to circle around the outside of the wagon wheel, following a well-worn dirt path, then to cut through some trees near the restrooms.

I turned around and slipped past the rear of the Hulk.

I didn't take a flashlight since there was a nearly full moon. I cleared our campsite through a couple of trees behind the RV and turned left onto the dirt path. The path wound in and out of the Quaking Aspens and came near to the creek gurgling in the background.

I left the path and crossed a patch of lawn and then entered a small grove of pines where it was pretty dark. Lights from the restrooms flickered about 500 feet ahead, but I was moving fast and focused on the store lights just beyond that.

I made it to the store in record time, bought the chocolate and graham crackers and headed back to the Hulk.

I passed the restrooms under the canopy of pine trees and stepped over a fallen log. My foot caught under something heavy on the other side, and I was thrown forward, landing on the ground with an "Umpf!"

"Damn," I said, spitting out dirt.

I propped myself on my elbows, wondering if anyone had seen me. *Story of my life!* I thought.

As luck would have it, there wasn't a campsite within close range. Perhaps just this once I'd be the only witness to my mishap.

I pulled my legs forward to get my knees under me, but had to yank my left leg over whatever it was that had tripped me in the first place. And whatever it was was large. When I'd freed my leg, I rolled onto my side and glanced back.

Something lay in front of the log behind me. I peered at it in the dark, trying to make out what it was. As my eyes focused, I realized that two half-lidded eyes were staring back at me!

"Aaaargh!" I screamed, scrambling to my feet.

A man lay on his back, his head turned in my direction. My heart thumped so wildly, I found it difficult to breathe. I inched forward and leaned in to get a better look at his face and then gasped.

It was the skinny guy with the ponytail from across the road–the one who had come out for a smoke.

Very little light penetrated the pine trees above, so I couldn't tell if he was breathing or not. A black splotch in the middle of his forehead made me curious. I reached out to touch it and came away with something wet on my finger.

"Oh my God!" I uttered, rubbing my thumb and index finger together.

I stumbled backwards in shock. He'd been shot. Nervous, I glanced around, wondering if whoever had done this was nearby, but it appeared that I was alone.

The thought of help had me reaching for my phone to call the police, but then I realized I'd left it back at camp. A lightbulb went off in my head–I needed reinforcements.

I grabbed my bag of treats and ran back to the Hulk. It was a miracle I arrived unharmed, given my history, but I stumbled back into the light of the campfire out of breath.

"What happened to you?" Blair asked, noticing my dirty jeans. "No, let me guess, you…"

"I found a dead body," I blurted.

CHAPTER SEVEN

"A dead body?" Doe parroted me and then laughed. "Of course you did. You don't have to make excuses, Julia. You fell, didn't you?"

"Yes…over a dead body."

I dropped the paper bag onto the table and reached out to grab the Daiquiri from Blair's hand, tipping it up and finishing it in one gulp.

She watched me in alarm. "Your hand is bleeding," she said, getting out of her chair.

Rudy stood up and came around the fire pit. "Are you okay, Julia? You don't look so good."

"Is no one listening to me? I saw a dead body!" I was sucking air in like a vacuum.

Blair grabbed a napkin and handed it to me. I used it to wipe the blood off my hand.

Doe pushed Tinker Bell off her lap and got up. They all gathered around me.

"Okay, what actually happened?" Rudy demanded.

"I'm telling you. I tripped over a guy on the ground," I said in a hoarse whisper. "In fact, I think it was one of the men from that motorhome across the street." I pointed to the Jayco RV.

The three of them turned in unison to look at the RV across the road.

"He's not there," I snapped, getting their attention back. "He's lying on the ground up by the restrooms. It looked like he'd been shot in the forehead."

"Come and sit down, Julia," Doe said, trying to take my arm.

"No!" I said too loudly. I lowered my voice. "We need to report it. I just came back to get you guys. I don't want to do this alone."

"Why don't we just go tell the other people he was traveling with?" Blair said, gesturing to the Jayco RV.

"Are you kidding me?" I squealed. "They could be the ones who killed him."

Blair blanched. "Okay, maybe you should take us there?"

I nodded, swallowing. "Okay. C'mon. But someone needs to call 911. And we need a flashlight."

As Blair went to the side compartment for a flashlight, Rudy pulled out her phone. "Are you sure about this, Julia? I don't want to call the police…well, if there isn't a dead body back there."

"I saw what I saw," I whispered obstinately. "He had a bullet hole in his head."

"Okay," Rudy said, beginning to dial.

Blair came back with the flashlight. "Let's go."

Rudy reported the incident to the 911 dispatcher as everyone followed me back past our RV and through the trees. We turned onto the path and a minute later, veered off toward the small grove of trees.

"Okay, right up here," I said, heading for the big pine tree. "Here's the log. He's right here…uh…what?"

The body was gone.

"So, where is he?" Blair asked, flashing the beam of light on the ground.

"He was right there," I said, pointing to the spot next to the log.

I glanced around the area, thinking that perhaps I had the wrong spot. I didn't. The body just wasn't there.

"Maybe he wasn't dead," Doe offered.

"No, he was. I saw a hole in his forehead, and his eyes were open, staring at me."

Rudy was still on the phone with the 911 operator. She put her hand over the phone. "Did you check if he was breathing?"

"Um…no. I was too shocked."

Blair used the flashlight again to study the patch of dirt at our feet. "There's no blood on the ground."

I followed her gaze. "He was lying on his back."

"If he'd been shot there'd be blood on the ground," she said.

We all stared at the area around our feet, using the flashlight to survey a six foot area. The ground looked undisturbed.

"Look, Julia," Rudy began. "Maybe I should call off the police."

"No, I know he was here."

"You have been through a lot lately," she said in a patronizing tone.

"And you *have* had a Daiquiri," Doe added.

I stared at each of them in turn. "I didn't imagine this."

"But there's no one here," Blair said. "What are we supposed to do?"

"I don't know," I replied with a raised voice. I felt frustrated and a little bit panicked that I'd made a mistake.

The wail of a distant siren sounded, making everyone snap around in the direction of the store.

"Oh, great," Blair said. "How are we going to explain this to the police?"

I gave a deep, defeated sigh. "I'll talk to them. It's my mistake–if it *is* a mistake. I'll go up to the entrance to meet them."

"We'll go with you," Doe said.

"Thanks. They're here," Rudy said into the phone. She flicked off her phone. "Let's check around as we go. Maybe we're just in the wrong spot."

We spread out and moved in the direction of the campground entrance. By the time we made it to the store, a squad car had just arrived. The officers had turned off their siren and lights as they rolled past the information booth.

When they pulled up to the store, I stepped forward. Two dark-haired officers emerged from the squad car. The driver was in his thirties. The other was balding and looked to be in his early forties.

"We're the ones who called you," I said to the driver. "I thought I saw a dead body."

He had heavy features and a cocky swagger to his step. His thick eyebrows lifted, revealing piercing blue eyes.

"You *thought* you saw a dead body?" he asked, not even trying to hide his skepticism. "And your name is?"

"Julia...Julia Applegate."

The other officer had come around the car and was eyeing each one of us in turn–probably attempting to size up our truthfulness, or sanity. He had a dark complexion and large brown eyes. His eyes lingered on Blair, who seemed almost comical in her pajamas. When the store clerk pushed open the door behind us, he waved her back inside.

"I'm Officer Ranch," the younger officer said. "This is Officer Romero. Tell us what happened."

I took a deep breath before beginning. "I came up to the store by the back path and cut through the trees. On my return trip, I stepped over a log and tripped over something on the other side. When I turned around, there was a man lying on the ground."

"You tripped over the log or the body?" he asked.

"The body," I said with emphasis.

"Where was this?" Officer Romero asked.

I pointed behind the store. "Back there. Past the restrooms."

"Let's go see what you found," Officer Ranch said, beginning to step past me.

"Um…he's not there anymore."

He stopped, turned and furrowed his brow. "What do you mean?"

"The body is gone. I didn't have my phone with me, so I went back to our campsite to get my friends."

"I'm actually the one who called 911," Rudy said, stepping forward.

The officers glanced at her and then back at me.

"And?" Officer Ranch asked without trying to hide his sarcasm.

"I brought them back to the *exact* spot where I tripped."

"And he wasn't there," Officer Ranch said, finishing the story.

"Right."

"Why did you think he was dead in the first place?" Officer Romero asked with more compassion in his voice.

I shifted my gaze to the girls and then back again. "Um…because it looked like he'd been shot in the forehead. I touched it and my finger came away with blood." I held out my index finger. "See?"

Neither of the officers blinked or laughed, which I guess was a good thing, but they didn't look at my finger, either.

"Tell you what," Officer Romero said. "Let's get your names and contact information first. Then, we'll go back to look for ourselves."

"There's no one there, officer," Rudy spoke up.

"We'll take a look, anyway," Officer Ranch said, barely looking at her.

We gave them all the information they needed, which Officer Ranch noted in a small notebook. Then, I led them back the way we'd come, stopping at the big tree. The officers used their own flashlights to survey the area, spreading out for several feet beyond the log.

"There's a broken branch up here," Officer Romero said, pointing to the stub of a tree branch right above the log. "Could the man you saw have run into this and passed out?"

"Maybe," I said, looking up at the branch.

"There's no blood on it," he said, flashing his light at it.

"Did you recognize the man on the ground?" Officer Ranch asked, snapping off his flashlight.

"Yes," I said, brightening up. "I was sure it was a man from the campsite across the road from us."

"Let's go see if we can talk to him," he said. "We'll follow you."

The six of us traipsed back through the trees onto the dirt path along the creek. As we emerged from behind the Hulk into our campsite, I pointed across the road. "He came from the campsite over th…what?"

The Jayco motorhome was gone!

"It appears that campsite is empty," Officer Ranch said, stepping past me and slipping his thumbs through the heavy belt around his waist.

"There really was an RV there," Doe said in her measured CEO voice.

"It's not there now, however," the officer replied with a less than an encouraging expression.

Blair walked toward the road and looked both ways. "They're long gone. They left a cooler behind, though," she said, pointing to the blue cooler sitting under the picnic table.

"Don't you find that weird?" I asked the officers. "I mean, they were there half an hour ago. Who leaves in the middle of the night like that? And leaves stuff behind?"

Officer Romero shrugged. "Maybe they just stopped here for dinner. Or, maybe they'd been here a couple of days. Did you just get here today?"

"Yes," I replied. "This afternoon,"

"Were they here when you pulled in?"

"Well, yes," I said.

Officer Ranch glanced around our campsite. His gaze stopped when he saw the Daiquiri bottles.

I followed his gaze. "No, I wasn't drunk."

"But you *had* been drinking," he said.

I felt my defenses rise, and I stepped toward him with a raised finger. "Look, I know a thing or two about dead bodies." My foot got caught under the leg of the picnic table, catapulting me into the arms of Officer Ranch. He grunted, lost his footing and stumbled backwards into his partner. All three of us went down like a set of dominoes, one on top of the other. I lay chest-to-chest with him.

"Oh, dear," I exclaimed.

I rolled off of the officer, feeling my face burn. Officer Ranch leapt to his feet as if it had never happened. Officer Romero was a little slower to get up.

"I'm so sorry," I mumbled as Rudy reached out a hand to help me off the ground.

My face had to be a deep shade of red, although it was dark enough I doubted anyone would notice. But who cared? The damage was done. I'd just taken down two police officers.

There was silence as both officers readjusted their shoulder radios and belt equipment and then shook their legs out to readjust, well, their *other* equipment.

Finally, Officer Ranch said, "How much *have* you had to drink?"

"She's just a little accident prone," Blair said, stepping in to give me support.

"Look, I tripped over a log and now a table leg, but not because I was drunk," I snapped at the young officer.

"Except that now I smell like alcohol," he said, sniffing the front of his shirt.

Damn!

"I spilled a little earlier," I said, gesturing to my blouse.

"Mrs. Applegate, what did you mean when you said you know a thing or two about dead bodies?" Officer Romero asked.

"Nothing," Blair said, this time stepping in front of me. "She's dating a cop and her ex-husband happens to be the gov..."

"A politician," I said, slapping her arm. "Look, I saw a man lying on the ground. I don't know where he went, just like I don't know where that motorhome went. But I am not crazy, and I am not drunk."

The officers and I had a bit of a standoff until a whirlwind appeared behind them. My eyes shifted to the whirlwind with suspicion. It came up from the road and then whipped through the campsite, blowing Blair's plate of crackers to the ground and swirling its way toward us.

"Chloe, no!" I said between clenched teeth.

"What?" Officer Ranch asked.

Chloe ignored me. The whirlwind enveloped us, blowing everyone's hair askew. A heartbeat later, it was gone.

"What the heck was that?" Officer Ranch asked, brushing dirt off his shirt and smoothing down his hair.

I exhaled in relief as I straightened the collar on my blouse. "Probably just Chloe," I replied without thinking.

"Who the heck is Chloe?"

My head popped up. "She's just…uh…just…"

"The wind," Blair interrupted me, stepping forward. "You know, like that song. *They call the wind Mariah*," she sang lightly. "We call the wind…um, Chloe," she said with a little smile.

He stared at her in disbelief and then looked around at each of us in turn. "You've got to be kidding me. I'm about to write you all up for…"

"What?" Rudy asked sharply.

He shot her a quick glance. "For disturbance of the peace."

"We haven't disturbed anyone," Blair replied.

"You've disturbed *me*."

Another gust of wind arose by the campfire. This time it picked up the discarded crackers from Blair's plate and swirled them into a cyclone. The small cyclone advanced on us again.

Blair, Rudy, Doe and I stepped aside to let it pass this time. The tiny tornado continued until it stopped in front of Officer Ranch, whose eyes bulged in surprise. He didn't move until the small cyclone exploded, showering him with a burst of dust and cracker crumbs.

He coughed and spit out dirt. "What the hell is going on here?"

The rest of us shared a look, and then I shrugged in submission. "Do you believe in ghosts?"

Officer Romero dropped his head and chuckled quietly. On the other hand, Officer Ranch glared at me, running a finger under his lip to clean it out.

"You know I could find a reason to lock you up," he said spitting out the crumbs. He reached for his handcuffs and took a step forward.

His partner placed a hand on his shoulder. "No reason for that, Chuck. Let's go check in with the front office and see about that other RV. There's nothing else we can do here."

Officer Ranch paused, locked eyes with me for one more second and then relented.

"We *will* write this up. And if we hear any more out of you ladies, there will be consequences. I'll put the report on the police blotter so any law enforcement department within three states will see what nutcases you are."

"C'mon, Chuck. They're harmless. Let's go."

Officer Romero turned and left the campsite, while Officer Ranch continued to stare at me. He held it for one more second and finally followed his partner. As he entered the road, he twisted his head back one last time. And then, something tripped him. He skipped a couple of steps before landing face down on the pavement.

I gasped and clamped a hand over my mouth. I heard similar exclamations from my friends.

Officer Romero turned in surprise. "You okay, Chuck? Did the ghost get ya?" He snorted a laugh and then offered his hand to his partner.

"Shut up." Officer Ranch rebuffed his help and got back up on his own. He turned to us with an angry stare.

I lifted my hands in defense. "Hey, it wasn't us. We're all the way over here."

Rudy and Blair had hands up to mask their laughter.

"Police blotter," he spat. "Don't forget. I have all of your names." He turned and stomped away.

"Good going, Julia," Blair quipped. "Now we have a record."

"Can he do that?" I asked when the officers were out of sight.

"Yes," Rudy said with her mirth fading. "A police blotter is a written public record of all police calls on any given day. He can record every detail."

"Great. Now I'll be the laughing stock of the Coeur d'Alene police and every police department this side of the Mississippi." I turned to the motorhome in a huff. "I think I'll take a shower."

"Julia," Doe said, trailing after me. *"We* believe you saw something."

"Okay," I said over my shoulder. "Still going to take a shower." I climbed the steps and slammed the door behind me, leaving everyone else outside.

I knew I was acting like a teenager. I just couldn't help it. I was frustrated. I was embarrassed. And I was confused.

But I wasn't crazy.

I had seen a man on the ground. Maybe he wasn't dead. Then where was he? And why had the Jayco RV left so suddenly?

CHAPTER EIGHT

When I emerged from the small, steamy bathroom twenty minutes later dressed for bed, everyone was settled in the main living area. Someone had made popcorn, and the smell wafted in the air making my mouth water.

"Hungry?" Rudy asked.

She and Blair were sitting at the dining table, while Doe sat in one of the swivel chairs with Tinker Bell in her lap.

"Come and sit down." Blair patted the seat next to her.

I grabbed a bowl from one of the cupboards and slipped into the seat next to Blair.

"Sorry about before," Rudy said. "I was mostly laughing at that cop. He was a piece of work."

Doe chuckled. "I have to admit that I enjoyed watching him take a header," she said, stroking Tinker Bell's head. "He was just a little too full of himself."

I pursed my lips. "It's okay. I'd laugh, too, if I wasn't so sure I tripped over a guy lying on the ground. I just don't know what happened to him."

"Maybe he walked into that branch, like the cop said," Blair suggested. "He fell just before you got there, but was just too drunk to get up and then managed to stagger away after you left."

"Then why did they all leave so suddenly?" I asked, referring to the Jayco RV.

"I don't know," Rudy admitted. "That was weird."

I scooped out some popcorn, and Rudy pulled out a board game from the cupboard above our heads. "Let's forget about it. How about some Scrabble?"

I laughed. "Are you kidding? How can we play Scrabble with you? You have the vocabulary of Ernest Hemingway, Emily Bronte, and F. Scott Fitzgerald all rolled into one. We don't stand a chance."

She gave me a self-satisfied smile. "To be honest, since Hemingway wasn't known for his vocabulary, I'd prefer Henry David Thoreau or T.S. Eliot. And I was never a Bronte fan."

"Then I'll take Emily Bronte," Doe said, raising her hand. She put Tinker Bell on the floor and came to sit next to Rudy. "And maybe Charles Dickens."

I smiled. "I guess I'll take Agatha Christie and Arthur Conan Doyle."

"Don't forget L. Frank Baum," Rudy added.

Everyone knew the Wizard of Oz was my all-time favorite movie. My apartment was filled with collectibles and movie posters from the world of the yellow brick road.

"Not really," I countered. "I love the movie, but to be honest, I've never actually read the books, even though I own a full set of them."

"No kidding?" Rudy said. "That surprises me. How about you, Blair?"

Blair had opened the bag of Scrabble letters. "Dostoevsky."

The three of us stopped and stared at her. Our silence made her look up.

"What?" she asked, her pretty blue eyes glancing back and forth between us.

"You never cease to amaze me," Rudy said, shaking her head. She began to help with the game. "But don't forget…with Blair's memory, she'll probably beat us all, anyway."

During our first murder investigation, we had learned that Blair had a photographic memory; she'd merely glanced at the pages of an important book and then recreated a complicated chart days later. Her ability to remember dates, recipes, and the names of nail polish colors suddenly made perfect sense.

"Are you feeling better, Julia?" Doe asked in a quiet voice. "You and I have both just gone through a terrible ordeal." She reached over and placed her hand over mine.

"And you haven't been sleeping well," Blair said.

"I'm fine. Maybe I just have murder on my mind too much these days. Now I'm seeing dead bodies everywhere."

"I think you're being too hard on yourself," Rudy said. "Doe's right. You both need a rest. That's partly why we thought this trip would be a good idea. A change of scenery."

"With lots of fresh air," Doe added, taking a cleansing breath.

"And some laughter," Blair said.

I chuckled. "Then let's get this game started so I can laugh myself silly when I misspell the first important word."

We played for about an hour. Blair did, in fact, win. Doe put the game back in the overhead compartment, and Blair turned on the TV to catch the late news. The station had just cut into the report from a young female D.C. reporter from earlier in the day. She was standing in front of a big brick building with a microphone stuck in Senator Owens' face.

"Ooh, turn it up," I said to Blair.

She flicked the remote control to increase the volume.

Senator Owens was short, perhaps five foot six, with thinning, gray-black hair brushed back at the forehead. Thick-rimmed glasses accentuated his dark eyes, making them look like pools of oil. He wore a navy blue suit with a red tie and kept pushing his glasses up his broad nose as he spoke.

"Yes, I've been in touch with Amy's mother," his voice boomed out. "We're both cooperating as much as we can with the police."

"Has there been a ransom notice?" the reporter asked.

Owens hesitated, glanced at someone off camera and then said, "Ransom? No. But I'd do almost anything to get her back. Now, if you'll excuse me, I'm due at a rally."

He turned away and disappeared into a big SUV. As the vehicle pulled away, the reporter turned to the camera.

"That's it, Bill. Back to you."

The regular news broadcast resumed, and Blair reduced the volume. "You've got to be kidding me. What does, '*we're both cooperating with the police as much as we can*' mean?"

"Good question," Doe said, putting Tinker Bell back in her lap.

"Did you notice how he hesitated before answering the question about the ransom?" I asked. "I wonder if they *have* heard from the kidnappers, but just don't want to say anything."

"I have a hard time believing anything that slime ball says, and I doubt he would do whatever was necessary to get his daughter back," Rudy said. "In fact, he emphasized that he'd do *almost* anything to get her back. A real father would have stood there as long as it took and do whatever he could to appeal to the kidnappers. Let's face it. He just cut the interview short so he could make it to a rally. He's an egotistical son-of-a-bitch."

"Well, I for one would just as soon leave all that stuff behind," Doe said. "We're on vacation. That means no murders and no mysteries."

"And no egotistical sons-of-bitches," Blair added with a smile.

The cupboard above the table popped open and the Scrabble box fell out again, spilling a handful of letters onto the table in a seemingly random order. I glanced down and inhaled a breath .

"Look," I said, pointing to the letters.

Seven of the letters clearly spelled out one word.

D.E.N.T.I.S.T.

CHAPTER NINE

We assumed it was Chloe who had spelled the word; we just had no idea why. Perhaps she didn't like dentists. We laughed it off and went to bed.

The next morning I awoke to the sound of someone in the bathroom. I rolled over and opened my eyes. Rudy was just drawing her legs out from her sleeping bag on the pull-out sofa bed.

"Morning," she mumbled.

"Good morning," I replied, stretching my arms above my head.

The bathroom door opened and Blair appeared with toothbrush and toothpaste in hand. She and Doe had shared the bedroom, which was equipped with two single beds.

"How'd you guys sleep?" she asked in a quiet voice.

"Pretty good," Rudy replied.

"Me, too. Is Doe awake?"

"Yes," a voice said.

Tinker Bell bounded into the main part of the RV and jumped onto my bed to greet me. She stuck her cold nose under my hand, asking for a pet. Doe stood in the bedroom doorway, already dressed.

"You guys want to use the bedroom to get dressed?" she asked. "I'm going to take Tinker Bell out."

"Yeah, that would be nice," I replied.

We spent the next twenty-five minutes dressing, brushing teeth, rolling up sleeping bags, and putting the table back up. Since we were anxious to get going, breakfast consisted of April's cinnamon rolls and some fruit.

After we'd finished breakfast and cleaned up the few dishes, we unhooked the water and electricity, put away all the chairs and climbed aboard for the second leg of our trip.

Blair was driving, and I decided to ride up front with her. As I settled into the big swivel co-pilot's chair, I glanced out the window at the empty campsite across the road, wondering again about the incident the night before.

"I still wonder why those guys left in such a hurry last night. It just seems so strange."

"Hold on a minute," Blair said, climbing out of her chair. She exited the RV and ran across the street to the cooler sitting underneath the picnic table.

"What's she doing?" Rudy asked coming up behind me to peer out the big front window.

"I don't know."

A minute later, Blair was back. "That cooler is empty except for a bunch of used needles in the bottom of it. Those people are druggies."

Doe grimaced. "Well, then, I'm glad they left when they did. We should stop and tell the store though, so they can dispose of the needles. Too many kids in this park."

"Good idea," Blair said, climbing back behind the wheel.

"Hey," Doe interrupted us. "We never decided what to do about Tinker Bell." She held the little dog in her arms.

"We could stop in town and try to find a shelter," Rudy said.

"Don't most shelters put them to sleep within a few days?" I asked.

Doe's dark eyes opened in horror. "No way. I'm not letting some shelter euthanize this little dog."

Tinker Bell seemed to sense Doe's stress level and reached up and licked her chin.

"We could stop at some of the homes we saw along the road to see if they recognize her," Rudy suggested.

"No," Blair said, putting the big rig in gear. "That will take too much time. You said the gal at the store said she'd been running around here for at least a week and no one had come looking for her. I say we keep her."

"I agree with Blair," I said. "At least with us, she'll be safe."

"What about when we get to Chicago?" Rudy asked skeptically.

I glanced around at Doe.

"Then I take her home," she said.

We all shared congratulatory looks.

"Bully for you," Rudy said.

"Welcome aboard, Tinker Bell!" Blair announced as she started the engine and pulled out of the campsite.

We reported the needles to the manager at the store and then began the next leg of our trip, following I-90 across the northern part of Idaho into the great state of Montana. As I suspected, Doe had brought some work with her and pulled out a report and her reading glasses.

"What are you reading?" I heard Rudy ask her as Doe opened the folder.

"It's a report on solid waste disposal," she replied.

"Sounds enthralling," she said. "I'll wait for the sequel."

I snuck a glance at Rudy. She gave me an eye roll, and opened the book she was reading. It was Doris Kearns Goodwin's biography on Abraham Lincoln, *Team of Rivals,* and I knew she was reading it for the second time. I smiled to myself. One more example of our diversity.

It was lunchtime when we pulled into Missoula. We slowed down to pass through town, and Rudy took the opportunity to call Elliott, her ex-husband. They chatted quietly for a few minutes. We heard her giggle once, which prompted a look between Blair and me in the front seats. When she hung up, she got up and poked her head in between us.

"Elliott says Joe Masterson is beside himself. They haven't seen Dylan in more than two days. Apparently, he was pretty upset about the break up with Amy. He was scheduled to go to a community college in Boston, close to the college Amy was going to so they could still be together."

"Do they think he's hurt himself?" I asked in alarm.

"I don't know. Elliott says the kid has a history of threatening to leave home. They think he might have done it this time."

"I would think that once it became public Amy was missing, he would come back."

She blew out a breath. "No doubt it makes him look guilty. Elliott said he'd keep me posted."

÷

We spent the night outside of Bozeman, Montana, in a big KOA campground. This one had thirty or forty tent sites and an equal number of RV slots. It had a swimming pool, a store, and a playground in the middle of a huge lawn at the center of the park. Our campsite bordered the big lawn.

The park was filled to capacity and there was activity everywhere. It was Doe's night to cook. She planned to whip up a fresh green leaf salad with mandarin oranges and walnuts to go with barbequed salmon. Doe took the time to dress the table again so we could eat outside in style and enjoy the sights and sounds of the campground around us. She also took the campsite's grill into the RV first to scrub it in the sink.

"Well, frankly, I can't complain about that," Rudy said, watching her through the small window above the sink. "I've never been thrilled about using the grills in public parks."

"Me neither," I said. "Bravo for Doe."

÷

We shared a great meal, with some fine wine and were just finishing when my cell phone rang. It was David.

"Hey, Babe," he said.

I chuckled and got up from the picnic table to go over to one of the camp chairs for privacy.

"Hello, yourself. How are you? How's the case?"

"Not much to go on, I'm afraid. Dylan Masterson is still missing."

"I know. Rudy's ex knows his dad. Do you really think he had anything to do with Amy's kidnapping?"

He sighed. "Not sure. He was pretty distraught after he and Amy broke up. That was the night before she disappeared. He called a friend and said he was coming over, but never showed. And his parents said he never went home."

"He could just be on a bender," I suggested.

"Sure, but for two days?"

"How is Senator Owens taking all of this?"

I didn't like the guy, but I wouldn't wish this on anyone.

"Like I said before, he won't leave his beloved office in D.C., so the FBI is talking to him there. They're also looking into anyone who is close to him."

"Why? Do they suspect another Senator or a staff person?"

"Right now everyone is on the list."

"How would someone in D.C. know where a teenage girl would be at ten o'clock on a Saturday morning all the way out in Washington State?"

"Simple. The senator emailed his daughter the night before. Her birthday was Sunday, and he wanted something delivered to her on Saturday. She told him she'd be at the park all day."

"Wow. So it could be anybody."

"Yes. He told at least one member of his staff about the delivery because he had to reschedule it. And the woman he told just happens to be camping somewhere in upstate New York, and we can't talk to her."

"Jeez. It's like you're blocked at every turn."

"That's not all," he said. "Being the popular politician that Owens is, he's also had several threatening letters and voice mails. The FBI is checking into all of that, too."

"It's never simple is it?" I said.

"It would be a lot easier if we at least knew why she was kidnapped. Right now, as far as we know, it could be some random stalker who took her."

"We watched part of Owens' news conference last night. He said there had been no ransom calls. Is that right?"

"Not as far as I know. We have the Dunphy's sitting by the phone. That's her mom and stepdad."

"So it could have been someone who took her to…" I stopped as a small chill rippled down my spine.

"Don't go there, Julia," he said, cutting me off. "We have an FBI task force set up. Homeland Security is even involved since it involves a U.S. senator."

"Juuuulia!"

The familiar voice that trailed across the campground like a banshee's cry made me jerk around. When my eyes focused on the source, I gasped.

"I've got to go, David. Believe it or not, Goldie is here. I'll talk to you tomorrow."

We hung up, and I returned to the table to find Doe nearly choking on her last bite of salmon. I patted her on the back to make sure she didn't pass out. I might have been surprised by Goldie's sudden appearance, but Doe looked stricken.

We watched my neighbor, Goldie Singleton, approach our campsite from the other side of the park. She was accompanied by another Mercer Islander, Aria Stottlemeyer. Not my favorite person.

Goldie waddled up to the campsite, waving her stubby little hand. "Helloooo," she called.

When she'd made it to the table, I said, "Uh…Goldie, what in the world are you doing here?"

"Did you follow us?" Blair sniped.

Goldie's eyes perked up. "Good one, Blair. No, we're goin' to a genealogy conference in Chicago. Didn't I tell you, Julia? Aria, here, is quite the genealogy expert." She nodded towards her companion. "She's related to the Duke of something-or-other."

"It's the Duke of Norfolk," Aria said with a slight twitch to her lip.

"Really? I had no idea," I murmured, glancing toward Aria.

That explained her imperious attitude.

Goldie was shorter than me and heavier in the hips. In fact, she carried her weight like a couple of saddlebags, hence the waddle. On the other hand, Aria towered over her like a skinny beanpole. While I found Goldie quirky and entertaining, Aria was another matter. She worked at the Mercer Island post office and enjoyed making other people uncomfortable. She not only liked to comment in public on the few extra pounds I carried, she had once found a way to interject the need for the Mayor to trim his nose hairs at a City Council meeting. How does someone do that?

I gave her a brief smile. "How are you, Aria?"

Her thin lips stretched into what would have to pass as a smile. "Fine. Where are you ladies going?"

"The Aberdeens have moved to Wisconsin," Rudy replied. "We're driving their motorhome across country for them."

Aria prided herself on knowing everything about everyone on Mercer Island since much of the information passed through the post office. Right now her Groucho Marx eyebrows arched in surprise.

"Really? I didn't realize the Aberdeens had moved."

Rudy chuckled. "You realize nowadays that most people learn stuff through social media, Aria. Not through the mail."

She grimaced. "They still have to file a change of address form."

"I bet you're happy to get away," Goldie said, changing the subject. "After what you just went through with that maniac." She shook her head. "I don't know how you were able to get outta that basement, Julia. I woulda peed my pants."

Doe got up. "I need to get something inside."

I watched Doe return to the motorhome with Tinker Bell right behind her. Doe could only tolerate Goldie's unbridled energy and quaint remarks in small doses. Apparently, she'd reached her limit.

"So...what are you guys traveling in?" I asked, not interested at all.

"Oh, oh," Goldie uttered. "Aria has a camper truck." She whirled around and pointed across the green space to a brown, three-quarter-ton pickup sitting in a campsite on the other side of the playground. It had a camper shell on it that extended over the truck cab.

"That looks cozy," I said. *No it didn't*, I thought. I'd last about half an hour in such close quarters with the two of them. "Where's Ben?"

Ben was Goldie's husband and our neighborhood conspiracy theorist.

"Oh, he's home takin' care of the gnomes." She snorted a short laugh, as if she'd just told a joke.

Goldie lived on about an eighth of an acre and had hundreds of gnomes on her property, both inside and out. Her house was called the Gnome Home by neighbors, and kids loved to sneak onto her property to move them around, I assumed just to drive her crazy.

"What about Betsy?" Rudy asked, suppressing a smile.

Betsy was Goldie's shotgun, which she'd used in February to shoot holes in my hand-stamped copper ceiling. To be fair, she'd done it in order to stop a man from killing me. But, while I appreciated the rescue, I still mourned the loss of my pristine ceiling.

Goldie frowned. "I wanted to bring Betsy, but Ben made me leave her at home. He was afraid I'd get in trouble carryin' her across state lines."

"Good call," Rudy said.

"Besides, everyone within a thirty mile radius will be safer," Blair said with a sweet smile.

"Another good one," Goldie said, laughing.

I stood up. "Well...it's good to see you guys. I hope you have a great trip. We need to get dishes done," I said, beginning to stack plates.

Blair and Rudy took their cue and jumped up to help.

"Yes, you guys have fun at the conference," Rudy said. "We'll see you back on the island." She headed for the motorhome with the empty salmon platter in her hands.

"Oh, sure, sure," Goldie said, shifting her weight from one foot to the other. "Well, you guys have a good trip."

"You, too, Goldie," I said. I gave her a quick wave. "Drive carefully. And enjoy the conference."

"Tell the Aberdeens to make sure and get that change of address form in," Aria said with a scowl.

Goldie and Aria left, crossing the playfield back to their camper. We huddled up in the Hulk, watching them go.

"Great," Blair said. "Now we're stuck in here all evening."

"Who'd have thought we'd run into them?" Doe said, flopping into one of the swivel chairs.

"So, I guess no campfire tonight," Rudy lamented.

"Not unless you want company," Doe said.

I glanced at her. "After my mishap with the marshmallow, maybe it's better anyway."

CHAPTER TEN

We spent the rest of the evening studying the map, discussing our route, and calculating how much time we might have for sightseeing. April called late to fill me in on things at the inn.

"I miss you," she said. "Especially because the visiting children have decided this is just one big playground."

I chuckled. "Patience, my dear friend. Patience."

"You don't understand. They literally think the inn is their playground."

There was a scream in the background and the sound of running feet.

"What was that?" I asked in alarm.

"Madeline!" a voice called out before April could answer. "Stop that! Preston, come here right now."

"Emergency! Emergency!" a tinny voice squawked in the background.

That last one was Ahab, our African grey parrot. His utterance was followed by two sets of high-pitched screams and then loud female crying.

"What in the world is going on?" I demanded.

"I told you," April whispered into the phone. "The Butlers have the son and daughter from Hell. I mean it. And the Griffins have an eight-year old boy that makes Attila the Hun look like Bambi. Add to that a sixteen-month old baby who is teething and we're in never-before-charted waters."

"Who's crying right now?"

"That's Madeline. She's eleven and won't need to go to college because she has a bright future as a grifter."

I choked on a laugh. "April! You've got to be kidding. She's only eleven. You think she's a con artist?"

"Ooooh, yes," April whispered. "She pits the boys against each other and then bats her big brown eyes at her mother and plays the fool. Right now, she's working her mother big time in the living room, staining your beautiful carpet with her fake alligator tears."

"I'm sure it's not that bad," I said.

"You have no idea. Besides all of that, the dogs have been imprisoned in the guest house because these kids don't know how to walk. It's not in their vocabulary. They run everywhere, and the Doxies chase them, nipping at their heels. All we need is a lawsuit because one of the dogs finally connects with an ankle."

Her description kept me chuckling. "I'm glad you put the dogs in the guest house. How is Ahab doing?"

"He's picked up Madeline's high-pitched scream. Somehow it's different than his siren sound. It scares the hell out of me. We moved his cage into the kitchen to keep him away from the kids, but I broke my favorite mixing bowl this morning when he let out a shriek."

"I'm sorry, April. I wish I could be there to help."

I heard her sigh on the other end. "No, you don't. And I'm glad you have an opportunity to relax. Listen, I just wanted to tell you that Mr. Fidelio said he can't break ground on the reception hall for another week or so. A project he's working on in Federal Way had some problems. I'll let you know when they get back to it."

"Okay," I said. "I'd like to be home for that, anyway. And I'm sorry I'm not there to help you. I bet you're not sleeping much."

"Sleep? What's that?" she said with a chuckle.

"All right. Hang in there, and don't get run over by a runaway kid."

She chuckled. "Got it. Maybe you could send me a Navy Seal or two for support. Take care and have a good trip."

We said our goodbyes and hung up.

I went to bed that night picturing Navy Seals rappelling down the side of the inn with night vision goggles ready to corral the kids.

÷

The next morning, we left early enough to miss seeing Goldie and Aria. I felt badly that we were avoiding them. After all, Goldie was my neighbor. And then I considered Doe's nerves and decided it was the right good choice.

As a nod to Blair, we pulled off into Billings so she could visit the place she had met and consummated her relationship with her current husband. All she did was get out of the Hulk and have us take a picture of her in front of Joe's Bar & Grill. She then had us take a picture at the motel next door in front of number 14. The whole event was a little bit of a letdown, but she texted the pictures to her husband and then giggled helplessly when he responded.

No one asked about the exchange.

We followed I-90 South to Fort Smith and then took a side trip to the Bighorn Canyon National Recreation Area as planned. Blair volunteered to make lunch and brought bologna sandwiches to a picnic table overlooking a deep, wild canyon, framed by an upland prairie. It was a clear, sunny day with a warm breeze. I'd brought the binoculars Caroline had loaned me and used them to study the awe-inspiring red rock formations.

"Look over there!" I said to my companions.

I handed the binoculars around so everyone could view a pair of bighorn sheep standing precariously on an outcrop of rock that hung over the winding river below.

"Watching them gives me the same feeling in the pit of my stomach whenever I see you wearing heels," Blair said with a smirk, handing the binoculars back to me.

"Funny," I responded.

We took a few pictures and then climbed back aboard the Hulk and hit the road. As we crossed the border into the northeast corner of Wyoming, we threw open the windows to allow the crisp, pine-scented air to fill the RV.

It was just after three o'clock when we pulled into the historic town of Buffalo, Wyoming, driving under a banner for the Clear Creek Summer Fest scheduled for mid-July. As we rolled down the main street, I snapped a picture of a life-sized bronze sculpture of a rodeo rider ready to tie a calf, with his trusty horse holding the line firm.

When I realized we were passing a string of antique stores, I called out to Blair. "Wait! Can we stop?"

"Sure," Blair said. "I'll see if I can find a place to park."

Blair found a space on a side street under a row of trees big enough for the Hulk. I marveled at her ability to parallel park that thing without so much as a scratch to the surrounding cars.

We grabbed our purses, put a leash on Tinker Bell and headed back down the sidewalk.

The town was filled with tourists who were strolling in and out of shops, consuming enormous ice cream cones, or sitting on benches enjoying the hot summer afternoon. I spent a glorious hour and a half browsing through two antique stores, making several strategic purchases. Doe followed me around, holding Tinker Bell in her arms. She made only one purchase, a lovely old sterling silver necklace with three blue topaz stones.

On the way back to the RV, I stopped in a small bakery to buy some treats for later. We returned to home base, where I unloaded my bags and spread out my finds on the dining table. They included an old sheriff's badge, a spittoon, two rusty branding irons, a lethal-looking vintage hay knife, a couple of rusted horse bits, and the pièce de resistance, an old photograph circa 1900 of a group of ranch hands castrating a bull.

"I've always wondered how a male can do that to another male," Blair mused, staring at the old photo.

"What do you mean?" Doe said, missing Blair's point.

"Cut their…"

"Got it!" I cut her off instead.

Doe chuckled. "Well, I've never seen anyone spend money so fast. All I found was something for my sister-in-law's birthday. Julia, on the other hand, emptied the store."

"I did not. I just knew what I wanted as soon as I saw it. I can already picture the vignette I want to create at the inn with a couple of old wagon wheels I have."

The ground floor of the inn was peppered with a host of antiques for sale. It was a big part of our business. Every couple of months I created a display by the front door as a way to showcase items that could be grouped together. The thought of a western scene, perhaps with a bale of hay or two, was forming in my mind.

"What'd you get, Blair?" I asked.

"A paper," she said, plopping down on the sofa. She snapped open a copy of *USA Today*. "I wanted to check on Owens' daughter. See if they've found her."

"You didn't do any shopping?"

She glanced up, creasing her perfectly penciled brows. "I'm not into antiques or souvenirs. Now, if there'd been a Tiffany's in town,

I would have been there in a heartbeat." She flipped one of the pages.

I turned to Rudy. "What about you? Find anything interesting?"

Her eyes lit up as she held up a dusty old book. "First edition of *The Great Gatsby*."

"Oh, my God, are you kidding?"

I reached out to take it out of her hand.

"It's missing the dust cover, a couple of pages, and the binding is torn, but I don't care," she said with a Cheshire Cat grin.

"You scored big-time," I said. "Good for you."

"Humpf," Blair snorted from behind us.

We turned to her.

"What is it?" I asked.

"The kidnapping story has already been relegated to the third page. Apparently they haven't found her." She looked up at me. "This is interesting, though. It says the police have interviewed her boyfriend, Dylan. He remains a person of interest because he doesn't have an alibi for the morning she went missing."

"That's good. I mean at least they've found him. When I talked to David yesterday, he was still in the wind."

"Don't they say if you don't find a person who has been kidnapped within the first 72 hours or so, the likelihood they'll be found alive drops dramatically?" Doe asked.

"Actually, it's only 48 hours," I replied. "After that, the trail can go cold and they may never be found."

"Then I feel sorry for that girl's family," Doe said. "I can't imagine what they're going through. And we can only pray that someone somewhere sees that girl and reports it."

"Does the article say anything about a woman who works for Owens?" I asked. "The FBI wants to talk to her, but she's camping somewhere in upstate New York."

Blair scanned the rest of the article. "Here's something. Owens' staff has all been interviewed except one assistant who is on vacation. A Roberta Stephens. She's backpacking in the Adirondack Mountains with her boyfriend. The FBI is hoping she'll call in. It gives a phone number."

"So the possible suspects are Amy's boyfriend and maybe this staffer," Rudy said. "Not much to go on."

"David said they're also looking at her stepfather. His business is in some trouble. Maybe he's hoping to get some money out of Senator Owens."

"He'd have to use an intermediary," Rudy countered. "Otherwise, Owens would know who he is."

"It seems pretty callous to kidnap your own stepdaughter in order to save your business," Doe said.

"Depends on how he feels about her," Blair said. "Remember, she's a teenager. I bet she's pretty tough for both of her parents to live with right now."

I smiled. "Sounds like you've had some experience in that regard."

"Let's just say that knowing how my dad felt about some of the boys I brought home when I was seventeen, I wouldn't have put the thought of abduction past him. He wasn't very successful in locking me up at night."

"Is that where you learned to use handcuffs?" Rudy asked with a snort.

Blair gave her a sly smile. "No. That's where I learned to get out of them."

÷

We took the turnoff for Mt. Rushmore after lunch and disembarked to join the throngs of tourists filing up the long walkway that extended under the Avenue of Flags. It was a cloudless day, with a crisp blue sky, and although the sculptures of the four presidents seemed small compared to photos, they were framed by the beautiful Black Hills of South Dakota, making them awe-inspiring nonetheless.

After taking several photos, including one in which we framed Blair's head in between Roosevelt and Lincoln, we joined the crowds of visitors in the gift shop. I bought a small copper bell with a color picture of the sculpture lacquered on it for Amelia, hoping she wouldn't drive her mother insane. I also found a gift I thought would bring a smile to April's face. It was a key chain with a small flask attached to it. The flask was emblazoned with the heads of the four presidents, and the thought of giving it to her made me laugh.

"What's so funny?" Rudy said, coming up behind me.

I showed her the key chain. "April is having an difficult time with a few of our guests," I said. "I doubt I'll have to explain the significance when I give this to her. What did you find?"

Rudy held up a flimsy pair of handcuffs. "For the princess."

I snickered. "You really are a wicked old woman, but knowing Blair, she may actually appreciate the gift."

"And have a way to use it," Rudy said with an evil grin.

By late afternoon we were checking into the Happy Camper Trailer Park in Rapid City, South Dakota. Because Rapid City is so close to Mt. Rushmore, it's noted for its elaborate Fourth of July celebrations. In fact, almost every small town within the surrounding area boasts of having one.

Rudy had made reservations at this particular campground because it was situated on the banks of a lake and offered its own fireworks show. Within a very short walk, we would have a front row seat.

We ate inside the motorhome so clean-up would be quicker and we could get down to the lake. When dinner and dishes were finished, we grabbed jackets, blankets, lawn chairs, flashlights and a cooler with a couple of bottles of wine and headed for the water. We contemplated taking Tinker Bell, but in the end, decided to leave her behind in case she might be spooked by the noise. Doe had bought her a rawhide chew toy at the gift store and tossed it to her new best friend just before we left.

It was a short walk to the small recreation lake. The sun was setting, and the shore was already filled with groups of people spread out with picnic baskets, small barbeques, coolers, chairs, and blankets of their own. A heavy barge, on which the fireworks were stacked, floated in the middle of the lake. A rim of green hills and trees framed it from behind.

Americana, I thought to myself. I just needed a hot dog.

Speaking of, a concession stand had been set up at the tree line. Since the temperature still hovered in the high eighties, a lot of people wandered away from it with ice cream cones, popsicles, big drinks, or colorful snow cones.

We found a vacant spot by a canoe rack and set up our chairs. Blair dug into the cooler and broke out a bottle of Riesling and handed out plastic tumbler cups. I brought out the box of cookies I'd bought at the bakery in Buffalo. I opened the top and passed it around, offering a mixture of miniature chocolate chip, oatmeal raisin, and snickerdoodles to my friends. When Blair ignored the box and passed it on to Doe, I surprised her with a small bag of sugar free brownies. She rewarded me with a smile.

"Thanks, Julia. I appreciate you thinking of me."

"I thought of you, too," Rudy said. She reached into her jeans pocket and pulled out a plastic bag. "Just for you," she said, giving me a knowing wink.

Blair knit her brows as she took the bag. Clearly, she suspected an insult. When she opened the bag and pulled out the handcuffs, she burst out laughing.

"Oh, Rudy, I always knew you cared about me more than you let on," she said. "Thanks. I know just what I'll do with these."

"And who you'll do it with," Doe emphasized with a mischievous glint in her eye.

We chatted amongst ourselves and people-watched as the sun sank below the mountains in the distance, leaving an orangey-pink glow behind. As we reminisced about fireworks displays when we were kids, told funny stories and generally enjoyed each other's company, I felt the heavy weight of the past month or so begin to lift from my shoulders. This is what I lived for: the warmth of my family and friends.

The fireworks were set to begin at nine-thirty. At quarter after the hour, the sight of all those ice cream cones took its toll, and I had to have one of my own. I asked if I could get one for anyone else. No one took me up on my offer.

I climbed the sloping lawn to the tree line and got in line behind two women who between them were big enough to blot out the sun. Okay, that was unkind. But, in comparison, my few extra pounds seemed inconsequential.

As I waited for the line to inch forward, I glanced around. To my right, an Asian family had staked out the area on the other side of the concession stand. There was a mom and dad with three toddlers–two boys and a girl. The little girl looked about four years old, and I couldn't help but smile. She reminded me of my daughter, Angela, at that age. I sighed at the anticipation of having my own grandchild someday and thought I should give Angela a call to check in.

I shifted my weight and turned to the left where four teenage boys were hanging around a big boulder, laughing and setting off smoke bombs, irritating anyone who passed by.

The line inched forward again when my cell phone went off. It was David.

"Happy Fourth of July," he said when I answered.

"You, too. Are you doing anything?"

"No. We're still embroiled in this case. We've had to run down multiple potential sightings of the girl, none of which panned out. But so it goes. What are you doing?"

I explained where we were and how soon the show would start.

"It always makes me feel like I'm in a war zone," I said, referring to the fireworks. "I'm glad you found Dylan, though. He didn't have much to say, I take it."

I kept inching forward as people left the line. Two girls joined their mother a few people in front of me, slowing it down again.

"He says he drove around all night after he and Amy broke up and ended up in the park about four in the morning. He fell asleep and didn't wake up until almost noon."

"So, he was there, in Luther Burbank Park when she was abducted?"

"Yep. But no one was with him, so no alibi. We're keeping him under watch."

"What about the woman who is backpacking?"

"Haven't found her yet. However, we learned that Owens planned to fire her when she got back."

"Did she know that?"

"Yes. His Campaign Chair confided in her."

"Why was he going to fire her?"

"She worked for his campaign and was in charge of paying invoices and tracking donations. They found out she'd been pocketing some of the smaller donations and raiding the petty cash."

"Whoa. Do you think she could be pissed off enough to have his daughter kidnapped?"

David sighed. "I don't know. According to the Campaign Chair she wasn't well-liked. She was a bit of a rabble-rouser, and her boyfriend is one of those weekend militia guys. If she was mad enough, she could have talked him into helping her with it. But, there has finally been a ransom notice."

"Hey, lady, move up!" a kid behind me snapped.

I whipped around and realized the two big women in front of me had left, leaving a gaping hole between me and the order counter.

"Sorry," I mumbled to the kid behind me. "Oh, shoot. I want to hear about the ransom note, but I've gotta go. Let's talk tomorrow."

I hung up and quickly moved up to order a Rocky Road cone. A minute later, I was heading back to the canoes when a couple of kids almost ran me over. I stopped short to let them pass.

As I waited to be sure I had a clear path, a familiar face crossed in front of me. My head whipped around to follow the man who carried a large cup of beer.

I refocused my eyes and took a quick breath.

It was the skinny guy with the ponytail from the Wolf Creek Campground walking away from the other concession stand line. He was wearing baggy jeans and a ball cap pulled backwards, along with a dirty tank top that showed off fully tattooed forearms.

My heart fell as my gaze followed him. Not because he wasn't dead. I guess that was a good thing. I was disappointed because I *had* been wrong.

As I watched him, a young boy bumped into him, spilling his beer. He turned angrily as the kid ran away, and I noticed that underneath the hat stretched backwards was a bandage on his forehead.

Ah ha! I thought. He must have run into that branch just like Officer Romero suggested. I hadn't been crazy. At least he'd been there on the ground, though not exactly dead.

He disappeared on the other side of the canoes.

I stood for a moment, narrowing my eyes as I watched him. I returned to my friends, but instead of stepping to the left where our group was sitting, I lingered at the end of the canoe rack, peeking around to the right. Sure enough, he had joined the red-haired woman. They were positioned at the end of the rack alone. No sight of the beefy guy with the beard.

I made a quick decision.

I stepped to the left and handed my cone to Blair, while I grabbed the back of my chair and dragged it towards the end of the canoe rack. Rudy looked over with a furrowed brow.

"What are you doing?"

"Uh…I just want to make sure I can see everything."

I planted my chair in the dirt, took back my ice cream cone and glanced to my right. Sure enough, I could just see the legs and feet of the two people I hoped to overhear.

I sat down as a loudspeaker crackled and a booming version of the national anthem burst forth, forcing all of us to stand. The music ended, and a voice said, "Welcome to Happy Camper's annual Fourth of July celebration. Sit back, relax and enjoy the most spectacular fireworks display this side of Mt. Rushmore."

There was a lull in the crowd as everyone took their seats again. Meanwhile, I leaned forward, licking my cone and listening to see if I could hear anything from my right.

And I did.

"We should have never gotten into this, Eva," the man said. "And now we have to go all the way to Chicago. That wasn't part of the plan."

"It *will* work," the woman replied. "And we're going to make a ton of money."

"But *we're* taking the biggest risk. And this Yoda guy Monty is always talking to is pulling all the strings."

Two girls ran in front of me, screaming, so I missed Eva's response.

I leaned forward more, straining to hear.

"Monty has things under control," she said. "I trust him."

"What about the side trip he wants to take to Lake Cleary?"

"He said they have to pick something up. That's all," Eva replied.

"I don't like it...don't trust...new guy...Roy..."

Once again, the two girls screamed, and I missed a portion of his sentence.

"Monty can control Roy," Eva replied. "You worry too much. And you need to stop drinking. Monty doesn't like it."

"Monty doesn't own me. And this Yoda is trouble. I'm telling..." *Boom!*

I flinched, almost dropping my cone.

The first huge firework exploded in the darkening sky above us, putting a halt to anymore eavesdropping. The first big firework was followed by three smaller ones in red, white, and blue. For the next thirty minutes, we sat in rapt attention until the show played out to the music of Tchaikovsky's *1812 Overture*.

By the time the show ended, it was dark. The sky around us was filled with smoke, and the air was dense with the smell of sulfur. People picked up blankets and chairs and began leaving the beach area, chatting amongst themselves.

As we headed back to the Hulk, I held back a moment to watch the couple next to us. They veered off to the left. Ponytail Guy stumbled once and bumped into the red-head. She pushed him away. They disappeared through some trees to another part of the campground. Since I didn't have an excuse to follow, I caught up to the others.

Minutes later, we were back at the Hulk. Doe was about to put a leash on Tinker Bell to take her for a walk.

"Let me do that," I said sharply.

Doe gave me a curious look. "I'm fine taking her."

"I need the exercise," I lied.

She still looked at me funny, but handed over the leash. "Okay."

"I'm going to get a fire going," Rudy said. "We never got those s'mores the other night, and now I want one."

"I'm going to take a shower," Blair announced.

"Well, then, I'll get the graham crackers and marshmallows out," Doe said.

I grabbed a flashlight and a baggie (just in case) and climbed out of the motorhome with the dog. We walked down the main road until we reached a fork. I glanced both ways, wondering which way to go. I decided to turn left, thinking it seemed more in the direction the two had gone.

Tinker Bell stopped once to pee and then walked in front of me, tail wagging. We passed families roasting marshmallows, rolling out sleeping bags, washing dishes, or sitting at picnic tables sharing popcorn and drinks. Nowhere did I see the Jayco motorhome with the red and blue stripes.

I was getting discouraged when I hit a curve in the road and there it was, hidden around the corner in the last RV slot.

My heart skipped a beat.

I couldn't explain what it was about these people that made me so suspicious, other than I'd thought Ponytail Guy (as I now thought of him) had been shot in the head. But, now, I wondered about what I'd heard by the canoes. What had the woman meant by, *"We're all going to make a lot of money?"* Were they selling drugs in addition to using them?

I paused in the middle of the road wondering what I should do. Then I remembered–I was out walking a dog. The white motorhome was the last in the row of campsites, bordering an area with grass and trees.

Perfect.

I proceeded forward as my heart rate sped up.

I'd never been good at covert actions, even when Angie was younger. I'd once tried to sneak up on her and a couple of her girlfriends when she was a teenager, hoping to overhear their conversation about a boy she liked. My foot rolled over a pencil on the floor, throwing me off balance. I stumbled forward with a cry of alarm and landed face down in the hallway, right in front of the girls. Angela just looked over at me and said, "Hi, Mom."

As I approached the white motorhome, a raised voice made me look that way. Eva and the burly guy I now thought was Monty were sitting at the picnic table, Eva's red hair illuminated by a camp lantern. A tall guy with a shaved head, who must have been Roy, the new guy, had Ponytail Guy pushed up against the RV.

"I swear, if you don't stop drinking, I'll kill you! We have too much to lose," he snarled.

I stopped and glanced their way. Roy seemed to sense my presence and turned. He let go of Ponytail Guy and stomped over to a chair by the campfire. Ponytail Guy rubbed his neck and stumbled around the end of the camper and off toward the lake.

I turned away and kept going until I stepped over the curb and into the dirt, my heart hammering.

What was going on with these people?

I purposely wandered to my right so I was hidden by their motorhome. I allowed Tinker Bell to sniff around and came up along the backside of the Jayco. Ponytail Guy had disappeared into the dark, so I decided to sit down on a big flat rock near the curb.

I'd no sooner gotten comfortable than a loud knocking made me turn toward the RV. Someone from inside the motorhome was banging on the wall.

"Dammit!" a voice growled from the other side of the vehicle.

I heard the motorhome door open and slam shut. Even though all the curtains were closed, I turned away in case someone looked out. I listened carefully.

There was the soft murmur of a female's voice. Then a male voice snarled, "Shut up! Eva, get in here!"

The motorhome rocked as Eva entered. She said something, but I couldn't understand it. The male replied, "Just do it unless you want to blow the whole operation!"

The motorhome rocked again, and the door slammed. It was quiet for a moment. Eva spoke to someone, but again I couldn't hear what she said. The motorhome rattled a bit as someone moved around inside. Eva, I assumed. A moment later, there was a soft cry and then all went silent.

"What the hell are you doing here?"

I jumped to my feet and spun to my right. Monty stood in the dark, his ugly face cast in shadow.

"I'm just walking the dog," I choked out. "I didn't mean to bother anyone."

"Well, you're bothering me. You're in our campsite."

"Actually, I'm not in your campsite," I said, glancing over to the curb that served as the dividing line.

He stepped forward, making me back up. Tinker Bell jumped in between us, barking and lunging at him. I pulled her back.

"Move on. And take your mutt with you."

The anger in his voice was menacing. I had no doubt this man would harm me if I didn't comply.

"I…uh…"

"I mean it," he snapped, throwing up his hand in front of my face. "And take this mangy animal with you."

He kicked out at Tinker Bell, connecting with her shoulder. She cried out. Instead of retreating however, she whirled around and tore into his ankle with a vengeance. He cried out in pain and stumbled backwards with the dog still growling and attached to his sock. I interceded, grabbing hold of the snarling, snapping dog and pulled her back. She wouldn't let go, ripping his sock.

"I'm sorry, but that was your fault," I said, holding her up.

He was bent over, grabbing his ankle. "I'm going to report you and that rabid dog. He'll be impounded."

Since I knew he was bluffing, I decided to bluff back.

"I'm happy to make the call. Let's get the police out here and let them decide whose fault this was."

He grew quiet, staring at me in the dark, his left eye pulled down at the outer corner as if it had been injured at some point.

Count to three.

"Just get the hell out of here."

"No problem."

My heart was racing, but I began to back up, feeling the need to keep my eye on him. When I got to the curb, I turned and left. I glanced back once. He was still staring at me from the shadows.

I passed the campsite. The man named Roy turned in my direction as Eva emerged from the motorhome. She stopped at the bottom of the steps, staring at me. Monty limped around the corner of the RV and stopped, completing a threatening tableau.

As a chill snaked down my back, I turned and retreated up the road, feeling three sets of eyes watching me.

CHAPTER ELEVEN

When I got back to our campsite, Rudy had a roaring fire going. She and Doe were sitting in chairs chatting and enjoying the outdoor ambience. I put Tinker Bell down, and she pulled at her leash to get to Doe, so I let her go. She ran and jumped into Doe's lap.

"Hello, little girl," Doe said with affection, ruffling her fur. "Hey, wait a minute." Doe used her fingers to hold the little dog's head to one side. "What's this?" She looked up at me, her brows pinched with concern. "What happened, Julia? This looks like blood on her nose."

The door to the Hulk opened, interrupting us. Blair emerged in pajamas and slippers again, drawing a comb through her wet hair.

"Where have you been?" she asked me.

"I took Tinker Bell for a walk."

"Sure you did," she said with a single lift to her eyebrows.

"I repeat, what happened?" Doe demanded.

I glanced over at Rudy, who was poking at the fire. "Don't you want to give me the third degree, too?"

She smiled and continued doing what she was doing. "No. Seems like they're doing a pretty good job of it."

I heaved a big sigh. "Okay, the white motorhome is here."

"Really? The one that left so quickly the other night?" Rudy asked, leaning back in her chair. "And you just happened to see it on your walk...the walk Doe was going to take until you snatched the leash out of her hands?"

I pulled one of the chairs over to the fire and sat down. "Okay. I saw that skinny guy with the ponytail from the Jayco motorhome down at the fireworks show earlier. The one I thought was dead."

"So, he's alive," Doe exclaimed.

"Apparently." I didn't want to revisit my mistake about his death and so kept going. "He was there with the red-headed woman. Her name is Eva."

"So that's why you pulled your chair to the end of the canoe rack," Doe said.

"Yes," I admitted. "I saw him at the concession stand and then watched him go sit on the other side of the canoes."

"Did you hear anything interesting?" Blair asked, sitting on the picnic bench, facing the fire. "Like anything about their drugs?"

"He said something to her about them taking all the risk."

"What would that mean?" Doe asked.

"I have no idea. He said it wasn't going to work, whatever it was. She replied that 'Monty'—I think that's the name of the stocky guy with the beard—had it under control and they were all going to be rich."

Everyone perked up at that little tidbit of information.

"So you took a walk to find their campsite," Rudy said. "And you must have found them. What happened?"

I took a deep breath. "There's a third guy with them now. I heard Ponytail Guy say something earlier about a guy named Roy joining them. And that another guy named Yoda was pulling all the strings. And get this…they're going to Chicago."

I let that sink in a moment.

"So we may see them again," Blair said.

"Yes. Anyway, when I was on my walk, Roy and Ponytail Guy were in a big argument. Roy had Ponytail Guy up against the motorhome and threatened to kill him."

"Sounds like a fun group," Doe said. "But I want to know where this blood came from."

"I went behind the motorhome to an area where there are no campsites. I sat down on a rock to let Tinker Bell sniff around. Monty showed up and ran me off."

"What? Why?" Blair asked.

"Maybe because I heard some weird stuff a few minutes earlier. Almost as soon as I sat down, I heard banging from inside the motorhome, as if someone was kicking or knocking on the wall."

"Maybe they were fixing a door or something," Blair offered.

"No," I said, shaking my head. "I think it was Monty who went inside right away and told whoever it was to shut up."

"Do you know who he was talking to?" Rudy asked.

"No. All four of them were outside."

"So there's a fifth person," she said.

"Yes. And Monty yelled for Eva. He told her, '*just do it or you'll blow everything!*'"

"That doesn't sound good," Doe said. "Then what happened? Get to the part about the blood."

"Before I knew it, Monty was by my side. I never even heard him come up. He said, '*What the hell are you doing?*' Then he ordered me to leave."

"He doesn't have any right to do that," Rudy said.

"I told him that, but he wasn't kidding. He stepped forward as if he would force me to leave. That's when Tinker Bell came to my rescue."

Doe perked up. "What do you mean?"

"She jumped in between us, and he kicked her. She tore into his leg."

"What?"

"Don't worry. Tinker Bell got the best of him. She went after his ankle, ripped up his sock and made him cry out like a baby. Anyway, that's why she has blood on her."

Doe's dark eyes were opened wide. "My goodness. She attacked him?"

"Yeah. Once I separated her from his ankle, he threatened to report her and have her impounded." Doe's face registered alarm, so I put up a hand to calm her. "Once again, don't worry. I challenged him to call the police, and he backed down."

Doe's face beamed with pride. She ruffled the dog's fur and leaned in to nuzzle her. "What a good little guard dog."

Blair and I smiled watching her, but Rudy sat back in her chair, a thoughtful look on her face. "I wonder what all that means," she murmured.

"I don't know, but there's something wrong with that group. I just know it."

"It's those bug antenna again," Blair said.

I turned to her. "No. You said my bug antenna was for finding dead bodies, and we all know how well that went. That guy is very much alive."

"Well, we know they're into drugs," Blair said.

"It's nothing that concerns us," Doe said with a slight reprimand. "We don't need to get involved."

"They'll probably be leaving tomorrow, anyway. Just like us," Rudy said.

I sighed with disappointment. "I know."

"Then I vote for s'mores," Rudy said, jumping up and grabbing the marshmallows off the table.

÷

It was Wednesday morning, and Blair offered to make pancakes and sausage for breakfast. When she announced she needed milk, I offered to walk up to the store. I found the little general store that sat next to a single gas pump. As I turned the corner and passed a big metal ice chest, I was surprised to find the Jayco motorhome there. Monty was outside pumping gas.

I turned my head as I went inside, hoping he wouldn't notice me, but I passed Eva on her way out. She carried a bag full of groceries and gave me a hard stare as she stepped through the door.

The refrigerator case was at the back of the store, so I quickly grabbed a quart of milk and returned to the checkout counter. The motorhome was still there, but Monty was climbing back behind the wheel.

The clerk put the carton of milk into a paper bag and handed it to me. I thanked him and approached the screen door, keeping my eye on the motorhome. As I stepped outside, the RV pulled away from the pump.

And…then it happened.

The curtain covering the back window was flung aside and the face of a young girl with dark hair appeared. Something pulled at the corners of her mouth, and her eyes were opened wide. She banged on the window with the flat of her hands and seemed to be trying to scream.

Then just as suddenly, she was yanked away from the window. The curtains were thrown shut, and the motorhome drove away.

CHAPTER TWELVE

I paused for a moment, unsure of what I'd seen. As the motorhome rumbled up the road, my mind struggled to understand.

Was that just a kid playing around? Maybe the kid that was banging on the wall the night before? Or was a girl being held hostage?

I hurried back to the Hulk and burst into the main cabin. Everyone stopped to gape at me.

"What's wrong?" Doe asked.

"I saw that motorhome again. They were leaving." I reached out to grab the counter to steady myself. My heart was hammering. "There was a girl inside. I think she was trying to get out."

"What do you mean?" Rudy asked.

"It was a teenage girl. It looked like she had a gag in her mouth…she was banging on the window."

My friends, *my best friends*, grew quiet and just stared at me.

"Don't you get it?" I insisted. "I think they might be holding a girl against her will."

Rudy got up from the couch and put her hand on my shoulder. "Julia, you need to let it go. They may not be very nice campers, but I doubt they've abducted someone."

"But you heard what they said last night."

"No, *you* heard what they said," she corrected me.

I spun around to address Doe and Blair. "Think about it. That thumping noise last night could have been that girl."

"Julia, why would someone abduct a young girl and then take her camping?" Doe asked with a dismissive chuckle. "I mean, you're not making sense. Don't kidnappers take their hostages to some abandoned warehouse or something? You're probably just getting this confused with the reports of Senator Owens' daughter."

"Oh my God!" I said, my eyes popping open. "Do you think it's her?"

"Whoa!" she said, holding up a hand. "No, I don't. I just meant you're conflating the two."

I dropped into one of the swivel chairs. "But the comment I heard out by the canoes about them getting a lot of money fits with an abduction," I argued.

"It also fits with selling drugs," Blair said.

"Maybe they're delivering her to someone," I argued. "Maybe they're sex traffickers."

"In a motorhome?" Blair almost choked on a laugh. "C'mon, Julia. Get real. I can just see the police chase now."

"Stop making fun of me." I slammed the grocery bag on the game table and took a deep breath. "Here's your milk. I'm not hungry. I'm taking a shower before we leave."

Once again, I let the splash of warm water wash away my anger and anxiety. When I'd finished, I emerged dressed and ready to go. There was no friendly banter between us this time. The girls were just finishing breakfast, and the tension hung in the air like smoke. I put my toiletries away and repacked my suitcase as they pulled the dirty dishes together and began to get ready to leave.

I joined the silent effort.

As a group, we had occasional disagreements, but we rarely had fights. This felt like a fight. And I was at the center of it.

A half hour later we were back on the road. This time, Doe was driving and Rudy was riding shotgun. I was in one of the swivel chairs, while Blair sat at the breakfast table using her big makeup mirror to apply her eyeliner. The tension was palpable. I noticed Blair glance at me a couple of times.

I pulled out my mystery book feeling like the odd man out. I treasured my friendships with Doe, Rudy, and Blair, and for the first time I felt the friendship beginning to splinter. Tears began to form at the thought, and I turned to the window to hide my distress.

I just wish I was sure of what I'd seen. Was I trying too hard to turn this into something it wasn't? It was a strange group of people traveling in the Jayco RV, to be sure. The guy called Monty had anger problems. Ponytail Guy drank too much. They were involved together in something that was going to earn them a bunch of money. But were they kidnappers? The girl I'd seen might just as easily have been their daughter or niece playing a prank.

I wiped away a tear and sighed, feeling a different weight lay heavy on my shoulders now.

Once I dug my teeth into something, I had a tendency to hold on. I knew that. It sometimes got me in trouble. It appeared this was one of those times. I had to decide if I was going to allow it to drive a wedge between me and the people I relied on most.

Soon, we were passing over the Cheyenne River and crossing into the center of South Dakota. I continued to watch the scenery pass by as I contemplated my options and was barely aware of Blair getting up to go to the bathroom. A few minutes later, a pair of arms enveloped me from behind. I felt Blair's cheek against mine as her Vera Wang perfume flooded my nostrils.

"You're the best of us, Julia," she whispered. "Don't let our cynicism stop you. Call David if you need to and tell him what you heard. And don't worry…we'll always have your back." She kissed my cheek and returned to the dining table where she pulled out a book.

I gave her a thankful smile and took her advice. I pulled out my cell phone and dialed David's number. As I waited for him to answer, I realized the last thing he'd said to me was that Owens had received a ransom note. With all the hoopla about Monty and crew, I'd forgotten that.

My heart fell when the call went to voice-mail. I left a quick message and hung up frustrated.

I contemplated opening my book to get lost in someone else's mystery, but my mind wandered back to the haunting image of the young girl in the window. I realized I had a mystery of my own to solve. *Who was she? And was she in trouble or playing some silly game?*

I decided to pull out my iPad. I googled the kidnapping case. It wasn't hard to find multiple articles and a picture of Amy Dunphy.

"What'd you find?" Blair asked.

She had put her book down and was watching me.

"A picture of Amy Owens, or Amy Dunphy. That's her name now."

"Is it the same girl you saw in the motorhome?"

"I don't know. I didn't get a very good look at her. She did have dark eyes and dark hair, though, so it could be her."

I stared at the photo, trying to place her into my memory of the girl in the window. Amy Dunphy looked to be in her late teens and had wide-set dark eyes and shoulder length, curly dark hair.

"She looks a lot like her dad," I said. "It could be the girl I saw. It happened so fast, though. And she was partly obscured by the curtains and whatever she had in her mouth."

"You think we should have reported it to the police, don't you?"

I looked up and paused before saying, "I don't know. At that very moment I was sure she was in danger. Now, I'm not so sure." I let my tablet drop back onto the table. "I mean, it could have been a kid screwing around. Maybe she's a trouble maker. Maybe that's why she was banging on the wall the night before. Some kids are like that...out-of-control. It just happened so fast. But I suppose if we'd reported it, we might have looked like fools again."

Blair frowned. "Especially when you're the only one who saw her, and we don't know where the motorhome is now. Sorry. I wish I could be more help."

"I know. Thanks."

She returned to her book, and I picked up the iPad and continued to stare at the face of Amy Dunphy, wondering if I had been that close to helping her, but couldn't.

You have lots of time to do nothing on a long road trip, so I decided to use my time to dig deeper on the internet.

I found an article from the *Seattle Times* on Amy's disappearance. There wasn't much more information than what we already knew, but there was more about Owens himself. Senator Owens had divorced his first wife, Trina, eight years earlier for a younger woman he'd been having an affair with–his campaign manager.

I smiled to myself. *Been there done that.*

Graham had divorced me and then married a woman almost thirty years younger. I didn't know what the Owens' relationship had been like before they split up, but Graham and I had gotten along well right up to the divorce, and we still did. We had just drifted apart emotionally and sexually, leaving a chasm of indifference between us.

The journalist who had written the article about Owens however, had done her homework. Owens had suffered through a nasty divorce from Trina, partly because of the affair and partly because he owned a pharmaceutical company worth almost a billion dollars. His wife not only wanted custody of their young children, she wanted half his assets. In the end, she'd gotten custody of Amy and her brother, Brad, along with the house on Queen Anne Hill and two million dollars to keep her happy. For a guy worth that much money, though, I thought she'd gotten stiffed. If you're used to a certain lifestyle, you can quickly blow through two million dollars, especially in Seattle where the cost-of-living is one of the highest in the country.

The article went on to report that after the divorce, Owens had married his campaign manager and continued his upward climb in the Republican Party. The article delved into his rise in the business world, too. Between 1999 and 2010, his company had been sued three times for gouging patients by charging exorbitant drug prices. Owens had also been sued twice for sexual harassment and was once accused of murder.

What? That got my attention.

I leaned forward, focusing on the text. A suit had been filed against Owens early in 2003 by the family of a young man who had died in a tragic accident in West Seattle when he fell from the roof of one of the office buildings. The accident had occurred in the eighties when Owens was working for Camden Pharmaceuticals. He and three other co-workers had gotten very drunk at an office party and found their way onto the roof.

The lawsuit had accused Owens of playing a role in the accident. The boy who died, Steven Phipps, was gay. Owens had mercilessly bullied him prior to the incident. He had not only called Phipps ugly names, but had been seen leaving notes on the windshield of his car suggesting that gay people ought to just be done with it and commit suicide. His boss had disciplined him twice.

God, what a monster, I thought.

On the night in question, witnesses claimed that Owens had shamed the young man into stepping onto the ledge of the building, even though the boy was dead-drunk. The boy got dizzy and fell.

Owens' lawyer had questioned why the family had waited so long to accuse Owens of such a heinous crime, and eventually the suit was dropped. I smelled a payoff. Nevertheless, it painted an unflattering picture of a man who had aspirations of occupying the Oval Office.

I sat back, thinking.

Could one of those situations have been the motivation for someone getting revenge?

I decided to do more research.

Amy had a Facebook page. I scrolled through her posts and many of her pictures.

She liked to post tutorials about how to do makeup and had posts about some of her favorite musical artists. There were also pictures of Amy with her mom, her stepdad, her brother, her boyfriend and her friends.

Her mother was an attractive woman in her fifties, with auburn hair, high cheek bones, and a full mouth. She looked happy and contented in the photos, making me wonder how devastated she must feel right now at the prospect she might lose her daughter forever. After all, Amy could have been abducted by a deranged serial killer as easily as someone who wanted revenge because of something her birth father had done. It might even be more likely.

Amy had tagged herself on Facebook as being in a committed relationship with Dylan Masterson. Dylan had a bit of a bad boy look—dyed black hair, pierced nose, and a chain tattoo around his neck. I had a feeling he wasn't a favorite at family functions. In fact, he didn't appear in any of the family photos.

One of Amy's recent posts implied that Dylan had had a run-in with the law. She lamented that since pot was legal in Washington State, things like cocaine should be, too. I remembered that David had mentioned something about drugs. *Could Dylan have gotten into debt with drug dealers and abducted Amy as a way to pay off his debts?*

According to Facebook, Amy planned on going to Simmons College in Boston. I looked up Simmons College. It was a women's liberal arts school. Glancing back at some of her pictures with her friends, it surprised me she would have picked a women's college. She seemed like too much of a partier for that. Then I remembered that Dylan had planned on going to the community college there.

Her mother's Facebook page was pretty sparse. The now Mrs. Dunphy had grown up in Bremerton and graduated from the UW. She shared some of the same family photos on her wall as her daughter, plus a few pictures of her and her second husband, Grant Dunphy.

I zeroed in on him momentarily, flipping through pictures in which he was featured. In most of those, he appeared distant from others in the photos, as if he was uncomfortable or just a loner. In one picture of the family at the beach, his eyes had drifted in the direction of Amy, clad in a teeny white bikini. The lasting image of him appearing to leer at his stepdaughter prompted a chill to run the length of my spine.

There was something else though, that made my heart skip a beat.

Grant Dunphy looked familiar. His eyes. His nose. The beefy shoulders. He looked like Monty, the man traveling in the white motorhome!

Damn! Now, my adrenalin was flowing.

I looked Grant Dunphy up on Facebook. He didn't have a page, but Trina's page had mentioned the Dunphy Construction Company, so I looked that up. It was located in Kirkland, a wealthy community about fifteen minutes northeast of Seattle. Sure enough, there were a few pictures of him on the company's website. Each time I saw him the nervous queasiness in my stomach grew.

He looked enough like Monty to be related!

"You okay?" Blair asked, looking up from her book again.

"Yeah," I replied, feeling a little breathless. "Look at this." I got up and eased into the seat next to Blair. "Who does this guy look like?"

I angled my tablet so she could see the picture of Dunphy. She stared at it a minute, scrunched up her pretty pink lips in thought and then said, "He looks like the guy with the white motorhome."

"Bingo! I think so, too."

"Who is he?"

"That's Amy Owens' stepdad."

Blair's eyebrows lifted. "Well. Well. Well. Do I smell some kind of conspiracy theory brewing in that mysterious head of yours?"

"Don't make fun of me."

"I don't mean to," she said, placing a hand on my arm. "You know, maybe you should tell David about all of this if you think you saw Amy Owens in that motorhome."

I slumped back against the seat. "I tried to call him earlier, but it went to voice mail. What if he doesn't believe me?"

"He'll believe you, Julia. His cop's brain will look at it rationally. It might at least put you at ease."

I nodded. "Okay. I'll try him again."

I pulled out my phone and got up and went into the bedroom. I dialed his number. He answered on the second ring.

"Hi, Julia. Listen, I can't talk right now. Can I call you back?"

"Um...sure."

I hung up, disappointed again and returned to the main cabin.

"That was fast," Blair said.

"He couldn't talk. Something must be going on. Maybe they've found Amy."

"That would be wonderful," she said. "Hang in there. He'll call back when he has time."

I sat across from her at the table and picked up my iPad again.

Senator Owens had a Facebook page through his office. It had over two thousand followers and gave his bio. Owens had graduated from a small college in Florida with a degree in business. He currently sat on the Board of Regents there. I googled the school and found he was also one of the school's largest donors. He'd donated over $3 million to have a new School of Business named after him. The picture showed the building overlooking Trinity Lake.

I flicked through dozens of campaign and rally photos. Once again, my heart rate sped up when I saw a red-headed woman standing in the background of several pictures. I leaned in. None of the photos showed her clearly, though. Her face was often turned to the side or she was blocked by someone else.

"Look at this, Blair," I said, turning the iPad to her. "What do you notice in these three photos?" I pointed to the ones in which the redhead stood in the background.

Blair's eyes shifted back and forth between all three images. Then her eyes lit up. She reached out with her index finger and pointed. "The redhead."

"Exactly!"

"You don't think...I mean you can't see her too well. Does she look like the woman in the motorhome?"

I hunched my shoulders. "I don't know, but I don't believe in coincidences."

"Well, when David calls, tell him everything, Julia. Whether he believes you or not. You need to get this off your chest. Otherwise, you're not going to be very much fun for the rest of the trip." She gave me a mischievous smile and went back to her book.

÷

The landscape we passed over the next couple of hours went from flat to rolling hills. We stopped for gas and lunch in Mitchell, a small town about two-thirds of the way across the state. Rudy announced we also needed to dump the waste water.

Since she had a list of public dump stations across the country, she had pulled into a gas station that offered one behind the convenience store. After we filled the big tank with gas, we pulled the Hulk around to the back of the building. This was the first time we'd dumped the waste water, so we were all a little nervous.

We got out and walked around to the other side of the RV, where there was a compartment holding the sewer hose. Rudy put on rubber gloves and pulled out the three foot hose with its swivel adaptor and took off a 3" diameter metal cap from a pipe underneath the RV. She screwed an elbow adaptor onto a circular connector at one end of the hose and a second adaptor at the other end. Then she snapped the hose into the pipe underneath the RV.

"Okay, Julia, can you snap that end into that hole?"

She pointed to a metal cap in the cement.

"Um…is there another pair of gloves?"

She stripped hers off and handed them to me. "Here, take these."

I put them on and did as she asked, opening the metal cap and snapping the other end of the hose into the dump hole.

We had been instructed by Nathan Aberdeen to empty the black water tank before the gray water tank. The gray water tank, which was the dish and shower water, would wash out remnants from the black water tank.

"Ready?" she asked.

When I nodded, she pulled a lever under the motorhome that would release the black water. The motorhome shook a little. Then, we heard the rushing of waste as it flowed down the big tube into the dump hole. The four of us waited patiently, looking everywhere but at the hole that extended underground.

That is, until the hose popped off!

"Oh, God!" Doe screamed, jumping back.

Everyone shrieked and bounced away as waste water spewed out of the RV and all over the ground, splashing everywhere. We must have looked like we were dancing a jig, since we did it in such perfect unison.

I was far enough away that I hadn't gotten splashed, but I glanced over at Rudy as she wiped down her shirt.

Uh, oh!

There was nothing we could do to stop the flow, so we watched in dismay until it slowed and then ceased. When it finished, the four of us stood there staring at the biggest, brownest, smelliest mess ever.

Our stunned silence was interrupted when Rudy pointed at something lying at the foot of the RV. It had once been white. And it had once been a tampon.

"Whose is that?" she asked in shock, still pointing at it.

Count to three.

We all turned to Blair.

Her eyes opened wide as her hands came up in defense. "Are you kidding me? Don't the Aberdeens have a daughter?"

"Yes," Rudy said, turning back to the mess. "God, what do we do now?"

I glanced around and found a water hose hanging over a hook nearby. "I guess we hose it into that grate."

"Wonderful," Doe said, glancing at her feet.

I could just picture Doe's tennis shoes either going into the trash or the campfire that night.

"At least for once it wasn't my fault," I said, walking over to get the hose.

"What do you mean?" Rudy retorted. "You pulled the hose out and put it into the hole."

I turned on the water and came back over to hand her the nozzle. "Yes, but you're the one who screwed the hose onto the motorhome, and that's what popped off. Have fun washing it down."

CHAPTER THIRTEEN

I left the others with a small smile playing across my lips and walked around to the AM/PM to get a Pepsi on tap. It was hot and humid and dumping human waste all over the pavement had made me thirsty.

Our mishap had been shielded from view by the building, so no one in the store commented on it when I went in. I got my drink and then took my time wandering the aisles, contemplating buying a Snickers bar or a small bag of cookies. The Snickers bar won.

As I came out, ready to rip open the Snickers, the Jayco motorhome passed the gas station heading east. I sucked in a gulp of air and ran out the door and around the building back to the Hulk.

"We have to go!" I called out, coming around the side of the RV.

The dump hose still lay on the ground, and Rudy was just returning the water hose to the hook. Doe and Blair looked on.

"C'mon, we gotta go!" I repeated.

"Why?" Blair asked, turning towards me.

"The white motorhome just passed. We have to follow it."

They shared an indulgent look between them.

"Julia," Doe began.

I put up a hand. I'd had it. They didn't believe me. Or worse, they didn't care.

"If you're not going after them, I am." I whirled around and hurried into the Hulk.

"Julia! Wait a minute," Rudy yelled after me.

All three of them followed me back into the RV. I'd already made it into the driver's seat, slammed my Pepsi cup into the cup holder and had the keys in my hand by the time they made it inside.

"Hang on," I warned, starting the engine.

Before they'd even found seats, I pulled away from the dump station with a jerk. Blair had barely gotten the door closed and had to hold on as I twirled the big steering wheel and made a hard left turn, circling the building.

"Julia, are you nuts?" Rudy demanded. "We left the dump hose back there."

"I'll buy a new one," I said.

"And we left the cap open," Doe said.

"Then I wouldn't use the restroom if I were you. Could be messy."

I had to sit forward in the seat in order to plant my foot solidly on the pedal. I turned right, bumping over the curb as I left the gas station parking lot. The Jayco was six cars ahead of me. I didn't have to weave in and out of traffic to follow it, since I could see it above the other cars.

"What are we going to do when we catch up to them?" Rudy asked, slipping into the seat next to me.

The anger vibrated in her voice.

"I don't know. I just want to know where they're going."

"What if they turn off onto some side road? We have to be at the Aberdeens," she said.

"A girl's life is more important," I snapped back.

"Shouldn't we talk about this?" Doe said quietly from behind me. "We're a team, Julia."

"None of you believe me. I'm not sure I believe me, anymore, but I need to know if what I think I saw was correct. If I was, then that girl is in danger. If I was wrong, I'll take the heat."

We followed Monty and his crew out of town at a leisurely pace, continuing east on I-90 for about forty minutes. Inside the Hulk, it was quiet. I had drawn a line in the sand with the others, maybe even creating a gap I might never close. I just couldn't seem to stop myself—I needed to find out about that girl.

As I followed the motorhome, Rudy went to change her blouse. By the time she came back, I had pulled off I-90 and entered the small town of Faraday. The Jayco RV pulled into a McDonald's and stopped. I slowed down, but kept going. As we passed the fast food restaurant, their door opened and Eva and Ponytail Guy got out and went inside.

I turned right at the next light, thinking I'd circle around the block and come back. I entered a residential neighborhood with narrow streets and cars parked on each side, forcing me to slow down. I had to navigate the parked cars, which I'm sure put everyone on edge, remembering the orange cones at the practice track.

When I got to the end of the street, I whirled the big steering wheel to make a sharp right turn. The motorhome swayed as I took the corner fast. I cut the corner too close and hit the stop sign. The impact ripped the side mirror off, and it flew into the street.

"Julia!" Rudy yelled. Her head whipped around as the mirror hit the pavement.

"I'll pay for that, too," I said, returning my eyes to the road.

I hunkered down, drove to the end of the block and turned right again, this time without ripping anything off the Hulk. A few seconds later, I made it back to the main street. I could tell the others were concerned, maybe even angry, but I didn't care.

I was on a mission.

We approached the McDonald's again. The Jayco was still there, so I pulled to the curb and left the engine running.

"Now what?" Rudy asked with barely restrained anger.

"I don't know. We wait."

I stared at the front door to the fast food restaurant, while Doe and Blair remained silent and Rudy fumed in the background.

Faraday was a very small town. As I glanced around, I estimated that not more than five or six hundred people lived there. By the looks of the businesses around us, we were also in the main part of town. The McDonald's looked like the only fast food restaurant.

"Julia," Doe finally said behind me. "This could get dangerous."

I sighed. "I know, but it can't be more dangerous than what that girl might be facing."

The door to the McDonald's opened. Eva and Ponytail Guy came out carrying several bags of food. As the two approached the motorhome, Ponytail Guy happened to look over in our direction.

He stopped mid-stride, staring into the front window of our RV.

I turned away, as the others moved away from the windows.

Too late. He'd made us.

He scowled and climbed into the Jayco. Within seconds, whoever was driving backed up and sped out of the parking lot, making a hard turn onto the main road right in front of us.

"Let me drive," Blair said, touching my shoulder.

I turned. She was standing behind me, with those blue eyes set in an iron stare as she watched the retreating motorhome.

"Oh, no," Rudy complained. "C'mon, you guys. This is a 40-foot motorhome, not a sports car."

"We'll be fine," Blair said, switching places with me.

She put her seat belt on, shifted the Hulk into drive and pulled expertly into traffic, following the white motorhome. The Jayco picked up speed, but didn't return to I-90. Instead, it continued out into the country.

We followed at a brisk pace.

I sat on the sofa behind Blair, leaning forward to see through the front windshield.

Blair kept us within three cars of the motorhome. At one point, the back curtains parted and a face appeared. It wasn't the girl, though. It was Eva peering back at us.

A few minutes later, the Jayco made a right turn onto a country road.

Blair followed.

Now there were no cars in between us.

The white RV accelerated again. We barreled down the road, both motorhomes rocking back and forth as we took the curves. Doe, Rudy, and I held on tight.

The road was narrow and hilly as we passed homes and farmland. We drove like that for about a mile before coming upon a set of railroad tracks. As we approached the tracks, the lights began to blink and the bell clanged.

They didn't slow down.

"Blair?" I cautioned.

"Blair?" Doe repeated.

A train approached from around a hill to our left, speeding toward us. The railroad track barriers began to drop.

Blair's foot reached for the brake.

The motorhome in front of us smashed through the barriers as they descended, barely missing the train that rumbled past a moment later.

Blair brought the Hulk to a screeching halt, throwing open cupboards in the main cabin. Dishes and canisters of sugar, flour and cereal flew out. The canisters broke open, layering the carpet with their contents, while some of the dishes hit the counter and shattered.

"Damn!" Blair said, slamming her hands against the wheel.

Doe glanced at me, her face white.

"We need to stop this," Rudy said, looking around at the mess behind her. "I promised to deliver this thing in pristine condition."

"We can clean it up," Blair said, never taking her eyes off the train as it lumbered past.

The train was a transporter and took a full minute to pass. By the time it did, the white motorhome was long gone.

Blair pulled slowly forward over the tracks, careful to avoid the broken barriers. The road we followed was lined with trees and wound around more farms and a few barns. We passed two cross streets, where Blair slowed down, but the white RV was nowhere in sight.

She continued for another couple of miles, but we were just going deeper into the countryside. By the time the road began to climb a steep hill, she turned the big rig around. A minute later, she pulled over to the side of the road and stopped.

The four of us sat in silence, probably contemplating a range of thoughts. Rudy was pissed off. Doe was concerned. Blair was disappointed she'd lost her quarry. And me? I felt deflated.

Finally, Rudy spoke up.

"Now what?"

"You have to admit something's wrong, Rudy," Blair said, turning in her seat. "Otherwise, why would they have risked being hit by a train in order to get away from us?"

I glanced at Rudy. She had also turned in her chair and was staring at the beautiful carpet, now marred by food and glass shards. She looked like she had just lost a championship basketball game. She inhaled a deep, cleansing breath and looked up at us.

"I agree. I repeat...now what?"

CHAPTER FOURTEEN

Rudy's question prompted a long pause as we each considered a potential way forward. If the others were like me, the adrenalin was still coursing through their veins, and my mind was a blur.

"Can we take a short break? That was scary, and frankly, I need a moment or two to process what just happened. We whizzed past a fruit stand back there. Why don't you guys do a little shopping, while I clean up in here? We can huddle up afterwards."

"Fine," Rudy said with a grim expression. "But I'll drive."

Blair shrugged and relinquished the captain's chair. Rudy slipped behind the wheel. She started the engine and pulled back onto the winding road without a word, stopping several minutes later when we got back to the main road. A large produce stand sat at the corner.

"I'll help Julia," Doe said to Rudy. "Can you get some grapes and a couple of nectarines?"

"Sure," she replied with a tight lip.

She and Blair climbed out while Doe and I stayed behind. Doe watched them move away from the motorhome, and then said, "Just give her some time, Julia. She's feeling responsible. The bonds of our friendship are a lot stronger than a big green motorhome."

"I hope so," I said, picking up a broken bowl. "I didn't mean for all of this to happen." I leaned over and scooped up more broken glass and dropped it all into the trash can. "Now I don't know what to do. Rudy is furious. Those people nearly got themselves killed. And there may be a girl in danger, and yet we have no way to help."

Doe put her hand on my shoulder. "We'll figure it out together– like we always do."

I looked up at her elegant face. Once again, she looked perfect. Thick salt and pepper gray hair that never seemed to move. And deep, dark brown eyes with long thick lashes that needed no enhancement.

"Are you mad at me, Doe?"

She smiled gently. "No. I know you too well. Your heart is in the right place. And you're not like Blair. It's not in your nature to take big risks, so something is driving you on this. Which means your instincts are probably right."

By the time Rudy and Blair returned, we had filled the trash can and used a small battery operated vacuum to get the top layer of stuff off the carpet.

"Looks better in here," Blair said, stepping inside. She was munching on an apple and held another newspaper under one arm. "Anything I can do?"

"No, I think we've done as much as we can right now," Doe said. "We'll have to empty this trash can, but thanks."

"It looks like we'll have to stop somewhere to get the carpet shampooed," Blair said, sitting at the table to open her newspaper.

Rudy had just climbed aboard holding a bag filled with produce. She glanced at the stained carpet, her face a mask of defeat. She turned without comment to put things into the refrigerator.

"I'm so sorry, Rudy. I'll make this right. I promise," I said again.

She paused. "I know you will," she said staring into the refrigerator.

"I'm sure the Aberdeens have insurance that will pay for all of this," Doe offered, snapping the small vacuum into a holder attached to the wall. "They'll have to replace the counter over here by the sink, though. It got chipped."

Rudy glanced at the counter behind her, inhaled and then sighed, closing the refrigerator door. She turned to me and crossed her arms over her chest. "I think you may have been right about this, Julia."

Doe raised an eyebrow at me and gave me a nod of encouragement.

"I just wish...I just wish..."

"What?" I asked her.

She sucked in a full breath. "I don't know," she said, exhaling. "I just wish there had been a better way to convince us." Her eyes surveyed the damaged carpet. "How am I going to explain all of this to the Aberdeens?"

I glanced at Doe and Blair for help, but they looked as helpless as I felt.

"Rudy, I promise that if I have to personally pay for every single repair, I will. I'll even pay for an increase in the Aberdeen's insurance if that happens."

She gave me a brief, crooked smile and then stepped around me and dropped into one of the swivel chairs. "Let's face it, something is very wrong with those people. Otherwise, why would they have risked their lives like that? They all could have been killed, so they must be hiding something. I just wish I knew what it was. Did anyone think to get their license plate number?"

"I got the first two letters," I said.

"I was focused on not killing us," Blair said, opening her paper.

"Well, maybe the first letters will help," Doe said. "Have you talked to David lately?"

"No. I've called, but he's busy."

"Well, I think you should call him again and give him whatever you have."

"What?" Blair erupted, staring down at the *U.S.A. Today* on the table in front of her.

"What is it?" I asked, moving over to her.

"There's an article about a man found shot to death in his mountain cabin in North Bend."

"Washington?" I asked.

"Yes."

North Bend is a community just east of Seattle, on the approach to the Cascade Mountains.

Why is that important?" I asked.

Her eyes were skimming the article. "Hold on. Uh…it says here that he lived all alone outside of North Bend." She read some more and then looked up with raised eyebrows. "His son reported that along with some money, his dad's old…white…motorhome was stolen."

"You've got to be kidding," I said, pushing in to sit next to her.

She turned the paper around so I could see the article. I skimmed the text and then pointed a finger at the fourth paragraph. "Wow, listen to this. *'The only thing missing besides the money is my father's old Jayco motorhome.'*" I looked up at my friends. My body had gone cold. "He says it was white with a red and blue stripe."

Rudy stood up and came to the table. "When?"

My eyes returned to the report. "They think it was either Friday night or Saturday morning. His body wasn't found until yesterday."

"Amy was kidnapped Saturday morning," Rudy said. "You *were* right, Julia. And that means they've already killed someone."

"Which also means they won't hesitate to kill the girl if they're confronted," Doe said. She was sitting on the sofa with Tinker Bell in her lap. The dog seemed to pick up on her anxiety and nervously licked her hand.

Blair pulled the paper back. "It says here that the old man was found in his kitchen. The keys to the motorhome were gone. He thinks maybe they killed his dad for money to buy drugs and took the motorhome as an afterthought."

"And we don't know where they are now," I lamented.

"At least now we have confirmation," Blair said, looking at me. "The police need to be looking for *that* motorhome."

"They probably are," Rudy said. "I'd assume they have an APB out on it."

"Then why are these guys driving across the country without anyone stopping them?" I asked.

"The authorities might only be looking for it in Washington State and states that border Washington, thinking they wouldn't go that far."

"Call David," Doe said. "He needs to know. While you do that, I'm going to take Tinker Bell out."

She put the leash on Tinker Bell and left the motorhome. I pulled out my cell phone and dialed David's number. It was just after 1:00 p.m. local time, so it would be 11:00 a.m. there. It rang twice before he answered.

"Franks here," he said in a gruff voice.

"David, this is Julia."

"Hey, hi," he said, his demeanor changing. "I'm sorry I had to cut you off earlier. It's been pretty busy around here. Anyway, I miss you. How was the 4th of July show?"

"Never mind that. I'm calling for a different reason. I'm going to put you on speaker phone, if that's okay."

"Sure...um...is everything all right?"

I pressed the button to put the call on speaker. "Okay, can you hear me?"

"Yes. What's wrong, Julia? I don't like the tone of your voice."

I looked at Rudy and Blair for support as I began my tale. "You're not going to believe this, but I think we know who abducted Senator Owens' daughter."

There was a short pause. "Uh…go on."

"We've run across an old motorhome several times on the trip. The people driving it are not very nice people. More importantly, I saw the face of a young girl at the back window as they were leaving a campground this morning. She was banging on the window and appeared to be trying to get out." I paused to swallow and take a breath.

"A young girl? A kid?"

"No, sorry. She looked more like a teenager. I didn't get a very good look at her."

"Okay, keep going."

"She was pounding on the window and trying to scream."

"What do you mean, trying to scream?"

"It looked like she had a gag in her mouth."

"You could see the gag?"

"Well, not very well. Something was in her mouth. That's what I thought it was."

Count to three.

"Hold on."

There was the sound of a chair scraping the floor, and then David mumbled to someone with his hand over the receiver. Rustling. More chair movement.

"Julia, I've invited Detective Abrams to listen to this. I filled him in, so go on. What did the girl look like?"

It amazed me how quickly he could transition into his investigative mode. Detective Abrams was the lead detective at the Mercer Island PD, and David's boss.

"She had dark hair and dark eyes," I said. "I only got a glimpse of her before someone pulled her away from the window and closed the curtains."

"Julia, this is Detective Abrams. Are you sure this wasn't just some kids playing a game?"

"I wasn't sure at first, but we've run into these people several times. They parked across from us in the first campground we stayed in. We saw two men and heard a woman, but no children or teens. When they left, they left a cooler behind with a bunch of used needles in it, though."

"Needles?" Detective Abrams asked. "Did they seem like they were on drugs?"

"Uh…no. Not at all. We saw both men with beers in their hands, but that's all."

I decided not to try and describe the incident with Ponytail Guy lying on the ground, thinking it was just a distraction.

"Anyway, we crossed paths with them again at an outdoor Fourth of July show. I overheard them say something about a third man they didn't like joining them, and a guy named Yoda who is apparently in charge. They also said they were going to make a lot of money and that they were going to Chicago."

"They didn't say how they were going to make the money?" David asked.

"No. Just that they were going to make a bunch of money. I happened to walk past their campsite later and saw all four of them outside, and *then* heard someone banging on the wall inside the motorhome."

"You didn't engage with them, I hope," David interjected.

"Uh…no, not really. Anyway, this morning I was up by the store as they were leaving. That's when I saw the girl in the window, just before they left the campground."

"That's the last time you saw them?" David asked.

"No. We passed them in a small town where they stopped for lunch and followed them when they came out. They realized what we were doing and ran from us by playing chicken with an oncoming train."

"They actually slammed through the barriers," Blair shouted over my shoulder.

The two men mumbled something to each other on the other end of the phone.

"Okay. What about the motorhome?" Detective Abrams asked. "Describe it."

"It's an old white Jayco motorhome with a red and blue stripe. It sounds like the one stolen from that old man in North Bend."

"Is it a Washington license plate?"

"Yes. I just got the first two letters–XT," I replied with an apologetic tone.

"That's okay. That will help," Detective Abrams said.

"Tell us again who's in the motorhome with her," David said.

"Four men and a woman," I replied. "The guy who seems to be in control is a big, beefy guy with dark hair and a dark beard. His name is Monty. And, David…he looks just like Amy's stepdad, Grant Dunphy."

"What?"

I recognized the incredulity in his voice. He was probably wondering how I would even know what Grant Dunphy looked like.

"You've been on the internet," he said in a measured tone.

"Yes. There's a lot of time to kill on the road. Once I saw the girl at the window, I had to know more. The likeness is uncanny. Anyway, they're traveling with a woman–a small redhead. She goes by Eva. The second man has sandy blonde hair he wears in a ponytail. We don't know his name, but he's about medium height and drinks a lot. Every time we've seen him, he has a beer in his hand. And he wears a baseball cap. The third guy is bald, and we think that's the guy named Roy."

"Good job," Detective Abrams said.

Blair nudged me and whispered, "Tell him about the red-head in the photos."

I shook my head no.

"Okay, but you're not to engage with these people at all, Julia," David commanded. "Do you understand? We'll follow up."

"But, David…"

"Stay out of it," he snapped. "If you're right, they've already killed the owner of that motorhome."

"I know," I said. "We read about it in the paper. That's why we called."

"Then let the authorities deal with it. We'll notify the right people."

"Okay. Will you let me know if you find anything out?"

He hesitated, but then said, "If I can. Just forget about this now and enjoy the rest of your trip."

He thanked me and we hung up.

"Why didn't you want to mention the red-head in those photos?" Blair demanded.

"What photos?" Rudy asked.

I heaved a sigh, realizing that not everyone was up to speed. "There's a woman in some of Owens' campaign photos who might be Eva." When Rudy's eyes lit up, I added, "But you can't see her very well, so it's hard to tell. And I've never gotten a very good look at the real Eva. I don't want to send them on some wild goose chase."

Rudy gave me a warm smile. "Good for you, Julia. Reason is winning out."

A knock on the door startled us. I got up to open it and sucked in a quick gasp when I found Goldie and Aria standing there with expectant expressions on their faces.

"Ooh," Goldie cooed. "Fancy seeing you guys again. How's yer trip goin?"

I turned to share a slightly horrified expression with Blair and Rudy. I turned back and replied. "Fine. Just fine."

"Doesn't look fine," Aria said. She crossed her skinny arms across her skinnier chest. "You're missing a rearview mirror. What'd you run into?"

"That was my fault," I said. I glanced past them to see Doe ambling down the sidewalk in our direction. Tinker Bell tugged at the leash. "I was...uh, turning a corner and cut it too close. I hit a stop sign."

"Don't think the Aberdeens will like that," Aria said, raising a bushy brow and drawing her thin lips into a straight line.

She was wearing a bright orange golf shirt, a visor and plaid Bermuda shorts that exposed her knobby knees. A perfect outfit for the town's busy-body.

I inclined my head and gave her a dirty look. "I'll pay for the repair."

"They also won't like the fact you lost your dump hose," she said.

"Huh?" I mumbled. I was distracted by Doe who had seen our guests and stopped to loiter on the other side of a tree.

"We noticed it when we pulled up," Aria continued. "The compartment that holds your dump hose is open, and the hose is gone. In fact, the entire door to the compartment is gone."

I seethed a little inside as she pushed her point. "We'll get that fixed, too."

Goldie peered through the screen door past me to Rudy and Blair. "The rest of you are bein' pretty darned quiet. What's goin' on?" She followed my gaze to where Doe's pepper gray hair was visible on the other side of a narrow tree. "Might as well come back, Doe," Goldie called out. "We're not leavin'." She planted her hands on her broad hips to make her point.

I sighed, knowing she meant it. Goldie could be stubborn as a mule, and Aria stood behind her with her chicken-bone arms still crossed over her chest in a sign of protest. If we didn't want to stand there and argue with them, we'd have to invite them in.

"Why don't you come inside?" I offered with a begrudging smile. I opened the screen door and waved to Doe to come back.

"Lordy, what happened in here?" Goldie said as she came up the steps. She was staring at the cereal, pancake flour and ketchup ground into the once beautiful carpet. Aria spotted the wastebasket, which overflowed with broken glass. "What in the heck *did* happen in here?"

When Doe came back in and closed the door, Blair and I sat down at the dining table, while Rudy and Doe sat on the small leather sofa.

"Why don't you guys take a seat?" I said, gesturing to the two swivel chairs. "We have a bit of a story to tell."

Aria and Goldie slid into the two big chairs opposite us. I paused a moment and then said, "I'm pretty sure I saw that girl who was kidnapped at Luther Burbank Park the other day—Senator Owens' daughter."

There was no sugar-coating it. If we were going to tell them, I figured it was better to just get it over with.

Goldie's eyes popped open. "You're kiddin' me."

"No. We've already reported it to David, and he's going to follow-up with the proper authorities."

"What happened?" Aria said in a rather demanding tone.

I gave a deep sigh, wondering how much I ought to tell them. I decided it didn't make any difference and so repeated the first part of our story, including my tripping over Ponytail Guy and calling the police.

"The guy was dead?" Aria screeched.

"No. I was mistaken. We think he was just drunk. He was gone when I brought the others back."

"Ohhh, I get it," Goldie murmured, giving Aria a knowing look. "One of your senior moments," she said with a giggle.

God, would I never outlive my reputation for being a klutz?

"What about this girl?" Aria asked. "When did you see her?"

I snuck a glance at my friends. "I was the only one who saw her. And since no one believed me about the dead body, no one believed me when I said I'd seen the girl either. So we just went on our merry way."

"And?" Aria prompted me. Her razor thin lips were pressed together and those beady eyes were filled with skepticism.

"We saw the motorhome again a little while ago when we were at the dump site," Blair said. "Julia decided we had to follow it."

"And that's when you lost the dump hose," Aria said, as if that was the whole point to the story.

"Yes," I hissed with irritation. "The dump hose is gone."

"But then they ran from us," Blair said. "In fact, they almost got themselves killed in the process."

"So you reported it to David," Aria said. "What real proof do you have that they've done anything wrong?"

I reached over and grabbed the newspaper. "There's an article in here about a man who was killed in North Bend. The only thing stolen was a motorhome that sounds just like the one these people are driving."

Aria took the newspaper from me, glancing down at the article. "Did you get the license plate number? I would've gotten their license plate number," she said with a twitch to her lip. "Then you could match it up."

We all exchanged looks of frustration.

"I got the first two letters and gave them to David," I said.

"The license plate was bent," Blair said in our defense. "And frankly, we were kind of busy trying to catch them without getting killed."

"Sounds a little like us," Goldie said with a quick shake of her head.

"What do you mean?" I asked.

Aria took her eyes off the newspaper and reached out with her foot and kicked Goldie's ankle.

"Oh…uh, we had our own situation yesterday," she said, rubbing her ankle.

"What do you mean?" I wanted to know.

"Just that Aria almost killed a guy on a motorbike."

All heads swiveled towards Aria. She shifted uncomfortably and lifted her chin, pointing that blade of a nose toward the ceiling.

"I didn't almost kill him. There were two motorcycles behind me, but I only saw the one in my left rearview mirror. I was keeping an eye on him as I changed lanes…and I forced the second motorcycle off the road."

"Oh, dear," Doe said. "Was anyone hurt?"

"No, but they were mad," she said.

"Real mad," Goldie added with an emphatic nod.

"I pulled over to apologize," Aria said with an annoying sense of righteousness. "They got off their bikes and started pounding on the side of the camper and yelling insults."

"So we ran," Goldie said. "And they chased us."

"They pulled up on either side of us, yelling obscenities and threatening us as we drove," Aria said. "We wouldn't have gotten away, except we came into a town where a parade was about to begin. That cut them off."

"Yeah, so we hid in a little restaurant for a couple of hours hopin' we wouldn't see 'em again," Goldie said.

"And did you?" Rudy asked.

"Not so far," Aria said. "I have a couple of dents in the side of my camper shell from where they hit it with their fists, though."

"So we both have battle scars," Doe said. She glanced around the interior of our RV. "Ours are just a little worse than yours."

"And yours has to do with a major case again," Goldie said with renewed enthusiasm. "So what are we goin' to do about this abducted girl?"

"We?" the four of us echoed together.

"Sure. We could help you look for 'em," Goldie offered. "Aria's good at this stuff."

"She almost killed someone on the road," Rudy argued.

"Almost," Aria stressed with a raised index finger.

"David has already told us to stay out of it," I said. "Besides, we don't even know where they are."

"What does this motorhome look like again?" Aria asked. "At least we could be on the lookout for it. Especially if they're headed to Chicago."

"Just like the article says. It was an old white Jayco motorhome, maybe twenty-five feet long with a red and blue stripe. First two letters of the plate are XT."

"Look," Aria said. "Let's exchange cell phone numbers so we can report in if one of us sees them."

That seemed reasonable, so we all got our phones out and programmed in each other's phone numbers.

"Where are you guys staying tonight?" Goldie asked.

"On the other side of Onalaska," Rudy said. "At the Black River Campground."

Aria nodded. "Okay. We'll see you there."

When they'd left, Doe said in a hopeful tone, "Maybe the campground will be full."

CHAPTER FIFTEEN

We drove for a few hours without stopping, allowing the scenery to pass by without comment. It was pretty quiet inside the Hulk, with each of us harboring our own thoughts. We skipped a formal lunch and instead snacked on fruits and veggies.

Aria followed us. After a while, she dropped further and further back until we couldn't see her anymore.

By late afternoon, we passed the town of Blue Earth, Minnesota, with a population of just over 3,000, one of which was a giant statue of the Jolly Green Giant.

"The Hulk would feel right at home here," Doe said as the sign disappeared in our rearview mirror–the one we still had.

Rudy pointed to a directional sign announcing the exit for the town of Winnebago. "Look, his cousin lives just north of here."

I felt the fog of dispiritedness lift as the small jokes brought smiles to our faces. Ten minutes later, Blair spied a sign for a country store and deli.

"I'm hungry for some real food," she said. "Anyone care if I stop?"

"Sounds good to me," Doe said. "Tinker Bell needs to go out anyway."

Blair took the exit off the highway and turned onto a frontage road that ran parallel to I-90. She pulled up to Jake's Country Store & Deli. The building was designed like a western storefront, complete with a covered boardwalk, wooden bench and a couple of old whiskey barrels out front. A small parking lot sat off to the side of the building. Blair turned onto the side street and parked at the curb.

"Can someone grab me a turkey on wheat and an apple?" Doe asked.

"Sure," Blair said.

We climbed out and entered the store, releasing the tingle of a bell above the screen door. The only person in the store was a tall guy behind the counter sitting on a stool reading a book. He had broad shoulders and a neatly trimmed beard. He appeared to be in his late fifties and had dark, smoldering eyes that looked up when we swung through the door.

"Do you have any premade sandwiches?" I asked him.

"Sure thing," he said in a rich bass voice. "Just made them this morning. Check the cooler in the back. We also have some hot stuff up here," he said, pointing to some shriveled hotdogs rotating on some spokes.

"Thanks. We'll check the sandwiches."

He held my gaze for a moment as I followed Rudy and Blair down the center aisle. The three of us perused the selection of sandwiches, picked out what we wanted and grabbed individual bags of potato chips and an apple for Doe. We had just paid for everything and were moving towards the door when I realized I was out of Pepsi.

"Just a sec," I mumbled to Blair's back. I turned and hurried down to the back of the store again. Since there wasn't a soda fountain, I had to find the right cooler. I grabbed a bottle of Diet Pepsi and came back up the aisle to pay for it. Of course, the candy and snack section at the checkout counter caught my attention, and I paused to contemplate whether to get a bag of sour fruit balls or a small bag of popcorn for later. I got them both and dropped them on the counter.

The guy behind the counter, whose name tag read *Jake*, rang up my purchases. As he dropped them into a paper bag, he asked, "Where you folks going?"

I'm five foot two and had to crane my neck to look up at him. He had short curly hair that was gray at the temples and he was dressed in jeans, a plaid shirt, and suspenders that stretched over a barrel chest.

"Madison," I replied, tearing my eyes away from his gaze. "We're delivering a friend's motorhome."

"Madison's nice this time of year," he said, handing me the bag. "Be sure to see the Monona Terrace Convention Center there, if you can. The original design concept was Frank Lloyd Wright's. He was born in Wisconsin, you know. Worth the trip if you have the time."

I nodded and said, "Great idea. Thanks."

The suggestion surprised me. He didn't seem like the type to appreciate fine architecture. I snuck a glance at the book he was reading, which was lying on the counter. It was Ron Chernow's *Alexander Hamilton*. I left the counter and swung open the screen door.

"By-the-way," I said turning back. "You're Jake, the owner?"

"Yep. Going on fifteen years," he said with a grin.

I smiled back at him. "Nice place."

I let the door close and turned towards the side street. I was reaching into my bag for the hard candies, when out of my peripheral vision, I saw the Hulk off to my left–*leaving!*

My head came up with a jerk.

The Hulk was crossing the dirt barrier between the frontage road and I-90, chasing the Jayco motorhome, both throwing up rocks and dirt in their wake. My mouth dropped open as I watched both vehicles bounce and sway over the uneven ground, leaving me behind.

I reached into my purse to grab my phone as they both made a hard left turn and disappeared up the highway, but realized with despair that I'd left it on the table in the motorhome.

Damn!

I stood there, feeling like a lost puppy.

I sighed and plopped down on the big, wooden bench in front of the store window with a nervous twitch in my stomach. *How long would it take them to notice I was gone?*

April's warning not to get left behind played in my mind.

The afternoon was warm, and a few flies buzzed around my head. The rhythmic sound of traffic on I-90 reached me as cars passed going both directions. I glanced at my watch. It was 4:37 in the afternoon.

The roar of a motorcycle engine startled me, and I glanced to my right. Aria's truck and camper appeared along the frontage road at a fast pace. Right behind her were two guys on big motorcycles. Aria took the corner by the store's parking lot at almost full speed, making the camper sway precariously. Goldie sat in the passenger seat, her eyes wide. She glanced my way and gave me a quick, nervous wave as they disappeared up the street.

I listened to the fading sound of the engines feeling like I was watching TV. Moments later, the grinding engines came up on my left, as Aria and her pursuers came down the opposite side street.

Aria ignored the stop sign and made a sharp left turn, disappearing around a curve a half block away. The motorcycles followed.

The screen door opened and Jake stepped out.

"You see all sorts of weird things out here," he said, watching the bikers. "She must have pissed someone off. What happened to your ride?"

I gestured off towards I-90. "They left me."

He chuckled. "Sit tight. They'll figure it out and come back."

"I don't know," I said with a shrug. "They're chasing some people we think are criminals."

His thick brows lifted. "Really? You live an exciting life."

This time, I chuckled. "You have no idea." In a high-pitched stage voice I mimicked, *"Nancy, every place you go, it seems as if mysteries just pile up one after another."*

"Who was that supposed to be?" he asked.

"Carolyn Keene wrote it in *The Message in the Hollow Oak*," I replied. When he gave me a blank stare, I added. "Nancy Drew."

"Ah," he said with recognition. "You're a mystery reader."

"Yeah. And now it seems like they follow me around. Mysteries, I mean."

"Well, there's a turn off not too far ahead. Your friends will be back. Mind if I sit down?"

I scooted over. "Be my guest." I pulled out the bag of popcorn. "Want some?"

He laughed. "Naw. I have to watch my figure." He used one enormous hand to pat his stomach. "You know, a year ago there was a massive police chase right here. Four or five squad cars chased a guy in a stolen red Mustang. He kept taking the off ramp, coming back by here and then going out onto the highway again."

"Did they catch him?" I asked, ripping open the popcorn bag.

"Yeah. He finally did a tail spin right there," he said, pointing to the dirt strip between the highway and the frontage road. "Turned that nice Mustang over about three times."

We were interrupted when the Jayco motorhome came barreling back along the frontage road, whizzing right past the store going in the opposite direction.

A heartbeat later, Rudy and the Hulk appeared behind them, streaking past us without stopping.

"Looks like they found the off ramp," Jake said, his head swiveling to watch the RV. "Seems like you might be in for a bit of a wait, though."

"Guess so," I said, taking a handful of popcorn.

"By the way," he said, reaching out with his hand. "I'm Jake Weatherly."

I took his hand in mine, aware that he was wearing some pretty sexy aftershave. My heart fluttered as I said, "I'm Julia…from Washington State. Seattle area."

"Seattle? Space Needle…built for the 1962 World's Fair."

"Is there anything you don't know?" I asked with a chuckle.

He gave me a warm smile and leaned into me. "I don't know your last name."

My face grew suddenly warm. "Applegate."

He leaned away. "Isn't that the name of your governor? Gray, or Garth, or…"

"Graham," I said.

He gave me a guarded look. "You're not married to him, are you?"

"Was," I said. "He's my ex."

His dark eyes lifted. "Then I'm sitting with royalty."

A laugh erupted from my throat. "Not anymore. Now he lives with a thirty-four year old who wouldn't know Frank Lloyd Wright from Michelangelo."

He gave me a look of appreciation. "You're familiar with Michelangelo's architecture? How he broke out of the classical style?"

"No, I thought he was just an artist."

He threw his head back and gave me a deep throated laugh. "I like you, Julia Applegate. I'll be sorry when your friends realize they've left you behind." As his laughter subsided, he asked, "By the way, who are they chasing?"

"Some people we think might have abducted a teenage girl," I said, swallowing the popcorn.

"No kidding. Why do you think that?"

"I saw the girl's face at the window. It looked like she was trying to get out."

"Humpf," he grunted. "Should we call the police?"

My eyes lit up. "Maybe. How fast would they get here?"

He shrugged his massive shoulders. "That's hard to say. We're served by the State Police. There are three officers for this whole area, and they might all be at the county fair right about now."

"Oh," I said despondently. I glanced out to the highway. "Well, maybe it wouldn't hurt. It might be awhile before they come back, anyway."

He pulled out his phone. "What kind of evidence do you have? I can guarantee they won't come unless you can pretty much prove what you saw, and they'll charge you if you call them out unnecessarily."

I put my hand over the phone in his hand. "Never mind, then. We don't have any proof. I just saw a face at the back of a window, and she looked like she was in trouble. I assume the people in that RV will get away from my friends soon and disappear again, anyway."

Jake returned the phone to his pocket. "Sorry. When you're out in the middle of nowhere, services are sketchy."

"I don't understand why these guys just don't take off down the highway, though," I said, referring to the Jayco motorhome. "Why do they keep circling back here?"

"Probably because that big motorhome of yours has a bigger, newer engine, and they know it. They're going to try and lose it on some of the curves, maybe even make them tip over." That gave me a start. "Also, staying on the highway draws attention to them." He glanced around. "If you'll notice, we don't have any neighbors. Just a lot of overgrown country."

The roar of motorcycles grabbed our attention again. Aria appeared from our left, coming back along the frontage road with the motorcycles on her tail. At the same time, the white motorhome appeared to our right with Rudy chasing it. The two sets of vehicles crisscrossed right in front of us.

"Jeez, this is like watching the Keystone Cops, just without the background music," I said, whipping my head back and forth.

"Yup," he said. "Happens like that sometimes."

As Rudy whizzed past us this time, I saw Blair look in my direction. *Had she noticed me?*

Jake chuckled. "Maybe I will have a handful of that popcorn."

I handed it over. "Be my guest."

"So what's the story with the camper and the motorcycles?"

"The women in the camper are friends of ours from back home. The woman driving pissed off the bikers when she almost ran one of them off the road."

He took a handful of popcorn and handed the bag back. "Well, as they say…*angry people are not always wise.*"

I turned to him. "Who said that?"

"Jane Austen," he replied. "*Pride and Prejudice.*"

I smiled. "You're an interesting man, Jake Weatherly."

"I try to keep up," he said, looking out on the roadway again. "Most likely one of 'em will be back soon," he said. "There's a circular dead end a couple of miles up there," he said, pointing left. "Unless they go back over the highway. That could take a while." He munched on his popcorn.

"So you like architecture," I said, gazing out on the two roadways in front of us.

"Yeah. Architecture reflects our culture, you know. In fact, a person's house says a lot about their personality."

I handed him some more popcorn. "I own a Victorian bed and breakfast called The St. Claire Inn. It probably says everything you'd want to know about me."

He dropped a few kernels of popcorn onto the wooden deck under our feet and a small whirlwind picked the kernels up and swirled them off the platform. He didn't seem to notice, but I suspected it was Chloe trying to insert herself into the conversation.

In the distance, the white motorhome and the Hulk passed us on the highway going east again. We watched them without comment.

"You know, the Victorian period was laced with mysticism," Jake continued. "How do you feel about the paranormal?"

My heart jumped at the thought he might have noticed Chloe's presence after all.

"Well, my inn is a validated haunted location."

"No kidding," he said again. "Have you seen any ghosts there?"

"Several times," I said, glancing around. I wondered what Chloe might do next. "In fact, at least one of them seems to have come with us on our trip."

The screen door flew open with a bang at my comment. We both whipped around to look at it.

"That would be Chloe," I said, sitting back again.

"Not so fast now," he said with a chuckle. "That door opens with a slight breeze."

The door slammed shut as if in response to his comment. Then it opened and closed in quick succession six times.

"How 'bout that?" I challenged him.

"Nope. Never saw that. Your Chloe has a sense of humor."

"Yes she does," I agreed with a smile.

The Hulk appeared to our left, returning alone and much more slowly this time. Rudy was driving and turned the corner, pulling into Jake's small parking lot.

"Well, your friends are back. Thanks for the popcorn…and the show," Jake said, getting up. He stuck out his hand, and I happily put mine in his. "Have a good trip," he said. "Hope you catch those guys."

He returned inside the store. I stayed where I was, feeling just a little smug that this, for once, hadn't been my fault. Moments later, I heard the sound of the RV door slam shut.

Count to three.

"Julia, we're so sorry," Doe exclaimed, hurrying around the corner with the others right behind her. "We didn't realize that you…"

I stood up and stopped them with a raised hand, making all three of them slide to a halt. "Really? You drove off without me?"

Aria roared into the parking lot with the bikers close behind. She came to a screeching halt, killed the engine and the two women jumped out of the camper and raced up to the front of the store to mingle with us. Safety in numbers, I guess.

The bikers clearly weren't afraid of a bunch of older women. They swung their legs off the bikes and began a slow march up to the store, sunglasses obscuring their eyes, helmets still on their heads. They made it to the end of the boardwalk when the screen door banged open behind us.

The bikers stopped short.

Jake stood with a big shotgun held loosely in the crook of his elbow. He didn't say a word. He didn't have to. The two bikers threw a dirty look at Aria and Goldie and returned to their bikes, revving their motors in a sign of protest as they disappeared up the road.

All heads swiveled to the big man with the shotgun.

"Girls, I'd like you to meet Jake," I said. "He's into architecture."

CHAPTER SIXTEEN

When I introduced the girls to Jake, Blair's eyes lit up like flood lamps. She was dressed in skintight jeans and a cerulean tank top that was two sizes too small. She dropped a bare shoulder and leaned forward, exposing the cleavage that left most men breathless.

"So nice to meet you, Jake," she crooned, holding out a perfectly manicured hand.

I grabbed her bony shoulder and spun her around. "I'll meet you all in the motorhome." I gave her a push, which she rewarded with a scowl. The five of them shuffled off the boardwalk and disappeared around the corner, leaving me to turn to Jake. "Thank you. You are a pleasant surprise out here in the middle of nowhere."

He grinned, bringing a sparkle to those smoldering eyes. "And you've brought a few moments of rare excitement to the slow river of my life."

I shook my head. "Where did you learn to be so poetic?"

"My mother believed that to be articulate, you had to read first. Therefore, our home was filled with books from every walk of life."

"Wise woman," I said.

He reached out and grasped my hand. The warmth of his touch sent a shiver up my arm.

"Take care, Julia Applegate. And remember, '*A little terror goes a long way.*' So be careful." When I didn't respond, he added, "Dean Koontz."

I smiled, gave his hand a squeeze and left, feeling the raw magnetism of his presence linger behind me. When I came around the corner of the building, I was stopped short by all five of my friends waiting for me with looks of restrained mirth. Well, all but Aria. I wasn't sure she'd ever smiled in her life.

"Should we call David?" Rudy asked with a snicker. She was leaning against the Hulk.

My eyebrows shot up. "What? No. Why? What are you talking about?"

"C'mon, Julia, that's quite a man back there," Blair said. "And he clearly had an eye for you."

I brushed past them with my chin stuck in the air and opened the motorhome's door. "Do you want to find those killers or not?"

The group followed me into the Hulk, allowing their chuckles to fade. We spread out around the main cabin to discuss our next move. Aria was still nervous about the motorcycle guys, and so we decided to follow her to the campground. It would be a good two-hour drive by back roads, which we thought would be the safer route. Doe would drive and take us up I-35 to 14 and over to Whitewater State Park and finally down to Onalaska.

Goldie and Aria returned to the camper. As Doe backed out of the parking lot, my cell phone pinged. It was David. A flush of adrenalin washed over me as I answered the phone.

"I have the license plate number of that old man's motorhome," he said, and then read it off.

"Damn! It's a different number," I said, writing it down.

"That doesn't mean you weren't right about those people, Julia," he assured me. "They could have just switched license plates. We're checking to see if the partial plate number you gave us matches anything that might have been stolen in the area."

"Okay," I said, my face still burning with guilt at my attraction to Jake. "Thanks."

"You okay?"

I perked up. "Sure. Just disappointed. I thought we had them. Hey, by the way, you mentioned yesterday that Owens had gotten a ransom notice."

"Yeah. It was a crudely written letter," he said.

"What do you mean?"

He laughed. "Like an old Charlie Chan movie. Someone cut out letters from a magazine and glued them to a sheet of paper."

"Any finger prints?"

"One. They ran it through AFIS. There wasn't a match."

"Which means what?" I asked.

"Just that the person has never been fingerprinted for anything."

"Too bad."

"Well, call me if you see the guys again," he said.

I cringed, thinking about the vaudeville chase that had just taken place in front of Jake's store. "Well, actually, we…"

"Hold on." He put his hand over the phone and mumbled something to someone in the background. "Sorry, Julia, I gotta go. Love you." He hung up.

Uh, what?

I lowered the phone, all thoughts of Jake and the killers gone. My heart soared. David had just used the "L" word.

David and I had been dating less than six months. Although our personalities seemed to fit like a glove, neither one of us had expressed our feelings to that extent yet.

I set the phone on the table, staring at it, barely aware we were back on the road again. Blair looked up from where she sat across the table.

"What's wrong?"

"What? Oh, nothing," I said, not wanting to reveal my innermost thoughts. "But…uh, I guess Monty and crew switched out the license plates on the motorhome." I pushed the slip of paper with the license plate number over to her. "This was the old man's license plate number."

Her blue eyes skimmed it. "Too bad. What else did David have to say?"

"Um…he mentioned they received a weird ransom letter."

"For how much?" she asked.

"He didn't say. He had to get off the phone. Listen, I'm hungry. I think I'll get the sandwiches."

I needed something to distract me, so I got up and grabbed some paper plates and handed out everyone's sandwiches and chips.

I sat down and took the wrapping off of my sandwich and opened my chips. As I crunched on a barbeque chip I glanced out the window at the passing scenery. "It's pretty out here, don't you think?"

"Too quiet," Blair said, glancing out the window.

We were on I-35, heading north, passing small towns and open country. When we cut off onto Highway 14, we passed lush green pastures where several horses grazed peacefully in the early evening shadows. An old red barn sat in the background of one piece of property alongside a small, white farmhouse with a broad front porch. A sign posted at the end of a long drive read *Honeydew Farms*.

I glanced at the farmhouse as it disappeared behind us and imagined what it would be like to sit on that front porch with David.

We left Honeydew Farms behind and passed through a tiny, neglected town that included a gas station with a single tired gas pump, a small grocery store, a post office and an antique store.

My head swiveled at the sight of the antique store. I couldn't help but wonder what treasures lay hidden within, and silently wished we had time to stop.

We continued on for a half hour or more. After lunch, I pulled out my bag of sour fruit balls and popped a green one into my mouth, savoring the bite of sour apple.

As the orange sun disappeared behind a crooked line of hills in the distance, leaving streaks of dark red behind, we passed a sign for the town of Lake Cleary. The name rang a bell, but for the moment, I couldn't remember why. I was too focused on David's last two words and the lingering tingle of Jake's touch. I waved my hand in front of my nose to capture the scent of Jake's aftershave. My heart fluttered at the enticing aroma.

My cell phone pinged again. I grabbed it, thinking it might be David. April's name popped up. I bit down on the candy to get rid of it and cried out in pain. "Ow!" My hand flew to my jaw as I dropped my phone on the table and swiped it on with my other hand.

"What'd you do?" Blair asked.

I shook my head. "I don't know," I said, cradling my jaw. I spit out the candy and pressed the speaker phone button, my hand still cradling my jaw. "How are you?"

"Going crazy," she said.

A high-pitched siren sounded in the background.

"Ahab?" I asked.

Our African gray parrot liked to imitate a police siren. He'd learned it from living with his first owner, an elderly woman who watched a lot of cop shows.

"Yes. He's reacting to the kids. I swear, Julia…I'm ready to fly out and meet you wherever you are and join you on your trip. I need some quiet time."

Blair and I shared a guarded look.

"Uh…yeah, sure. We're just laid back and enjoyin' the ride."

There was a long moment of silence from April.

"You're totally lying," she said. "What's going on?"

"Um…nothing, other than just breaking my tooth." I was rubbing my jaw.

"This is me, Julia. Remember? What's going on?"

I shrugged and gave Blair a look of defeat. "Let's just say we've had an interesting trip so far."

"I know you. That means you're in the middle of something dangerous. What is it?"

"Actually, we're just chasing some people."

"What do you mean chasing some people? Why?"

I took a deep breath. When I exhaled, I said, "Because we think they abducted Senator Owens' daughter."

"You…what? Wait a second. You've got to be kidding."

"And don't forget my tooth," I blubbered.

There was a long moment of silence on the other end of the phone.

"Did you hear me?" I whined at her.

"Of course I did."

Count to three.

I felt a sudden catch in my throat. "Hey, you may know me, but I know *you*. Why are you being so quiet?"

"Uh…I had a weird dream. It was convoluted. There was something about your tooth, a short guy with dark hair and dark eyes, and a crazy dentist. The dentist reminded me of the Steve Martin character in *Little Shop of Horrors*."

"Oh, God," I said with a laugh. "Well, bingo on the tooth, but I don't plan on allowing a crazy dentist to drill on me."

"No. That's not all," April continued more seriously. "I saw something else. I didn't know what it meant at the time, but…"

"What?" I prompted her.

April had a sixth sense. She often knew things before they happened or answered the phone before it rang. It was her dreams that often predicted dire events, though, so my heart rate accelerated.

"I was near a railroad track in the dream," April said. "There were two men chasing me. A girl was crying somewhere. And…"

My heart began to race now. "What? Go on," I said, eyeing Blair, who was listening closely.

"Like I said, these things are always confusing," April said. "They're hard to understand. Anyway, a short dark-haired guy was speaking at a microphone and the two men had a gun. I couldn't see the girl, but the men started to chase me, and I fell off a cliff and rolled down a hill and into a tree."

"A cliff and a tree? In the middle of the railroad track?"

Dreams were confusing, but this sounded absurd.

"I didn't say it made sense, Julia. Anyway, after I hit the tree, I ran through the woods until I found an old barn. The entire time I heard the girl crying. Then, the two men came out of the woods. One of them tripped over a dead guy with a ponytail lying on the ground."

I'd been holding my breath and finally let it out. "No. He wasn't dead. Just stunned."

"What do you mean? How would you know?"

"Because, I'm the one who tripped over him. You were dreaming about me. But...he wasn't dead. He's very much alive."

"No, Julia, he's not. He's dead."

"April, it was a big mistake. We've seen him since then."

"I'm telling you, Julia, the guy with the ponytail *is* dead. I'm sure of that. There was a hole in his forehead."

"Yes, I know. He ran into the branch of a tree a couple of nights ago. I..."

"Julia, stop! I had this dream earlier *today* when I took a break and dozed off in the guest house. You weren't anywhere in this vision."

A chill ran the length of my spine. "Seriously?"

"Yes. And you need to be careful. I woke up in a cold sweat, and that doesn't usually happen."

"Okay. We'll be careful. In fact, I've talked to David. He's aware of our situation...well, most of it. Was there anything else?"

"Yes. Just before I woke up the police surrounded that barn with their guns drawn. The girl was still crying. There was a gunshot and the crying stopped."

"As if the girl had been killed?"

"That's what I thought."

"She was shot by the police?"

"I don't know. It was confusing, like most dreams."

"But you think the girl was killed?"

"Yes. I felt a deep sadness when that happened."

I paused for a moment, soaking it all in, my heart hammering. "Was the short dark-haired guy Senator Owens? That sounds like him."

"I don't know. I just know this all felt very real."

"Okay, thanks, April." There was a loud crash on the other end of the phone. "What was that?"

"Oh, damn!" she said. "Please don't touch that," she called out to someone. "I gotta go."

"Well, now you know that our life isn't any more orderly than yours right now. Take care."

"You, too," she said. "I'll check in with you later. And wait until you get home to get your tooth fixed."

"Don't worry. I will."

I turned off the phone and sat back, rubbing my jaw. "What do you think?" I asked Blair.

"Who knows? She got the guy you tripped over right. And your tooth."

"And the railroad tracks," I added.

"Yeah. But what does the rest of it mean?" She watched me massage my jaw. "How'd you break your tooth?"

"I bit down on a piece of candy and felt it crack."

"Does it hurt?"

"It did when it happened." I paused and carefully pushed my tongue against the molar. The tooth moved. "Shoot. I think I did break it. I don't have a dentist anymore. Dr. Pearl retired."

Blair's blue eyes twinkled. "I have a great dentist. Dr. Ford. He has an office downtown on Elm Street."

I gave her a pouty look. "Does he have nitrous oxide, so I won't feel anything?"

She gave a soft laugh. "Yes, Julia. You'll have to eat on the other side of your mouth until you get home, though."

"Maybe I'll lose a little weight." I forced myself to stop touching my tooth with my tongue. "Weird though. Chloe must have known I was going to break my tooth, too. Remember the Scrabble letters?"

Blair was tapping her fingers on the cover of her book and didn't seem to have heard me. "You know, I think you should call David back and tell him about how we chased the Jayco motorhome around Jake's store. At least the police should know those guys are in the area."

A nervous jitter skittered down my core. "Um…okay. I guess that's a good idea."

I didn't want to call David back yet. I hadn't had time to process his last words. I was afraid that maybe I'd misheard him. I knew I'd have to talk to him sooner or later, so I reluctantly dialed his number.

"Hey," I said, when he answered. "I know you're busy, but we saw that motorhome again. In fact, we chased them around..."

"It's okay, Julia," he said in a rush. "That's why I had to get off the phone earlier. They've found the old man's motorhome."

"What? Really? Where?"

"In a ravine up on Snoqualmie Pass. There's a team heading up there now."

"You're sure?"

"Yeah. They were able to ID the license plate from up above. It's down a steep slope, and it will take an entire crew to bring it out."

I slumped back against the seat with a heavy feeling of disappointment. "Well, okay, then. I wonder who these people are we've been chasing, then."

"Who knows?" he said. "They might be carrying drugs or something, and that's why they ran. Stay away from them."

"What about Amy Dunphy?"

"She's still missing. We're still looking closely at her boyfriend. We're bringing him in today to talk to him again. I like him for it."

"What about her stepdad?"

"There's nothing yet to suggest he's involved. There is a text from her older brother that we're looking into, though."

"Brad?"

"Yes. How do you know his name?"

"Internet," I replied. "What was the text?"

"He's underwater financially because of gambling debts. The text was about that. He wanted to borrow money from the senator, but Owens said no. Might give him a reason to try and extract money from him."

"You think her own brother would abduct her?"

"He's only related by marriage. He's Grant Dunphy's son, so, yeah, it could happen."

"All right, then. I'll let you get back to business. I'll talk to you later."

We hung up. There were no words of affection this time. The disappointment inside me turned quickly to sadness, and a tear threatened to form in the corner of my eye.

"I need to use the restroom," I mumbled.

I slipped out of the bench seat and hurried to the bathroom. Once inside, I grabbed some toilet paper and wiped at the tear. *Damn!* I always did that–read too much into what people said. Most likely, David had said, "*Love you,*" just as a way to say goodbye.

I sighed deeply, flushed the toilet to complete my ruse and returned to the main cabin. As I did, Doe called over her shoulder, "We're almost out of gas, and it's getting dark. There's a Chevron station up ahead. I'm going to get gas now since it's almost on empty. That way we won't have to fool with it in the morning. Can you call Goldie?"

"Sure," I said, happy to have something to do.

I got on the phone and called Goldie to let them know we were taking the next off-ramp to get gas. Doe pulled the big rig off the interstate and slowed down as she entered the small town of Kasson. I was considering getting out when she stopped for gas to buy more Pepsi when Rudy shouted out from the front passenger seat, "Look, there's the Jayco!"

She was pointing ahead of us and to the right.

Doe took her foot off the gas, drifted to the right side of the road and pulled up to the curb next to a small diner. The Jayco sat thirty feet or so away from us, parked at the side of the diner.

"Tell Aria to pull over," Rudy said to me.

I gave Goldie the instructions, and Aria pulled to the curb about half a block ahead of us.

"What do we do now?" Blair asked, turning to look through the side window at the motorhome.

The diner faced away from the street and towards a gas station that shared the same lot. The parking slots in front of the diner were full. I presumed that's why the Jayco had been backed into one of the three parking slots on the street side of the diner, with its nose blocking our view of the diner's front door.

"We should call the police," Doe said.

"Wait," Rudy said. "Not yet. We don't want anyone to get hurt. If the police show up, those guys could kill the girl, maybe even take hostages inside the restaurant."

"Shouldn't that be for the police to decide?" Doe argued.

"What can we tell them?" Rudy countered. "That we *think* these people are holding a girl hostage and that they're driving a motorhome stolen from an old man they killed in Washington State? What happens when they ask us for proof?"

"Wait. I just talked to David," I said. "They found the old man's motorhome. It's in a ravine up on Snoqualmie Pass."

Rudy turned a deflated look in my direction. "So this isn't even the old man's motorhome," she said gesturing to the RV in question.

I shook my head.

"Great." She slumped into one of the swivel chairs.

"What about the fact they keep running away from us?" Blair asked. "Why would they do that?"

"I still think they're holding a girl hostage, even if it's not Amy Owens," I said. "And she needs our help."

"I agree that under normal circumstances we should call the police," Rudy said. "We've already made fools of ourselves with the police in Spokane however, so I'd like to keep our names off the police blotters in South Dakota if we can. Sorry, Julia."

"Apology accepted," I said with a shrug.

"So...what do we do?" Doe asked with a somber look.

"We need to find out if there is a girl being held captive, no matter who she is. I say we go see what's inside that camper," Rudy said.

The rest of us reacted with undisguised shock.

"Seriously?" Doe asked. "We're going to break into their motorhome?"

Rudy shrugged. "If we call the police with what we suspect, even if they believed us, they would need a search warrant to get inside. We need some proof."

I realized for the first time that Rudy was enjoying this. As a lifelong investigative reporter, she loved digging deep into things. This was a mystery she wanted to solve.

"What's the plan?" I asked. "One of them could be in there with her."

Rudy was staring at the white motorhome, her small brown eyes narrowed in thought. I could tell that big brain of hers was running on overdrive.

"You and Doe can sneak around to the other side of the Jayco and watch the front door of the diner in case whoever is in there comes out. Blair and I will go up to the RV and knock. If no one answers, we'll get inside."

"What if they locked it?" Doe asked. "If the girl is in there, I'm sure they locked it."

"We'll get inside," Rudy said more firmly. She got up and pushed past me to rummage through the kitchen drawers.

"Interesting way to park," Blair said, peering at the motorhome. "Backing in, I mean. I guess they want to be able to get out of there fast."

"We'd better hurry," Rudy said, coming back with something in her hand. "They could just be ordering take out, and we don't know how long they've been in there."

The gas station and mini-mart sat at the rear of the big lot, facing the road, with two lines of gas pumps in front of it. The diner sat to its left.

The four of us hustled out of the Hulk. Doe and I scooted around the rear of the Jayco and moved into the space between the diner and the RV.

The diner was small, with a single window on the street side next to us. No light shone from inside, so it was probably an office or storeroom, keeping us safe from prying eyes. As I poked my head around the front corner of the building, I saw a car pull up next to one of the gas pumps in the middle of the lot. On the far side of the convenience store was a motorhome and a couple of cars, all with for sale signs in their windows.

By now, the sun was low on the horizon, leaving the two of us in a heavily shadowed tunnel between the Jayco and the building.

While we watched for the burly guy they called Monty, Blair and Rudy went to the street side to access the door of the RV. I heard a short knock, followed a minute later by the creak and sway of the RV.

"What are we going to do if they come out?" I asked Doe, as we peered around the corner.

"I don't know. We didn't figure that out," Doe said. "It's not like we do this for a living."

A moment later, Rudy tapped me on the shoulder, nearly making me jump out of my skin.

"No one is in there," she said in a hoarse whisper. Blair loomed behind her.

"Then let's see if she's inside the diner with them," I said.

"How do you propose we do that without them seeing us?" Doe asked in a raised voice.

I could tell this covert stuff was putting a strain on her sense of orderliness; after all, you didn't do this sort of thing in a boardroom.

"Listen, I'm the shortest. I'll sneak up to that front window and peek inside. The cars in front of the building will block me from the street and anyone at the gas station."

"What if they're sitting right next to the window?" Blair asked.

"I'll be careful. I can do this. If she's not with them, then this was all a big mistake and we can leave."

Rudy put a hand on my shoulder. "Wait a minute. Call Goldie. She and Aria have never been seen by this group. They can go inside and let us know who is in there."

"Good idea," I said.

I pulled out my phone and called Goldie to explain the situation. Within seconds, the two of them hustled around the back of the white motorhome to join us. Now there were six of us crowded in the small space between the Jayco RV and the wall of the restaurant.

"They're inside?" Goldie asked. "This is so excitin'."

"No, it's not," I chastised her. "The girl might be in there with them. All we need you to do is find out if we're right."

"And you'll need to hurry," Rudy said. "They could come out at any minute. So be careful."

Goldie nodded and the two of them went inside. We waited impatiently as we peeked around the corner, only to flinch back when the restaurant door opened and an elderly couple appeared. They got into a small pickup by the front door and pulled out. We flattened ourselves against the wall of the building to avoid detection.

"This is ridiculous," Doe said. "I feel like I'm in a bad movie."

Finally, my cell phone pinged.

"Yes?" I said, answering it.

"We see two men at a table eating," Aria said. "One is a big bald guy. He's wearing a plaid shirt. The other one is kind of a beefy guy with a beard and a bad eye."

"That's them. No girl? No woman with red hair?"

"No," she said. "But we're seated at the counter. Oh, wait a minute." There were several seconds of excruciating silence. "She's with them!" Aria whispered into the phone. "The woman with the red hair just came out of the restroom. She's holding onto the girl's arm. God, she doesn't look good. In fact, she looks drugged. But, Julia, she has blond hair. I thought you said the girl had dark hair."

"She's there," I said breathlessly to the others. "They must have put a blond wig on her or dyed her hair."

Rudy exhaled in exasperation. "Then we're right back where we started. For all we know, that's their niece or something. Tell Aria to get out of there and go back to their camper to wait for our signal."

I relayed the instructions to our new cohorts. A moment later we heard the restaurant door open and close. Goldie and Aria appeared in the parking lot. They glanced our way but kept going towards the street.

"What do we do now?" I asked Rudy. "And where's Ponytail Guy?"

"I don't know. Let's get back to the Hulk and move it so they don't see us," Rudy said. "We'll have Aria follow them when they leave, and we'll hang back."

We started back the way we'd come, when I stopped them. "Wait a minute. What's that?" I said, pointing past Rudy to the side of the Jayco.

Everyone turned toward the motorhome.

There was something dripping onto the pavement just below where the sewer hose was kept. My nose crinkled in disgust considering what it might be, but I pushed past Rudy and leaned down to zero in on it.

"Oh, my God!"

"What is it?" Blair asked from over my shoulder.

I extended a finger toward the liquid.

Blair slapped my hand away. "Don't touch that!"

"Something's wrong here." I rose up, scanning the perimeter of the compartment. There was a gap at the upper right corner, as if something inside was pushing against it. I reached out and released the latch.

The door popped open, and something heavy fell out, making me jump back as it hit the pavement with a thud.

I screamed.

Blair screamed.

Rudy and Doe screamed.

Ponytail Guy lay frozen into the shape of a fetus at our feet. Only this time, he had a real gunshot wound in his forehead.

"Oh, shit!" Rudy murmured.

"My God, is he dead?" Doe asked, peering over Rudy's shoulder.

"Are you kidding? He has a big hole in his head," I replied.

"Where have we heard that before?" Blair asked cynically.

"Yes, but this time he was folded into the compartment that normally holds the dump hose," I said, my voice rising.

"Okay, stop arguing," Rudy snapped, glancing around. "We have to figure out what to do."

"I say we get out of here," Doe said, glancing around.

"No, now we have evidence," Rudy said. "Now we *should* call the police."

"Wait a minute," I said. "This changes everything. Blair, you heard April's dream."

"What dream?" Rudy demanded.

"April called and told us she had a dream that Ponytail Guy was dead."

Rudy's face was compressed into heavy skepticism. "How did she know anything about Ponytail Guy?"

"She didn't. That's the point. He showed up in her dream...dead." I pointed to the dead guy at our feet by way of proof. "She also dreamt about a girl and two guys with a gun, but the most important thing was that just before she woke up, the police arrived and the girl was killed."

A heavy silence floated in the air.

"She's right," Blair finally said. "That's what April said."

"If they killed Ponytail Guy, what's to stop them from killing the girl if they think they're cornered by the police?" I asked.

"What can we do?" Doe asked.

I turned to Doe. "I say we put the body back and..."

"I'm not touching that thing!" Blair screeched.

"Wait, hear me out. We put him back and let them get back on the road. Then we call the state patrol and report a drunk driver with something red dripping down the side of their motorhome." I raised my eyebrows as if to say, "*Get it?*"

"That could work," Rudy said. "But we have to hurry."

"I still don't want to touch him," Blair said, folding her arms in protest.

"I'll help," Doe said, stepping around me. "I just want to get out of here before someone sees us."

Doe leaned down to grab his shoulders, while Rudy slipped her hands under his hips. I cupped my hands beneath his knees. With a hefty grunt, we began to lift him. Doe squealed when blood smeared her sleeve. She yanked her arm back, dropping his shoulder.

He tumbled to the pavement again as we all lost our grip.

"Crap!" she said. "Sorry."

"Why is he so stiff?" Blair asked from the safety of her position behind us.

"Rigor mortis, you idiot," Rudy snapped. "C'mon, let's do this."

We bent down to try again and got him halfway to the compartment before realizing how hard it would be to get him back inside. He was, after all, stiff as a board and folded up like a pretzel.

"Wait," Rudy said. "Put his shoulders in first."

"No, I think we should tip him up," I said.

"Did you see how he was stuffed in before?" Rudy asked in a strained voice.

"No! He just fell out."

"I can't turn him," Doe said. "If I do, I'll lose my grip."

"C'mon, let's just shove him in," I said, straining under his weight. "I can't hold him anymore."

We got him to the lip of the compartment, fighting to hold him steady.

"Okay, on three...shove him in," Rudy said.

Rudy counted to three, and we pushed.

Rudy got his butt in, but he started to tip forward. Rudy turned and leaned her entire body against his, holding that half of his body in position. She was gritting her teeth with the strain. I tried tucking his feet in.

In the background, I heard the diner's front door open and close and looked up in time to see people crossing behind the cars parked in front of the door. I saw a head swivel in our direction, but the group kept going.

"Quick, we need to finish this," I said. "Someone's going to see us."

"He's not going to fit!" Rudy snapped.

"He's got to fit." I turned to Blair. "Blair, see if you can reach over and fold his head in."

She gave me a horrified look. "His head with the big hole in it?"

"Yes, Princess!" Rudy retorted. "Quit being so dainty."

Blair reached out a hand to delicately tip his head down.

Doe was facing the other side of the parking lot and let out a gasp.

"What?" I asked.

"It's them," she said breathlessly. "They just left the restaurant and are crossing the parking lot."

I turned to look, losing my hold. Ponytail Guy fell to the pavement with a splat.

"Damn!" Rudy exclaimed.

"Never mind that," I said.

The four of us left our dead friend and inched forward to look over the cars parked in front of the diner. Sure enough, Monty and crew were crossing in front of the AM/PM, weaving their way through the gas pumps.

"Where are they going?" Doe asked.

"Straight for that other motorhome," Blair said, pointing.

Eva had her arm around the girl's waist, while Roy dragged her forward by the arm. Monty was in the lead.

They got to a gray and white Tioga motorhome with a 'for sale' sign in the front window and paused. Monty looked around and then jimmied the door open.

"My, God. They're going to steal that other motorhome," Doe said.

"Makes sense," Rudy said. She glanced behind her. "Why keep driving one that has a dead body in it?"

"That's pretty brazen, though," Doe commented.

"Not really," Rudy replied. "All of those vehicles for sale are parked out of the line of sight of anyone in the store, and people at the gas pumps aren't paying attention."

It took them less than thirty seconds to get the door open and climb inside. A few seconds later, someone removed the 'for sale' sign from the window and Monty had the engine going. He pulled the motorhome past the store and toward the street.

"Tell Aria to follow them," Rudy said.

I grabbed my phone again as we ducked down behind the cars and peeked around the front of the Jayco to watch them enter the roadway and turn right.

I quickly explained the situation to Goldie and told her to follow the gray and white motorhome that had just passed them.

"Roger that," she said.

Once their RV had disappeared up the street, we scrambled back to the Hulk. This time, Rudy got behind the wheel. As a fierce competitor, she didn't like to lose. To her, this had become a competition.

"Uh…isn't anyone concerned we just left a dead body back there?" Doe asked, glancing out the window at the Jayco RV.

"Can't worry about that now," Rudy said. "We can't lose them."

She pulled away from the curb with a jerk, swerved around a slow moving car in front of us and revved the engine to give pursuit. I watched her for a moment, thinking that perhaps I'd unleashed a monster.

We hadn't gone more than a few blocks when Doe cried out, "Rudy...remember? We're almost out of gas. We're not going to get very far."

Rudy mumbled an expletive and slammed her fist against the wheel. "Fine." She turned to me in the co-pilot's chair. "Let Aria know. She'll have to keep on their tail."

I nodded and once again dialed Goldie to give her an update.

"Roger that," Goldie said again.

I rolled my eyes when I hung up. "Goldie thinks this is a game."

Blair leaned forward from the main cabin. "Julia, could you have been mistaken about the color of the girl's hair?"

I turned to her. "I don't know. It happened so fast. Maybe that's not Amy Owens, but some other poor girl they kidnapped. We could be looking at a sex trafficking ring or something."

"God, I hope not," Doe said.

"What are we going to do when we find them?" I asked Rudy.

Rudy sat in the pilot's seat tensed as if ready to spring forward. Her jaw muscles were clamped shut, and her hands gripped the large steering wheel as if she were squeezing the life out of it. Watching the few cars around us, it made me a little nervous to have Rudy driving.

"Rudy?" I whispered again. "What *are* we going to do?"

She turned towards me with her small brown eyes squinted in a fierce stare. "Help that girl. Any...way...we...can."

CHAPTER SEVENTEEN

Rudy was one of those people who had a rough exterior, matched by a personality that always hummed with a little bit of adrenalin. And yet, she was also someone who kept her emotions in check. She was measured. Focused. She made reasoned decisions. We relied on her for that.

Right now, however, she seemed a little unhinged. The sense that these people might outsmart us had pushed her over the edge, and that underlying tension was seeping out through her pores.

"How are we going to save the girl? We can't confront them," I said. "They have a gun."

"And they're not afraid to use it," Doe said from the swivel seat by the window.

"We'll find a way," Rudy snapped. "We always do."

I turned back to the road ahead. We were still off the interstate, and there wasn't much traffic. When the yellow fuel light indicated we were about to run out of gas, Rudy pulled into a Chevron station and slammed on the brakes. Blair got out to pump the gas.

As the rest of us waited in a tense-filled RV, my phone rang. It was Goldie.

"Where are you guys?"

"Not sure," she said. "We're in a residential area. It's getting dark and difficult to see the street signs through all the trees. And we haven't been close enough to get the license plate number."

"Okay. We had to stop to get gas. Call us back when you figure out where you are and we'll catch up."

"Roger that," she said a third time.

"Looks like we need to wait," I said to the others. I related the rest of what Goldie had told me. I tried to relax into my seat, feeling like, once again, we were heading into a danger zone with few resources to back us up.

"Why do you think they killed Ponytail Guy?" Doe asked from behind me.

I shook my head. "I don't know. Maybe because he just didn't fit in. Remember, I heard him complaining to Eva at the Fourth of July celebration. Then I also saw Roy push him up against the motorhome. They clearly weren't on friendly terms."

"Maybe he drank too much," Doe said. "Every time we saw him he had a beer in his hand."

"And then there's the night Julia thought he was dead," Rudy said. "He must've been dead *drunk* when he ran into the tree." She gave me a brief nod of approval, as if to apologize for her earlier skepticism.

"Creepy, though, how April called that one," I added. "She knew nothing about these guys at the time. That's also why I take her at her word when she says she saw the police shoot and the girl died. I think we need to be very careful."

The door to the Hulk opened and Blair climbed back in. "What do we do now?"

Doe sighed as she glanced at Rudy. "I don't know, but I feel like our legal liability is stacking up fast. I'm not sure we're going to be able to explain our way out of any of this. Especially the dead guy we just left on the pavement back there."

Rudy started the engine and pulled the Hulk over to the side of the parking lot, where she killed the engine again. The raw intensity of her exterior had softened, and she seemed to be breathing easier.

"We wait," she said. "We'll hear one way or the other from Goldie where they are and then we can catch up."

There was a long moment of silence as Blair plopped down on the leather sofa.

"Well, I need something to eat," I said.

I went to the refrigerator to grab the grapes we'd bought earlier. I ran them under water and then brought them to the table in a bowl. I took a couple before offering them to Doe.

"You know, we have no idea where they went," Doe said, breaking off a small bunch. "They're in a motorhome that no one knows they have, and it's getting late. They could just pull off somewhere up by the lake and lay low for the night."

"Wait!" I said with a grape halfway to my mouth. "I remember now. I heard Ponytail Guy say something during the fireworks. He mentioned a side trip Monty had to make to Lake Cleary."

"So they're purposely going to the lake for some reason. And it may have nothing to do with the girl," Rudy said thoughtfully. "I wonder what that's all about. The good news is they don't know about Aria and Goldie…yet. Keep your fingers crossed they don't figure out they're being followed."

Blair sighed. "What a trip this has been. We thought we were just taking a simple trip across country."

Doe chuckled. "When has anything we've done ever been simple?"

"Well, at least none of us are in any danger this time," Blair said, reaching over for a bunch of grapes.

I glanced around at my friends. We were all exhausted, frustrated, and deflated.

We needed a rest.

As I munched on a grape, my phone rang.

"They got away from us," Goldie reported when I answered. "We're up by Lake Cleary. We got cut off by a truckload of kids. The motorhome pulled up a hill and disappeared."

"Where are you?" Rudy called out.

"Just a sec," Goldie said.

We could hear her conferring with Aria.

"We're at a crossroad—Forest Glen and Sparrow Road. Do you wanna meet us here?"

"Yeah. We'll find you." Rudy turned to Blair, who already had her cell phone out looking up the streets.

"Okay, follow this road," she said, slipping into the co-pilot's chair. "Then turn left at the first stop sign."

Rudy followed Blair's directions until the GPS voice took over, telling her what to do. Several minutes and several turns later, we found the spot where Goldie and Aria were waiting.

The intersection was two country roads surrounded by open fields and two structures on opposite corners. Across the street from us was a large ranch-style home with a sloping driveway. The lights were on and a pickup sat in the driveway. To our left was a closed auto repair shop with a fenced junkyard behind it.

Rudy found a wide space in the road and pulled over in front of Aria's camper, next to a sagging wire fence. Seconds later, our door opened and Goldie and Aria climbed in.

"We lost 'em," Goldie said with disappointment.

She and Aria plopped into the swivel chairs.

My heart sank. "Can't we do something?"

Goldie shrugged. "We could split up and drive around looking for 'em."

"It's getting late," Doe said. "It will be dark soon." She glanced at her watch. "Maybe we should call and report in to David."

"C'mon, you guys. I didn't think you'd give up so easily," Aria complained.

Her dark eyes glinted in the low light. She was loving this.

I heaved a deep sigh. "But we don't know where they are."

"We have the atlas," Blair said, opening the glove box. "Since we know they're going to Chicago, they'll have to circle back at some point." She pulled out the atlas and joined me at the table, opening the map book and flipping pages.

"Okay, here we are. Lake Cleary," she said, pointing to a spot on the page.

Rudy had left the driver's seat and slipped into the seat next to me, while Aria, Goldie and Doe looked over Blair's shoulder.

"It looks like the lake is surrounded by hills, and Forest Glen Road winds up around the lake," she said, tracing the road with her finger. "There's another small town, Gateway, on the north side of this stretch of forest."

"Look here," I said, pointing. "Forest Glen circles all the way around the lake and comes back out to Sparrow Road. And Sparrow Road is blocked on the west by this nature preserve."

"Which means there's no other exit," Aria said. "The roads that split off around the lake are all dead ends," she said, pointing toward the map. "Nothing cuts all the way through to Gateway."

"We have them!" Blair said. "That road has to be a good five or ten miles long. All we need to do is to wait here until they double back."

"Or we could just call the state police and let them know," Doe interjected.

Her dark eyes looked sad in the waning light, or tired, as if she was fighting a losing but important battle. She and I had just barely missed being killed by a madman a few weeks earlier. Now, we were chasing a group of thugs who had already killed two people and who we believed may have abducted a young girl. Doe lived in an ordered world. With three murder investigations already under our belts and now this, her ordered world was unraveling.

"We need to see this through, Doe," I said. "We can't risk a young girl's life."

We locked eyes for a moment, and then she nodded. "I know."

Everyone became animated again.

"Okay," Rudy addressed Aria. "Why don't you and Goldie follow the motorhome up that road and around the lake? Check the side streets and see if you can find them. We'll stay here, just in case they come back. We'll move the Hulk over by that repair shop, where they'd be less likely to see us if they circle all the way around and come back on Sparrow Road."

"Okay," Aria, said. "But hold on. I have a couple of walkie-talkies. They're faster than the phones." She left the Hulk and hurried back to her truck. A minute later, she returned and handed me a black walkie-talkie. "Keep it tuned to channel 2," she said. "You just press here when you want to talk and release the button to listen. They're top end and have a 35-mile range, so we should be good."

I nodded. "Thanks. I got it," I said, wondering why she had walkie-talkies in the first place.

"Okay," Aria said. We'll see if we can find them. We'll be in touch."

The two of them exited the Hulk and returned to their truck. After they'd pulled out and around us, Rudy backed up the motorhome, pulled up next to the old building on the other side of the street, but left the engine running. If Monty and his crew came back down Forest Glen Road the way they'd gone up, they would see us, although they might not notice us in the dark. If they circled all the way around the lake, we would be blocked from view as they came east along Sparrow Road.

Blair volunteered to go outside with the binoculars and give us a heads-up if she saw the motorhome approaching from Sparrow Road. She jumped out and hid around the corner of the building. We had waited only a few minutes when the walkie-talkie crackled.

"Mama Bear calling Green Bay," Goldie's voice called out. "Come in Green Bay."

I pushed the button to talk. "Who the heck is Green Bay?"

"You guys," she responded.

I sighed and rolled my eyes at Doe. "Okay, what's up?"

"Nothing. We haven't seen them. There's a bunch of homes up here and some roads that do cut off, but they're dead ends."

"So they'd still have to come back this way."

"Right."

"Okay, we'll hold tight," I said. "Keep looking."

"Okay," Goldie said. "Over and done."

"That would be over and out," I said with a sigh.

The minutes dragged on until a half hour had passed. Inside the Hulk, the air was tense as we waited, and it looked like Blair was also getting anxious standing outside. Either that or she had to pee. She kept shifting her weight from one foot to the other.

A sharp rap on the door startled us. I opened it to find a tall, middle-aged police officer standing outside.

"Good evening, ma'am," he said tipping his hat.

"Hello," I responded tight-lipped. My heart was in my throat. "Can I help you?"

He looked around me into the RV. "I wonder if you could step outside."

I glanced behind me at Doe and Rudy. "Um...sure. All of us?"

"Yes, ma'am."

We filed out of the Hulk and lined up outside. By now, the sun was down and the corner street lamp had come on. A a second officer came around the back of the RV with Blair in tow.

"What is this about, officer?" Doe asked, holding Tinker Bell in her arms.

He had his notebook out. "We've had a complaint."

"A complaint?" I said.

"Yes, m'am. From one of the neighbors." He nodded across the street to the house with the sloping driveway.

I glanced that way and saw the curtains at the front window move. Someone was watching us.

"Can I have each of your names and the license of the person driving?" the officer said.

We glanced at each other and then rattled off our names. He took his time writing them down, while Rudy went back inside to get her license.

"What's going on?" Rudy asked after he'd checked her ID. "Have we broken some law?"

"No, ma'am. Not yet," he said, flipping his notebook closed. He nodded to the home kitty-corner from us. "The neighbors said you were acting suspiciously."

"Suspiciously. Us?" I protested in an innocent tone.

"Yes, ma'am. They were concerned. They saw this woman hiding behind the building there," he nodded toward the auto repair shop. "And your big motorhome was just sitting here with its engine running."

He stopped talking at that point, turned to us, hooked his fingers through the loops in his belt and stared, waiting.

Count to three.

"Well, we weren't doing anything wrong," I finally said.

"What *were* you doing?"

Now, it was us who just stared.

"We're waiting for a friend," Blair blurted out.

"Why were you hiding?"

Blair's demeanor quickly changed. One of her shoulders dropped. Her head tilted to the same side, and she crossed her arms, clamping her breasts together.

"Officer," she purred, stepping closer to him. She stood right under his chin, lifting her baby blues in his direction. "I think you'd agree that I shouldn't just stand out by the road all alone. There are a lot of good 'ole boys trolling these streets. I was watching for our friends, so I kept to where I was protected. That's all." Blink. Blink.

It worked.

He coughed once, glanced at her cleavage and then stuttered, "Uh…yes, of course…not, I mean. I…uh, well we'll let the neighbors know you're just waiting for someone." He stepped back and put his notebook away. Then, in an effort to reclaim the upper hand, he said, "But I wouldn't stay here too long. Best to move along as soon as you can." He gave us a nod, handed Rudy's license back, and the two officers returned to their cruiser, which was parked behind us.

We all clambered back into the RV as they drove over to speak to the complaining neighbors. We watched them get out of the car as the home's front door opened. They had a short conversation with a man and then left.

"Phew, that was close," I said as the man closed the door.

"No kidding," Doe said. "Thanks, Blair. Once again, you rock."

She smiled demurely. "Thanks. But we still don't know where Monty and crew are. And those cops might come back to check on us."

We waited another fifteen minutes before the walkie-talkie crackled. I reached over and pressed the button.

"Hi, Goldie."

"Mama Bear to Green Bay," she said.

"Yes, I know, Goldie," I said with a deep sigh. "What's up?"

"We found them!"

CHAPTER EIGHTEEN

According to Goldie, she and Aria had driven up several dead-end streets around the lake and finally spied the gray and white Tioga RV parked in the driveway of a small house that looked empty. They couldn't tell if anyone was in the RV, or if Monty and the others had gone into the house, but all lights were off–both in the motorhome and in the house.

"Okay, we're coming up," Rudy said. "Where are you?"

"Dunno," she said. "You'll pass a small store on your right. It's the second street past the store. Turn right. You'll come up a hill, and then you'll pass another, shorter street that cuts off to the left. They're at the end of that street. Hold on." We heard Aria's voice in the background, and then Goldie added. "Aria's got her infrared glasses out to see what that street is." We all shared an incredulous look at the mention of infrared glasses. There was more mumbling, and then Goldie said, "Okay, the street that cuts off the one we're on is called Sterling Road. See you soon."

We followed them up Forest Glen, passing fancy, multi-level homes at the water's edge to our left, flanked by tall aspen and oak trees. Smaller cottages sat along the road to our right, overshadowed by steep hillsides filled with tall pines and low vegetation.

The two-lane road twisted and turned for several miles. With no street lights, it was slow going, especially because we had to keep a look-out for the store. Finally, we found a small market tucked into a hillside, surrounded by trees. Even though it was after ten p.m., a group of young people hung out in front of the store, while cars pulled in and out of the dirt parking lot.

We passed the store and found the road we needed on the right. It was called Broadview Street. We made the turn and climbed a winding hill into a residential neighborhood. Aria's camper was parked almost at the top of the hill, just past Sterling Road. We pulled around a cul-de-sac and parked behind her, facing downhill. As Rudy turned the wheels to the curb and cut the engine, our door opened and our co-conspirators climbed in.

"So what does it look like up there?" I asked them.

"Both of these streets end with a circle," Aria said. She had changed into a black turtleneck, camouflage cargo pants, a bomber jacket and combat boots, making me wonder what she expected to happen that night. "There are about eight houses on Sterling," she said. "It appears half of them are empty. I think a lot of these places are vacation homes, so people are probably in them sporadically."

"And the house where the gray motorhome is parked looks empty?" Rudy asked.

Aria nodded. "There's no car out front or in the carport, and all the lights are off. It's just the motorhome in the driveway."

Rudy sat back, thinking. "I wonder if this is the extra stop Monty was talking about."

"Shouldn't we just call the police now?" Doe asked once again. "Seems like we've done our job."

Blair and I shared a concerned glance. April's dream loomed large in my mind.

"I'd like to find out if the girl is actually Amy Owens," Rudy said.

My heart skipped a beat. "I would, too. Maybe they're all just drug dealers, and that's why they ran."

"All the more reason why we should call the police," Doe argued, her facial muscles tensing.

"Remember April's dream and what we learned when Julia was held captive in that church basement back in December," Blair said, recalling our first murder investigation. "The police can't get a search warrant without evidence. The most they could do right now is knock on the door and ask questions. All these guys would have to do is to lay low and not answer the door."

"And then they might kill the girl," I said. "I don't want to take that chance."

Doe sighed. "What do you think we can do? Besides get *ourselves* killed in the process?"

"We could sneak up there and peek through the windows," Blair offered. "Maybe we can see Amy. If they had a wig on her in the restaurant, they might take it off inside the home."

"I take it you're willing to be the one to go check," Doe said with a slight challenge to her voice.

"Yes, I am," Blair said.

"So am I," I added.

"I'll go," Aria said, raising her hand.

"No," Rudy said. "You should stay here. If they come out again, they'll likely turn down the hill, and you and Goldie can be ready to follow them again."

Aria sighed with disappointment. "You're right."

Oh well, there went the need for combat boots.

"Okay," Rudy said. "Blair and Julia can launch from here. We have the walkie-talkies and our phones." She leveled a serious look at Blair. "You're going to have to be quiet, though. If you use the walkie-talkie, whisper. Better yet, back away from the building before you try to communicate with us. If it's an emergency, do what you have to do."

I could feel the tension grow around me again, and goosebumps prickled my arms. I glanced at Blair. "You okay with this?"

She bit her lower lip. "Yeah. They're drugging that girl, and God knows what else. We need to find a way to help her." She turned to Doe. "We can do this, Doe."

She held Blair's gaze for a moment and then sighed. "Then here's to safe passage," she said with resignation, reaching out her hand.

The rest of us placed our hands over hers as if the six of us were about to burst forth onto a football field. Instead of a team chant, however, we squeezed each other's hands. Then, Aria and Goldie quietly returned to their camper.

Blair and I were both dressed in jeans and tennis shoes. Blair had put on a lightweight jean jacket over her tank top, so I reached into the closet to grab my own jacket. Blair dug through the drawer for the flashlight.

I grabbed my phone and dropped it into my right pocket. When I did, I felt a packet of Kleenex and the small compass knife Chloe had wanted me to take. My stomach clenched at the thought that Chloe had known I might need a knife. But it gave me a strange sense of resolve and comfort that the ghosts had my back.

Blair gave me a nod. "We're ready," she said, turning to Rudy.

"Okay. All you're doing is confirming that it's Amy," Rudy said. "Nothing else. Don't go all commando on us. If she's there, we call David, who will call in the police."

"Why David?" I asked with a start.

"Because the local police would be more likely to believe him," she said with a shrug. "We don't have any real evidence."

"Got it," Blair said. "Be back soon."

Blair's optimism didn't match the nervous twitch in my stomach. In fact, my adrenalin production was on overdrive, making my hands shake. I swallowed hard and followed Blair outside.

The temperature had dropped, although it was still muggy, and a slight breeze brought the smell of campfires and lake water as we passed Aria's camper. We nodded to the two dark figures in the front seat. I thought I saw the shadow of Goldie's hand as she raised it in salute, then we turned the corner to start up Sterling Road.

Only the first few houses had lights on, and there were no street lamps. Fortunately, the nearly full moon bathed the area in a golden hue. We walked with purpose, as if we were just two neighbors out for an evening stroll.

When we got to the cul-de-sac at the end of the road, Blair stopped and pointed. The stolen motorhome was parked in the driveway of a small stucco home framed by large hedges. There were no lights and no movement anywhere.

"Let's get up close to the motorhome first," she whispered. "If it's unlocked, we can check inside."

I nodded.

As crickets chirped away in nearby bushes, we followed the curb around the circle and then broke off and tiptoed up the driveway, coming along the right side of the RV. Blair raised a hand, telling me to stop. We listened for a moment, but heard only the crickets. She pointed at me and then to the building.

She was telling me to watch the building while she went into the motorhome.

I nodded and took a step past her.

The Tioga was a cab-over style motorhome. Blair tried the door. It opened with the hint of a rattle. She pulled open the screen door. When no alarms went off and no one appeared, she slipped inside.

My heart thumped so hard that my chest vibrated. Behind me, the RV rocked and creaked. I tensed. Outside, there were only the comforting sounds of a rural night.

A moment later, Blair reappeared and shook her head.

No one was inside.

I swallowed hard. That meant we had to approach the house.

We inched away from the RV toward the building. It was small–maybe 1200-square feet. The curtains were closed at both front windows, and no light leaked from behind them. Blair ignored the front door with its small ivy wreath, and veered into a carport. She peeked into a side window, but everything was dark in the front part of the house. We moved through the carport and approached the rear of the building where the faint sound of voices put us on alert.

Blair threw out her arm to stop me.

She pointed to a sliver of light that shone through the blinds at a back window.

We took a step forward. The sound of a door opening at the back of the house had us hustling off to the right to duck down behind two large trash cans.

A voice boomed out, "We'll be back soon. Keep an eye on her." We peered through a gap between the trash cans and saw Monty and Roy emerge around the back corner of the building.

"What are we gonna do about her?" Roy asked, stopping in the carport to light a cigarette. "We're gonna have to get rid of her soon."

I put my hand over my mouth to avoid gasping. *They were going to kill Amy.* Blair squeezed my other hand in warning.

Roy inhaled and then exhaled a plume of smoke, which curled up into the air around his bald head. I felt the heat rise in my belly.

"Not yet," Monty said. "We need her to control the girl."

No, they were talking about Eva!

"Shit, I can stick that kid with a needle," Roy said, sucking on the cigarette. "We don't need her for that."

"Sure, and kill her in the process. Eva's a nurse. She knows how much to use to keep the little bitch quiet."

"Yeah, but we left the drugs in that old motorhome. We don't have enough left to keep her quiet until we get to Chicago."

"That's okay. We're picking up something in a few minutes that'll do the trick."

Monty's cell phone rang. He reached into his pocket to grab it. "Mclaughlin," he said, making a half turn away from Roy. "Yeah…What?…Shit. Okay. Where?…Wait. There's too much security there. That wasn't part of the deal." He paused to listen. "Really? Half a mil…each?" He glanced over at Roy. "Okay. Yeah, I got it." He hung up and dropped the phone back into his pocket.

"What?" Roy asked.

"That was Yoda," Monty said, turning back. "He's pretty pissed. He said the senator isn't cooperating. Yoda wants us to get rid of the girl and then meet him in Chicago. He has a plan to go after Owens instead, Saturday night."

Roy's bloated features flexed into an ugly grimace. "What plan? Are you sure this guy's legit? Getting rid of a senator in the middle of a big meeting like that will be dicey. There will be cops everywhere."

"He's legit. And he just offered us enough money to make the risk worth it. Look, we have a pickup to make. Then we take care of the girl. We have to be in Chicago tomorrow afternoon."

"Do I need to get a tux?" Roy asked with a chuckle.

"Dunno," Monty said, starting to move again. "I guess we'll find out when we get there. Yoda will call us tomorrow morning."

They left the carport, climbed into the Tioga, started it up and backed out of the driveway. Blair fired up the walkie-talkie, calling Rudy.

"Roy and Monty are coming your way in the motorhome," she whispered. "They're going to pick something up. And Rudy, we've confirmed it's the senator's daughter. We heard them say so."

"Okay, c'mon back," Rudy ordered.

"No. When they come back, they're going to kill her. We need to get her out of here. Call the police."

CHAPTER NINETEEN

Blair clicked off the walkie-talkie and pocketed it.

My eyes opened wide. "Wait. What? We're going to try to get her out of there?"

"I can handle Eva," Blair said. "C'mon. We don't have much time."

She left the safety of the trash cans, forcing me to follow. We crept along the side of the building and toward the backyard.

We followed a narrow concrete walkway around the back corner of the house, ducking down as we passed the windows. We got to the back door, which opened onto a small patio scattered with folding chairs and a glass-topped patio table.

The outdoor light above the back door was off, but the blinds on the small window had been angled partially open, allowing the inside light to shine through. The lock on the door had been broken.

We positioned ourselves on either side of the door and slowly rose up to peek through the blinds.

Inside was a small den, decorated with big, soft furniture. Framed photos of the lake hung on walls painted a forest green. To the right was a kitchen with a butcher block island and a silly black and white wall clock designed to look like a cat's face.

Eva sat in a big leather recliner angled toward the corner to our left. She was watching TV, using the remote to change channels, oblivious to our presence.

Slumped on the sofa on the far wall behind her was Amy. Dressed in a pair of shorts, tennis shoes, and a tank top, her hands and feet were tied, and she had a gag in her mouth. Her head had dropped forward, and the wig had been removed, allowing her dark hair to tumble around her shoulders.

As we surveyed the scene, panic welled within my chest. I knew Blair. She was fearless. And I could tell she was assessing the situation. I remembered Rudy's comment that Blair shouldn't "go all commando." Apparently her warning had fallen on deaf ears.

Blair pushed me behind her and then turned to whisper, "I'm going to get Eva's attention. When she opens the door, I'll grab her and pull her out. You get in there and use that knife of yours to free Amy."

I nodded with a big lump in my throat. As she turned away, I reached into my pocket and brought out the small knife Amelia had given me and opened it, my heart thumping. We pressed ourselves into some bushes under the window, and then Blair tapped on the window.

It seemed like an eternity before the door knob turned, and the door cracked open. Eva's head appeared, her eyes searching the darkness outside.

"Monty?" she said.

Blair sprang into motion.

She grabbed Eva's wrist with lightning speed and yanked her forward. As the small woman stumbled out the door, Blair whirled around in front of her and gave her a quick jab to the face. She crumpled to the pavement, blood oozing from her nose.

Damn!

"Go!" Blair ordered.

I gingerly stepped over the stunned woman and headed for Amy.

The sharp knife cut the ties at her feet and wrists, releasing her. I turned to get Blair's help, but she was dragging Eva across the patio.

I poked my head outside. Blair had just pulled the handcuffs Rudy had given her out of her pocket. She handcuffed Eva to a pipe extending from the lower part of the building and then rushed back inside with me.

"Okay, let's get out of here," she demanded.

Together we pulled an unconscious Amy off the sofa and each took one of her arms. I snatched Eva's hoodie off the recliner and slipped Amy's arms into it. She was small–not much bigger than me–but limp and awkward to move. I put my arm around her waist, while Blair slipped her arm under Amy's shoulder.

I looked over at Blair. She nodded once, and the three of us stumbled toward the open back door.

We staggered into the cooling night air and made it to the back patio before the walkie-talkie crackled. We stopped. Blair balanced Amy on her hip and reached into her pocket to extract the device.

"Yeah," she said.

"Blair!" Rudy's harsh whisper called out. "Get out of there. They're on their way back."

"Shit!" Blair exclaimed, shoving the walkie-talkie back in her pocket. She looked around. "C'mon!"

We began hauling Amy toward the backyard and the forest beyond, her limp feet dragging along the ground.

"Where are we going?" I asked, struggling to keep up.

"We can't go back the way we came," she said.

We reached the end of the lawn and stepped into a dense copse of trees and bushes. Branches scratched, prodded and probed us, and berry bushes snagged our clothing as we pushed through. It was difficult to hold onto Amy, and just when I thought we'd lose our hold on her, we broke free of the foliage. Good thing, because we were practically dragging her behind us by this point.

"Pick her up," Blair snapped.

We yanked her to her feet and then kept going. We'd only made it a few more yards before we heard the soft rumble of the kidnapper's motorhome's engine behind us.

That spurred us on.

Since Blair was much taller than me, she was able to lift Amy higher, pulling her feet off the ground. Together we propelled her forward.

Although we'd left the thick foliage behind, we still had to weave between trees and bushes. We stumbled over strands of ivy and broken tree limbs, and were slapped a couple of times by branches. Amy moaned and seemed to come half awake at one point and tried to pull away from us.

"No!" Blair whispered. "Amy, we're here to help you."

When we heard shouts from the house behind us, we picked up the pace, veering left to avoid a thick patch of bushes studded with large rocks. We circled around them and then...I stepped off into thin air, pulling the other two with me.

We fell, tumbling and rolling down a steep hill. I slammed into a big rock and then rolled over it, knocking the air out of my lungs. When it was all over, I lay on my back, staring at the stars trying desperately to catch my breath. I rolled onto my right side with a groan.

Amy was about four feet away on her stomach, head toward the bottom of the hill. She wasn't moving. I could just barely make out Blair below her.

Faint voices got us moving. Blair rose and scrambled back up the hill to Amy. I sat up and shook my head, then stood holding my ribs to help Blair get Amy back to her feet.

"C'mon. We have to hurry," Blair said in a hoarse whisper, glancing to the top of the hill. "They're coming."

We stumbled to the bottom of the hill and waded through a shallow stream, silencing a chorus of frogs. We pushed to the other side as the voices grew stronger above us. Once across, we struggled up a small rise and dropped down behind a large boulder.

Both of us were breathing hard, which brought tears to my eyes because of the pain in my ribcage. Amy was slumped against the rock, groaning. I put my hand over her mouth to keep her quiet. The voices remained at a distance for a few seconds, and then they were gone.

We waited a good minute, and then Blair tried the walkie-talkie.

It didn't work. It had been smashed when she rolled down the hill. She tossed it into some bushes, sighed with frustration and leaned back against the rock, breathing hard. "Now what?"

I pulled out my cell phone and swiped it on. No bars.

I gave the same despondent sigh. "Why don't we try to get back to that store?"

She turned toward me. "How? I have no idea where we are."

"The police should be coming soon," I said.

"Or not," Blair said. "We're out in the country. Who knows which law enforcement agency covers this area?"

"We could stay here for the night. Go back the way we came in the morning."

"No. Amy can identify them, and so can we. They'll come after us."

A muffled "pop" startled both of us. It was a gunshot, and we stared at each other in the dark.

"Eva," I said with some remorse.

My phone lit up and began to play, *Rock Around the Clock.* An uninvited chill ran the length of my spine.

I quickly swiped on my phone and put it to my ear. "Mom?"

"Get out of there! Someone's coming for you."

"I know, Mom. I...we don't know where to go."

"I hear water. Follow the water. Now!" she snapped, and then the phone went dead.

"C'mon," Blair said, jumping up. "We need to get as far away from here as we can."

I struggled to my feet and then we each took one of Amy's arms.

"Okay, on three. One. Two. Three."

We pulled Amy up and left the relative safety of the boulder. I couldn't help but glance to the top of the hill behind us. A shaft of moonlight illuminated a rocky, steep slope that seemed to extend forever in the opposite direction. Somehow, we'd missed running into the few trees on the hill. We were lucky to be alive. The flash of a wavering light several hundred feet away made me grab Blair's arm and point in that direction.

"Time to go. What'd your mother say?"

"Follow the stream."

"Okay, let's go."

The stream curved in and out of a gulley with steep hillsides rising on either side. The light behind us disappeared as we turned the first bend. Ash and oak trees spread their canopy of branches above us, while the trickle of water serenaded us as we stumbled forward. We traveled a good quarter mile up-stream before stopping to rest.

We gently lowered Amy onto the ground, and then I plopped down onto a large boulder holding my ribs. "Do you think we're safe yet?" I asked between gulps of air.

"No," Blair said, slumping onto a big rock. She was holding her right wrist. "We're a loose end they'll need to tie up. We need to keep going."

"I need to catch my breath," I said. "Give me a second. What's wrong with your wrist?"

"It's bleeding pretty badly," she said. She stripped off her jacket and then removed her tank top. She wrapped the tank top around her wrist, tucking it in to secure it. She started to put her jacket back on, but struggled. I got up and helped her get her arms in and then button it up.

An owl hooted above us just as a bat whipped past my head, making me duck. As I lifted my head again, a small, floating light behind us made me freeze.

"They're here!"

Blair spun around as she buttoned the last button on her jacket and stared into the darkness.

"No, that's a glow bug. Look," she said, pointing to several more tiny lights flitting around a bush that extended over the water.

I stared with fascination as the small fireflies bobbed back and forth like disembodied ghost lights. When a grunt echoed down the valley, my heart nearly stopped.

"Was that a human or an animal?"

"Doesn't matter. Let's go," she replied.

We grabbed Amy again and continued to struggle forward. I was groaning with pain when we broke out of the gully and into a large glen some ten minutes later. An old barn stood to our left, with a broken-down cabin behind it in the dark. A shattered down fence ran along one side of the two buildings, and two tall electrical poles stood at the front and back corners of the property. Although there was a large scoop light mounted above the double doors of the barn, everything remained ominously dark.

I looked around with alarm. "This reminds me of April's dream. Do you think it's safe?"

"Who knows? But we're not safe out here in the open, and we might find something in there we can use as a weapon."

As she began to move in that direction, the sound of a splash some distance behind us startled me. Someone was coming up along the stream.

"Go ahead of me!" Blair said. "I've got Amy."

I ran ahead while she put her arm around Amy's waist and practically lifted her off the ground, hauling her forward.

I made it to the barn without tripping. One big barn door was open. I ducked inside. Blair was only a few steps behind. I tried to close the door behind her, but it wouldn't budge, so we veered to the left, away from the opening.

The stale odor of old hay and rotting wood washed over me as my eyes adjusted to the dim light. We were in one big room with a vaulted ceiling. Windows on either side allowed rays of moonlight to cut through the darkness and frame the interior. Farm equipment, hay bales, and old wooden barrels loomed in the shadows.

Blair pulled Amy over to an old bale of hay and dropped her gently behind it. She pulled out the flashlight and began scanning the area around us. She spied an old wagon wheel propped up against the wall with several spokes missing and sprinted over to it to pick up one of the spokes from the floor. She slapped it against a hay bale to make sure it was solid.

"Aren't we sitting ducks in here?" I whispered with trepidation, glancing toward the big double doors.

"Probably. But we don't have the energy to go much further, and we can't out run them. We'll have to make a stand." She handed me the spoke. "You take this one. I'll find another one, and we'll split up."

She hurried back to the wagon wheel and found a second spoke. I waited, feeling numb with fear at the thought we would have to engage with these killers. I was having trouble breathing, and didn't know how much good I'd be, anyway.

And then an image appeared that gave me hope.

A hazy glow appeared behind the bale of hay, near Amy. It was the image of a woman dressed in a long, white nightgown, a dark braid of hair draped over her see-through shoulder. She had her hand resting on Amy's head.

Elizabeth!

Elizabeth was Chloe's mother and had died in the same fire that had killed her daughter and one of her sons. Chloe had made herself known on this trip several times, but I hadn't been sure Elizabeth's ghost had accompanied us. But like any mother, she probably wouldn't have let Chloe go alone. The thought almost made me smile.

"Blair," I whispered, pointing as my body flooded with relief.

Blair turned around and stopped short. Elizabeth looked at us, her image illuminating the space around Amy in a halo of light. She nodded once, just as a gravelly voice rang out from outside the barn.

"Amy! If you're in there, you'd better come out. We won't hurt you."

My heart leapt into my throat. It was Monty. I'd recognize that growl anywhere.

I pulled my phone out and stared at it, willing my mother to call. "Please, Mom," I whispered. Seconds passed. And then, the phone lit up. I swiped it on before it could play her signature song.

"Mom! We need help," I whispered into it before she could speak.

"I know, Button. What's happening?"

"We're in a barn in the mountains. We rescued a young girl, and there are two men outside who want to kill us." I was nearly in tears, and choked on my final sentence. "Can you do *any*thing? Please."

"Amy!" Monty yelled again.

I whirled toward the voice, my body now humming. Blair rushed over to my side.

"He doesn't know we're in here with her," she whispered. "He thinks Amy escaped alone."

"Amy!" he yelled again. "You won't get away."

I still had the phone to my ear. "Julia," my mom said quietly. "Is Elizabeth there with you?"

My head swiveled in the direction of our resident ghost, who still hovered protectively behind Amy.

"Yeah. How did you know?"

"Really, Julia? We have the same address. Just give her a chance. She knows what to do."

"I'm only going to count to three, Amy, and then we're coming in," Monty yelled.

There was a gun crack, and a bullet crashed through the window above me. I let out a short scream as glass shards rained down around me. My cry won me an angry slap from Blair. I clasped my hand over my mouth.

"You got her!" Roy said from outside.

"I hope I killed her," Monty replied in a low voice.

Blair moved to the side of the barn doors, holding the wagon wheel spoke firmly in her hand, ready for battle. I froze, my heart banging in my chest. I wasn't sure what to do until a low hum brought me to attention.

It was coming from the scoop light above the barn doors. I wondered if Mom had come through for me after all. Affecting all things electrical seemed to be her single biggest talent from the other side. The low-level hum became a loud buzz, and then the light sprang to life, bathing the area in front of the barn in a glaring, yellow glow. We could hear mumblings of alarm from the two men.

"Careful, Amy," Monty warned. "Don't do anything rash."

Monty mumbled something to his partner. I stretched my neck to peek out the now broken window and saw the two men standing about sixty feet in front of the barn, squinting into the light.

"C'mon, Amy. Don't make us come in there."

There was a moment of near silence. Then the scoop light above the doors exploded, sending sparks and shards of glass several feet into the air. The men cried out and jumped back.

"Shit!" Roy said.

"Okay, Amy, I guess we'll have to come in," Monty yelled.

I saw Blair tense, and my heart jumped into my throat.

And then a sizzling, spitting sound made me look up toward the electrical pole, which I could just barely see through the window. The cord running from the scoop light to the pole had split away from the lamp and had begun to rotate in the air, sending hissing sparks flying in several directions. There were more cries of alarm from the two men, who backed away from the hot wire as it waved back and forth in the air right in front of them.

"Shit! What the hell is going on?" Roy yelled, stumbling away from it.

"Let's rush the place and finish this!" Monty yelled.

He didn't have a chance, because the cavalry arrived!

Elizabeth skyrocketed through the open door to hover in front of the barn in all her eerie glory. And I do mean eerie.

Her nightgown billowed in the air around her, and her bare feet were several inches off the ground. A ghost's face and extremities appear blotchy, because the body isn't solid. So Elizabeth didn't look very friendly hovering above them like that.

"Damn! What the hell?" Monty yelled. He backed up so fast he fell on his butt.

"It's got to be some kind of trick," Roy said, staring wild-eyed at the apparition.

Elizabeth continued to glisten in the darkness, her white night dress flowing around her in unearthly splendor. And then she even surprised me; she threw her arms out to the side and emitted a bone-chilling cry that turned my body cold.

"Shit!" Monty yelled, backing up again.

"Shit!" I murmured.

Monty began firing at Elizabeth. I ducked, as the bullets went wide, clipping off pieces of the barn. When the gun's magazine was spent, he threw the weapon at her, but of course, it passed right through her.

He watched it happen and scrambled to his feet.

"Let's get outta' here," Roy yelled.

The two men turned and ran back up the gulley and disappeared.

I slid to the floor, tears of relief springing to my eyes. When I looked up, Blair was leaning against the barn door, her body slack with exhaustion.

Before we could speak, Elizabeth appeared at the barn door again, her image flickering in the shadows. She glanced at me, and then darted back to Amy. She reached down to brush her ghostly fingers across the girl's forehead, then leaned in to give her a kiss before her gossamer image faded and was gone.

CHAPTER TWENTY

Once the excitement was over, my cell phone jingled *Rock Around the Clock.* I answered and put my mom on speaker.

"Thank you, Mom," I said, choking up. "What would I do without you?"

"A question I ask myself often. It feels like the danger is gone. Are you okay?"

"We're fine. I assume you were responsible for the fireworks display."

"Yes, but you really need to stop doing this, Julia."

"What do you mean?"

"Getting involved with bad people. What happened to the nice, quiet girl who liked baking and arts and crafts projects?"

I chuckled, which sent a sharp pain through my ribcage. With a wince, I said, "I don't know. She's all grown up now and dating a cop."

"Sounds like I'll have to have a talk with him."

"No!" I blurted. "No talking to David. It's not his fault. In fact, he'd like me to live a safe and orderly life. I just keep running into these things."

"All right, Button. I've gotta go. Stay safe."

"Thanks, Mom."

I hung up the phone and struggled to move over to where Amy was still slumped against a hay bale. I dropped down next to her.

"So what do we do now?" I called over to Blair.

Blair came over and sat on the hay bale next to Amy. "I say we stay here tonight."

"Don't you think they'll be back?"

"Would you?"

I chuckled. "I guess not. Good, because I'm exhausted. And my ribs are killing me."

"Sorry, I didn't even ask. What happened?"

"I hit a rock when we rolled down the hill. I think I cracked a rib."

"Oh, jeez. A cracked tooth and now a rib. I'm sorry, Julia."

"Well, what about you? How's your wrist?"

She lifted her right arm with the blood-streaked tank top wrapped around it. "I think it's okay. It might need some stitches, though." She dropped her hand again. "Why don't you sleep first? I'll keep watch."

"No, I can stay awake." I was completely lying.

Blair smiled. "Don't worry about it. I'm fine for a while. I can keep an eye on Amy. Hand me your phone, and I'll wake you in a couple of hours. Just don't snore. If they come back, we don't want them to hear us."

"Very funny. Thank God for Elizabeth, though. I sure like having my own Seal Team 6."

"No kidding," Blair agreed.

I handed over my phone. "You know, I include you in that metaphor. You really do rock, Blair."

She smiled. "Thanks. Now get some sleep."

I curled up on the ground between two bales of hay, confident that Elizabeth and my mother would watch over us. I was asleep within minutes.

÷

Blair woke me several hours later. I had to pry my eyes open, but willingly took my turn holding vigil.

It was chilly in the barn. The humidity had lifted, and I had to wrap my arms around myself to keep warm. I glanced over at Amy, glad I had grabbed Eva's hoodie and put her into it.

As the night turned into early morning, rodents and small animals rustled in the walls of the barn or in the bushes outside. Every time I heard a noise, I flinched, visualizing a pack of wolves circling the barn, or Monty and Roy returning to finish the job. The aroma of the decaying hay was oddly relaxing though, and I kept nodding off. I had to pinch myself every so often to keep awake.

I decided to use the time to think about Rudy and the others. *What were they doing? Were they okay and looking for us?*

Finally, David's image floated into my mind, and I felt wrapped in his loving embrace. The mere thought of him warmed my insides. I only hoped I'd make it out of this alive so I could express my own affection for him, as he had for me. Yes, I would take that chance. After all, Jake was eye candy, but David was French chocolate, and everyone knows how much I love chocolate.

Eventually, the sun sent rays of light through the windows to reveal discarded farm equipment, rat-infested grain sacks, and horse tack scattered around the barn. Outside, a pair of crows began an argument, breaking the morning silence. When Amy stirred and opened her eyes, I sat up.

"Amy, are you okay?"

She turned bleary eyes my way, and her face contorted with confusion and fear. "Where am I?"

"We rescued you," I said, nodding toward Blair.

Blair woke when she heard voices and sat up. She shook her head and rubbed her temples.

"Morning," she mumbled.

"Who are you?" Amy asked, glancing back and forth between us.

Amy's face was pale, and there were scratches and bruises across both cheeks and down her legs. The dark eyes that would normally look at life with the optimism of a teenager were dull and lifeless.

"My name is Julia. This is Blair. I saw you in the window back at that campground, and we've been following the people who abducted you ever since."

She shook her head as if to clear it and placed her hands on her forehead with a look of pain on her face. "My head's so fuzzy. They kept drugging me."

"We know. It should wear off quickly now," I said. "You are Amy Owens aren't you?" When she nodded, I asked, "Do you know who they are, the people who took you?"

"No," she said. "One of them grabbed me from behind when I got out of my car and threatened to shoot me if I tried to run. I never got a good look at him. They stuck a needle in my arm right away."

Tears began to roll down her cheeks at the memory. I threw my arm around her shoulders. "It's okay. We've got you now."

"But we need to get out of here and back to our friends," Blair said. She took a deep breath and rose, dusting off her jeans. I noticed her teeter slightly.

"You okay?"

"Yeah," she replied. She took the blood-stained tank top off from around her arm and dropped it onto a hay bale.

"How does it feel?" I asked her.

She studied the long incision on her forearm. "I don't think it's that deep. At least it stopped bleeding."

I climbed to my feet, holding my ribs. "Okay. I've got to pee. I'll be right back."

I grabbed the pack of Kleenex out of my coat pocket and found a broken-down farm wagon a few feet away. When I came back, I offered the Kleenex to the others. They each took their turn, and then we left the safety of the barn and went to the stream to wash our hands.

There was a low-lying fog in the glen, but the sun was already beginning to break through. We took drinks of the fresh creek water and then Blair splashed water on her arm to wash off the blood. She dried it gently against her jeans.

Again, I watched her take a deep, cleansing breath. Her face was drawn and pale and most of her makeup was gone. Though still pretty, she looked profoundly tired.

"You don't look so good, Blair. You need something to eat."

"I'll be okay," she said. "You don't still have the knife Amelia gave you, do you?"

"Yes," I said. I reached into my jacket and pulled it out. "How will that help us?"

She took it from me. "The compass. Remember that map we looked at? There was a town called Gateway just north of the lake."

While Blair held the small knife with the tiny embedded compass, I tried my phone again. Still no bars. Blair rotated her body until she was facing north.

"That way," she said pointing forward.

A dirt road wrapped around the run-down cabin and extended away from us. She started forward, faltered and almost fell. I reached out and grabbed her.

"Blair! Sit down a minute."

I helped her lower herself onto a log.

She gave me a less-than-reassuring look. "I'm okay. We've got to go."

"Wait," I said, reaching into my other jacket pocket. I'd remembered the Snickers bar I'd bought at the gas station so many hours before. "It won't fill you up, but it will help."

I handed it to Blair, who ripped it open and bit off a third of it. When she swallowed, a sense of relief played across her face. She tried to hand it back.

"No. You finish it." I turned to Amy. "You okay with that? She's a diabetic. She needs to eat."

Amy was staring longingly at the candy bar in Blair's hand, but she glanced at me. "Of course. I'll be fine."

I turned back to Blair. "Eat."

She gave me a grateful look and finished the candy bar. As the color returned to her face, she got unsteadily to her feet.

"C'mon. Let's get out of here."

We avoided the road, just in case Monty and Roy decided to come back. Instead, we followed another deer path up the valley. It was much easier traveling without having to drag Amy, although she, too, wasn't too steady on her feet. Once she even had to stop because she felt like she was going to throw up. I assume it was the drugs. Blair took the opportunity to rest with her.

"How are you feeling?" I asked her.

A brief smile flickered across her face. "Much better, but I'll have to eat some real food soon."

"Then let's keep going."

Overnight, the pain in my ribs had spread to my back, which made each step difficult. Still, we made good time.

We followed the deer path through the glen and then back into a forest of pine trees and undergrowth. Rabbits scuttled across the path as we trudged along, and birds twittered in the trees above us. Despite the fear and anxiety from the night before, the morning felt invigorating.

An hour into our trek, we approached a steep hill. I stood back, looking up at it. "God, I hope we don't have to climb that."

Blair checked the compass. "Yeah, I think we do. Hopefully, it's the last leg of our trip, though."

I took the deepest sigh I could without generating pain, and said, "Okay, let's get it over with."

We began the climb, doing switchbacks as we went. My labored breathing made me stop twice, and a couple of times I had to use low branches from small trees to pull myself up. A couple of times my foot slipped, giving me a start. I retained my footing, leaned forward and kept going.

Two-thirds of the way to the top, my foot skidded out from under me, and I almost tumbled backwards. Amy grabbed my hand and stopped me from falling. As a cloud of dust rose around me, she pulled me forward, supporting me the last fifty yards.

By the time we'd made it to the top, I was done. I'd never thought I was out of shape. This experience had me pledging to start an exercise program as soon as I got back home.

Blair also looked more weathered than I'd ever seen her. Her face was pink from exertion and glistened with sweat.

"You two rest. Let me do some checking around," she said, taking deep breaths. "I'll be right back." She disappeared down another small trail.

"She's pretty amazing," Amy said, watching Blair's disappearing figure.

"You have no idea."

I found a fallen log and sat down, deciding to use the time to learn a little more about the girl we'd risked our lives to save.

"They didn't *hurt* you, did they?" I asked carefully.

"You mean sexually?" she asked in alarm. "No. At least, I don't think so." She sat next to me, reflecting a moment on her imprisonment. "No. I don't remember anything like that. I remember a woman, though. She would move me around, feed me and take me to the bathroom." Her pale face twisted in disgust. "She treated me almost like a baby." She smelled her armpits through the hoodie. "Ugh. I need a bath."

I smiled. "She was a nurse. I think that's why they recruited her. They promised her she'd make a lot of money."

She nodded. "That sounds right. She's the one who kept giving me the shots." Amy reached over to rub the inside of her left elbow. "I still feel kind of...I don't know, disembodied. Do you know why they took me?"

I shook my head. "No. It has something to do with your father, though. We overheard them say he was being uncooperative. Do you know what that would mean?"

She flinched as if she'd been slapped. "Uncooperative?"

"Yes. That's what one of them said."

Her eyes blinked away tears. "No," she said. "I don't know what that would mean, other than he's pretty powerful in the Senate. Maybe they want something from him politically."

Her initial reaction made me wonder what her relationship was like with her father. From what I knew of him, he didn't seem like a warm and cuddly guy.

"The police thought maybe your boyfriend, Dylan, had something to do with it."

Her eyes got as big as saucers. "Dylan? No way. We broke up that night, and he was pretty upset. But he's a good guy. And he's a pacifist."

"I'm sure they found that out," I said. "You have no idea who might be connected to this? How about your stepfather?"

"My stepfather?" she said, offended. "Why do you ask that?"

I realized I had to tread lightly. "Just that one of the men who took you looks just like him. Does your stepfather have a brother?"

"Um…yeah. Martin. But…he'd never do anything like this."

"Are you sure? Are either one of them in any financial trouble?"

She thought a moment. "I don't think so. Martin lives in Los Angeles. He owns a bar down there. And my stepfather has a construction company."

The sound of a footfall made us both look up. Blair appeared on the trail. A smile lit up her tired and worn face.

"I see buildings at the bottom of the hill. I'm pretty sure it's the town of Gateway. Julia, check to see if your phone works now."

I pulled my phone out and swiped it on. "Hallelujah!" I exclaimed. I dialed Doe's number and was ecstatic when she answered.

"Julia? Where are you? We've been worried sick."

"We're okay!"

"Oh, my God. They're okay," she cried out to the others. "Where are you?"

"Wait. Here's Blair."

I handed the phone to Blair.

"Get the atlas out," she said. "Look just north of the lake. There's a small town called Gateway. We're on a hill just above it. We'll call back when we get to the bottom. Meet us there."

Blair hung up the phone and handed it back to me. "C'mon. I need a cup of coffee and a very large omelet."

CHAPTER TWENTY-ONE

It took us ten minutes to travel across the top of the hill and another ten to safely descend it. It was steep and slippery in places. As is often the case, going down felt harder than climbing up. My calves burned and each step put pressure on my sore ribs.

Once again, Amy came to my rescue when I slipped and almost fell, swirling up a cloud of dust. She grabbed my arm to steady me and then held onto me the rest of the way down. Once we'd made it to the bottom, she had to pause.

"You okay?" I asked her.

Her face seemed even paler than before.

"Yes," she said with a deep breath. "I just don't feel so good."

"C'mon. You'll feel better when we can get you something to eat."

It took another few minutes to wade through scrub brush and dry grass to reach the first outlying metal building.

We came up along the side of it and emerged into a space at the back of a boat shop. The three of us crossed through an alley littered with old boat wheels, a few empty steel barrels, and some rusting outboard motor parts, before we made it onto the main street of the small town of Gateway.

Our small band of travelers stood there for a moment, soaking it in.

We were safe.

"There," I said, pointing across the street.

A small café with red-checkered curtains in the windows sat next to a gas station. We hurried across the street and entered the restaurant.

Several sets of eyes glanced our way when we came through the door. We must have looked like something out of a Tolkien novel. After all, we were covered in dirt, scratches and bruises.

The clock on the far wall said 7:15. We took a large table in the back and gratefully sat down, ignoring a few brief sneers at our appearance. I pulled out my phone and called Doe again, telling her where we were.

"Be sure to bring my purse. Because we're ordering breakfast."

"Okay," she said. "Rudy thinks it will be a half hour or so before we get there."

I tried straightening my hair and found a piece of straw buried near the crown of my head. I pulled it out and threw it on the floor just as a young waitress arrived. She glanced at it and then said, "What would you like?"

"I'll take a stack of blueberry pancakes, sausage, and hot tea," I replied. "And where are your restrooms?"

She cocked her head to the right. "Down the hallway."

I glanced over at Amy who looked relieved to sit down. "Get whatever you want."

"Can I have two waffles and bacon? And a glass of milk."

The waitress wrote it down and then turned to Blair, who was using a napkin to wipe dirt off the backs of her fingers.

"I'll take a Denver omelet and hash browns," she said. "And some orange juice."

While we waited for the food to arrive, we took turns going to the ladies' room to wash up. Once the food did arrive, we dug in without any ceremony. There was little conversation; we were all too busy satiating our hunger. I'm not sure blueberry pancakes had ever tasted so good to me.

We had just finished eating when the doorbell jingled, and the remaining four members of our group burst in.

Blair and I jumped up to share hugs with them, me protecting my ribcage. They pulled up chairs and sat down with us.

"This is Amy," I said, putting my arm around her.

She looked up with a shy smile, while I proceeded to introduce the others. She nodded to each one, and I noticed tears beginning to form in her eyes.

"Thank you," she mumbled. "I can't believe you all risked so much to help me." She used the back of her hand to wipe her eyes.

"Thank Julia," Doe said, reaching out to grab her hand. "She's the one that insisted we pursue their RV. The rest of us weren't even sure you were in there."

I gave Doe a grateful smile.

Amy turned to me and started to cry again. "I don't know how to thank you."

I smiled and gave her a hug. "Don't go all the way to Boston for college," I whispered in her ear. "Your mom is going to want to keep you close for a while."

She smiled and nodded.

"So what now?" Aria asked.

"Have you called your mother yet?" Doe asked.

Amy shook her head. "I'm afraid to," she said, wiping her tears away. "We had a big fight the night before I disappeared. I said some really ugly things to her."

I took her hand. "Trust me. You mother won't care." I looked up at my friends. "But I have an idea. I don't think we should call her mom just yet."

"Why not?" Rudy asked. "She has to be worried sick."

"The two men who chased us last night thought Amy had escaped by herself. They didn't know we were with her. *And* they think they injured her when they fired a round into the barn. For all they know, she's still lost out there in the wilderness injured or even dead."

"What's the point, Julia?" Doe asked.

"Maybe I'm thinking too much like a mystery writer, but we heard Monty say they needed to get to Chicago by tomorrow night. Someone named Yoda said that since he couldn't get Amy's father to do what they wanted, he would go after him directly. If they don't know whether Amy is safe or not, she remains a threat, and it might just knock them off their game."

"And in the meantime?" Rudy asked.

"We keep Amy with us. I'll call David. Maybe the police can go to her home and tell her parents privately."

"We can't do that," Rudy said, shaking her head. "We need to get her to a hospital. We should have already taken her."

"No!" Amy said. "I'm fine."

"You don't look fine," Rudy said. "And the police will want to interview you. Maybe even save your clothes and get pictures of your arms," she said, nodding toward Amy's elbows.

Amy's eyes flashed with fear as she turned to me. "Please. I want to stay with you. I...I..." Her composure began to disintegrate as tears rolled down her cheeks, creating rivulets of dirt. She even began to shake. "I can't be left alone. I...I just can't." She burst into sobs.

"We won't leave you," I said, putting my arm around her again, holding her tight. I turned to Rudy. "We can't leave her behind. She'd be all alone until her parents could get here."

"And we need to get to Chicago," Blair said. "Someone is still after her father."

"We could split up," Aria suggested.

"No," I said. "We're a team in this. It's the only way we've survived so far."

"Then what do we do?" Doe asked. "And no matter what you say, Amy needs to call her mother."

I sighed. "We keep Amy with us. Let's get on the road. We'll preserve her clothes and take photos of her arms and anything else we have to."

"And you think the police will accept that?" Aria asked skeptically.

I rolled my eyes. "No, but I'm not willing to leave Amy here."

"Neither am I," Blair said. "We risked life and limb to save her. I'm not abandoning her now, but we do have to get going. We're the only ones who know what these people look and sound like."

"I agree," I said. "We need to be in Chicago. I'll call David from the road. He can talk to her parents and then she can call her mom."

"I'm okay with that," Amy said, wiping her eyes. Her hands still shook, but she took a cleansing breath. "I want to do whatever I can to get these guys."

The waitress arrived with our bill.

"I've got it," Doe said, pulling out her credit card.

"Thanks, Doe," I said.

"Okay, let's get on the road," Rudy said. "We're supposed to be at the Aberdeens' in a couple of hours." She turned to Amy. "I bet a shower would feel good."

She smiled. "Yes. Thanks."

It was 8:35 by the time we made it to the sidewalk ready to board the Hulk.

"Wait a minute," I said, throwing my arm out to stop Rudy. I was staring at the roof of the motorhome. From where I stood, it looked as if the air conditioner had been ripped halfway off. In fact, it was hanging part-way off the side of the roof and there was a deep scar running along the upper wall of the RV, where a portion of the siding had been peeled away. "What the heck happened?"

Doe suppressed a laugh. "Rudy happened."

I turned to my little athletic friend, who was already blushing.

"Hey, we were driving around looking for you. It was pitch black out, and I drove under a big oak tree that hung low over the road."

"More like she drove into it," Goldie said, rolling her eyes. "We were right behind her."

"Good going, Rudy," Blair said with a giggle.

"Listen, we were worried sick about you guys," Rudy said in her own defense.

"As well you should have been," I said. "But now, I'm keeping score."

Once we were back inside the Hulk, Blair found clean jeans and a t-shirt that would fit Amy and gave her soap and shampoo to take a shower. We also gave her a trash bag in which to put her dirty clothes.

"If you'll let me," Blair said, "I'll go with you to take pictures before you wash all the evidence away."

She nodded and the two went into the small bathroom.

As Rudy pulled away from the curb, I went to the back bedroom to take a look at my ribs. Doe came in behind me and saw the big bruise that extended across the right side of my ribs and wrapped around my side.

"Oh, Julia, that doesn't look good," she said.

"A large rock and I had an altercation," I said with a groan. "The rock won."

"It's probably too late for ice. You might want to tape it, though."

"Let's wait until I can grab a shower at the Aberdeens' first."

"Okay," she said. "Let me know when you're ready and I can help." She sat down on the bed. "Listen, Julia. I'm sorry if I was the constant nay-sayer in all of this. You were right all along, and I'll never doubt you again. I'm proud of you. You saved that girl's life."

My throat began tighten. "We did it together. I don't know what I'd do without the rest of you."

She got up and we hugged, separating when I winced.

"Sorry. Come out and relax a bit," she said.

We returned to the main cabin, and I sat in the swivel chair. As we traveled, a rumbling noise coming from the roof of the RV made me nervous.

"Is that the air conditioner?" I asked Doe.

She smiled ruefully. "Yes, but I wouldn't say any more about it to Rudy. It wasn't her finest moment."

"I think I'll call David," I said. "Can I borrow your phone? Mine's almost dead."

"Sure." She pulled her phone out of her big black bag and gave it to me as I plugged mine into a charger.

"Okay, give me a minute. By the way, didn't you guys call the police last night?"

"Yes, but this area is covered by the state patrol, and they were all at the county fair. Anyway, after we saw the stolen motorhome leave in a big hurry, we decided to go find you. What we found was Eva."

I paused with the phone in my hand. "You found Eva?"

"Yeah," she said glumly. "That's when Rudy called David. *He* got a response. A squad car arrived within a few minutes. You know they shot her."

"We heard the shot," I said with a shake of my head.

"Okay, just give me a minute."

I left the table and walked back to the bedroom and dialed David's cell phone. When he heard my voice, he said, "Julia! Thank God you're okay."

"I'm fine. Well, not perfectly fine. I think I cracked a rib. Never mind about that. Listen, I don't have time to tell you the whole story, but we saved Amy Owens."

"Rudy said she thought you had. She didn't know where you were, though. Is Amy with you?"

"Yes."

"Her parents will be thrilled."

"That's what I wanted to talk to you about."

I explained my idea and why I thought it would help the situation.

There was a brief pause before he said, "I get it. Good thinking, Julia. I need to let her parents know, though. We can't keep something like that a secret from them. We can keep it out of the media, though. When do you think you'll be done with the Gateway police?"

My heart missed a beat. I took a deep breath. "We haven't talked to them. We're on our way to Wisconsin. We have to deliver the motorhome to the Aberdeens, and then…"

"Wait. What?" he erupted. "Julia, this was a kidnapping!"

"Believe me, I know, David. I almost got killed saving her." He was quiet on the other end of the line. I took another deep breath and lowered my voice. "We discussed taking Amy to a hospital, but she freaked out. We never would have gotten her there. She doesn't want to be alone with all those strangers. We put her dirty clothes into a plastic bag though, and Blair is taking pictures of her arms where they shot her up with drugs. But we are not turning her over to the police right now at her own insistence."

"Okay," he said in a resigned voice. "I don't like it, but I'll call the Chicago PD and let them know what's going on. They're going to want to interview her, though. I'll see if I can get her parents there, too. I'll call you after I talk to them."

"Okay. We'll meet you in Chicago tomorrow. And David...I...I..."

"I know," he said in a lowered voice. "Love you, too."

My eyes burned as I hung up. He'd said again what I couldn't bring myself to say. I would have to rectify that.

I returned to the table. Blair had finished with Amy.

"What did he say?" Blair asked.

"He's on board with the idea and will meet us in Chicago tomorrow."

"So let's have it," Doe said. "How did you two rescue her?"

We sat down and related how we had tricked Eva and freed Amy. We spoke loud enough that Rudy could hear us from the driver's seat.

"You rock!" Rudy called out from the driver's seat.

"But why are you so scratched up?" Doe asked.

So then we had to explain how we had escaped into the forest, tumbled down the hill and fled up the stream bed.

"Boy, I only remember bits and pieces of that," Amy said.

She had come out of the shower with wet hair, looking decidedly better. She wore Blair's jeans folded up at the bottom and a crystal blue t-shirt.

"You look beautiful," I said.

She smiled shyly. "The pants are too long, but they'll do." She put the shampoo and soap on the counter and came to sit at the table. "Now I know why I have big bruises on my legs, though."

"That's how I injured my ribs," I said, gesturing toward my midriff.

"How did we get in the barn?" she asked.

I continued the story. When I described Elizabeth's and my mother's intervention, Amy almost choked.

"Seriously?" Her pretty brown eyes were opened wide. "Ghosts?"

"Yes, but you may not want to tell anyone else about that. We all accept the paranormal in my life. Others may not. It's up to you."

She smiled, exposing a slight overbite. "I'm good with that. It will be our little secret. But, dang, I wished I'd seen that."

The bottle of shampoo flew off the kitchen counter and landed on the floor. Amy spun around in surprise. When the bottle began to spin in a circle, her mouth hung open in shock.

"Amy, meet Chloe," I said.

Her eyes were the size of computer discs. I got up and put the shampoo into the sink. I turned to Amy. "By the way, the police are going to let your parents know you're okay and then you can call your mom. We're keeping it all on the down-low, though."

"Is that a mystery term?" Blair said with a smirk.

Amy laughed. "Okay. I'm in."

My phone rang. I pulled it off the charger and opened it. It was David.

"You're good to go. Amy can call her mother. I've also spoken to the Chicago Police. They want us to meet at the downtown precinct. They'll need to know what you know if they're going to have any chance of protecting Senator Owens. He's already been warned not to attend the dinner tomorrow night, but apparently he's ignoring the warning."

"Okay, what time do you get in?"

"I get in around noon local time. I'm going to join the Chicago PD and the FBI for a walk-through of the conference facility. We'll all meet back at the precinct at two o'clock."

"Okay, we'll meet you there."

"Julia," he began, "I know you have to go to Wisconsin, but be careful. This was too close."

"Hold on."

I got up and took the phone into the bedroom. "We'll be careful," I said. "And I promise I'll call you if we see them again. I didn't mean to snap before."

"No worries," he said.

"But I do worry," I said. "I know I push things too far for you. I don't know how you put up with me."

"Julia, you…"

"No," I said. "This time, I have to say it. You mean more to me than you can ever know, David. And I can hardly wait to see you so I can tell you how I feel in person. I'll talk to you tomorrow."

I hung up before the conversation disintegrated into a sentimental mess. I had to keep focused.

When I returned to the main cabin, I said to Amy, "Your parents have been notified, so you can give them a call. I still need to charge my phone, but you can use Doe's."

Doe handed Amy her phone.

"Thanks." She got up and went back into the bedroom and closed the door.

"Julia, why don't you get a shower now?" Doe said. "Then we can tape your ribs."

I glanced over at Blair, eyebrows raised. "Okay with you?"

"Absolutely. I've already washed out the cut on my arm. I can grab a shower at the Aberdeens'."

I've never taken a shower that felt better. As the water washed away the dirt and grime, my spirits soared. *We'd saved a young girl's life.* I got a little teary-eyed myself at the thought and was happy I had the shower water to wash away any tell-tale sign of my emotions.

I emerged in clean khaki pants and a yellow blouse. Amy had returned to the kitchen table, so Doe joined me in the bedroom to tape my ribs with an ACE bandage. When we both came back out, Rudy was already leaving the interstate.

"We'll be at the Aberdeens' in about forty-five minutes," she said from the front seat.

"How are we going to explain the damage?" I asked her.

I saw her clamp her jaw shut and press her lips into a straight line. "Just tell the truth," she finally replied. "What else can we do?"

÷

It was almost noon by the time we pulled up the hill to the gray split-level house in an upper-middle class neighborhood just outside of Madison. Rudy had called Nathan Aberdeen earlier to let him know what time to expect us. She hadn't told him anything else, however, so there was a level of anxiety in the motorhome that would rival the first trip home with a new boyfriend. We had discussed stopping to get the motorhome cleaned, but decided it wouldn't make much difference. There would be no sugar-coating how much damage we'd done to his prized possession. And I had no illusions it would go over well.

Rudy pulled to the curb, angling the wheels so the Hulk wouldn't roll backwards down the steep hill, although at this point, a little more damage wouldn't have mattered.

Aria parked behind us.

As Rudy killed the engine, the front door to the house flew open and Nathan and his wife stepped outside and came down the steps.

I watched from inside the motorhome as their expressions changed from open and welcoming to confusion and then slowly to abject horror. Their footsteps slowed, and then they came to a complete stop. Their mouths actually hung open.

Rudy was the first to disembark. The rest of us followed, including Amy. We all gathered at the end of the walkway, with Goldie and Aria bringing up the rear.

By the time we were all assembled, it seemed that Nathan had regained the use of his vocal chords and blurted out, "Oh, my God, wha…what happened?" His eyes were fixated on the roof. His jaw opened and closed a couple of times without sound.

Rudy stepped forward. "Let me explain, Nathan."

"You destroyed it," he said moving right past her.

His long legs faltered as he took each step. He looked like he was part of the walking dead. I imagined he felt that way, too.

"No…well, yes, we did kind of destroy it," Rudy said, turning to follow him. "But there's a very good reason. I'm sure once I explain, you'll…"

"I trusted you," he said, still staring at the motorhome.

Rudy turned to me and nodded at Amy. I took the girl's elbow and moved her into Nathan's range of vision. "Nathan, this is Amy Dunphy. She's Senator Jim Owens' daughter," I said quietly, trying to get him to look at her.

It was Mary Aberdeen who responded. "The young girl who was abducted?"

"Yes," I said. "We saved her from the people who were going to kill her."

I stopped talking at that point. I figured there would be time later for a detailed account. Right now, they just needed to know the basics. In other words, their motorhome had died in service to keeping a young girl alive.

"We're so sorry, Mary," Rudy said, turning to Nathan's wife. "We really didn't have a choice, though."

It seemed Nathan Aberdeen hadn't heard a word we'd said. He stumbled the rest of the way down the walkway and up the steps into the motorhome.

"Mary, we'll get it repaired. I promise," Rudy said. "But we didn't have a choice," she repeated. "They were going to kill her."

Mary Aberdeen's green eyes had locked on Amy. She reached out a hand and drew the girl in. "Are you okay, sweetheart?"

Amy's face and arms were still marred by scratches and bruises, topped off by the deep circles under her eyes.

"I'm okay now," she said quietly. "What these ladies said is true, though. I owe them my life."

Mary threw her arm around Amy's shoulders, but it was a plaintive whimper from inside the motorhome that caught our attention. A moment later, Nathan appeared at the doorway to the motorhome and stumbled back down the steps. I think he was about to cry.

"It looks like a war was waged in there," he said. "The carpet, the countertops, the upholstery, the, the…"

"Oh, for heaven's sake, Nathan, give it a rest," Mary snapped at him. "This girl has been through hell, and her life is more important than your stupid motorhome. I'm taking her inside. You can stay out here and cry like a baby if you want to." She turned to us. "Our daughter is at camp, so between beds, sofas, and a roll-away cot, I think we'll have enough room for everyone. What time do you have to leave tomorrow?"

"We have to be in Chicago by two to meet with the police," Rudy said. "The people who took Amy are still after her father, and he's making a speech tomorrow night."

Mary nodded and then said, "Okay. It's about a two and half hour drive, so let's get everyone cleaned up. We're barbequing chicken later for dinner, and I have a blueberry crisp for dessert. How does that sound, Amy?" she asked, tightening her arm around the girl's shoulders.

Amy gave her a brief smile. "Good. Thank you."

"Okay, let's get you all inside." She stopped and turned to me with alarm. "They're not still chasing you, are they?"

"No. They disappeared last night and don't even know we have Amy."

She released a cleansing breath. "Okay. Good. Have you had lunch?"

The group followed her up the walkway towards the house when a protracted metallic groan stopped us. We all turned just in time to see the air conditioner slide off the roof with a 'fingers on a blackboard' screech. It crashed to the pavement in front of Aria's camper.

Everyone stared at it for a brief moment and then turned without comment and followed Mary into the house, leaving Nathan outside to give the air conditioner its last rites.

CHAPTER TWENTY-TWO

It felt good to be stationary, if only for the night. While several of the girls used the afternoon to take showers, I threw some laundry into the washer and then planted myself in a recliner to take a well-deserved nap with the Aberdeen's cat, Cooper, curled in my lap.

By late afternoon, I had repacked my suitcase with clean clothes and refreshed my spirits. Mary was in the kitchen preparing dinner, so Rudy and I joined her. We helped cut up lettuce and vegetables for a salad, while we related the story about how we rescued Amy.

"How did you have the guts to follow those people?" Mary asked, putting chicken breasts on a plate. She shook her head. "I would have been scared to death. And frankly, Nathan would never have gone for it. Once we're on the road with a destination in mind, there are no side trips. He's like a man on a mission."

"I suppose you're talking about me."

Nathan walked in from the deck with the fire starter in his hand.

"Julia and Rudy were just telling me their story. They went through some pretty incredible stuff."

"I don't doubt it," he said cynically. His eyes shifted to the window over the sink to stare at the Hulk parked at the curb. "So what are you going to do now? That young girl needs to get home to her parents."

"They're meeting us in Chicago," Rudy told him. "The killers don't know whether Amy is dead or alive. We hope to use that to keep them off their game."

He turned to her. "What do you mean y*ou're* going to do that? I would think the police would take over."

I was beginning to dislike Nathan Aberdeen. Of course, he had a good point; normally the police *would* take over. I didn't let the fact he was right assuage the irritation I felt every time he opened his mouth, however.

"We're the only ones who know what these guys look like," I replied, throwing some croutons on the salad. "We can help the police identify them."

"Someone could recognize Amy, though," Mary said.

I hadn't thought of that and glanced at Rudy, who gave me a shrug.

"I guess we'll have to figure out a disguise."

Mary wiped her hands on a dish towel and headed for the door. "I'll be right back."

A moment later she returned with two wigs in her hand: a short black one, and a long blond one.

"Janey has three or four of these. She likes to change up her looks when she goes to parties. Do you think one of these would help?"

I reached for the short black wig. "Yes. They've already used a blond wig on her, so I'll see if she'll wear this one. Thanks."

Nathan had opened a cupboard to pull out a new jar of barbeque sauce and turned to his wife with a hard stare. "Haven't we done enough?"

The tension in the room rose quickly. Mary put one hand on her hip and lowered her chin to stare at her husband.

"We owe it to that girl to do everything we can to help," Mary said with a steely edge to her voice. "What if it had been Janey who had been abducted? Now, are you just going to complain, or do you have something positive to offer?"

His eyebrows shot up. "Are you kidding? I've already sacrificed my…"

"Not one more word about that motorhome," Mary snapped, pointing a finger at him. "These women need our help."

While I didn't think much of Nathan Aberdeen, I was sad Mary Aberdeen now lived a thousand miles away.

When Nathan didn't respond, she said, "What about Omar?"

"What about Omar?" he countered, clearly flummoxed.

She turned to me. "Omar is Nathan's new best friend. He lives next door. He's a retired Navy Seal and teaches self-defense at the community center. Sounds to me like you ladies could use some counter-moves. Judging from some of your adventures on Mercer Island, I presume you have no intention of just backing out of this."

Boy, did she have me pegged.

"We don't have a game plan, yet," I said.

"It sounds to me like you need to attend that fancy dinner," she said with a short nod. "And if you do, you'll be putting yourselves back in danger. Omar might be able to help."

God, I liked this woman.

Mary turned to her husband with an expression he interpreted immediately.

"I'll go see if he's home."

He stomped out of the kitchen. A moment later we heard the front door close.

"Jeez, you should teach kindergarten," I said with appreciation.

She gave me a full-throated laugh. "Seventeen years. Second grade."

÷

By dinner time, we shared drinks on the back deck, while Nathan barbequed and Amy played in the yard with Tinker Bell and Boomer, their Golden Retriever. Cooper had found a home in my lap.

"How are you going to get into the dinner?" Mary asked, sipping her wine. "Don't you need to be part of the Republican elite?"

There was a pause, as Doe, Rudy, and Blair turned to me.

"What?"

"You can call Graham," Rudy said. "If anyone can get us into that dinner, he can."

"Of course," Mary said, as if just remembering I had once been married to the Republican governor of Washington State.

"Tell him Rudy is writing an article for the Huffington Post about our trip across country and thought attending the dinner would make a great focal point," Doe suggested.

"Why can't you say I'm writing it?" Blair asked in a huff. "At least I'm a registered Republican."

Everyone turned to stare in unison at Blair.

"What?" she said in her defense. "I could write an article like that."

"Of course you could," Doe agreed. "But why would you?"

Blair thought a moment, shrugged her pretty shoulders and then said, "Good point."

"I'll call Graham," I said. "I need to tell him the truth, though."

"Okay, say Graham gets us all get into the dinner," Aria spoke up. "Then, what?"

"We keep an eye out for Monty and Roy," Rudy said. "We don't know who Yoda is."

"We'll need to spread out," Doe countered. "How do we talk to each other?"

"Too bad you don't have some of those intercom things I always see on the police shows," Mary said, nibbling on a carrot stick.

I noticed a quick, knowing glance between Aria and Goldie.

"What is it?" I challenged them.

"I might be able to help," Aria said.

All heads turned to stare at Aria.

"How?" Blair asked.

"Come with me," she said.

We left our drinks on the table and followed Aria out to the camper. She unlocked the back door.

"Wait here," she said.

Aria climbed in and left the door open. She turned to face us, got on her knees and pulled back the carpet on the floor in between the sink and the breakfast nook. She slipped her index finger into a notch in the floor and pulled up a piece of flooring.

The rest of us leaned in to look and then gasped.

There was a compartment under the floor filled with a bunch of strange devices.

"You don't have any weapons in there, do you?" Doe asked with alarm.

"No, of course not," Aria replied.

"What is all that stuff?" I asked.

Aria looked at me with a satisfied grin. "Spy gear."

There was a long, silent pause.

"Why in the world do you have spy gear?" Blair asked.

"Tell 'em, Aria," Goldie said, egging her on.

Aria sat back on her heels. "I used to work for the ATF."

I don't know what I thought Aria was going to say, but working for the ATF wasn't it. I looked at her with new found respect–or horror–I wasn't sure which.

"That was a number of years ago," she said. "It was back when I lived in California. I was right out of college and just worked there for a few years. But I became kind of fascinated with it all."

"Okay, but why do you own this stuff now?" Rudy asked pointedly.

Aria hesitated and then said, "I belong to a group. It's called Spy Academy. We practice covert operations on the weekends."

A slight breeze tickled my ear. Music floated from an open window up the street. I also thought I heard the ticking inside Rudy's head, which meant it was about to explode.

"I'm going back inside," she said, shooting Aria a poisonous glare. She turned on her heel and left the group.

"Ignore her," I said to Aria. "Do you have anything in there we could use to communicate with each other at the dinner?"

"Yes." She leaned down and reached into the compartment, bringing up a box. "These are individual intercoms, just like Mary said. I have four of them, so we'll have to share. With these, we can be anywhere in the building and still speak to each other."

I turned to Mary with a smile. "Ask and 'ye shall receive.'"

"I had no idea," she said.

"I also have some infrared gear, but that won't help since we'll be inside a lit room."

"Have any Tasers?" Blair asked, leaning a shoulder into the doorway.

I turned to her in shock. "You want to use a stun gun on someone?"

"I wouldn't have any problem zapping one of those guys. And neither would you."

"I don't have any Tasers," Aria said. "Sorry."

"I think that's a good thing," Doe said. "I'm not sure I want to be anywhere near Blair if she's carrying a charged Taser."

"Humpf," Blair snorted.

"That's okay," Mary interjected. "Nathan said Omar will come over after dinner to help you practice some defensive moves. Hopefully, that will be enough."

"Defensive moves will be good," I said, turning to go back inside. "Because with Blair along, I think we have the *off*ensive moves covered."

We returned to the backyard and enjoyed barbequed chicken, rice and salad. Omar showed up around seven o'clock.

He was in his early forties and of Middle Eastern descent. He was maybe 5' 11", with rippling muscles underneath a tight t-shirt and loose sweat pants. I thought that, like Blair, he bought shirts a size too small in order to emphasize his physical attributes.

Blair noticed it, too.

She was sitting at the patio table staring blankly at Amy and the dogs as they chased each other around the yard, when Omar arrived. She turned a lazy expression in his direction. Once her eyes swept across his muscle-packed body and dark, handsome features, she came instantly alert. In one fluid movement, she was out of her chair and heading his way.

I chuckled to myself. He had no idea what he was in for.

"Everyone," Mary began, "this is Omar Khouri."

He nodded to us each in turn as we introduced ourselves. Blair leaned in to grasp his outstretched hand and placed her other hand on his muscular shoulder.

"It's so good to have you here, Mr. Khouri. We have soooo much to learn."

She batted her eyes and pressed her fingers into his shoulder muscles. He glanced at her cleavage, looked up and smiled at her briefly, and then stepped back.

Uh-oh. What did that mean? I'd calculated that there were only about ten percent of men unaffected by Blair's feminine wiles. Was he part of the ten percent? I glanced at Blair and noticed the flirty smile quickly disappear.

"I hear you need some instruction in case you get into an altercation," he said to the group.

"It would be more accurate to say *when* we get into an altercation. At least when you're speaking of these two," Rudy said, pointing a finger at me and Blair. "Despite their age."

Mary chuckled in the background.

Omar shrugged. "Age has nothing to do with it. Rapists and thieves are looking for a weak target."

"I'm never a weak target," Blair said, crossing her arms over her ample chest.

He smiled at here again.

"It's still good to be prepared," he said, allowing his eyes to linger a moment on her accentuated cleavage. "Why don't we get started?"

We followed Omar to the lawn and he arranged us in a half circle in front of him. Nathan and Mary remained on the deck with Amy, Boomer and Tinker Bell.

"Remember that first and foremost you want to keep someone away from you," Omar began. "Be alert at all times. It's called intuitional awareness. In other words, be aware of your surroundings. And don't be afraid to stop, turn, and confront someone you think is following you."

"Frankly, the situations we've found ourselves in haven't given us a chance to stop someone," Doe said.

He nodded, as if he understood. I suspected Nathan had filled him in on our most recent adventure.

"Okay." He gestured for Blair to step forward. "As someone comes at you, move in and go for their throat, because that's how they breathe. Bend your arm and bring your hand in for a swivel strike." He showed how Blair could slam him right in the throat with the inside of her hand. "Be sure to follow through with your entire body and put your weight behind it." He pulled Blair forward as if she had moved against him. Her breast slammed against his chest, and once again, he just smiled.

I adjusted my opinion–he wasn't one of the ten percent. He was one of the ninety-percent.

"What if they get hold of us?" Rudy asked.

"Okay, let's practice how to get out of a choke hold," he said.

He asked Nathan to come down to help with the demonstration. When Nathan was in place, Omar had Nathan loop his right arm around his neck, locking it place with his left hand.

"Okay, it looks like I'm stuck. But watch. I turn my head towards my attacker, which helps to open up my airway, and tuck my chin down. Then, I'm going to use leverage and grab his elbow like this."

Omar grabbed Nathan's elbow, and then using his left hand, he grabbed Nathan's wrist.

"Then, step to the side with your right leg and back with your left." He took a quick step to his right, ducked down and stepped back, wrapping his left leg around Nathan's right leg. "Twist you head inward, like this." He turned his head until it popped out of the choke hold.

"Wow," Blair murmured. "I like that."

"I'm not done," he said. "I kept hold of his wrist. You want to seize and control. Now, I pull it up like this." He pulled Nathan's arm up behind his back at an awkward angle, making Nathan wince. "And, then, I come in for the kill." With a quick jab of his knee into the back of Nathan's right leg, he brought Nathan to the ground.

"Then we finish him off." Omar used a closed fist to fake a sharp jab right into Nathan's temple. "Okay, let's practice it."

We spent thirty minutes breaking the moves down one by one and practicing them until we had them down pat. By the end of the hour, Omar had us change partners.

"Most likely, your attacker will be bigger than you," he said. "You can't be intimidated by gender or size."

So we each had to work with him or Nathan. Goldie worked with Omar and had a bit of a mishap. She popped out of the head hold, lost her balance and flew into the middle of a hydrangea bush.

I got Nathan, who grabbed me a little too roughly. I responded in kind. I grabbed his elbow, ducked down, stepped back and twisted my head out of his hold. Then I jacked my leg up and kneed him in the...well, I missed the back of his leg and hit something far more vulnerable. The kick forced him to the ground, groaning, with his hands holding his privates.

Other than that, I felt pretty good about my practice.

CHAPTER TWENTY-THREE

Nathan disappeared into the house, I assumed to get some ice. We thanked Omar, and Mary served dessert. Afterwards, she said goodnight and went to check on her husband. I caught Amy yawning in front of the T.V. with Boomer on the couch next to her.

"Why don't you go to bed?" I said. "Tomorrow will be another big day. You'll get to see your parents."

I sat down at the end of the sofa. Boomer lifted his head, looked at me, and dropped it back into Amy's lap.

Amy gave me a wan smile as she dug her fingers into the fur on Boomer's back. "I'm excited about seeing my mom, but my stepdad is pretty distant. He's just waiting for me to go off to college so he can have my mom all to himself."

"You and your mom are close?"

She smiled. "Yeah. It's always been me and her. My dad was never around. He was always either working or running for office. That's why I felt so bad when she and I argued the other night."

"Tell me about your dad. What's he like?"

She paused a moment. "He's driven, I suppose you could say. I don't remember him coming to any of my school events when I was little. That was my mom's job. But I would sure hear from him if I came home with a grade he didn't like." She turned sad eyes to me. "And, yet, I love him. I don't want him hurt."

"Of course you don't. He's your dad."

"Yes. And one day, I hope to make him proud."

"Oh, Amy, I know he's proud of you. You're a beautiful, smart girl. I'm sure he's been torn up about your abduction."

She laughed through her tears. "You don't lie very well, but thanks." She sat up, displacing Boomer's head. "I think I'll go to bed. Thanks, again, Mrs. Applegate."

"Please, call me Julia."

"Julia," she said. "I'll see you in the morning."

Boomer followed her up to bed.

The rest of us spent the remainder of the evening around the kitchen table discussing the upcoming dinner.

"Hey, I don't want Amy to hear me, but look at this." I pulled up her stepfather's construction company website on my iPad. "This is Amy's stepdad. Look like anyone?"

"Yes," Doe said, her eyebrows clenched. "Monty."

"That's what Blair and I thought."

"Boy, shave off some of his hair and they look enough alike to be brothers," Rudy said. "You don't think he's involved, do you?"

I showed the picture to Aria and Goldie. "I have no idea. I've already told David so he can check him out. Maybe it's a coincidence. She told me earlier he was probably happy she was gone so that he could have her mother all to himself."

"I wonder if they've arrested Amy's boyfriend," Rudy said.

"I have a hard time thinking an eighteen-year-old is Yoda," I said. "Whoever Yoda is, he has to be someone with the authority to tell Monty and Roy what to do *and* the money to pay them." I glanced at my watch. "I think I'll call Graham. It's eight o'clock at home."

I left them and went to the kitchen to make the call. As always, Kitty, his thirty-something wife, answered the phone, making my teeth grind.

"Hey, Julia," she said in her lazy drawl. "I heard you're on a trip." She chuckled as if she'd made a joke. "Get it? On a trip? Washington is a pot state now." She laughed hard enough to probably send snot out her nose.

I couldn't stand it.

"Actually, Kitty, the phrase to be *on a trip* had to do with taking LSD, not smoking pot."

"Yeah, I know. I don't take drugs…except the stuff my doctor gives me."

"What does your doctor give you?"

I knew I would regret the question the moment I asked it, and I pictured her staring at her fingernails as she talked to me.

"Oh, you know. Stuff to help me sleep. And I take that Garcinia Cambodia stuff to help me lose weight."

I did a face plant with my hand.

"It's not Cambodia," I said. "Oh never mind."

"I also do that cleanse thing. And I take these pills to strengthen my hair. You should try that stuff, Julia. It really works. My doctor also wants me to take iron, so I do that. And, of course, once a month, I take Doan's pills because I get a back ache."

I clenched my jaw muscles so tight, they were burning.

"But you should see all the stuff Graham takes," she said. "He takes a handful of vitamins every day. Sheesh. He's almost a pill-popper."

I stopped grinding my teeth. "Speaking of Graham…any chance he's there?"

"Yes, but he has a terrible cold. In fact, now he's taking pills for that!"

"Maybe I could talk to him. It won't take long."

"Oh, okay. Just a sec."

I drummed my fingers on the kitchen table as I waited. A moment later, the voice that had started my engine each day for over twenty years came on the line.

"Hey, Julia. What's up? I thought you were on a road trip."

"I am, but we have a situation."

There was an audible sigh and then a sniffle.

"What is it this time?"

I explained about Amy's abduction and subsequent rescue, minus things like breaking and entering the motorhome, knocking out Eva, or the intervention by the ghosts.

"Wow, good for you, Julia. Why haven't I heard anything about it on the news?"

"Because we're keeping it quiet. The two men who abducted Amy think she escaped on her own and may be either dead or lost out in the woods. If she doesn't surface, it could give us an edge."

There was a moment of silence.

"Was that Detective Franks' idea?"

And there it was–a swift shot at David. Graham had done it a few times before, despite the fact he had been dating Kitty during the last few months before our split and married her almost immediately after our divorce.

"No, it was my idea, but David agrees, so please don't say anything to anyone. We're meeting with the Chicago police tomorrow afternoon to decide how to proceed. These men are still after Senator Owens."

"He's the keynote speaker tomorrow night."

"That's why I'm calling. I'm hoping you can get us into the dinner."

"You want tickets for all four of you?"

"Six of us. Goldie and Aria are with us."

I heard him blow out a sigh. "That's a tall order. From what I understand, the dinner is pretty much sold out."

"Can you try? This is important, Graham."

"I'm surprised this new boyfriend of yours would put you in such a dangerous situation."

A flutter in my chest made me pause, since David didn't even know I was planning on attending the dinner.

"Uh…we're the only ones who can ID these guys."

"Okay, let me see what I can do. I doubt I can get you all at the same table, though."

"That's okay."

"Tickets are $500 each. Are you prepared to pay that at the door?"

"Yes."

"Okay, I'll get back to you, probably tomorrow afternoon. I'm flying out first thing in the morning."

"Okay. Thanks, Graham. You sound like you have a cold?"

"Yeah. I'm almost over it, though."

"Well, be sure to tell Kitty you need some drugs for your *trip*."

"What? Why?"

I smiled. "Oh, just for the fun of it."

CHAPTER TWENTY-FOUR

The next morning, the smell of coffee and bacon greeted me as I sat up and stretched. Rudy and I had slept on a pull-out sofa bed in the downstairs den. After we got dressed, we joined Nathan and Mary for breakfast. Everyone else had finished and gone out to the motorhome to remove the camping gear and box it up. Mary had offered to mail everything home.

"How did you sleep?" Mary asked as she set a plate of hot waffles on the table.

"Really well," I replied, glancing at Nathan.

I wondered how he had slept after my errant kick to the family jewels. He kept his head down, choosing to concentrate on his breakfast rather than engage with me.

"Have you rented a car?" Mary asked.

Rudy speared a waffle with her fork. "Enterprise is going to drop off a big SUV in an hour." She glanced over at Nathan, who hadn't even acknowledged us. "Nathan, if you'll get a repair estimate, we'll pay directly so your premiums aren't affected."

He didn't respond right away, instead shifting his eyes to his wife, who remained silent.

"Actually, I talked with them this morning," he said. "I explained the situation. I'm not sure they believed me, but they said if we get an official statement from the police verifying your story, it won't affect my premiums." He put his fork down and sat back. "Of course, they agreed only after I threatened to go to the media." A small smile played across his lips. "But don't worry. I swore them to secrecy until all of this becomes public."

A feeling of relief rolled over me. Perhaps the Aberdeens' memory of our visit would be relegated to the stuff of legend and not painful images like the motorhome and my unfortunate mistake during our defense training.

÷

Enterprise arrived at 8:30. Rudy returned to the rental agency to fill out the paperwork. She was back a half hour later. By then, the rest of us were ready to go.

Since the Aberdeens' daughter was about the same age and size as Amy, Mary had given Amy some clean clothes to wear. By 9:00, we were hefting suitcases and bags down the walkway and into the big Suburban. Aria and Goldie would follow us to Chicago in their own camper truck. Once there, we would hand off Amy to her mom at the downtown police station, where we would also meet up with David.

Doe hugged Tinker Bell and then handed her off to Mary, who had offered to keep her until Doe could drive back on Sunday.

"Please take care," Mary said to all of us. "And thank you for what you did for Amy."

Amy suddenly ran up to her and threw her arms around her neck. "Thank you so much, Mrs. Aberdeen."

Mary gave her a good hug. "We were happy to help. Stay safe, now."

Nathan stepped forward and handed Rudy a slip of paper. "You mentioned you were only able to get rooms on the outskirts of town. I know a guy. I rented three rooms for the six of you at the downtown Hilton for two nights. I hope that helps." He paused and then finished with, "Just get these guys."

Rudy smiled and nodded. "Thanks, Nathan. We'll be in touch."

We pulled away from the curb, waving our goodbyes and hit the road for the last portion of our journey.

As planned, we made a quick side trip to Waukegan to drop off my mother's ashes at the Chase Funeral Home. Blair accompanied me to the office, where we were met by a tall, slender woman with eyes the color of violets. She took us outside to the columbarium—a long, curved wall in the middle of the rose garden with individual niches that held cremation urns. My mother had long ago paid for one next to my father. I had ordered an inscription for the face plate with my mother's name, inclusive dates and her favorite quote, *"When life gives you lemons, squeeze them in people's eyes."*

We found my mother's niche on the far side of the wall. My throat swelled as the woman removed the granite faceplate, revealing an empty stainless steel box, which would be my mother's final resting place.

"I'll leave you alone a moment," she said, stepping away.

I nodded, realizing suddenly I was unable to speak.

"Me, too," Blair said, placing a hand on my shoulder. "I'll meet you inside."

Once I was alone, I could smell the rich aroma of the roses closest to me. I glanced at the serene surroundings, thinking, "*This will be a nice place for my mom.*"

I stepped forward and placed the blue porcelain urn into the small metal enclosure and stood back, thinking of my mother. If she had been there in person, she would have made some snide comment about me imprisoning her. And, then, she would have cackled, taken a long draw on her cigarette and coughed.

The memory made me smile.

This is what my mother had wanted. Twice, when she'd called me on my cell phone after her death, she had asked me to take her home. She wanted to be next to my father–the only man she'd ever loved. I hoped that bringing them together this way didn't mean I would never hear from her again.

As if on cue, my phone pinged to alert me to an incoming text. I pulled it out and thumbed the message open. A chill fluttered across my skin as I read it.

"*Thanks, Button. Stay safe. And BTW, the man you're looking for is closer than you think.*"

The light went out on my phone, and she was gone.

I felt the blood drain from my face. *Damn, my mother had learned how to text from the great beyond!* And, then, a second chill rippled down my back. *Wait a minute! Did she mean David was closer than I thought? Or had she just warned me about Yoda?*

I put my phone away and closed my mother up in the niche. I stared for a moment at the small plaque with the cynical quote and then smiled. It was so like my mother.

I pressed my hand on the cold metal for a moment, silently saying my goodbyes.

With a solemn breath, I removed my hand and watched my handprint fade away. I returned to the office, and we were on the road again a few minutes later.

÷

We arrived at the Hilton just after noon.

Rudy and Doe bunked together, while Blair and I took the room next door. Goldie and Aria took the third room down the hall. We quickly unpacked. Amy donned the black wig, and then we met downstairs at the café for a quick lunch.

"You know, even if Graham gets us into the dinner, we don't have anything to wear," Doe said as she toyed with her salad.

"I assume we don't want David to know we're even going," Rudy said.

"He'll have to know," I said.

My phone pinged, interrupting us. When I answered, it was Graham.

"I could get four tickets to the dinner."

"Okay, thanks. We'll try to make that work. Do we just give our names at the door?"

"Yes, and do me a favor. Pretend you actually *are* Republicans. These are my colleagues, Julia. So, don't start any arguments with anyone."

"Graham! I think you know me better than that. I would never embarrass you."

"Right. Like the time you told my lieutenant governor that redistricting was a conservative plot to turn the country red."

"Well, it is."

"Maybe. But not something you say at a black tie Republican fundraiser in front of the RNC state chair. It tends to ruffle feathers. So be on your best behavior. You're going to be in red state territory."

"Got it. I'll see you tonight." I hung up and glanced around the table. "We're in."

÷

With two big conferences in town, we figured it would be difficult to get cabs for seven of us. The Public Safety Headquarters, which housed both the Chicago police and fire departments, was only a few blocks from our hotel, so we decided to walk.

David had landed and would meet us there. We were to ask for Detective Mankiewicz when we arrived.

It was a few minutes before the appointed hour when we approached the huge, box-like structure with its brick trim. With hundreds of glass windows glaring down on us, it was easy to be intimidated by this building, especially when you considered that Chicago has one of the highest murder rates in the country. This had to be a very busy place.

I stopped everyone on the sidewalk for a moment before going in.

"What's wrong? Do we need to get our story straight?" Doe asked me.

"No. Well, maybe. I just don't want to mention how Elizabeth and my mother helped us. If there's any mention of ghosts, the police won't take us seriously."

"You're right," Rudy said. "But what are you going to say about how you avoided getting killed out there in the wilderness?"

I looked over at Blair for help. She perked up. "We'll just say we used my tank top to stop the bleeding on my arm and then left it behind when we hid out back. Because Julia cried out when they began shooting, they probably found the tank top and thought *Amy* had been shot. Then, they left the barn looking for her, leaving us behind. Nothing else about the story has to change."

I glanced at Amy. She shrugged. "I'm good with that. After all, I only know what you told me, anyway."

"Okay, works for me." I took a deep breath. "Let's go."

"Dylan!" Amy shouted, spinning away from us.

She sprinted towards the end of the building, following the fleeing figure of a tall, slender man wearing a hoodie.

"Amy!" Rudy yelled, taking off after her.

Amy disappeared around the corner, with Rudy hot on her heels. A moment later, Amy reappeared, almost bumping into Rudy.

"Amy, who was that?" I asked, coming up to her out-of-breath. "Who were you chasing?"

Her pretty face was screwed up in disappointment. "That was Dylan. Why would he run from me?" She seemed on the verge of tears again.

Rudy and I shared a concerned look.

"What do you mean that was Dylan? Wouldn't he be at home?" I asked.

She shrugged. "I don't know, but I'm sure that was him." She stomped a foot and a tear threatened at the corner of her eye.

I put a hand on her shoulder. "Listen, right now we need to get you inside before anyone recognizes you."

We led her to the entrance and pushed through the big front door into an enormous marble-floored lobby. We approached a large reception desk, where multiple receptionists stared at computer screens.

"We're here to see Detective Mankiewicz," I said to a middle-aged woman with her hair pulled into a tight bun.

"Name?" she asked, her eyes never leaving the computer.

"Julia Applegate."

"Just a moment."

She picked up the phone and spoke to someone. When she hung up, she had us sign in and fill out name tags before telling us to take the elevator to the second floor.

When the elevator dinged and the door opened, David and José were waiting for us.

Um, what?

"Julia!" David said. He took a step forward as if to embrace me, and then stopped when my six companions flowed out behind me.

But I wasn't looking at him.

"José, what are you doing here?"

My handsome maintenance man stuck his hands into the pockets of his Chinos and shrugged. "Detective Franks called me and said he needed me to come along."

David turned to me. "I brought him for back-up. He *is* a black belt in some martial art, isn't he?

"Yes. But…"

"So…he's assigned to you until we catch these guys." He cut me off as I started to object. "I know you, Julia. You're going to go to that dinner whether I want you to or not. Am I right?"

I blew out a sigh. "Yes."

"Then, José will be your shadow. The police and FBI don't have any extra personnel."

"Fine." I reached behind me and drew Amy forward. "David, this is Amy Dunphy."

Amy turned in his direction, her pretty eyes downcast.

David reached out and took her hand. "Sorry, Amy. It's good to meet you." He was studying the cuts and bruises on her face. "We should have you checked out by a doctor."

"No. I'm okay. Thanks to Julia and the others."

David put his hand on her shoulder. "Okay. You're a very lucky girl. Would you like to see your mother? She's waiting."

Her eyes opened with anticipation. "Yes."

A warm smile eased across his face. "Then, let's go."

"What about my father? Senator Owens?"

David shifted his weight and looked momentarily uncomfortable. "We haven't told your father you've been rescued. We didn't think we could keep it under wraps if we did. He has too many people around him, but he'll be told the minute it's safe to do so."

"But, I..." she started.

"Look," David interrupted her. "We don't want these guys to change their plans. This could be our only shot to catch them in the act. We've talked it over with your mom and stepdad."

"Okay, I understand," she said. "Is my father at least accepting protection?"

"He says he has his own private security and knows that we'll be there tonight in full force. C'mon, your mother is anxious to see you."

I reached out and grabbed Amy's hand as we followed David down a long hallway. When we reached the last door on the left, David stepped past a uniformed officer posted outside and opened the door.

"Here you go," he said, gesturing inside.

The room was small, with a large, rectangular wooden table in the middle. On the far side sat the man and woman I had trolled on the internet—Amy's mother and stepfather.

Trina Dunphy jumped up and rushed around the table to embrace her daughter, tears running down her face. Her stepfather stood awkwardly at the table. It was hard not to look at him and think of Monty. After all, Amy had said her stepfather had a brother whose name was Martin. Could his nickname be Monty?

As I studied his face, he glanced at me and then away.

Had we already told the bad guys Amy had been rescued? That made me think of Dylan. *Was he actually in Chicago?* Too many coincidences to be, well, coincidental.

I decided to focus for the moment on the hard-fought reunion in front of me.

Trina Dunphy had her arms clamped around her daughter's shoulders, as if she would never let go. Amy didn't seem to mind.

They were both crying and apologizing for the fight they'd had the night before Amy went missing.

I glanced over at David, and he nodded toward the hallway. We slipped back outside and closed the door. That's when I noticed someone new had joined our group.

"Julia, this is Detective Mankiewicz," David said, gesturing to the newcomer.

Detective Mankiewicz was as tall as David, but more slender, skinny in fact. He had a pleasant face, dark brown eyes, short dark hair combed straight back from his forehead and a pencil moustache that reminded me of William Powell in the old Thin Man movies.

"Let's step across the hall," he said.

We left Amy with her mother and the patrol cop and crossed into a larger conference room. As the others crowded through the doorway, I pulled David to the side.

"David, we just saw Dylan downstairs, in front of the building."

"Amy's boyfriend?"

"Yes. Well, *we* didn't see him. Amy did–or she thought it was him. She took off after him, but he disappeared. I thought you had him in custody."

"We had to let him go. There's no actual evidence connecting him to the kidnapping, other than he was in the park at the same time. Give me a minute. I'll tell Detective Mankiewicz."

The seven of us spread out around the table, while David conferred off to the side with Detective Mankiewicz. The detective stepped back into the corridor to call the patrol officer over. He said something to him and then came back inside and closed the door.

"Okay, who wants to begin?"

CHAPTER TWENTY-FIVE

"I think this is mostly Julia's story," Rudy said in response to the detective's prompt. "She's the real hero here."

There were murmurs of agreement, which I accepted with a gracious smile.

"Just because I'm the one who saw Amy first."

"Why don't you start at the beginning," Detective Mankiewicz said.

He sat with his pencil poised to write when the door opened and a young man in a dark suit entered. Detective Mankiewicz looked up.

"Come in Agent Mathers." He turned to us. "Everyone, this is Special Agent Mathers from the FBI. He's going to sit in on the interview."

Agent Mathers wore a dark suit and tie and was probably in his late thirties. I wasn't sure I'd recognize him if I saw him in the hallway ten minutes after we left the room however; he was that bland. He gave us a brief smile and then sat at the end of the table.

I shifted my gaze to David. He gave me a quick nod. "Go on, Julia."

I took a breath and began our tale. I described in detail the first night we saw Monty and his crew at the campground outside of Spokane and the subsequent misdiagnosis of Ponytail Guy's death.

"We called the police," I said. "But, frankly, we looked like fools when the body and the motorhome disappeared. One officer even threatened to lock us up if we caused any more trouble. It's one of the reasons we avoided calling the police after that."

Detective Mankiewicz nodded and made a note. "Okay, what happened next?"

I recounted everything that happened on the Fourth of July and the next morning when I saw Amy's face at the window.

"I was so startled I just stood there as the motorhome drove off," I said apologetically. "To be honest, I wasn't a hundred percent sure of what I'd seen. I just couldn't get her image out of my mind, though. So I started googling information about Amy's family and became more and more convinced my first impressions were correct. But no one else believed me," I said, eyeing my friends. "That's why, when I saw the Jayco motorhome pass us at a gas station, I went after them. I'm really too short to drive something that big, and…well, I…"

A short chuckle erupted from David, prompting a sharp look from me. He quickly sucked it up and glanced down at the table.

Rudy spoke up. "Let's just say that once we're done here, we hope you'll give us a copy of the formal report for the insurance company."

Detective Mankiewicz smiled. "I get it. Go on."

I described the close call at the railroad tracks and how that had brought everyone around to my belief that something was wrong with these people.

"Right after that we met up with Goldie and Aria again," I said, nodding to them.

"When did you see the Jayco motorhome again?" David asked.

I paused to think a moment. "At Jake's store. Um…well, *I* didn't really see them. Rudy did."

I gestured to Rudy to pick up the story, hoping I wouldn't have to talk about the cops and robbers chase or about Jake.

Rudy explained how she had gone after them in the Hulk.

"Oh, oh," Goldie said with a giggle. "That's where Rudy left Julia behind. She watched the whole thing while she flirted with the sexy guy who owned the store. Ow!" Her head snapped around to Aria, who was sitting next to her.

There was a moment of awkward silence as David's eyebrows lifted and those luscious brown eyes shifted my way.

"Listen, that wasn't the important part of the story," I said, hoping to deflect attention away from Jake.

I went on to describe how we spotted the Jayco motorhome again at the small diner early that evening, sent Goldie and Aria in to spy on them, and then found Ponytail Guy dead in the dump hose compartment.

"Why didn't you call in the authorities then?" Agent Mathers asked.

We all turned to him at the end of the table as if he'd just walked into the room.

"Um…because they marched right over to another motorhome in the parking lot and stole it. By now, we knew they had a girl with them, we just weren't sure it was Amy. We had to go after them."

Detective Mankiewicz put a hand up. "Wait a minute! What did you do about the dead body lying on the pavement?"

Count to three.

"We left him there," Doe finally admitted.

Detective Mankiewicz turned toward David with a look of incredulity.

"Don't look at me," David said with a shrug. "I wasn't there, but I know these women. When they're on the scent, there's no getting them off."

"That's what I'm afraid of," he replied. He turned back to me. "Please continue."

"We didn't get very far because we had to stop for gas, so Goldie and Aria continued to follow them."

I then related how we followed Aria and Goldie to Lake Cleary, found the stolen motorhome at the small house, overheard Monty and Roy mention Yoda, and freed Amy.

Detective Mankiewicz gave Blair an appreciative look when I described how she'd knocked Eva out. "You left her alive? Right?"

Blair nodded. "Yes. Her nose was bleeding, but that's all."

"Why did you have handcuffs?" Agent Mathers asked.

I think we all held our breaths at that one.

"I bought them at the Mt. Rushmore gift shop and gave them to her as a gift," Rudy said.

David turned a mischievous smile towards Blair.

"Anyway, we got Amy out of the house," I interjected. "But Rudy called and warned us that Monty and Roy were coming back, so we took off into the forest."

I explained how we heard the shots when we were down in the gully and then turned to Blair to let her finish the story.

She described how we fled up the streambed and took refuge in the barn. And then, she recounted the lie we'd concocted about leaving her bloody tank top behind when we left the barn to hide outside. There was no mention of the ghosts.

Detective Mankiewicz had taken copious notes. "Okay," he said, putting a period at the end of his last sentence. "What did the police have to say when they found this...Eva?"

"We were there for that," Rudy said, raising her hand. "They processed the crime scene and interviewed us. Of course, we could only tell them why we were there and what we *thought* might have happened, since Blair and Julia were missing."

Detective Mankiewicz turned to me. "Detective Franks told me that you didn't meet with the Gateway police. Why not?"

The six of us sat and stared at him. Funny how, when you're nervous about something, things like the air conditioning can sound loud.

"Frankly, Amy was too fragile. She wouldn't allow it, but we have her clothes, and we took pictures of her injuries."

Blair pulled out the plastic bag with her clothes and pushed it across the table to Detective Mankiewicz. "And here's my phone with the pictures."

"I'll take that," Agent Mathers said.

He took her phone to access her photos.

I looked back at Detective Mankiewicz. "Saving Senator Owens has to be the priority now."

"We'll handle that part of it, Mrs. Applegate," Detective Mankiewicz said.

"You don't understand," I said, leaning forward. "We're the only ones who can identify these guys."

"We'll get a police artist up here right away to help with a sketch. But it's far too dangerous to have you involved anymore."

"You can't keep us out of this," Rudy said quietly. "We've all risked our lives to save Amy. We're not quitting now."

"We'll be at the dinner tonight, anyway," I said. I stuck my chin out in stubborn resignation.

"You don't need to be at the dinner," he challenged me.

"Too late. Graham already got us tickets."

"And who is Graham?"

I rarely played the ex-husband card, but it was warranted here. I saw David drop his gaze to the table, as if trying to ignore my next comment.

"He's the Governor of Washington State...my ex-husband. Rudy is doing a story on the conference. So we're all going, whether you like it or not."

I avoided looking at David. Detective Mankiewicz remained quiet, as did Agent Mathers, who was busy doing something with Blair's phone.

"Okay," Detective Mankiewicz relented. "Since I can't lock you up for 24 hours, as much as I'd like to, you can be our eyes and ears in the room. Under no circumstances are you to engage with these guys, though. Understood?"

"Of course," I replied a little too quickly.

The door opened and a female officer stepped in. "Detective Mankiewicz, Senior Agent Preston is here from the FBI."

Mathers came to attention and handed the phone back to Blair.

"Excuse us," the detective said standing up. "This will be a joint operation tonight. Even Homeland Security is involved since it has to do with a sitting U.S. senator. Detective Franks, I'll leave you to prep the ladies. I'll send the artist up right away."

"Detective Mankiewicz," I said, stopping him at the doorway. "What about Amy?"

"We have an officer debriefing her now. She'll stay in our custody until after we secure her father. Detective Franks, can we have a word?"

The three men left and the door closed behind him. The rest of us waited impatiently, until David came back.

"What'd he say?" I asked him.

"That I'd be responsible for you, so you had better pay attention." His eyes shifted to José. "And you'll be on duty *all* night. Is that understood?"

"Got it," José said with a serious expression. "Do I get a gun?"

That went over like a lead balloon.

"Okay," I murmured. "What do we need to do?"

David grabbed a roll of papers that sat next to him on the table. They were the floor plans of the Sheraton Grand Chicago. We spent the next thirty minutes reviewing them. David pointed out the front, back and side entrances, restrooms, offices and meeting rooms. He identified where stairways and elevators were and where security checkpoints would be set up.

"There's a media center on the second floor mezzanine, here," he said, pointing to the plan. "But it will be closed. The only media in the room will be one cable news station and the AP. Also, there's a major construction site on the backside of the building. They're adding a new wing." He pointed to the area on the map.

"So no one will be coming or going through there," I said.

"No. All those rear doors and hallways will be blocked off. There will be twenty undercover agents and police officers in the building. They'll all be wearing these little gold leaf pins," he said, pointing to a small pin on the lapel of his suit jacket. "That's how you'll be able to identify someone if you need help."

"Okay, what do we do if we see Monty or Roy?" Blair asked.

"Text me," he responded. "Just the name and location. We'll pick it up from there. We'll distribute your sketches to all of our undercover officers."

"Okay," I said. "I'll make sure everyone has your number."

Aria opened her mouth to say something. I gave her a brief shake of my head. I didn't want her to mention the ear wigs.

"Any chance we can get two more tickets to the dinner?" Rudy asked.

He shifted a thoughtful gaze to Rudy. "I'll see what I can do."

David got up and left. As soon as he was gone, Goldie asked me, "Aren't you going to tell him about the ear wigs?"

"No. They only allow us to communicate with each other, not David or the police."

"Since we have four of them," Doe said, "we'll have to split up."

"Right. I was thinking that Blair and I would pair up. You and Rudy. And then Goldie and Aria. I'm not sure how we'll be seated, but I figure we can't sit down for too long, anyway. We'll work in pairs and keep moving around. Roy and Monty could be anywhere in the building."

"Who will use the fourth com?" Blair asked.

I turned to José. "You game?"

He grinned. "Sure. Just like *Law and Order*."

"Won't it look weird if we just keep roaming around?" Aria asked.

"People move around all the time at these things," Doe said. "You just have to look purposeful. You know, like you're going to get a drink. Going to the ladies' room. Pretending to see someone you know across the room. Stopping to chat with each other."

"Okay, but the six of us ought to have a code if we see Monty or Roy," Rudy said.

"Why do we need a code?" Goldie inquired. "I thought we were just going to text."

"That's to David. What if Monty is standing a few feet away from you? You can't text all of us or blurt out his name. So…maybe you say something like, *I can't live without chocolate*. The word chocolate would alert us that you've seen Monty. Get it?"

"Hey, chocolate is my line," I said.

She smiled. "Well, we should use something personal and true, not something that would raise an alarm."

Goldie's features lit up. "Oh, oh, I get it. *I can't live without chocolate* can be for Julia. But if I see one of them, I could say that chocolate *gives me the runs*."

Blair burst out with a laugh. "What? No."

"I don't think we need to be that literal," I said, holding back a laugh.

Her face fell. "I thought we were supposed to make it personal. You love chocolate, but I'm allergic to it."

Rudy said, "I was just using chocolate as an example. Let's use the weather instead. Okay? Don't say anything about the weather tonight *unless* you see Monty or Roy. If you mention the temperature, it means you've just seen Monty. If you mention rain, it means you've just seen Roy. Does that work for everyone?"

"Yeah," Goldie said. "Temperature is Monty. Rain is Roy. I get it."

The door opened and David stepped back into the room.

"Okay," he said. "We can get two of you in as wait staff, but you're going to have to get some appropriate clothes."

"No problem. We'll take care of it," I said.

"Okay, the sketch artist is on her way up. After that, do your shopping. José is going to need something to wear, too. I'll meet you at the Sheraton around six-thirty." He leveled a stare at me. "This could be very dangerous, Julia. We have no idea what they're planning or who they're working for. And that's the wild card. The person you call Yoda could be anyone in that room, or not be there at all. He could be giving orders remotely, so be careful. *Very* careful." He paused a moment, as if he wanted to say something else, but glanced around at the other faces staring at him and left.

CHAPTER TWENTY-SIX

"Goldie and I can be the wait staff," Aria offered, holding her phone. "I've already googled a restaurant supply store in town that sells uniforms."

I nodded. "Thanks, Aria."

We spent the next twenty-five minutes with the sketch artist and then left. It was almost three-thirty by the time we made it out into the humid afternoon.

"Listen, we'll have to get to the banquet hall early if we plan to blend in with the banquet staff," Aria said. "So we'll meet you there."

She nodded and hurried down the sidewalk with Goldie hustling after her.

"Then I guess it's time for us to do what we do best," I said to the others. "Shop."

The five of us spent the next ninety minutes at Saks Fifth Avenue, loading ourselves down with a suit and tie for José, and new clothes, shoes, stockings, jewelry, makeup, scarves, and wigs for us. Yes, I said wigs. If we were truly going undercover, we couldn't let Monty or Roy ID us first.

Since José was staying at the Park Hyatt, we parted ways on the street with a promise to pick him up a little after six o'clock.

Back in our rooms, we quickly took showers and got ready. At six o'clock we met in the hallway dressed in our finery. I had on slender leg velvet pants with an Irish green sequined top, accented with a short, blond wig with bangs.

"Damn!" Blair said. "You look fantastic, Julia."

I was grinning from ear to ear. "Thanks. I hope David recognizes me."

Blair gave me a quick double lift of her eyebrows. "Recognize you? He's going to want to jump your bones."

Doe and Rudy laughed and murmured their agreement.

"You look great with long, black hair," I said to Doe. "And that beaded jacket is stunning."

Rudy had chosen crepe pants and a bright orange chiffon blouse with a patterned scarf. She'd added a dark brown wig cut to her shoulders.

"I love those colors on you," I said to her. "I could never carry off orange."

"Thanks. I hope I can last in these new shoes, though," she said, wiggling her right foot.

"Humpf," Blair grunted. "That's why you should have brought some sensible shoes."

We looked down at her three-inch candy-apple red heels.

"Right, cuz those are so sensible," Rudy quipped.

"Well, you look terrific," I said to Blair.

"I just hope someone doesn't mistake her for a call girl," Rudy said.

Blair wore a short, red sequined dress cut down to her waist. Her long crystal beaded earrings caught the light and sparkled every time she moved. Instead of a wig, however, she had pulled her blond hair up in a stylish mess of curls on top of her head.

"So, no wig for you," I said.

"Naw. I have a feeling no one will be looking at my hair," she said with a sly grin. "C'mon. Let's go. We need to pick up José." She threw a lightweight black sequined shawl around her shoulders and spun on her shapely heels and headed down the hallway.

We decided to drive the rental car rather than try and get a taxi. Since I had done so little of the driving on the trip, I volunteered to take the wheel.

We found José at the curb of his hotel. He climbed into the backseat and Blair whistled.

"You look sharp," she said, referring to his black suit and tie.

"Just headin' out with my ladies," he replied with a grin.

Rudy laughed. "Should we call you Sugar Daddy?"

He cracked up. "Sure. If I'm the daddy, you're the sugar."

Rudy groaned. "Oh, stop."

"Let's get going and get this evening over with," I said.

I had already programmed the address for the Sheraton Grand Chicago hotel into the car's GPS and pulled into traffic. Within minutes, we crossed the Chicago River and turned left onto W. Grand Ave. Inside the car, we ran through scenarios of how Monty and Roy might get into the dinner. They could dress up as wait staff, or they could attend as guests.

"What if they dress up as security guards?" José asked. "I'm sure the event center will have heavy security."

"Yeah, they could do that," Rudy said. "There's also a media center. They could get fake media credentials."

"No. Remember the media center will be closed," I said.

"Still, we're going to have to move around the entire building," Doe said

"Do you have our ear wigs?" I asked, glancing across at Rudy.

She was riding shotgun and opened her fancy bag to bring out the small earpieces. She gave one to José, one to Blair and kept one for herself. Aria and Goldie already had the fourth one.

Rudy, Blair and José each placed them inside their ears. Rudy had the main switch in her bag and turned it on.

"Ooh!" Blair exclaimed with a jump. "Turn it down."

Rudy did as she was asked. "Is that better?"

"Yeah, perfect," Blair said. "Julia, I might give this to you when we get there. You can hide it under your wig. My hair is up, and it might show."

"Okay. No problem," I said, keeping my eyes on the road.

We were just about to cross the Chicago River again, when Rudy looked out the window and said, "Didn't we already cross the river?"

"Yes," I replied. I glanced over at the GPS. "We're still on track, though." I turned back to the road, carefully navigating the traffic around me as we rumbled across the bridge.

We discussed why Owens might be a target, including his abhorrent personality, until Rudy said, "Hey, Julia, this doesn't look like the right area." She was peering out the window again. "Hold on." She pulled up the address for the Sheraton Grand Chicago on her phone. "The Sheraton is on East North Water Street." She leaned forward to read the GPS on the dash. "You programmed in North *Walker* Street."

"Oh, shoot. I'm sorry. How far out of the way are we?"

"I don't know," she said, adjusting the address in the GPS. "Give me a minute."

She fixed the GPS, and the female voice told me to continue for six blocks until I got to W. Chicago Ave, where I would turn right.

"Okay, we're good to go now," she said. "And we still have a little time."

We continued for a few blocks until the GPS told me to turn right, and we crossed back over the Chicago River again.

"At least we're getting multiple views of the river," Blair joked, craning her neck to gaze at the water.

"Well, this tour company aims to please." As we came off the bridge, my nose crinkled up. "What the heck is that smell?"

"Smells like someone lit a smoke," José said.

"We must've passed a manufacturing plant or something," Rudy said. She cracked a window to let in fresh air. "This should help."

The night was warm and clear, so Rudy left the window open, clearing the bad smell. Slowly, however, the burning smell returned and kept getting stronger.

"Where is that smell coming from?" Doe asked, concern seeping into her voice.

"I don't know, but it's getting pretty strong," I said, keeping my eyes on the road.

"Oh, damn," Rudy said. She pointed to a thin trail of smoke coming from the dashboard.

"Oh, my God!" I said, glancing at the smoke.

A sizzling, snapping sound startled everyone. I flinched and took my eyes off the road and drifted into the next lane, prompting a horn blast from another driver. I swerved back into my own lane.

"Julia! Be careful," Doe reprimanded me.

I checked cars behind me, yanked the wheel to the right and pulled to the curb, killing the engine. Everyone threw open their doors and hurried out. The inside of the car had already filled with acrid smoke; it smelled like we had fried a major motor cable.

"What do we do now?" Blair asked, throwing the shawl around her shoulders.

"We could call Triple A," Doe offered.

"No," Rudy replied, glancing at her watch. "It's already ten after six. We need a ride."

"We're a few blocks from the Godfrey Hotel," Blair said, staring at her phone. "Let's just walk up there and grab a cab?"

"Okay, but what do we do about the rental car?" Doe asked as we set off.

"I'll call the rental company and tell them where it is," Rudy said. She looked up the number and made the call.

"You sure you're okay in those heels?" I asked Blair, glancing at her feet.

She erupted with a laugh. "Are you kidding? I could do a marathon in these."

We started off and turned right at the next light. Blair guided us to Huron Street, where a giant Rubik's Cube-like building appeared. The enormous steel and glass structure was jaw-dropping in its design. I was contemplating what Jake would think of it when Rudy pulled me out of my thoughts.

"There's the Tioga!" she yelled.

We all turned and saw the retreating tail lights of the stolen RV disappear into traffic.

"They're heading for the Sheraton," I said. "Damn! We have to hurry."

"We need a car," Rudy said.

"So where's a cab?" I said, looking around with desperation.

There were zero cabs parked in front of the hotel and none passing on the street.

"Damn!" I said again. "There are too many people in town."

José was eying the valet parking operation. "How badly do we need a car?"

I followed his gaze. "No. We cannot steal a car!"

"Why not?" Rudy asked. "We'll *borrow* a car and leave it at the Sheraton in pristine condition."

"Where have we heard that before?" Blair sniped

"Why don't we just call Uber?" Doe asked.

"It will take too long," José said.

"God, here we go again. Okay, what's the plan?" I asked José.

We were huddled together in front of a bistro a hundred feet up the sidewalk from the hotel's valet stand. José stripped off his suit jacket and handed it to me. He rolled up his sleeves and tucked his tie inside the buttons of his shirt.

"Give me a minute, but be ready." He glanced around and then walked confidently down the sidewalk.

There were two guys running cars that night, and they were extremely busy. José walked casually up to the front entrance of the hotel and waited off to one side. A tall skinny kid took the keys from a board behind the station and ran out and around the corner to retrieve a car. Just then, a Mercedes pulled in. The second young man handed the driver of the Mercedes a tag, took his keys, got in and pulled the car out the circular drive and turned left toward the parking lot. The car owner entered the hotel.

That's when José stepped in.

A black Cadillac pulled up and a couple emerged. José grabbed a tag and handed it to the driver as he got out. He took the man's keys and then got behind the wheel as the couple entered the hotel. José pulled out the circular drive, but turned right instead of left. He pulled to the curb where we were waiting.

Once more, my heart was hammering as we jumped into the car.

"One of these days our luck is going to run out," Doe said with a distinct edge to her voice.

José pulled away from the curb. "They'll never have to know the car was gone."

"Then, let's get there fast," she replied.

Blair had her phone out again. "Turn right at the next street." José followed her directions. "We're close," Blair said, staring at her phone. "Just a few more blocks."

"Okay, the sooner we get rid of this car the better," Rudy said. "I'm as nervous about this as Doe is."

The sharp sound of a siren made everyone whip around to look out the back window. Red and blue lights flashed two blocks behind us, coming our way.

"God, that was fast," I said in a panic.

"Don't worry," José said with his eyes on the rearview mirror. He spun the steering wheel, throwing all of us up against the left side of the car as he made a sharp right turn into a darkened alley.

"Whoa!" I said, holding my painful ribs. "Take it easy."

He rolled the car into the middle of the alley and cut the engine and lights. We all grew silent as we sat in a tunnel of deep shadows, flanked by piles of trash and a couple of dumpsters. The siren and flashing lights blasted past the alley behind us and kept going, bringing audible sighs of relief from everyone inside the luxury car.

"That was close," Doe said, flopping back against the seat.

"No kidding. Let's get out of here," José said. He started the engine and flicked on the headlights.

Everyone froze.

Three heavily-tattooed men blocked the front of the car, arms crossed, looking anything but friendly.

"Uh…Julia," Doe muttered.
Damn!

CHAPTER TWENTY-SEVEN

Tension flooded the car as we stared at the men illuminated by the arc of the car's headlights.

"Back up!" Rudy snapped.

José put the car in reverse, turned around and began to back up and then came to a screeching halt.

A fourth man stood behind us, blocking our path backwards. He held a baseball bat and slapped one end into his open hand.

"Damn," I said again.

We couldn't go around them. We couldn't go through them.

"What do we do?" I whispered with a nervous twitter in my throat.

"Shhhh," José shushed me. He turned back to the men in front of the car.

The three men stared back at us, unmoving. Tattoos covered exposed flesh, including one young man who had an angel's wing imprinted across his right cheek and down his neck. They all wore baggy jeans that looked ready to fall off. One was wearing a cloth headband, while another had on a baseball cap backwards. The tallest man stood a few feet off to one side. He had a shaved head and multiple large chains hanging from around his neck. He also had a gun tucked into his belt.

For the umpteen millionth time my throat constricted, and I felt like I couldn't breathe.

"Let me handle this," José said. He turned off the engine and opened the door. "Stay put."

We didn't argue.

He left the door open and approached them with his palms open and out to the side. He said something in Spanish and then glanced back at the car and chuckled, giving the car a dismissive flick of his hand.

What did that mean?

The men followed his gaze and then responded in Spanish. The guy with the shaved head pointed to the inside of José's wrist. José glanced at his hand.

José's arms were littered with tattoos, and I knew he had one on the inside of his right wrist that had always made me wonder if it was a gang marking. He'd come from a troubled past, growing up on the streets of Los Angeles stealing cars. But I had never felt comfortable asking him about the details, and truthfully, it didn't matter. Now, I wondered if that tattoo was going to help us or be our downfall.

Shaved Head Guy, as I mentally referred to him, pointed at the car with a look of appreciation. José glanced back and shrugged.

"What do you suppose is going on?" Doe asked nervously.

All four of us leaned forward, peering out the front window.

"It looks like they might be bartering for something," Rudy replied.

"Not us!" Doe said wide-eyed.

"Are you kidding?" I whispered. "We wouldn't be worth much."

"Speak for yourself," Blair said from the front seat, tucking a curl behind her ear.

The four gang-bangers, which I assumed they were, leaned in to talk in private. Shaved Head Guy nodded to José. José turned and came back to the car and leaned into the driver's side.

"Get out slowly and follow my lead. Wipe the car down as you go and bring my coat."

He turned and stepped back.

"Oh, God, this doesn't sound good," Doe lamented.

"C'mon, let's go," Blair said.

We climbed out of the car, using whatever we could to wipe door handles as we went. Blair scooted across the front seat to get out by the driver's side door and used her shawl to swipe the circumference of the steering wheel.

The three men watched with interest and then confusion as we emerged from the car.

What did they expect?

I remembered our credit cards, cash, and jewelry. But their stares turned to curiosity as we lined up next to José, and then...

They laughed.

What the heck?

The guy from behind the car moved up and joined his friends. He pointed at Rudy and said, "*Ella se parece a mi nanna.*"

His comment prompted uproarious laughter from the rest of the group.

It was pretty clear that *nanna* meant nanny. I bristled, despite our situation.

"What are they saying?" I asked José.

"Never mind."

"You got to be kidding, man," Shaved Head Guy said in English. "You say these your ladies? You mean your *old* ladies."

There was more laughter and obvious rude comments in Spanish from his colleagues.

José shrugged. "Hey, even old guys get lonely, man."

My mouth dropped open.

"Yeah, man, but they don't want to do it with their *mother*," Baseball Cap guy said, hooting with laughter again.

The rest snickered along with him. Then Baseball Bat Guy stepped forward to stand right in front of Blair. He was almost as tall as she was and eyed her up and down, his head tilted to one side.

Blair didn't move. She stood with one hip thrown out and followed the man's eyes as his penetrating look covered every inch of her body.

"This one ain't so bad," he said, leering at her with a broken-tooth grin.

Blair dipped one shoulder to lean into him. "At least you have an eye for quality, young man."

His dark eyes glinted. "Say, Mama, I bet you be a helluva ride."

"Back off," Shaved Head Guy said. "We have business to conduct here." He turned to José. "Like I said, we'll take the car. That's the deal."

"But…" I started.

Blair stomped on my foot. "Ow!"

José glanced back at the Cadillac. "Deal."

"Good doing business with you, homeboy," Shaved Head Guy said. "Give my love to the Santa Monica 13." An evil laugh erupted from his throat.

He stepped past José with a lingering smile and slid in behind the wheel of the Cadillac. His friends followed, undressing us with their eyes as they went. The guy with the angel tattoo nodded to me.

"You look like my fourth grade teacher, Mrs. Muñoz," he said with a seductive wink. "I always had a thing for her."

A twinge of disgust twisted my gut. He brushed my shoulder in passing.

When Shaved Head Guy started the engine, we moved to either side of the alley. The car began to roll forward, and Shaved Head Guy leaned out the window. "Take it easy, man."

The tail lights disappeared into the well of the long alley, and they were gone.

We just stood and stared after them.

"Well, easy come, easy go," Rudy finally said. She spun in the opposite direction. "Let's go."

"What about the Cadillac?" Doe said, turning to follow Rudy. "How do we explain that?"

"We don't. It's not our responsibility anymore." Rudy began walking out of the alley the way we'd come in.

Blair handed José his coat. "Nice job."

I grabbed Doe's elbow. "C'mon, Doe. The good news is that now you don't have to worry about getting arrested for car theft."

"Yes, but why do we always have to end up in dirty basements, tunnels, or rat-infested alleys?"

"Topic for another time," Rudy called out from a few feet ahead.

Blair pulled out her phone as we moved toward the street. "We're close to the Sheraton. And we're late, so we'd better hurry."

We left the claustrophobic darkness of the alley and within a couple of minutes came within sight of the NBC Tower and several other high rises.

"Just a couple more blocks," Blair said, glancing again at her phone.

"Jeez, if I'd known we'd be trekking to the dinner, I would have brought my tennis shoes," Doe whined.

Rudy looked at her watch. "It's 6:45. Why don't you call David?"

My phone pinged, making us look at each other in surprise. It was David.

"Where *are* you?" he demanded.

"We're almost there. We had a little…um…trouble."

"A *little* trouble?" Rudy said with a snort.

"What happened?"

"Nothing," I said, throwing a dirty look at Rudy. "Our rental died, and we had to get another…ride."

"Okay," he said with a sigh. "At least you weren't in any danger."

"No, no, we weren't in any real danger. José is with us and has everything under control. I'll text you when we get there."

"Okay, see you soon."

We hung up.

"You're going to hell for all the times you've lied to that man," Blair said over her shoulder.

I blew out a breath. "I know, but he'd worry more if he knew we'd stolen a car and then been car-jacked by four gang members. By the way," I said, turning to José, "how did you strike that deal so fast?"

"We had a couple of friends in common in California," he said with a private smile.

"Uh-huh," I said.

His smile grew into a grin.

We crossed the Chicago River one more time, this time on foot, and approached the Sheraton. As we neared the building, we were met with a large group of protestors marching in a circle on the sidewalk across from the entrance to the hotel. They were chanting and carrying signs calling for everything from gun control to a woman's right to choose.

"Oh, great," I said. "One more thing for the police to deal with."

The street was blocked off on either side of the building by patrol cars with their lights flashing. Officers lined the front of the entrance, and the valet parking had been moved beyond the blockade.

We crossed the street a half block away and then joined a throng of people climbing the steps to the entrance of the building. Men were dressed in tuxedos, while the women sparkled and shined in silks, velvets, sequins and jewels. We fit right in.

We had to pass through security to have our IDs checked and our purses searched and then walk through a metal detector. The alarms went off when Rudy went through and they hurried her off to the side. When they went through her purse, they found the controls to our intercoms.

"Call Detective Mankiewicz," I said. "He'll vouch for us."

The officer did that, and a few minutes later the young, slender detective showed up. I explained what Rudy had in her purse.

"We needed a way to communicate with each other. Nothing nefarious."

He gave me an exasperated sigh. "That's okay," he said, looking at the security officer. "Let them in."

Rudy got her purse back, and Detective Mankiewicz gave us a severe look. "I know Detective Franks gave you instructions, but I want to make something clear. This is not some game. These people are serious. They've already killed three people."

"You don't need to convince us," Doe said. "We're quite aware of the danger."

Her imperial attitude took him by surprise. He glanced at her and then nodded. "Okay. Let Detective Franks know you're here."

He left, and we approached the registration tables where they handed us our name tags and table assignments. Since we hadn't paid yet, we were directed over to another table where they took our credit cards.

When we were finally allowed into the foyer, Doe spoke up.

"Well, I for one, need to use the ladies' room."

"Me, too," I said.

The four of us used the restroom to clean up after our long walk. We returned to the foyer and backed up to a wall so that we could see the room. I texted David and told him we'd wait there.

"What happens if you see Graham?" Blair asked me.

A sudden panic welled in my chest. I'd forgotten I would have my ex-husband and current boyfriend in the same room. One was a governor and the other a cop. What could go wrong?

"I guess I'll cross that bridge when…"

"What bridge?" David asked, coming up behind me.

"Uh…the Chicago River bridge. We crossed it three times tonight."

Blair dropped her chin and pressed her lips together to hide a smile.

"And then our car almost caught fire," Doe said. She gave me a conspiratorial nod.

"That's right," I said. "We must have had a short or something in the dashboard."

He put a hand on my shoulder. "Well, I'm glad you're okay, but what's with the blond hair?"

"We didn't want to be recognized," I said, disappointed in his response.

"Okay, I get it. Good idea. Are Goldie and Aria here?"

"I don't know. We haven't seen them yet. But on our way here, we did see the RV with Monty and Roy," I told him. "They must be here somewhere."

"Governor Applegate!" someone called out.

Graham and Kitty had just gotten off the elevator and came through the main entrance into the foyer. They were surrounded by several members of Graham's staff, who were attempting to create a barrier between him and a couple of press people.

"I thought the press wasn't going to be allowed in here," I said to David.

"Not in the banquet room. This will be as far as they get."

Graham stopped in the middle of the foyer when a reporter stuck a microphone in his face. Even from where we stood, we could hear the question.

"Governor, what do you know about the abduction of Senator Owens' daughter?"

Much of the room chatter around him fell silent, and we perked up to hear what he said.

"The FBI and our local police are working diligently to find her. I have every confidence she will be brought home safe and sound. Thank you," he replied.

I released a sigh of relief that he hadn't revealed Amy's rescue.

Graham grabbed Kitty's hand and pushed past the reporter.

"He likes an audience," David murmured.

A part of me flared in defense. "Part of the job," I said as casually as I could. "Why don't we go inside and find our seats?"

"Okay. I'll be close by." He reached out and squeezed my hand. "Be careful."

"Always," I said as the warmth of his touch tingled up my arm.

David turned to José. "Stick close."

José nodded, and David left.

I turned to my friends and tapped my earpiece. "Okay, everyone turned on?"

"Julia!" Blair burst out in a laugh. "That's sounds like something I'd say."

"Fine," I said, blushing.

"I think we can all hear each other," Rudy said with a smile.

"Yes, we certainly can," Aria's voice came over the coms.

"Aria, where are you?" I asked.

"In the banquet room."

"Okay. Then let's split up. Keep your eyes peeled. Blair, you're with me."

CHAPTER TWENTY-EIGHT

The dinner was being held in the Chicago Room, a space where vendors normally display their wares and network with attendees during conferences. Since the Chicago Room was the only place that could accommodate a stage, entertainment and seating for 1,000 dinner guests however, the vendors had been moved to the grand ballroom.

The Chicago Room was oval shaped and open to a vaulted ceiling. The mezzanine, where there were offices and meeting rooms, overlooked the expansive area below. The second floor could be accessed by stairs at either side of the room and an elevator at the north end.

After going through the final check point, we entered the room. Round tables draped in white extended before us like a sea of lily pads. In the middle of each table was a red and blue floral arrangement, sporting a small American flag. Since the overhead lights had been dimmed, small red, white and blue LED lights hidden within the centerpieces sparkled like tiny patriotic glow bugs.

"I thought the Fourth of July was over," Rudy sniped.

"Down, girl," I said.

A band played from the north end of the room, where a stage had been set up to accommodate the speakers.

"Look at the stage," Doe said. "I feel I ought to salute."

She was referring to a backdrop composed of four large rice paper panels that framed the platform. The panels had been stenciled with a red, white and blue swirling ribbon accented with a splash of white stars and the words "In God We Trust." Directly in front of the panels stood the podium, which was dressed with patriotic fabric and a Republican Governors' Association logo.

"Almost makes my eyes water," I said. "This must be what they mean when they say draped in the flag."

I glanced up to the center of the high ceiling where three enormous crystal chandeliers hung in a row. Each was festooned with bands of white chiffon pulled across to the second floor railings where they were tied off and adorned with giant red fabric roses.

The room was already half full. Most people were milling about or standing in line at one of the four bars set up on either side. I recognized a couple of governors and senators, even the head of the Republican National Committee. It was going to be a who's who of Republican politics.

My liberal toes curled.

"Do you see Senator Owens?" Rudy asked, her gaze sweeping the room.

"No," I replied. "But, so far, I don't see Monty or Roy, either."

"It's time to split up," she said. "Stay in touch."

"Will do," I said.

Rudy and Doe began to gravitate toward the left side of the room, pretending to look for their table. Blair and I moved right.

"Our table is right there," I said to Blair, pointing a few feet in front of us.

It wasn't a surprise that we'd been seated in the back since we'd made last minute reservations. The table was empty, so we wandered further into the room.

As we weaved in and out among the guests, a dark young man approached in a gray suit with one of the gold leaf pins on his lapel. He gave me a slight nod as I silently slipped passed him without comment, relieved at the knowledge that law enforcement was in the room.

"There's Aria," Blair said. She nodded towards a large side entrance. Aria's tall, angular figure stood out next to a small folding table set up for discarded drink glasses.

"I see her." She gave me a slight nod. "I wonder where Goldie is."

"She's over here," Rudy said.

We located Rudy now across the room at one of the bars. Goldie was a few feet away helping another member of the wait staff set out water glasses. She looked comical stuffed into too-tight black pants and a white button-down shirt with a little black ribbon at the neckline.

"Not her best look," Blair said too loudly.

"Then it's a good thing she's too far away to hear you," Aria said through the earpiece.

I nudged Blair and gestured toward Aria. Blair gave her a quick look. "Sorry," she murmured.

"Let's focus on the task at hand," Rudy said. "Keep milling about."

Blair and I began to wander through the room and passed José standing against the wall watching us.

"Julia!" a voice rang out.

I whirled around to find the wife of one of Washington's state senators approaching me.

"What in the world are you doing here?" she asked with a slur.

"Oh, Penny, how nice to see you." She was alone and already a little sloshed. My mind was doing somersaults as I contemplated what I assumed would be the first of many lies I would be forced to tell. "Where's Richard?"

"Oh, he's schmoozing someone he thinks will give him money," she said with a smirk. "You know how it goes. It's all about the money. But what in the world have you done to your hair?" she asked, reaching out to touch the wig.

I'd forgotten about the wig and reached up to touch it myself. "Oh, I'm just having some fun. You know…when in Vegas…" I said, giving her a false giggle.

She threw her head back and cackled, spilling her drink down the front of her dress. "Oh, oops."

I'd known many spouses during my marriage to Graham who felt smothered by the life their husband chose and drank too much as a result. It made me feel sad for Penny, whose brilliant career as an interior designer had dissolved when her attorney husband had gone into politics.

"I understand," she said, wiping the drink off her silk dress. "I like to have a little fun on the side myself." She leaned in, flooding the air around us with the scent of the chardonnay in her hand. "We'll have to get together sometime and swap stories." She eyed Blair standing silently beside me, winked at her, and then slipped into the crowd.

"My God…she winked at me," Blair blurted in alarm. "What the heck did that mean?"

"I don't know, and I don't think I want to. Hey, Rudy," I said. "Since you guys have it covered in here, I think Blair and I should take a stroll out to the entrance again and check the hallways."

"Good idea," Rudy responded.

Blair and I weaved through the crowd toward two sets of double doors and pushed out into a wide, carpeted hallway. We took a look around and then headed back towards the main entrance.

We had just passed the men's restroom when a deep voice stopped us.

"Blond becomes you, Julia."

We turned to find Graham flanked by two of his body men. His eyes twinkled as he eyed my blond wig.

"How come you waited until now to show this sassy side of yourself?" he asked with a sly grin.

"I just wondered what it would be like to be irresistible. Speaking of...where's Kitty?"

The smile on his face fell. "She went ahead to the table. She doesn't really like these affairs. My guess is that she'll be on her phone most of the night. She's in a bidding war on eBay for an heirloom piece of jewelry she wants." He gave a slight shrug as if it was something he would have to endure.

"I may have liked these types of events more than Kitty does, but I was never very good at keeping my mouth shut. There's always a tradeoff," I replied.

He laughed. "That's true." He leaned in, coming close enough to overwhelm my senses with the seductiveness of his cologne. "You may have run a bit at the mouth, Julia, but I've never known a more articulate woman. I miss that."

When my eyebrows lifted, he stepped back. Graham's dark hair had turned mostly gray, and his tanned skin had deep lines from years on the ski slopes. But, like fine wine, he had weathered well; he was still one of the handsomest men I knew. He gave me a rueful smile and then turned to Blair.

"Nice to see you, Mrs. Wentworth. I hope you ladies find what you're looking for tonight. Stay safe."

He stepped away from us and continued back down the hall, his body men following.

"Well, well, well, Miss Julia," Blair said, watching him go. "If I didn't know better, I'd have to say that right now you have not one, not two, but three men on a string."

I turned to her. "Huh? Who's the third guy?"

"Jake?"

"What about Jake?" Rudy asked through the earpiece.

"Nothing," I snapped. "Forget Graham. Forget Jake." I started to walk away. "C'mon, we have work to do."

Blair and I made our way back to the entrance where people were still streaming in. We decided to hang back a few minutes to watch the newcomers. I glanced to my right and saw José leaning against the wall. He looked casual enough, but kept glancing in my direction.

"Our bodyguard," I said, nodding toward him.

"I noticed," Blair said. "He ought to join the CIA. I never see him following us, yet he always seems to be wherever we are."

Someone touched my elbow. I turned to find David. "Anything yet?"

"No. But the others are in the banquet room, including Aria and Goldie. We thought we'd check around out here. Any news on who you think Yoda is?"

He shook his head as his eyes scanned the room. "No. The CPD has been checking into Senator Owens' background and can't find anyone with a nickname like that."

"Could it be someone who *looks* like Yoda?" Blair asked.

David shrugged. "The reference doesn't seem to ring any bells with anyone. It could be a real name, a nickname, or a call name picked just for this job."

"What about Amy's stepfather? Anything on him?" I asked.

"No. Detective Mankiewicz said they're checking into his business, though. We'll see."

"Well, you'd better be ready to rock 'n roll," Blair said, nodding toward the entrance. "Here comes the man of the hour."

We followed her gaze to a large press of media who had surrounded someone entering the building. It was Senator Owens, and he was answering their questions on the fly. As he came through the doors and moved into the broad foyer, dozens of press, security guards, and staff followed. It was like watching a hoard of locusts.

"Clearly, he isn't taking this threat seriously," I said.

"Whether he does or not, he doesn't seem to care," David said.

"And he doesn't know yet about Amy?" Blair asked.

"No," David replied. "Which I'm sure we'll get ripped about later. But we thought if we told him, he would become even more careless." David put his fingers to one ear. "Hold on." He listened a moment. He had an earpiece in, too. It was probably linked to Detective Mankiewicz. "Okay," he said. He turned to me. "I'll be back." He gestured to José, who moved over to stand between me and Blair. "Stay close."

He left us and disappeared into the crowd. I turned to Blair.

"Let's get closer to Senator Owens. I'm curious how he's handling this."

The three of us followed the locusts to the check point at the entrance to the banquet hall. That's where security stopped the press. Senator Owens paused, and a female reporter threw out, "Senator Owens, what are you doing to help find your missing daughter?"

The crowd grew quiet, as a look of irritation swept across his dark features.

"I love my daughter and have every confidence the FBI will find her and keep her safe. But I have a responsibility to keep working on behalf of this country and my constituents. Now, if you'll excuse me…"

And with that, he turned and disappeared into the banquet hall.

"What he really meant to say was that he has a responsibility to elevate his image so he can run for President," a woman next to me mumbled.

I turned in her direction, but she had moved into the crowd with her companion, laughing. I watched them a moment, until a tall, slender man cut in front of me.

"Dr. Ford," Blair said. "What are you doing here?"

The man turned in surprise, his blue bow tie matching the blue of his eyes.

"Mrs. Wentworth…hello. How are you?" A faltering smile spread across his face. He glanced at me, and then turned his attention back to Blair. "I thought it was only your husband who followed politics."

"It is. I'm here with Julia," she said, referring to me. "This is Julia Applegate. In fact, I just recommended she come see you about a broken tooth."

"Oh, I'm sorry to hear about your tooth. I saw your husband a few minutes ago."

"Ex-husband," I corrected him.

"Of course," he said. "Are you a fan of Senator Owens? I understand he'll be the keynote speaker tonight."

"No. Not really. We're just..." I paused, realizing I didn't know what to say. He filled in the blank.

"You're just good Republicans," he said, finishing my sentence. I nearly choked. "Well, uh, actually..."

"That's right," Blair said, linking arms with me. "Where's Ruth?"

"Uh...I'm in town for a meeting and was invited by a friend. Ruth is at home with her caregiver," he said with a warm smile. He shifted his weight uncomfortably. "Well, it's nice to see you again, Mrs. Wentworth," he said with a nod. "I hope you enjoy the dinner."

"You, too," Blair replied.

Dr. Ford left us and moved into the crowd. I turned to Blair. "That's your dentist?"

"Yes. He's a great guy," she said. "He and his wife, Ruth, bought Dorrie Watts' old house."

"Why were you surprised his wife wasn't with him?"

"She has MS and he rarely leaves her side. Except to work, of course."

We pushed our way back into the banquet room and moved off to one side for a moment. My eyes were scanning the room.

"By the way, how *is* your tooth?" Blair asked.

I automatically swept my tongue across the inside of my mouth. "Okay. I'll need a crown, though. By the way, he seemed nice."

Blair snatched a stuffed mushroom off a tray of hors d'oeuvres as a waiter passed. "He is. He adores his wife and is very good with kids, although they don't have any."

"And he's in Mercer Island?"

"No. Downtown Seattle," she replied, swallowing the remainder of the mushroom. "Damn, that was good. I'm hungry."

We began moving back into the crowd and Blair found another waiter.

"I'll give him a call," I said. "We should have asked him when he'd be back in town."

"Well, trust me, you'll love him," she said, swallowing a small chicken bite. "He has a great sense of humor and is a collector like you."

We pushed through a dense group of people.

"What does he collect?" I shouted after her.

"Mostly science fiction memorabilia. His favorite is Star Wars." Blair stepped sideways past a circle of men deep in conversation. "He has posters, action figures, lunch boxes—you name it. I think he met Harrison Ford at one point, and their last names made him feel simpatico."

"I wonder why I don't have that connection with the Wizard of Oz."

"Oh, you do. I think of you as Glinda."

"At least not the Wicked Witch of the West."

We found an empty space next to a wall and stopped, still scanning the room. She grabbed another mushroom off a passing hors d'oeuvres plate.

"Well, Dr. Ford likes to tease me. He knows I've been divorced three times, so he always says goodbye by saying, '*May divorce be with you.*'" She chuckled. "It's pretty funny. And then I respond with, '*Funny, you are.*'"

She laughed until I grabbed her elbow, nearly knocking the mushroom out of her hand.

"What are you doing?" she snapped.

"Blair, why were you so surprised to see Dr. Ford here tonight?"

"Because he's not a Republican," she replied with an innocent shrug.

"Damn!" Rudy said into the earpiece.

"Why?" Blair asked me.

"Star Wars?" I said, giving her a 'don't you get it?' look. "*Funny, you are?*"

Count to three.

Blair's eyes lit up. "Oh my God! You don't think Dr. Ford is…"

"Yes, I do."

CHAPTER TWENTY-NINE

"God, I can't believe our bad guy is my dentist," Blair murmured. "After all, he's had his hands in my mouth."

"Forget that," I snapped. "We need to find him again."

"Where are you guys?" Rudy said into the earpiece.

"Banquet room. We're heading back to the entrance where we saw him."

Blair and I spun around to go against the incoming traffic. Once we were in the foyer, we stopped and looked around.

"Do you see him?" I asked.

"No," she said, craning her neck.

"Damn! Why don't you go down that hallway? And check the vendor hall. We'll go this way. Text me if you see him."

Blair nodded, and we split up. José still shadowed me, so I stopped to explain.

"Did you see that guy who stopped to talk to us a few minutes ago?"

"A tall skinny guy?" he said. "Blue bow tie."

"Yes."

"Right," he said, already beginning to swivel his head to survey the crowd. "You think he's the Yoda guy?"

"Yes. While you look for him, I'm going to alert David."

I wore my purse strap across my body; I pulled out my phone to text David with the information. He didn't answer. I tried again. No response. A nervous flutter took up residence in my chest.

"He's not answering. Let's go."

We moved down the long hallway, weaving our way through people near the bathrooms. Finally, we were alone in the hallway and stopped by a group of stanchions that blocked off the side of the building under construction. There was no Dr. Ford anywhere in sight.

With a sigh, I turned around.

"Not here," I said so the others could hear. "Rudy, he might have gone into the banquet room by one of the other doors. Keep a look out. He's tall and thin, balding, with a blue bow tie."

"Will do," she replied.

"You, too, Aria."

"I'm looking," Aria said. "I'll let Goldie know."

"Let's go back," I said to José.

We retraced our steps to the main foyer, where I texted Blair. She appeared a few minutes later from the other direction.

"Any luck?"

"No," she replied, still scanning the crowd. "But the vendor hall is closed."

"I've got the others looking for him in the banquet hall." I turned to José. "Why don't you check the men's restroom? We'll wait here."

"I'll check both of them," he said, heading towards the vendor hall first.

My phone pinged with a text from David.

"Where are you?"

"Main entrance," I texted back.

"I'll be there right away."

While we waited, Blair and I searched faces in the crowd. People continued to stream in through the main entrance, past security and up to the registration tables to get their seat assignments. Since the main set of elevators sat near the front doors, many people were coming up from the underground garage.

"We have to find him," I murmured.

A moment later a familiar voice called out and David emerged from the crowd.

I rushed over to him. "Did you get my text?"

"Which one?" he said, a little out of breath.

"We think we know who Yoda is," I said in a lowered voice.

His brown eyes popped open. "No. Sorry. The group of protestors outside has grown, and a couple of fights broke out between the competing sides. It's getting ugly out there."

"Can they keep it under control?" Blair asked, coming up behind me.

"I think so. It's just one more thing for us to deal with, though. Anyway, what do you know?"

I explained the encounter with Dr. Ford and why we believed he was the man we sought.

"That's a stretch," he said.

"No, it's not. Besides, what else do we have?"

"And Ford shouldn't be here," Blair said. "He's not a conservative."

David pulled out his cell phone. "Okay, do you know what direction he went?"

I pointed down the hallway. "That way, but he's not down there. José and I just checked. He could have gone into the banquet room by the side door. We were just about to go in and look for him."

"Do you think he suspects anything?"

I shrugged. "Not from us. He and Blair just greeted each other, and then he left."

"What does he look like?"

I described him. Meanwhile, José returned from checking the men's rooms.

"He's not in either one," he reported. "I saw a couple of guys with blue bow ties. Just not your guy."

David nodded. "Okay, I'm going to report in to Detective Mankiewicz and the FBI. We'll see what we can find out about him. What's his first name?"

"Mark," Blair replied. "His office is in Seattle."

"Will you shut down the dinner?" I asked.

"Not until there's a clear and present danger. It looks like you may be the only chance we have of finding this Yoda character, though. That's as far as you go, though. I mean it. Find him and report in to me immediately. Don't go near him."

"Okay. I promise. And we'll stay together."

David left to find Detective Mankiewicz, while we headed for the banquet room. The second time we entered, Rudy and Doe met us. The room was full now, and the band blared out some Barry Manilow tune.

Most people were seated and the wait staff had begun to serve dinner. Yet, there were still long lines at the bars and people continued to mill about. After all, the room was filled with people with money, and the politicians were working them.

"Julia!" Goldie interrupted us. Her voice came through garbled on the ear wig. "I think I see…um, I think it's…*very, very* hot in here."

I had to think a minute. Hot…temperature…Monty! I reached out and grabbed Blair's arm. "Goldie thinks she sees Monty."

"Where are you, Goldie?" Rudy asked.

"Near the front bar…on the side…room with…band."

I scanned the other side of the room and found Goldie two-thirds of the way down the room, holding a tray.

"Where's Aria?"

"She…um, had a bit…digestive problem. She gave me…ear thing. I dropped…in a glass of wine, so…not working…good." She tapped her ear, sending claps of thunder through the coms.

"Goldie, stop that!" Rudy snapped, as we both cupped our ears in pain.

"Sorry. Anyway… over there," Goldie said, nodding to her left.

My gaze shifted toward the bar where a man in a tuxedo stood next to a heavy-set woman wearing a long-sleeved gold dress. The man was partially blocked.

"C'mon," I said to my group. "We need to get closer."

The five of us circled the room, coming up alongside the bar. The man Goldie ID'd was facing the room, staring at a spot in front of the podium. Senator Owens was seated at the table directly in front of the stage.

"I'm not sure that's him," Blair said in a whisper. "No beard. And he looks, I don't know, taller."

As if he'd heard her, the man turned and vanished into the bar crowd.

"Shoot!" I turned to my cohorts. "C'mon. We need to get up higher."

We weaved in and out among the throng of drinkers and hustled up the stairs behind the bar. We came out onto the second floor landing near the middle of the room.

Only a few people stood on the walkway watching the festivities below. We ignored them and spread out along the railing, scanning the room.

"Anyone see him?" I asked.

"No," Doe answered. "The room is just too damned big."

"Rudy, you and Doe stay here. Blair and I will move to the other side. José, stay with me."

"Okay," he said.

Blair, José, and I hurried to the other side of the balcony, scanning the room as we went.

"Do you see him?" Rudy asked when we got to the other side.

"No," I replied. "What about you, Goldie? Have you seen him again?"

"No," she responded, still sounding like she was under water. "What? Julia, I've ...go back to the kitchen. What should...do?"

"Um...go. Just slip away as soon as you can. Or find Aria."

I saw Goldie duck past some people as she headed for the side exit. We continued to watch the room as the band played on. A few seconds passed before Goldie came back on the com.

"Julia!" she whispered in a near panic. "I see a...in a blue bow tie!"

My heart leapt into my throat. "Where?"

"He's in the hallway...the kitchen."

"Goldie thinks Ford is down by the kitchen," I said to Blair. "We need to get down there."

"We're closer," Rudy said from across the room.

She turned and said something to Doe, who spun around and disappeared into the stairwell. "Doe is going to go take a look," Rudy said.

We continued to maintain our watch until Doe's voice came over the coms, "I've...Goldie's ear wig. She...go back to the kitchen. I don't see Ford."

"Okay, stay down there in case he comes back," Rudy told her. "Be careful."

"Okay," she warbled on the com.

"I'm texting David," I said.

I sent David a quick message telling him we thought Ford might be in the area near the kitchen and that we might have seen Monty in the banquet room.

A sudden scuffle at the hall entrance drew our attention that way. Two security guards wrestled with a man holding a large poster. Alarmed voices rose throughout that end of the room.

"What the heck is going on down there?" Rudy said from across the room.

"I think it's a protester," José said.

My phone pinged with another text from David. "*Are you okay?*"

"*Yes. What's going on at the entrance?*"

"*A protester got through security,*" he texted. "*I've sent some people back to the kitchen. I'll let you know.*"

I put my phone away, reported to the others and went back to surveying the room below.

"It's like looking for a needle in a haystack," Blair said next to me.

"Let's do it in sections," I suggested. "I'll take the front third by the entrance. José, you help Rudy take the middle? And Blair, you take the far end. Text me if you see anything."

"Got it," she replied, pulling out her phone.

"Okay," Rudy said into the earpiece.

Blair moved toward the stage end of the room. I meandered toward the main entrance, all the while scanning the area below. José stayed where he was.

As I made my way to the end of the second floor landing, I decided to map the room below me by tables, stopping to inspect each one.

My heart jumped when I got to a table near the entrance. I saw the side of a man's face that looked like it could be Roy. I reached into my purse and took out the small binoculars and zeroed in on my quarry.

"See anything?" Rudy asked from across the room.

I shook my head. "No. I thought it was Roy, but it's not him. Keep looking."

We searched for another ten or twelve minutes with no luck. As the wait staff began removing empty dinner plates and waitresses brought in large trays of desserts, my phone pinged. I looked down to see a text from David.

"Something's happening out front. Stay where you are."

"They're getting ready to serve dessert," Rudy warned over the coms. "That means the speeches will start soon."

"I know," I replied, looking up from my phone. "Where the heck is he?"

I was standing directly above the main entrance now. The entire room was visible below me. Blair was two-thirds of the way down the landing, parallel to the stage. The closed media center sat at the end of the second floor balcony.

As the dessert was served, I meandered back towards José. He was standing next to a pole set up to hold heavy stage lights. The metal casings had been angled to send beams of light down toward the stage. Four more lights hung from a bar in the ceiling in front of the stage. This left the area behind the stage completely dark.

The band stopped playing as a short, rotund man appeared on stage. Blair meandered back towards us as the little man began to speak. The microphone squealed, making people reach for their ears.

"Good evening, everyone. Thank you so much for coming. My name is Steven Colby. I'm governor of the great state of South Carolina," he announced to a rousing round of applause.

Blair thumped my arm. "Hey, look at the guy standing just behind the band. That could be Monty," she said, pointing to the edge of the stage.

I lifted my binoculars to peer at a big guy dressed in a tuxedo. The man was clean shaven, with dark brooding eyes. "I'm not sure. He's in the shadows, so it's hard to tell."

My cell phone pinged again. I checked my text.

"*Where are you?*" David asked.

"*Second floor balcony, looking down on the crowd,*" I quickly texted back.

"*Where's José?*"

"*With us.*"

"*Okay, stay put. There's a big conflict out front.*"

I put my phone back in my bag. "The protestors must be acting up outside. Where the heck is Aria?" I asked the group.

"She's back, but they put her to work again," Doe said. "I think the com is working better. It must've dried out. Should I stay down here?"

"Yes," Rudy said. "Just in case."

"That *is* Monty," Blair said, nudging me.

The man behind the band had moved into the light. I lifted the binoculars and felt the blood drain from my face. "Damn! You're right. He's just shaved off his beard."

"Wait!" Blair said, grabbing my arm. "Zero in on that waiter."

I did as she said. A waiter had just stepped past Monty, handing something off to him. Monty wrapped his fingers around whatever it was and slipped it inside his jacket.

"The waiter just passed him something." I followed the waiter with my binoculars. He was weaving his way through to the bar. "Damn! I think that's Roy."

"We need to let David know," Rudy said. She had begun to run around the end of the landing in our direction.

"Okay, take these," I said, handing José the binoculars. I dialed David this time.

"Franks," he answered out-of-breath.

"We see Monty," I said in a rush. "He's standing alone near the stage. He's shaved off his beard. And a waiter passed him something. The waiter might be Roy."

"Okay. We have agents in the room. I'll let them know. But, Julia, I just got a call from Mankiewicz. They found a waiter in a closet. He's dead."

"Oh, my God," I murmured. "Roy must have killed him to get the uniform."

"Listen, I've got to find Mankiewicz and Agent Peters. He's the FBI agent in charge. I think it's time to get Senator Owens out of there."

"What about Monty?" I asked in a panic. "Can you get him?" I leaned over to José. He had the binoculars up. "Where's that waiter?"

"Behind the bar," he said.

I told David.

"Okay, I'll let the agents in the room know. It'll take me a minute to talk to the others, and then I'll get back inside and find you. Keep an eye on those guys."

I hung up, feeling my heart pound wildly in my chest.

"They found a dead waiter in a closet," I said to my friends.

Even José reacted with surprise. "Shit, I hope David gets here soon."

"What are we supposed to do?" Blair asked.

"David said they'll be coming in to take Senator Owens out. We're supposed to keep an eye on Monty and Roy."

Governor Colby had just introduced Senator Owens. Applause filled the room as Owens rose from his chair and headed for the podium. Two security officers accompanied him, remaining on either side of the stage. Four more men in suits stood against either wall with hands clasped in front of them. I noticed one put his hand to his ear, listening to someone.

The side door opened and Detective Mankiewicz approached one of the agents. He whispered to him. They nodded toward the bar.

As Senator Owens approached the podium, Governor Colby shook his hand. Owens stepped to the microphone.

"Thank you. Thank you," he said, tamping down the applause with his raised hands.

"We have to do something!" I said. "Owens is a sitting duck up there."

"But...what?" Rudy asked in a near panic.

As Owens thanked members of the Republican National Committee, there was another commotion, this time on the far side of the room by the bar.

"It's Roy," José said, looking through the binoculars. "Detective Mankiewicz took him out."

"One down," I murmured, watching a couple of agents begin to move toward the band.

"That Monty guy is gone," José said, shifting the binoculars to the band. He gestured to the spot on the other side of the room.

He was right. Monty had disappeared.

"Back there!" Blair said, pointing behind the stage.

There was empty space behind the stage, except for the lone shadow of a man moving behind the rice paper panels.

I called David again.

"Monty has gone behind the stage," I whispered into the phone. "There's no one back there, and Owens is on stage. Where are you?"

"I'm on my way," David said, huffing and puffing. "Mankiewicz got Roy out. He's coming back with a couple of officers to get Owens."

"What do we do?" I asked, feeling an overwhelming anxiety. "Monty is still in the room."

"Anything. Cause a ruckus," David shot back.

"But we're upstairs."

"Scream. Yell. Anything!" he ordered.

I was stunned by his commanding voice. "Um...okay," I murmured, hanging up. "David said to cause a ruckus."

The dark figure of Monty leapt onto the back of the stage. Only the rice paper screens stood between him and Senator Owens.

"What do we do?" Rudy asked urgently.

The side door opened and Detective Mankiewicz re-entered the room with two officers. Owens was droning with a bunch of platitudes about working on behalf of the American people until his microphone crackled and went dead, cutting him off mid-sentence. He tapped the mike, looking around for help. Governor Colby began to make his way back onstage.

"What's going on?" José asked.

A man's voice booming out over the PA system stopped everything.

"Don't bother trying to fix your mike, Senator. Like you, it's just a piece of shit."

Governor Colby paused. Owens looked behind him and then above him in confusion. People shifted in their seats, mumbling. Detective Mankiewicz was halfway to the stage when the main doors opened and David hurried in.

"Everyone stop where you are!" the voice said. "If anyone moves or approaches the stage, Senator Owens will die."

David skidded to a halt, his hand reaching for his weapon. Detective Mankiewicz paused. The room went silent, as my heart leapt into my throat.

"I tried to make you a deal, Senator," the voice went on. "Come clean, I said, and I wouldn't harm your daughter. But you wouldn't. You wouldn't even help your own daughter. All you care about is power and influence."

A very nervous-looking Owens began to leave the stage.

"Stop where you are, Senator! I mean it."

Owens paused at the edge of the stage.

"You may want to hear this," the voice continued.

There was a brief pause before a young girl's voice crackled over the PA system. "I want to go home. Why won't you let me go home?"

It was Amy's voice.

Owens reacted as if he'd been electrocuted. "You bastard!" he shouted to the ceiling.

"You're so righteous. But now you have only seconds, Senator," the voice said.

I turned to Blair. "Is that Ford?"

She was glancing around, as if trying to find the voice. "Yes, that's him. But where is he?"

"Well, he doesn't know Amy is safe," I whispered. "But we have to do something. Now!"

"I can swing down and knock Monty out of the way," Blair said, gesturing to the fabric draped from the chandelier to the railing. She reached over and began to unravel the fabric rose.

"God, is that the only way?"

"Do you have anything better?" she said, quickly pulling the fabric free.

"Wait, I'll take care of Monty," José said. "You guys get Owens." Without waiting, he turned and ran for the stairs.

Rudy put her hand on Blair's arm. "I have better aim, Blair. You know I do. I'm also lighter. C'mon, help me onto the railing."

Blair hesitated, and then handed Rudy the loosened band of chiffon. Rudy wrapped it tightly around each one of her wrists and then grabbed it in her hands. Blair leaned down to give her a boost. When Rudy stepped onto the railing, she teetered.

"Careful," I snapped, reaching out to steady her.

Rudy grabbed onto the light pole for balance and pulled the chiffon taught between her and the chandelier.

"Are you ready to confess, Senator?" the voice continued over the PA system. "About that night in Florida? About your fraternity pledges and the lake? Think carefully before you answer. *Your* life and your daughter's depend on it."

The adrenalin was thrumming through my veins. *How were we going to stop this?* I glanced at the banquet room below. Ford seemed to be able to see people in the room and what they were doing. *Could he see us on the second floor?*

I looked toward Monty, who was at the back of the screen now, his right arm crooked and his hand at his waist. He was pointing something at Owens' back.

"Hurry, Rudy! I think Monty has a gun!"

I looked helplessly at David, who was inching his way towards the stage.

"Remember, Senator, it's not your daughter I want to hurt," the voice said. "It's you. You're a bully. People have died because of you. It's time to come clean. I'll count to three. That's all I'll give you. Confess to the world…or you die. It's that simple. One…"

Owens shifted back and forth on the stage, unsure of what to do.

"Go, Rudy!" Blair almost yelled.

"Two," the voice said. "It's now or never, Senator."

Rudy took a deep breath and stepped off the railing as the voice said, "I'm sorry, senator. Three."

Time seemed to slow to a crawl as everything happened at once.

A door opened behind the stage, and José burst through, distracting Monty.

Rudy swung in a wide arc towards Owens as a woman in the crowd screamed. The chandelier jerked and rattled, and people pointed to the little Tarzan whizzing down toward the senator.

As José ran for the stage, Monty whirled back with the gun pointed at the senator.

Owens glanced up just as Rudy slammed into him, throwing him off the stage. She swung through, crashing into the drum set, clipping the shoulder of a band member and then swinging back to land in a tangled pile of music stands and chairs.

José leapt onto the stage and threw Monty down as his gun went off.

Detective Mankiewicz and the two security guards descended upon Owens to shelter him.

I caught David's eye and pointed behind the stage, yelling, "Monty!"

He rushed in that direction as people screamed and ran for the exits.

I turned for the stairs, but stopped when I noticed Blair searching the underside of the railing.

"C'mon," I yelled at her. "Let's go!"

"Wait!" Blair said, grabbing my arm. "I know where Ford is." She pointed to a camera bolted underneath the railing. "That's how he can see everything." She turned to the far end of mezzanine level. "He's in the media center."

I glanced that way. All the blinds were closed. A small light glinted behind the blinds.

"Oh, my God."

Blair kicked off her heels and ran. I followed. We got there just as the door opened and Dr. Ford poked his head out.

"Mark!" Blair yelled.

He swung his head in our direction and quickly retreated inside, slamming the door. The sound of a lock made us stop.

"There's a back door," Blair yelled. "I'll go after him. You cut him off if he comes back this way." She pointed to the hallway in front of me.

Blair ran past the front of the media center and turned down a parallel hallway. I took a moment to say into the earpiece, "Doe, tell David that Ford is heading toward the rear staircase. Blair's trying to cut him off."

I began to run. In my panic, my foot caught on the carpet. I stumbled and fell. *Damn!* Slightly stunned, I got back up and set out again, holding my ribs.

In the background, the sound of chaos and panic in the banquet room continued, and I could barely hear Doe's voice over the com in my ear. I came to the end of the hallway and stopped short, breathing heavily.

Dr. Ford stood at the head of a set of double stairs and an escalator with a gun pointed at Blair.

"I don't want to hurt you, Mrs. Wentworth," he said.

"What's this all about, Mark? Why are you doing this?"

"It doesn't matter anymore," he said in defeat. "Owens has gotten away with it for thirty years. Just like he gets away with everything."

Blair's eyes flicked in my direction and back again. "But what in the world is worth killing a young girl over?" She inched toward the balcony railing, making him turn towards her and away from me.

"The death of my little brother. The man is a monster. He can't have more power in this country."

I tip-toed out of the hallway and moved quietly up behind him.

"What about your wife? Who will take care of her?"

I noticed the gun begin to shake. I circled to my right, coming within inches of Ford's right shoulder.

"My wife died over two months ago," he said, choking back a sob. "I've lost everyone I love. And I invested everything I have into getting Owens. Nothing matters anymore."

A strong, sweaty hand grabbed me around my neck.

"Aaaargh!" I screeched, struggling to get away.

Ford spun around. Blair started forward, but he quickly stepped back so he could see both of us at the same time. He pointed the gun at her again. "Don't."

I smelled a blend of alcohol and cigarette smoke from the man behind me. His fingers dug into my flesh. I suspected it was Monty. He must have come up the side stairwell.

"Let's take them with us," Monty said. "It'll be good insurance."

Ford jerked the gun toward the elevator behind Blair. "Hit the button."

I was pushed forward as the man jabbed me in the back with what I assumed was another gun. Blair frowned and punched the elevator button.

When the doors opened, I was shoved inside and slammed against the wall. I turned to find the dark, hateful eyes of Monty staring down at me. His bad eye was bruised and swollen shut.

José!

"I don't like busybodies," he growled at me, his breath nearly knocking me over.

Ford forced Blair inside just before the doors closed. He hit the first floor button, and the elevator jerked as it began to descend. For five seconds, the air inside the elevator was thick with tension.

Ding!

I jumped when the elevator hit the ground floor and the doors opened. Ford poked his head out and looked both ways.

My mind was whirring. I remembered from the floor plans that this elevator was next to an exit that opened onto the construction site. Because of that, there was no one around. This exit had been blocked off, and everyone had run for exits that opened onto the street or to the garage.

Ford had planned well.

"Move," he ordered us.

I reached up to my ear, hoping I could say something to alert Rudy, but my ear wig was gone. Blair stepped out of the elevator first, with Ford right behind her. Monty took the opportunity to grab my upper arm and drag me out, twisting my arm mercilessly.

"Don't try anything funny," he said with the gun now pointed at my face.

We stepped to the left where a glass door led outside.

"Open the door," Ford told Blair.

When she did, he pushed her out and then followed. As Monty shoved me forward, I saw José running down the hall in our direction.

Monty didn't notice and shoved me out the door into the darkened construction zone. There was a van parked a few feet from the exit. The van had a construction company placard on the side. Ford had already thrown open the rear doors and was forcing Blair inside in her bare feet.

I stumbled forward over the uneven ground just as José flew out the exit door and launched himself at Monty again, landing a roundhouse kick at his hip. Monty went down on one knee, almost losing the gun. José was winding up for a second assault when Ford grabbed my blouse and yanked me to the back of the van with the gun pointed at my head.

"Enough!" he bellowed.

José stopped mid-kick, steadied himself, and turned to us, his face flushed.

"I'll kill her," Ford said. "I don't care if she is the governor's wife."

"Ex-wife," I choked out.

Ford twisted the fabric of my blouse even tighter, almost cutting off my breath.

"Get in," he said to José, waving the gun towards the interior of the van. "You just became more collateral."

Monty got to his feet. José gave me an apologetic look and shot a hateful stare at Monty.

Ford let me go and pushed me inside the van. I banged my knee on the way in, but then scooted back next to Blair, who was seated on a long, metal tool box. José jumped in and sat on the floor near the cab.

"I'll ride back here," Ford said to Monty. "You drive. Where's your friend?"

"Police got him."

Ford cringed. "Okay. He's on his own. But we need a new car."

Monty nodded. "I know a guy."

"There can't be any questions," Ford said, nodding toward the three of us.

"There won't be."

Ford climbed in with us, while Monty closed the doors and walked around and got into the driver's seat.

"Don't worry, this will be over soon," Ford said to us.

Pressure built in the pit of my stomach. Somehow that didn't sound so good.

Ford held the gun on us while he searched through a bag of trash in the back of the van. He pulled out a handful of rags.

"Turn around," he said to José.

José flinched forward, as if to attack.

"Stop!" Monty called out from the front of the van. He had his gun pointed at José. "Just do as he says."

Ford tied José's hands behind his back first, then mine, and then Blair's. He had two rags left. They were crusty with paint, but he used them to gag me and Blair.

While Ford did that, Monty used his phone to make a call. All we heard him say was, "We need a ride," and, "Okay."

Once we were secured, Monty started the engine and pulled the van out of the construction site onto a street behind the convention center. The three of us rocked back and forth as the van rumbled along under the street lights.

Silence fell inside the vehicle. We drove for five or six minutes, made a few turns, and entered a bad part of town where neon signs for bars and nude dancers flashed through the front windows. When we turned into an alley, darkness shrouded the interior, casting everyone inside in shadow.

Monty slowed and then stopped.

"We're here," he said as he killed the engine. "Give me a minute."

He left the van and disappeared from view. We heard a door open and then voices. A minute later, Monty was back.

"We're good."

The grinding sound of a motor broke the silence, as a big, metal roll-up door set into the brick wall next to us began to move. We couldn't see much from where we were, but Monty started the engine and backed the van through the opening.

He stopped the vehicle with a jerk and turned to Ford. "Okay, now we negotiate."

CHAPTER THIRTY

Ford looked at us. "Be good, and you could still get out of this alive tonight."

He opened the back door to the van and got out, closing the door behind him.

José got up and looked through the front window. His sharp new suit was dirty and the pocket was ripped. He emitted a low chuckle.

"Hang tight. We may be okay."

He turned to the back doors. A moment later, one of the doors opened. The face that stared in at us made me gasp. It was the guy with the angel tattoo spread across his neck–the one who said I looked like his fourth-grade teacher. His eyes opened in surprise when he recognized us.

"*Van a matarnos,*" José mumbled to him.

He nodded to José. "*Qué ha pasado?*"

"*Hombres muy malos,*" José replied.

The young man nodded again.

I glanced at Blair with a look of hope.

"Angel!" someone yelled.

"*Buena suerte,*" the young man murmured. He reached into his pocket and tossed something into the van. Then he closed the door.

Angel. His name matched his tattoo.

I glanced at the dirty floor, where a small knife now lay.

José turned and leaned back to draw the knife into his fingers. As he worked to slip it under the rag tied around his wrists, I peeked through the front window.

To the right of the van, Ford and Monty negotiated with our old friend, Shaved Head Guy, and the guy who held the baseball bat. The guy who wore the baseball cap backwards stood in the background.

We were in a large garage. Overhead lights illuminated a variety of cars parked against the far wall. Ford was eyeing a single car, a black Cadillac.

Damn!

It was the car we had stolen from the hotel and then had stolen from us. For someone who didn't believe in coincidences, I was beginning to reconsider.

I glanced back to José. He was working furiously at slicing through the rag that bound him. His hands suddenly popped apart.

"Turn around," he whispered.

I turned my back to him and he released me. Blair murmured something through her rag, and I released her. We both rubbed our wrists.

"Ugh," I said as I yanked the gag out of my mouth and wiped my lips. "Now what?"

"Just follow me and be quiet."

José carefully opened one of the back doors and swung it wide. A brick wall greeted us.

We slithered quietly out of the van, crouching low. Blair and I followed José around the back of the vehicle, which had been parked right next to a tool-laden work bench.

As we snuck along the side of the van, Angel appeared and we stopped. He glanced our way and gave a quick shake of his head.

We waited, hunched over and hugging the van.

Angel faced the rest of the garage. He casually crossed his arms over his chest as he listened and watched whatever Ford and Monty were doing with the other gang members.

While we waited, someone started a car engine and a yellow hot rod pulled up in front of the van. The loud engine was killed, and we heard the car's door open and close as our lungs filled with exhaust fumes.

Angel remained where he was and then dropped his right hand to gesture to us. We began to move. When José reached the front of the van, he paused.

There was a two foot space between the van and the hot rod.

He glanced up at Angel.

Angel stepped into the space, blocking us from view and prompting José to move again.

The three of us crab-walked past the opening. As soon as we passed, Angel began talking and moved back to his friends.

My heart was pounding now. We made it to the rear of the hot rod. The alley and freedom were only a few feet away. *Now what?*

"Stop!"

We froze. My breath caught.

Monty came up behind us. "Stand up."

We straightened up, and I snuck a peek at Monty. He held a gun. Ford and the rest of the gang members faced us from the other side of the car. Shaved Head Guy showed mild surprise when we appeared on the other side of the hot rod. He turned to Angel, who gave a slight shrug.

"How the hell did you get out?" Monty snarled.

"Doesn't matter," Ford said from across the room. "Bring them over here."

Monty stuck the gun in my back. "Get going, Grandma."

I saw Angel flinch, and a scowl covered his face.

Monty pushed us around the back of the car and over to Ford.

Ford turned to Shaved Head Guy. "We'll take the Cadillac."

"Hey, man, that's not a trade," Shaved Head Guy said. He jerked his head toward the van. "That's a piece of junk." He turned toward us. "If you take the Caddy, we want her, too," he said, nodding toward Blair.

"And I'll take her," Angel said, pointing to me.

"No," Ford said. "They're not part of the deal. Get them into the caddy," Ford told Monty, pulling his gun from his waistband.

Shaved Head Guy reacted with lightning speed. His hand shot out with a gun pointed at Ford, and there was a chorus of clicking noises as guns appeared in the hands of the rest of the gang members—including Angel.

I felt dizzy and a little bit nauseous.

Ford glanced around at the weaponry. "Looks like it's a standoff."

"You better not stiff us," Shaved Head Guy said to Monty. "We negotiated in good faith."

Monty hesitated and then turned to Ford. "You got any money to sweeten the deal?"

Ford paused and then looked at Shaved Head Guy. "Sure. We'll make this right. Hold on. Watch them," he said to Monty, meaning us.

He put his gun on a rolling tool cabinet and began to search his inside pocket for his wallet.

It was José's cue to act.

He was standing next to Monty and straight-armed his fist into Monty's temple. The beefy guy collapsed to the floor. José grabbed his gun.

Before Ford could react, Angel jumped forward and retrieved Ford's gun from the tool cabinet. Ford didn't miss a beat, though. He reached out and grabbed me, spinning me around and putting me into a choke hold, nearly cutting off my air supply.

"Stop!" he yelled. "I'll break her neck. I swear I will."

Everyone stopped. My eyes met Blair's. She gave me a reassuring nod.

And so I moved.

I took the biggest breath I could, tucked in my chin, bent forward and whipped my left foot around Ford's right leg. My head popped out of his grasp. I yanked his arm back and came up hard with my knee aimed at his...well, damn, I missed. Again.

Ford crumpled to the floor, grabbing his crotch.

Angel burst out in laughter. "Don't mess with Mrs. Muñoz," he chided.

I gave him a smile as I adjusted my blond wig.

Shaved Head Guy turned to José and nodded. "You want us to dispose of these guys for you?"

José looked at me, while Ford continued to rock back and forth in agony on the floor next to Monty.

"No. I'll call the police," I said, reaching for my phone.

"Wait!" Shaved Head Guy said. He gestured to the garage. "This our home. Our business."

"We should take them with us, anyway," Blair said. "I think there are a few law enforcement agencies who would like to talk to them."

"We'll need the van," Jose said to Shaved Head Guy.

"No problem. Emilio," he said to the man holding the baseball bat. Shaved Head Guy jerked his head to the right. "*Encontrar algo a la vez para arriba.*"

Emilio went to the wall work bench and pulled out a roll of electrical tape. He came back and tossed it to José.

José forced Monty's hands behind his back and wrapped them tightly before pulling him to his feet. He was awake now, but unsteady.

By this time, Ford was sitting on his heels taking deep breaths. José tossed the tape to Blair, who wrapped his hands as well.

"Get up," Blair told him.

Ford got painfully to his feet, and José and Angel perp-walked the two men to the back of the van.

I turned to Shaved Head Guy. "Thank you. You have no idea the good you just did. These guys abducted and drugged a young girl and were going to kill a U.S. senator."

He turned to his friends with open arms. "*Felicitaciones amigos*," he said with a broad grin. "*Somos heroes!*" They shared a hearty laugh, and then he turned to me, his amused expression lingering. "But we also saved a compadre's business. No?"

His eyes traveled to Blair, who looked a little more like a street walker after our ordeal. Mussed-up hair. One shoulder exposed. A tear in the hem of her very short red-sequined dress.

She gave Shaved Head Guy a seductive wink.

"Oh, that," I said.

"*Slavery still exists, but now it applies only to women, and its name is prostitution,*" he said under his breath.

"Excuse me? Was…that a…quote?"

He grinned, his eyes twinkling beneath all those tattoos.

"Victor Hugo," he said simply.

"Well, I'll be damned."

"C'mon. Let's go," José called out from the van. "I'll ride in back."

I turned back to Shaved Head Guy and extended my hand. "I'm surprised to find a gentleman on the back streets of Chicago." He took my hand in his. It was rough with callouses. "What's your given name?"

"Benito," he replied. "It means blessed. Do you bless me, little lady?"

I smiled. "I don't have the power to bless anyone, Benito. But *we* were certainly blessed to meet you tonight."

CHAPTER THIRTY-ONE

While José guarded Ford and Monty in the back of the van and Blair drove, I called David and told him we were safe. We arrived back at the conference center to find the protestors had dispersed. There was a police barricade, but we were allowed through.

We parked at the front of the building. Detective Mankiewicz and David rushed down the steps to meet us. As I climbed out of the van, David wrapped me in a quick hug.

"God, I'm glad you're okay," he murmured in my ear. He gave me a squeeze and said, "C'mon."

We joined the others behind the van. José had just emerged through the back doors, handing off Monty's gun to Detective Mankiewicz.

"Is one of these guys Yoda?" Detective Mankiewicz asked.

"Yes," Blair said, pointing to Dr. Ford. "Meet my dentist, Dr. Mark Ford, a.k.a Yoda."

Detective Mankiewicz waved to two police officers standing at the curb.

"Take these two into custody. Murder and kidnapping. Read 'em their rights."

The officers removed our prisoners from the van and took them away. Detective Mankiewicz turned to us, but David put up a hand.

"Look, detective, these women have been through a lot. I think we need to let them clean up and get some rest. We can talk to them in the morning."

He looked back and forth between us. "Okay, but I'm just curious, how were you able to get these guys?"

"Um…actually, José disarmed Monty," I said.

"And Julia took care of Ford," Blair added.

"What?" David asked. "How?"

"Oh, he grabbed me around the neck, and then I...here, let me show you," I said, reaching for David's arm.

"No!" Blair and José said in unison.

David turned to me. "What did that mean?"

I started to laugh. "Let's just say that Dr. Ford won't be fathering children anytime soon."

Detective Mankiewicz smiled and shook his head. "Amazing."

"C'mon, I'll take you back to the hotel," David said.

An officer brought up an unmarked police car, and the four of us piled in. As we began to pull away from the curb, I asked, "By the way, how's Rudy? I couldn't see what happened to her after she kicked Owens off the stage."

David was riding shotgun and took a deep sigh. "She's in the hospital."

"What?" I said, almost coming out of my seat.

"What happened?" Blair asked, leaning forward.

"She hurt her back and one of her knees. She'll be okay, but they wanted to keep her in the hospital overnight."

"Take us to the hospital," I demanded.

"No, Julia. I talked to Doe as soon as you called. They gave Rudy some painkillers. She's asleep. Doe wants you to go back to the hotel."

I sat back again. "Rudy is one brave woman."

"No kidding," Blair agreed. "I may not be able to tease her so much anymore. By the way, what happened to Senator Owens?"

David turned around from the front seat. "He was ushered out of the banquet room and taken to the police station, where he threatened to sue all of us the moment he learned we hadn't told him Amy had been found two days ago."

I shrugged. "Well, you can hardly blame him."

"That's okay," David said with a smug smile. "The FBI is considering charges against him for obstructing justice. Turns out that Ford contacted Owens at least twice, offering to release Amy if he would just go public with the role he played in the death of one Eric Ford during college. He never told Owens who he was, but at least Owens knew why she'd been abducted and should have had a pretty good idea who took her. And yet he stayed silent, which got a couple of people killed. I don't think he'll be suing anyone."

"What about that ransom note?" José asked.

"It was Owens' assistant, you know, the one he was going to fire?" he said to me. "It was her and her militia boyfriend who sent it. They'd heard about the abduction when they were camping and thought they could cash in on it."

"Jeez," I exclaimed. "What a bunch of crazy people out there. And Dylan? Was he ever here in Chicago?"

"No. Amy was pretty vulnerable. She must have seen someone that looked like him."

When we arrived at the hotel, David insisted on walking me to our room and said goodnight with a long, warm kiss.

"I'll talk to you in the morning," he said. "Be prepared to tell us the whole story, though."

I smiled sweetly. "Don't I always?"

÷

The next morning, we called the hospital to check on Rudy. She would be released at noon.

Aria and Goldie decided to catch the last few hours of the genealogy conference, so José joined Doe, Blair, and me for breakfast at our hotel. We took the time to craft a story for the police that avoided any mention of the Cadillac, car theft, or Benito's chop shop.

Amy and her parents met us in the lobby afterwards. Amy rushed up to me and threw her arms around my neck.

"Thank you," she gushed.

I stood back, holding her at arms-length. "We were happy to do it."

"Well, maybe not *happy*," Blair said with a brief smile.

Amy threw her arms around Blair, too, catching her by surprise.

Trina Dunphy stepped forward and placed her arm around her daughter's shoulders.

"We owe you all so much. I don't know what we would have done if we'd lost her."

Amy began to tear up. "It's okay now, Mom."

Grant Dunphy remained in the background. He snuck glances at Amy, a look of remorse on his face.

"Have you seen your father?" Doe asked. "He must be thrilled you're okay."

Amy's bright expression fell. "Um…no. He had to go back to D.C. He called me, though," she said, attempting to regain her enthusiasm.

Her mother's face was drawn with restrained anger. "Jim doesn't have time for anything but politics."

"That's okay, Mom," Amy said, grabbing her mother's hand. "I have you."

"And me," Grant Dunphy said, stepping forward. He put his arm on Amy's shoulder.

Amy smiled and put her hand over his.

"When are you heading home?" Doe asked, bringing everyone's attention back.

"This afternoon," Trina answered. "We're going to enjoy the rest of the summer before Amy goes off to college."

"No, Mom," Amy said, glancing at me and then back at her mother. "I've changed my mind. I'm going to take a year off. Then I'll apply to the U Dub."

She was referring to the University of Washington, bringing a broad grin to her mother's face.

"I'd love that," Trina said.

"Maybe we can get that new waterbed you wanted," her stepdad said, giving her shoulders a squeeze.

He was making an effort to connect with his stepdaughter.

"Really? Wow, thanks." She gave her step-dad a hug.

"Well, we'd better get going," Trina said. "Thank you again."

We watched the three of them leave and then I said, "Well, we need to go pack."

"I have an errand to run," Blair said. "I'll catch up with you later at the police department."

José went back to his hotel to pack, while Doe and I returned to our rooms to pull our things together. Then we all met Blair about an hour and a half later when we met to debrief with Detective Mankiewicz and David.

It was Detective Mankiewicz who grilled us. When we finished, we wrote down our version of events and left. David and I had already discussed staying until Monday, so he remained behind to help Detective Mankiewicz write up reports and wrap up the investigation.

Just before noon, we stopped by Aria and Goldie's hotel to say goodbye. They were back from the conference and were getting ready to head back to Mercer Island with all of Aria's spy gear.

"Aria, you were a great help," I told her. "Thank you."

Her bushy eyebrows clenched in the middle, as if she were confused by my comment. "We were glad to help. If you'd like, you guys could join me on one of the spy weekends."

"Oh," I said, surprised. "Well, maybe. Thanks," I said, thinking that was the last thing I'd ever do.

Blair gave a fake cough and said, "You guys drive carefully, now. No running motorcyclists off the road."

Aria gave her a dirty look, but Goldie chuckled.

"Good one, Blair."

We waved goodbye to them and caught a cab to the hospital. José waited in the hallway, while we went into Rudy's room. A nurse was just getting her out of bed when we walked in.

"Oh, my," I said at the sight of her.

She was covered in bruises.

"It looks worse than it is," she said, groaning as she swung her legs over the edge of the bed.

Doe had brought a change of clothes, so the nurse let us help Rudy get dressed. It wasn't easy. She was stiff and winced every time she moved an arm or leg. Once we had her safely tucked into the wheelchair, Blair produced a gift.

"This is for you," she said, handing it to Rudy.

Rudy gave her a suspicious look. "What is it? A bomb?"

"Of course not," Blair said with a furrowed brow. "Although, I might think of you now as the *bomb*. I think you're my new hero. What you did was pretty awesome, Rudy." When Rudy didn't say anything, Blair added, "I mean it. You saved a U.S. senator. Even if we do all hate the guy."

Everyone laughed.

Rudy ripped off the wrapping to reveal an old book with a leather cover and a slightly torn spine. Her small brown eyes lit up.

"Oh, my God. Blair...thank you." She glanced up, her eyes filled with tears.

"What is it?" Doe said, stepping around so she could read the book title. "Oh, dear, it's a first edition of *Little Women*."

I put my arm around Blair's waist and leaned into her. "No, Blair, you're the bomb."

÷

As I finish this story, I'm reminded once more of just how much my friends mean to me. I've always loved them for their charitable works, their intellect and curiosity, their humor and now, their bravery. Our friendship had withstood the road trip from hell. We would return home to pick up where we left off, although a little worse for wear.

We loaded Rudy into a taxi with José and sent them to the airport where they would fly home to Mercer Island. Blair, Doe, and I shared an early dinner, and then Doe rented a car and left for Wisconsin to pick up Tinker Bell and fly home the next morning. She also carried a copy of the police report to give to Nathan Aberdeen for his insurance company.

Blair would move to another hotel to meet Mr. Billings and attend the import car show, which began on Wednesday. I accompanied her to the lobby, where I gave her a hug.

"So you're staying over to spend some time with David," she said. "I hope that goes well. I worry about your relationship when you get involved in these murder investigations. It's got to be tough on him."

"I know," I said with a sigh. "Every day I wonder if he'll just finally say 'enough' and hang it up. I guess I'll just have to enjoy him while I can." I squeezed her hand. "Enjoy your time with Mr. Billings, too. You're lucky, you know. He adores you."

"All my husbands adore me," she said with a twinkle in her eye.

"Yes, they do," I said with a chuckle. "Yes, they do."

CHAPTER THIRTY-TWO

On Monday, David and I attended a charity game at Wrigley Field. It was an annual softball game between Chicago's police and fire unions. Proceeds would go to the local children's hospital.

David was proud to show off the iconic ballpark, with its ivy-covered infield walls. And the weather cooperated with cooler temperatures and less humidity.

"Is Detective Mankiewicz playing today?" I asked, as we settled into our seats with Cokes and hot dogs.

"Yes. He says he never misses it. There he is," David said. He pointed to the dark-haired officer who was just entering the field.

We were sitting above one of the dugouts. There were perhaps six hundred people in attendance, including lots of children. Since I hadn't seen David the night before, I hoped to gain a little more information about Dr. Ford and his motivations as the players warmed up.

"Did you learn any more from Dr. Ford?"

No one sat next to us, so David could speak freely.

"He was pretty forthcoming. His wife died a couple of months ago, so he thought he had nothing to lose by going after Owens after all these years."

"He told Blair something about Owens killing his brother."

"His younger brother, Eric, died in a swimming accident in Florida many years ago. Owens was president of the fraternity that Eric pledged. He was the ringleader of a group of frat boys that forced a group of pledges down to the lake late one night, made them strip and then threw them in. Eric Ford was terrified of the water. He almost drowned when he was young and only survived because big brother Mark saved him."

"And Mark wasn't there for him that time," I said with sadness.

"No. And Ford has never forgiven himself. I guess Eric was a sickly kid. He got bullied a lot in school. Mark looked out for him. He was devastated when Eric died. The only reason Eric joined the fraternity was because Mark had belonged to it.

"So he blamed himself?"

"Yes. Hazing was common back then, but there weren't any real consequences. Owens and a couple of other boys were kicked out of the fraternity, but not the school. His father had been a trustee, so he was pretty safe. And no one paid a price for Eric's death."

I sighed and slumped back in my seat. "That's what Dr. Ford meant when he told Blair that Owens got away with something thirty years ago, just like he gets away with everything else. Sad when you think about it."

David turned to me, his brown eyes narrowed. "Ford's a criminal, Julia. He abducted a young girl and was willing to have her killed. And he was willing to assassinate a sitting U.S. senator. He deserves to go away for a very long time."

"I know. Guess I'll be looking for a different dentist, though," I said, touching my broken tooth with my tongue. "Speaking of, how in the world did a family dentist get hooked up with thugs like Roy and Monty?"

"He hired them," David said, taking a bite of his hot dog.

"Like from Craigslist or something?"

"No," he said swallowing. "He did a lot of volunteer dentistry for the local jails."

My eyebrows arched. "Wow. Good source of professional help when you need it."

"Guess so."

"What did you learn about Eva and Ponytail Guy?"

"They were brother and sister. She met Monty McLaughlin at a club, and they began dating. He recruited her to administer the drugs because she was a nurse."

"Wow. Brother and sister. I didn't catch that one."

"Roy is Roy Powers. They were no dummies. That motorhome we found in the ravine had the old man's license plates on it, but when they pulled it out, it was a different motorhome. Anyway, Ford initially offered them a hundred thousand each. When he couldn't convince Owens to go public with what happened to his brother, he upped the ante to half a million each."

"Where'd he get that kind of money?"

"A huge life insurance policy on his wife."

"How did they get into the building with all that security?"

"Ford was in Chicago for almost two weeks planning this," David said. "He got his hands on the building plans and scoped out the construction site. When McLaughlin and Powers got to town, he was ready with construction clothes, work belts, and that van with the placard on the side. The two men drove onto the site Saturday afternoon...remember it was the weekend, so no one was there...and then got access to the building through the duct work for the new HVAC system. Once they were inside the new addition, it wasn't difficult to get into the main building. Ford also attended a small event at the hotel last week. He found a supply closet and got the door open using some of his dental tools."

"The man is smart. You'll have to give him that."

"Yep. He planted clothes just in case the abduction didn't work. McLaughlin got a tuxedo and a fake Republican National Committee ID tag, and Powers got a fake security uniform with a gun."

"I wonder why they killed the waiter, then."

"Maybe it was the one flaw in the plan. Powers was supposed to pass the gun to McLaughlin so he could kill Owens. I suppose he thought it wouldn't attract as much attention if a waiter did it. On the other hand, it sounds like Powers just likes killing people."

"What was he in prison for?"

David turned to me with a grim expression. "Murder."

"Jeez. Then I feel lucky none of us were hurt. What happens to Owens now?"

A couple shuffled into the seats in front of us. David leaned into me and lowered his voice.

"If Owens went to trial for what happened in Florida, it would be for involuntary manslaughter. The average statute of limitations for manslaughter is only two to four years, though."

"So he gets away with it?"

He shrugged. "The law isn't perfect."

I sighed. "I can understand why Dr. Ford was so frustrated."

"Julia, he decided to take the law into his own hands, and several people have now lost their lives, including an innocent kid who worked part-time as a waiter for the conference center."

I blushed with embarrassment. "I know. It just all seems so unfair."

He reached out and grabbed my hand. "Life isn't fair, but that's one of the things I like about you, Julia. You try to see all sides. I just don't think Ford deserves it. I also don't think Owens will get off scot-free, though."

"What do you mean?"

The players had taken the field and were getting in position to start the game.

"Not only is the FBI considering charging him with obstruction of justice, several investigative journalists are heading to Florida to dig into every inch of his background. His life is about to become a living hell, and I doubt he has a future as a Presidential candidate. Poetic justice for a bully."

"I'm just glad Blair remembered there was a back door to the media center. Otherwise, Ford would have gotten away."

David laughed. "She *is* a surprise…on so many levels. I have to admit that the talents you all bring to these investigations boggles the mind." He chuckled again.

I eyed him curiously. "Was that a compliment?"

He smiled. "Yes. For four women of a certain age, you're not just talented, you're creative. I never would have thought of swinging down from the second floor to save Owens."

"You told me to cause a ruckus."

"Yes, I did. And you did so with flying colors, literally." He laughed at his own joke.

"So do the girls and I need to go back to Lake Cleary or Gateway to meet with the police there?"

"Eventually, but this investigation will go on for a long time. You'll have to testify at trial, though. By the way, do you even remember the town you left Ponytail Guy in?" He gave me a sideways glance that was a mixture of reprimand and humor.

I grimaced. "Not really. Can't you find that out through all of your law enforcement buddies?"

He started to laugh. "Yes. We know where you left him, although he wasn't found until the next morning. You're going to have to have a conversation with the police there, too." He shook his head. "It seems you left a trail of murder and mayhem from Mercer Island to Wisconsin."

"Very funny," I said. "By the way, thanks for bringing José. He was more help than you know."

"Yes, well, he has more talents than I realized." He looked at me with a raised eyebrow.

I forced myself not to ask what his comment meant. The last thing I wanted to do was to unwrap José's many talents, including car theft. *Don't ask, don't tell* was my new mantra.

The game announcer saved the moment.

"Welcome everyone to Wrigley Field and Chicago's annual Children First Game between our first responders. Sit back, relax, and enjoy your afternoon."

As the players entered the field, my cell phone pinged. I had an incoming text. I pulled out the phone and thumbed open the screen to read it.

"Be careful. Danger is coming your way. Fast."

The light on the phone went out, leaving me flabbergasted. It was my mother again. *But what the heck did that mean? What was coming at me fast?*

The pitcher wound up and threw the ball wide. The batter didn't even swing.

"By the way, Julia, I think we need to talk," David said, leaning into me again. "I have a problem with your proclivity to get embroiled in murder investigations."

My mind was focused on what my mother had just said. "What?"

"You keep almost getting killed."

I pulled away from him with my heart in my throat. "What do you mean?"

"I mean I can't protect you, and it bothers me."

"You don't need to protect me," I said in a huff.

The pitcher threw another ball. The batter swung, but missed.

"Well, someone needs to. And because of that, I'm not sure I can continue with this relationship the way it is. I have to weigh risk and reward. And the risk is just too great compared to the time I get to see you."

My eyes began to burn, and my heart was exploding in my chest. *Is this what my mother meant? Was David breaking up with me?* I couldn't bring myself to ask. Instead, I turned away so he couldn't see the tears threatening to flow.

"Julia?"

"I guess you'll have to do what you have to do."

"What? No, Julia," he said, reaching for my hand.

Crack! The batter finally connected with the ball, sending it over the fence in our direction. I looked up in time to see it coming at me—fast.

My eyes opened wide. I heard David say, "Julia, I think we should move in togeth…"

Smack!

The ball grazed my forehead and my world went to black.

Damn!

The End

Let's Prevent Bullying

It just so happens that October is National Bullying Prevention month; the same month I'm launching *All Roads Lead to Murder*. When I began the Old Maids of Mercer Island mystery series I didn't plan on exploring a variety of social ills, but since I spend most of my everyday life doing just that, it has become a natural extension of who I am.

In that light, I wrote an article a few years ago for the Renton Reporter on bullying. In that article, I quoted *stopbullying.gov* that defines bullying as, "…unwanted, aggressive behavior among school-aged children that involves a real or perceived power imbalance. The behavior is repeated, or has the potential to be repeated over time." My article was directed towards the type of bullying kids experience in school, but you can see by this definition that it almost perfectly defines my character, Senator Owens. Hence, this note about bullying.

Unfortunately, bullying begets more bullying. It's only natural; it's a learned behavior. If no one challenges the *young* bully, he/she is allowed to grow up into a bullying adult. If that adult also happens to be financially or politically successful, then the bullying may change in nature, but its effects are no less harmful. Just take a look at our current political climate.

The effects of bullying can take a toll on our entire society. Children who were bullied, or were themselves the bully, are at a higher risk of suffering from depression, anxiety, panic disorders and antisocial personality disorders as they get older. In the most extreme cases, it has the potential to lead to acts of violence or even suicide. We've heard of too many such incidents as the result of cyber-bullying. (Don't get me started.)

Bullying is all about power, and bullies get away with bullying because we let them. I once worked with a psychologist who told me, "*People teach other people how to treat them.*" I didn't quite understand what he meant until a couple of close friends began to relentlessly tease and laugh at me one night in my apartment. I hate being teased. It makes me feel helpless, little and inconsequential. Even though I kept asking them to stop, they didn't. I decided that if I let it continue, I would be telling them that it was okay. *I would be teaching them how to treat me.* So I asked them to leave. They were stunned, but they never teased me again.

So what can we do to help stop bullying?

I quote from my article here: *Tell your child that if he/she sees someone being bullied, don't encourage it by watching. Tell them to eliminate the audience by leaving the scene and then telling a trustworthy adult. If it feels safe, encourage your child to disrupt the situation, perhaps by saying something like, "Your mom's here, you have to go." Children can set a good example by not bullying others. They can reach out to someone who has been bullied to let them know they are not alone. And always encourage them to participate in school anti-bullying projects.*

October is Halloween and the month for ghouls and goblins. How appropriate that it is also the month to talk about what each one of us can do to stop bullying.

Again from my article: *Have a conversation with your children. We can all help to stop bullying if we talk about it, keep our eyes and ears open, and report it when we see it. There are real-life consequences if we don't – and they can be worse than any horror movie shown on a Halloween night.*

Or worse than any book I could write.

Reviews

If you enjoyed *All Roads Lead To Murder*, I would be truly honored if you would take a few minutes to go back to Amazon and leave a review. Self-published authors live and die on the number of positive reviews our books receive. Thank you for reading *All Roads Lead To Murder*.

About the Author

Ms. Bohart currently runs the Renton Community Foundation, helping to facilitate millions of dollars in grants to address areas of need, such as the arts, healthcare, homelessness, kids-at-risk, and even pet care. She holds a master's degree in theater, has published in Woman's World, and has a story in *Dead on Demand*, an anthology of ghost stories that remained on the Library Journals best seller list for six months. As a thirty-year nonprofit professional, she has spent a lifetime writing brochures, newsletters, business letters, website copy, and more. She did a short stint writing for *Patch.com*, teaches writing through the Continuing Education Program at Green River Community College, and has written for the *Renton Reporter*.

All Roads Lead to Murder is her seventh full-length novel and the fourth in the Old Maids of Mercer Island mysteries. You can check out her other books, including the Detective Giorgio Salvatori mysteries, on Amazon.com. She is hard at work on the third book in that series. *The Essence of Murder* will take Giorgio and Grosvenor, his faithful Basset hound, into the dark worlds of vampirism and dog-fighting rings.

If you would like more information, please visit Ms. Bohart's website at: www.bohartink.com, where you can let the author know you'd like to be added to her email list to be notified of upcoming publications or events. You may also join her author page on Facebook.

Follow Ms. Bohart

Website: www.bohartink.com
Twitter: @lbohart
Facebook: Facebook @ L.Bohart/author

Made in the USA
Middletown, DE
18 February 2018